WILD RIDE

JENNIFER CRUSIE
BOB MAYER

crusie
MAYER

ACKNOWLEDGMENTS

We would like to thank

Our beta readers, Brooke Brannon, Heidi Cullinan,
Rachel Plachcinski, Lani Diane Rich, and Anne Stuart,

Debbie—for being Bob's better half,

Kennywood for giving us a place to start thinking
about Dreamland,

Joss Whedon for *Buffy*,

the Argh People who brainstormed the fortunes,
especially Carolyn T. ("Someone close to you has a secret to share"),
McB ("Th at's not a good look for you," "It's going to get worse
before it gets better"), and Karen F. ("He loves you all
he can, but he cannot love you very much"),

Mollie Smith for putting together the Crusie–Mayer website
and up with us,

Amy Berkower and Jodi Reamer of Writer's House
and Meg Ruley of the Jane Rotrosen Agency
for also putting up with us,

and

Jennifer Enderlin for being the best editor
any writer could hope for.

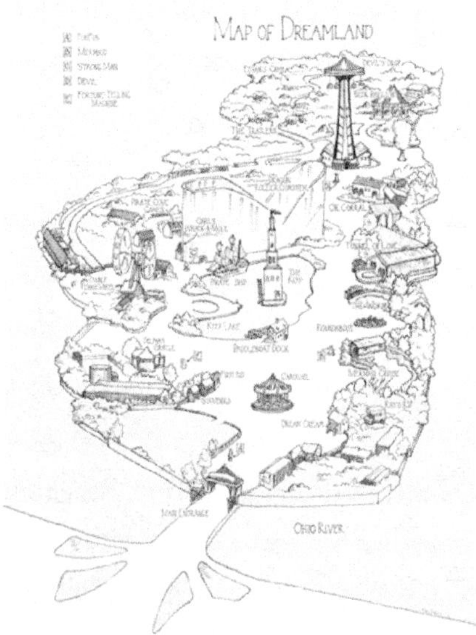

CHAPTER 1

Mary Alice Brannigan sat on the roof of the Dreamland carousel at twenty minutes to midnight and considered her work in the light from the lamp on her yellow miner's hat.

It was good.

FunFun, the redheaded clown sitting cross-legged next to her on the roof's peak, was fully restored again. Of all the clowns in the park, including the beautiful seven-foot ironclad Fun at the Dreamland entrance, this wooden one was her favorite: exuberantly happy, one yellow-gloved hand pulling back his striped blue-green coat to show off his orange-and-gold-checked waistcoat, the other flung above his head, reaching for the gold panpipes he'd lost long ago.

"Don't worry, baby," she said to him, patting her work bag between them. "I got your pipes right here."

He grinned crookedly down at her, or at least down toward the ground as a breeze picked up, biting with the chill of the Ohio October night. Mab pulled her canvas painting coat closer around her and looked out over the newly restored jewel box of an amusement park. It had taken her thirty-nine years, but now she was not only in Dreamland, she'd saved it. *Once I finish the Fortune-Telling Machine, I will have put this place back the way it was at the very beginning. I will* belong *here. I* rock.

And the best part was that she was surveying it all at night with no—

"You up there, Mab?" Glenda yelled.

—people around to spoil the moment.

"Stop what you're doing and come down here," Glenda called, the cheer in her voice sounding as platinum bright as her hair, and about as authentic. "We'll walk you back to the Dream Cream, see you get upstairs to bed. You need your sleep, honey."

Mab gritted her teeth. This was what she got for taking a break to gloat over her work: people showed up and shouted at her.

She pulled her bag closer and took out the pipes, careful not to scratch any of the five little golden cylinders. Then she fished a tube of fast-set glue out of the bag, stood up carefully, and reached to glue the pipes into the FunFun's empty fingers, tilting her head back so the light from her miner's cap shone on the hand.

A small black raven swooped down and perched on the clown's head.

"Beat it, Frankie," Mab whispered to the bird, trying to brush it away without dropping the pipes or falling to her death.

Frankie flapped his wings and rose above the clown and then settled down on the upflung hand, cawing at her like a cheese-grater dragged across a fire escape.

Cinderella got bluebirds doing her hair, Mab thought. I get ravens screwing with my work.

From below, Mab heard the raspy voice of Glenda's friend Delpha, an echo of Frankie's: "She's up there, Glenda. Frankie knows."

"I know, too," Glenda said, and then she raised her voice. "I'm not kidding, Mab, stop whatever you're doing up there *right now*."

Mab leaned in, holding on to the glue with one hand and the pipes with the other, and looked Frankie right in the eye.

"These pipes are going in that hand, bird," she told him, serious as death. "Do not get between me and my work."

Frankie watched her for a moment, his eyes steady and bright with intelligence, and then he cawed again, the sound going down Mab's spine like a rasp, and flapped off.

"Okay, then." Mab checked for the side of the pipes with the broken metal rod on it, reached up and squirted a generous shot of glue into the hole in the FunFun's palm, and slotted the broken rod into it. She held it for sixty seconds, ignoring demands to quit from down below, and then wiggled it a little to see if it had set.

The pipes clicked, the sound sharp in the night, as if the metal rod had moved into place, engaged a gear or something.

What the hell?

"Okay, that's it," Glenda said, the brightness gone from her voice. "I'm coming up there."

At fifty-nine, Glenda was probably in better shape than Mab was at thirty-nine, but it was dark, and Glenda liked a cocktail or three after six, and while she was often annoying, Mab didn't want her dead, so . . .

"Hold on." Mab capped her glue and put it in her paint bag and eased down the turquoise-and-blue-striped carousel roof to peer over the edge, gripping the gold scalloped trim for insurance.

Glenda stood on the flagstone below in the spotlight cast from the lamp on Mab's hat, one hand on her capri-clad hip, the other waving a cigarette, her spiky white hair glowing over her pink angora sweater. Beside her, ancient, black-eyed little Delpha looked up from under lowered brows, her improbably black hair slicked down on both sides of her sunken face like two strokes of black paint over a skull, the rest of her swathed in a dark blue shawl that blended into the night.

Frankie flapped down to sit on Delpha's shoulder.

Death's parrot, Mab thought. "Glenda, I'm almost done—"

"Done?" Glenda smiled up at her, tense for some reason. "But, honey, you shouldn't be doing anything up there—"

Somebody staggered out of the night and lurched into Glenda, who bumped into Delpha, who stumbled back and dislodged Frankie, who went for the staggerer, who screamed and batted at him.

Frankie flew to sit on the edge of the carousel roof beside Mab, and the guy looked up.

Mab saw brown hair, bleary eyes, and a dense five o'clock shadow over an orange Bengals shirt: Drunk Dave, one of the Beer Pavilion regulars who should have been out of the park when it had closed forty-five minutes before. He'd probably stumbled off to pee in the trees that rimmed the island and gotten lost. Again.

"Whassat?" Drunk Dave squinted up at her, and Mab realized that to him, she was just a big light in the black sky.

"This is God, Dave. Go home, sober up, get a job, and never get drunk again. Or you'll go to hell."

Drunk Dave's mouth dropped open, making him look even more slack-jawed than usual.

"Go home, Dave, the park's closed," Glenda said.

"Okay," Dave said, and staggered on.

"Come down, Mab, and we'll walk you back to the Dream Cream," Glenda said. "It's not safe for you to wander around alone."

"I've been walking around this park alone for months, and now you tell me it's not safe?"

"Well, there's Dave."

"I can take care of Drunk Dave with one hand wrapped around FunFun."

"And there's danger." Glenda waved her cigarette around vaguely. "It's . . . October."

"Right. The dangerous month." Mab shook her head, which made the light from the lamp on her hat swing wildly, and then she crawled back up the striped metal roof. The park people were just odd; that was all there was to it. It probably came from living on the grounds. You lived full-time in Dreamland, you got strange.

"Mab, get down here right now!"

"I'm *coming*!"

She fastened the flap on her work bag, made her way back to the ladder on the opposite side of the carousel, and climbed down to the flagstones that covered most of the park. Tomorrow she'd come out in the daylight and see the wood FunFun in all its finished glory, and then she'd move on to the Fortune-Telling Machine—

Something hard ran into her, and she lost her hat as she went down and smacked her head on the stone. "Ouch!" she said, and grabbed her hat and put it back on so that the light on it would stun the moron who'd knocked her down. "Damn it, Dave—"

Huge turquoise eyes gleamed down under iron-hard red-orange curls. A stiff turquoise striped coat loomed over her, metal protesting as it bent. Then the thing brought its red-orange lips together slowly and ground out "Mmmm" and then spread them apart with the sound of rending metal to say, "ab," its smile widening and its cheeks splitting as it jerkily held out its yellow iron-gloved hand to help her up.

"FunFun?" Mab said faintly.

The thing nodded, its head moving slowly up and down with a metallic squeaking sound.

Mab screamed.

*****

ETHAN JOHN WAYNE stared across the causeway at the locked iron gates that led to Dreamland as the sound of his taxi faded into the darkness. Something was missing on the other side of the gate, but it had been a long time since he'd been home, and he couldn't figure out what it was. Well, maybe they'd moved something. A lot of things changed in twenty years.

He rubbed his chest, feeling the scar that covered the Taliban bullet pressing on his heart. Dreamland was as good a place to die as any, and he had family here, which counted for something. What, he wasn't quite sure.

He dropped his rucksack to the ground, pulled out a leather flask, and took a good, long slug. Then he put the flask away and squared his shoulders to go back into the park. It wasn't much of a home, he thought, but at least it was peaceful, no people around to—

A scream rent the night. Ethan threw his vest on, grabbed his .45-caliber pistol from the pack, and sprinted for the entrance. He leapt as he reached the ten-foot-high wrought-iron gate, free hand reaching for the crossbar just below the top, and fell right onto his butt.

Cursing, he got to his feet and approached the gate, factoring in his inebriated state. *Mission planning, sir.* He tucked the gun inside his Kevlar vest so he could use both hands. It took longer to climb the damn thing than it should have, and when he got to the top of the gate, he tottered and almost fell again, but then he lowered himself and dropped the few remaining feet to the ground, narrowly missing the line of golf carts parked there. He drew his gun and ran across the causeway and down the midway toward the carousel, where he could see three people gathered.

He came to an abrupt halt when he saw his mother standing with her arm around a woman dressed like a bag lady in a long, bulky, paint-splotched coat and a yellow miner's hat.

"What's going on?" he demanded.

His mother turned, and her face lit up like it was Christmas. "Ethan!" she said, and flung herself at him, hugging him so tight that he couldn't get a breath. "What's this?" She pulled back and knocked her knuckles on his chest, testing out his body armor and making him wince, since she was banging right over his bullet. "Oh, I don't care, you're home!"

She flung her arms around him again, and Ethan patted the back of her fuzzy sweater and looked over her shoulder to see Delpha staring at him, with Frankie on her shoulder staring, too. "So you have returned," Delpha said. A flicker of a smile touched her thin lips, gone as quickly as it had appeared, but for her, it was like Glenda's bear hug.

"Yep," Ethan said. Out of the corner of his eye, he saw old Gus come limping up from the back of the park.

" 'Bout time you came home," Gus said gruffly in an overly loud voice, but he pounded Ethan on the shoulder just the same. "Good to see you, boy. You're just in time."

For what? Ethan wondered.

Glenda raised a tear-stained face. "How long can you stay? You have to stay a long time."

"I quit the Army. I'm staying," Ethan said, and Glenda looked startled, but then she must have decided not to look a gift son in the mouth because she let go of him and patted his chest again.

"I'm so glad." Her eyes welled up again. "Oh, I'm so glad. We even have a job for you! You can help Gus with security!"

"I don't want a job, Mom. I just want some peace and quiet." He looked around at them. "Who screamed?"

"I did," the bag lady said. "Sorry. Usually I'm very calm, but I got run down by a clown." She touched the back of her miner's hat gingerly. "I hit my head."

"Someone hit you?" Ethan said, feeling something that would have been outrage once. "Where is he?"

"No, it ran into me. . . ." She stopped, taking her hat off. "I think there's blood."

"Which way did he go?" Ethan said, and she said, "I don't know" at the same time Glenda said, "Let it go, Ethan."

Ethan started to speak and got one of his mother's famous Don't Argue looks.

"She hit her head and *hallucinated* the clown," Glenda said, enunciating each word clearly. Then she turned to the bag lady. "You *hallucinated it.*"

The woman blinked at her and then said, "Yes. I did."

"Okay," Ethan said, and reached toward her. "Let me check your head."

She stepped back. "I'm gonna say no on that."

"Mab, Ethan has been in the military," Glenda said proudly. "Ethan, this is Mab, she's restoring the park." She looked from Ethan to Mab and her smile faded. "You look . . . so much alike," she said, and then shook her head. "Never mind, I'm just so glad you're here."

Ethan looked at the bag lady. If he looked like that, he was closer to death than he'd thought. He said to the woman, "I'm trained in first aid," trying to move the whole thing along before he passed out from exhaustion and alcohol.

"No, thank you," she said.

Ethan circled around her to look at the back of her head. Her hair was a thick, red-brown choppy tangle—it looked like she hacked it off with a knife—but he couldn't see much blood, so it was probably just a scratch, not a scalp wound or else it would have been a mess. Scalp wounds were bad, hard to stop the bleeding. And then if the bullet hit bone . . . Ethan closed his eyes for a second.

"What are you doing?" the woman said, turning to look at him.

"You'll be fine. Who hit you?"

"A FunFun ran into me." She looked up at the carousel roof. "I was working on the FunFun up there, but he's still there, and anyway he's made of wood. The one that ran into me was a big metal-covered one, like the iron one by the gate. Did you see it when you came in?"

"No," Ethan said, now realizing what had been missing. The damn clown statue.

"Then it was probably that one. Of course, that's insane. I'm not insane."

"Right," Ethan said, glancing at his mother, who looked sane but worried.

"I told her to get off that roof," Glenda said, as if he'd accused her of not helping. "I *told* her to stop working." Whatever had rattled her before was gone, possibly because she'd gotten a grip and realized they didn't look alike.

Gus grabbed his arm and his attention. "Come on, I'll show you how to do the Dragon run. Now that you're here for good, you can take over."

"See," Glenda said to the woman, patting her arm. "Everything's fine now. Gus is going to do the midnight Dragon run, just like always. Everything's normal. No big iron, uh, robot clowns."

"Robot clowns?" the woman said. "This park has robot clowns?"

"No, no." Glenda patted again.

Patting, Ethan realized, was his mother's main form of communication. That and a wide array of looks.

"I'll take you back to the Dream Cream," Glenda told her. "We'll get that blood cleaned up, make you a cup of tea, you'll be good as new."

She gave Delpha a look, and Delpha nodded at her and then faded away from the carousel.

Glenda smiled at Ethan. "As for you, young man, you come right to my trailer when you're done with Gus. Tomorrow I'll get Hank's old trailer cleaned out and made up for you. You'll have a place of your own." Her eyes welled up again. "I'm so happy you're home, Ethan."

"Right," Ethan said. "Don't clean up the trailer, I'd rather sleep in the woods. Are you sure you're all right walking around here? If somebody's in the park—"

"We're fine," his mother said firmly, and he thought, *She knows who it was*. "I'm so glad you're back," she added.

"Me too, Mom," he lied, and made plans to get whatever the hell was going on out of Glenda once they were alone.

*****

Once he was away from the carousel, the park seemed darker than Ethan remembered it, and he realized it was because there was orange cellophane over the streetlights for the park's Screamland weekends, the reason for the skeletons somebody had strewn around along with—

A ghost flew in his face, empty-eyed and openmouthed, and he held off on drawing his gun as the pulley it was on yanked it back into the tree he'd just passed, not a ghost, just a skull beneath some white stuff that looked like fog but was probably cheesecloth.

"Geez," he said to Gus, and Gus nodded.

"Mab knows how to make a ghost," Gus said, and Ethan thought, *I know how to make ghosts, too,* as he relaxed his grip on his pistol.

He looked closer at the fence and saw the flickering red light of the infrared beam that had tripped the ghost, the same thing he'd seen in Afghanistan trip explosives. He shivered.

"Mab's uncle got her the job," Gus said as they headed down the midway to the back of the park. "Glenda wasn't too sure about her, since her uncle's Ray Brannigan, and you know them Brannigans, but once Mab got here, it was fine. Hard worker."

"Brannigans?" Ethan said, keeping an eye out for more trip-wire ghosts among the skeletons and giant spiders, which wasn't easy, given his current alcohol content.

"Yeah, you know, that crazy family, always trying to shut us down."

Ethan bumped into the fence and another ghost flew at him. He batted it out of the way as its pulley yanked it back into the trees. "Of all the times I could have picked to come home, I had to come for Screamland."

"What's that?" Gus said, cocking his head.

"I had to come home for Screamland," Ethan said in a louder voice.

" 'Course you did," Gus said. "Big party planned for Halloween 'cause that's when the park's gonna be all restored. We got media coming in Friday after next, get it on the news so a lotta people'll come." He sounded proud, like he talked about the media all the time.

"Great," Ethan said in a normal voice and noticed that Gus didn't hear. Well, he was old, and running the damn Dragon Coaster couldn't be easy on the ears.

The good news was the park would close after Halloween and stay closed until spring. He could stand two more weekends of the park full of screaming people and cheesecloth ghosts to spend whatever months he had left in solitude and quiet.

They passed the paddleboat dock. A figure moved in the shadows out there, watching them, and Ethan's hand again went toward the gun tucked into his vest.

"That's Young Fred," Gus said.

Ethan relaxed. "Related to Old Fred?"

"Grandson. Old Fred died 'bout seven years ago. Young Fred took over. He was only fifteen, but he stepped up." Gus raised his voice to call out to the boy on the dock. "What are you doing out here?"

Young Fred shrugged as he came closer. "Heard the commotion from upstairs. Everything okay?"

"Mab fell down," Gus said. "We gotta go run the Dragon." He jerked his thumb toward Ethan. "This here is Ethan, Glenda's boy."

On that, Young Fred came all the way down to the beginning of the dock. "I heard about you," he said to Ethan, admiration in his voice. "Big military hero. Navy SEAL."

"Special Forces," Ethan said, taking a dislike to Young Fred.

"Huh?" Young Fred said.

"Green Berets," Ethan amplified.

"What are you doing here, man?" Young Fred said, dismissing that. "You got out of here. Why would you come back?"

"He came back 'cause this is his home," Gus said, sounding peeved. "We gotta go. You get on up to your place now."

Young Fred took a last incredulous look at Ethan and went back to the boat dock house.

"He lives up there," Gus said. "Keeps an eye on the place. Good boy." He sounded doubtful on the last part.

Ethan looked past the dock to the Keep, the dark tower looming in the center of the paddleboat lake. The drawbridge, which usually touched down on the end of the dock, was up and there were no lights on in the restaurant on the main floor, which, if memory served him right, was unusual. Of course, his memory was temporarily being sat on by many slugs of Jack.

They passed the battered Fortune-Telling Machine that he had learned early was a complete crock, and Delpha's tent-shaped booth that he'd carved a hole in the back of so he could listen to Delpha tell fortunes, which were not a crock. Then the Double Ferris Wheel, where he'd grabbed his first kiss, and the Pirate Ship with its dozen jolly plastic pirates looking brand new, which was a testament to that Brannigan woman's skill; they'd been in pretty bad shape since the glorious afternoon when he was twelve and he'd beaten the crap out of them with a wooden sword and declared himself King of the Pirates. Then the games (Carl's Whack-A-Mole was still there) and the food booths (if he never had another funnel cake again, it would be too soon) and finally the struts and tracks of the Dragon Coaster, with its massive wooden dragon tunnel arching over the highest loop, waiting to swallow the cars on their last ascent, and the seven-foot iron-clad orange Strong Man statue in front of the Test Your Strength machine next to the entrance to the coaster. The whole place looked great except for the dragon tunnel at the top of the coaster that was still missing the jeweled eye it had lost before Ethan could remember.

Gus climbed the stairs onto the wooden platform and went into the small booth that controlled the ride. He threw a switch, and the thousands of tiny green lightbulbs that lined the course of the ride came alive.

Lit now, it looked smaller than Ethan remembered from all the times he'd sneaked out of Glenda's trailer at midnight to watch the Dragon soar, the times that Gus had told him stories of demons in the park and made him count the number of times the cars rattled at the end when they hit the dragon's tail. Five meant the park was safe, he remembered now. Demons all locked up. Gus had even given the demons names. Tura, the one that looked like a mermaid: Ethan had had some fantasies about her. Fufluns, the good-time demon. Two others he couldn't remember. And Kharos, the Devil.

It was a miracle he'd never had nightmares. At least not from his childhood.

The freshly painted blue-and-green cars were ready to go, their scales gleaming in the green lights on the tracks. Ethan stood with Gus on the platform as the old man pulled out his pocket watch and flipped open the lid.

"It's time." Gus shut the watch, stuffed it back into a pocket on his vest, entered the small booth, and hit the controls.

With a shudder, the cars began moving, heading toward the first turn, gleaming in the lights as they clattered up the incline over the Keep lake, the entire ride shaking as if it were going to fall apart, then swooping down into the curves. Ethan watched in silence until the cars were slowly crawling up toward the pinnacle of the last loop, the dragon tunnel, at least a hundred feet into the air, the wooden struts supporting the track shivering and creaking in protest. The Dragon wouldn't set any records for height. Or length. Or safety, Ethan thought, mesmerized by the creaking cars that sounded like they were going to collapse at any second. Perhaps they shouldn't be running it any more than they had to.

"Gus? Maybe—"

Gus waved him off, walked to the end of the platform, and unhooked the chain that closed off the service walkway. He stepped onto the walkway and then leaned over, putting the right side of his head right on top of one of the rails.

"Geez, Gus, that's dangerous," Ethan said, but the old man couldn't hear him, focused on the vibration of the coaster. Ethan walked over and stood on the walkway, prepared to snatch Gus out of the way if the old man didn't move before the Dragon came home.

The coaster went through the tunnel and roared down, racing into the high-bank corkscrew turn called the Dragon's Tail. The cars slammed back and forth on the rails and then splashed through the shallow water at the bottom toward the long straightaway leading back to the platform, and Gus stood up as it came in, his face grim in the light from the control booth.

"What's wrong?" Ethan asked, worried the old man was going to have a heart attack.

"Only four rattles." Gus headed back to the control booth, and Ethan followed close behind.

The Dragon pulled up to the platform, and Gus threw the lever, stopping it. The bars that kept people from falling out automatically lifted. He threw switches, powering down the ride, turning off the thousands of lights that lined the edge of the tracks, the pinpoint reflections in the water flashing out and leaving the lake lifeless. The park plunged back into darkness, a few streetlamps dotted here and there casting lonely cones of orange light through Glenda's cellophane.

Ethan put his hand on Gus's shoulder. "Come on," he said. "Let's go back to the trailers—"

He stopped, suddenly alert.

Nineteen years of Special Operations duty in the Army and three-plus years in combat: no amount of alcohol could wash those instincts away. Ethan fumbled for the pistol, finally pulling it out, the grip sweaty in his left hand. He blinked, trying to focus, searching back and forth, the muzzle of the gun following his eyes as he tried to see into the dark shadows. He grabbed Gus's arm. "Come on *now*," he said, and saw Gus looking at his chest, frowning.

He looked down and saw the tiny red dot of an infrared laser sight.

Oh, crap, he thought, and then the round hit him.

CHAPTER 2

Mab had let Glenda steer her to the Dream Cream and sit her down on one of the pink leather stools at the counter. She really wanted to keep going to the door to the back hall—one short flight up to her bed in Cindy's apartment and solitude and silence—but she was feeling dizzy and her head hurt and she'd read something once about not falling asleep with a concussion. Also, she needed to find out what had hit her. If the damn kids from the nearby college were pulling a prank with the iron FunFun statue at the gate that she'd spent eighty hours restoring, heads were going to roll.

She touched the back of her own head gingerly. It hurt.

"Let me get you a cold cloth," Glenda said. "You look kind of . . . gory."

"Thank you." Mab put her hat on the counter. The Formica was covered in retro pink swirls, so she stopped looking at it and tried to focus on the mirrored wall behind it, with its glass shelves of sundae dishes and milk shake glasses and the blackboard where Cindy wrote down the flavors for the day.

Glenda flipped up part of the counter and passed through to the other side. She took a clean dish towel out of the drawer, ran it under the cold water, wrung it out, and came back to stand behind Mab.

"Hold still," she said, and pressed it to the back of Mab's head, where it stung for a moment and then just felt good.

"That's nice," she told Glenda, and then the door opened and she heard her uncle Ray's voice saying, "What the hell happened?"

"She hit her head," Glenda said, her voice hard. She went around to the other side of the counter, looked at the bloody dish towel, and threw it in the trash.

Ray sat down on the stool beside her, his middle-aged muscular bulk crowding her. "You okay?"

"Getting there." Mab touched the back of her head again and then looked at her fingers. No blood. Things were looking up.

"What are you doing here?" Glenda said to Ray. "It's past midnight."

"Working late, like everybody else," Ray said, trying to sound jolly, which was not in his skill set. He jerked his head toward the back of the store and evidently to the yard beyond that, where he kept the small RV he used as an office. "Cleaning up some filing." He transferred his smile to Mab. "What a worker you are, Mary Alice. I told you she'd be great, didn't I, Glenda?"

Glenda nodded at Mab. "I'll make you a cup of tea," she said, and began to fill the kettle.

"Let me see your eyes," Ray said to Mab, and she turned and looked at him as he leaned toward her, big and sure and expensive in his Burberry coat with his miniature black-and-gold Ranger crest stuck to his lapel like a designer label.

He put his hand under her chin, which she hated, and she saw that his broad handsome face was getting puffy with age. She should tell him to stay away from close-ups with people. He looked a lot better from far away.

He peered at her. "You look all right. Pupils the same size. What happened?"

"A clown knocked me down." Mab pulled back from his hand as her head throbbed. "Can I have an aspirin, Glenda?"

"Sure thing."

Glenda moved down the counter, and Ray sat back.

"You'll be fine. You ready to start the Fortune-Telling Machine?"

"Yes," Mab said, and the door opened again and Delpha came in with her bird.

"Here you go." Glenda handed Mab the aspirin as Delpha sat down beside her, Frankie on her shoulder.

"It's as we thought," she said to Glenda. "He's gone."

Mab surveyed the people who surrounded her: Glenda, her platinum hair spiked up and her blue eyes tense; Ray, his shark eyes staring down at her from his beginning-to-bloat broad face; and Delpha with Frankie on her shoulder, her hollow eyes making her look as skull-like as the cheesecloth ghosts in the park. They all looked odd to Mab, as if they were only pretending things were fine. Frankie was the sanest looking of the lot.

"So who was this clown who knocked you down?" Ray said, trying to smile jovially at her, his tension obvious.

"I think it was the FunFun by the gate," Mab said, and Ray lost his smile.

"The FunFun by the gate? I thought you meant some clown of a guy—"

"She *hallucinated* that part," Glenda said, staring at him. "She hit her head and then she *hallucinated* the FunFun, so—"

"Well, hell, yeah, she hallucinated it," Ray said. "Iron clowns don't go running around, that's crazy."

He sounded weird, as if he were trying too hard not to sound weird.

"Weird," Mab said aloud.

"What?" Ray said, his eyebrows snapping together.

"I finished the carousel," Mab said, to get him on to something else before he drove the clown into the ground.

"Well, good for you," Ray said. "Now you can start on the Fortune-Telling Machine."

"I plan to," Mab said. "Could you go away now?"

"That's no way to talk to your boss," her uncle said, his geniality dimming.

Mab shook her head and then regretted it as her head pounded harder. "You are not my boss. I am my boss. I have done an outstanding job on this park, and tomorrow when my concussion is over, I will begin on the Fortune-Telling Machine, and it will be as fabulous as everything else I've done, and you will say, 'Thank you very much, Mary Alice,' and then I will go on to my next job, where I will also be my boss and where I will also do a fabulous job." She thought of the iron-covered FunFun by the gate, the beauty of the smooth stripes on his coat, the gleam she'd painted in his turquoise eyes, the lushness of the multiple glazes on his waistcoat. If somebody had damaged him—

"You have an interesting approach to employment," Ray said, an edge in his voice.

"I have an interesting approach to everything." Mab turned away from him and nodded at Glenda, nervously tapping her cigarette on the pack. "I'm okay now, I'll go upstairs to bed. You go see your son."

"I'll see Ethan in a bit, you sit and have some tea," Glenda said, but she looked toward the door.

"Ethan?" Ray transferred his gaze to Glenda. "He's here?"

"He just came home tonight." Glenda lit her cigarette. "Resigned from the Army. Big surprise."

"You should have told me," Ray said. "Why's he here now?"

Glenda inhaled and blew out a long stream of smoke away from Mab. "He. Just. Got here."

Mab slid off her stool and detoured around Ray to sit at the end of the counter and look out the mullioned windows into the empty dark street beyond. It was too dark to see clear out to the gate where the iron clad FunFun should be, but she could still see him as he'd looked when he'd hit her, larger than life, saying her name . . . "You know, when the clown talked to me, he split the metal on his cheeks. That's real damage, that's not going to be easy to fix. Good thing it was a hallucination." She caught sight of Glenda's face, her shock reflected in the window.

"He said your name?" Glenda said.

"The clown talked to you?" Ray said.

She swiveled the stool around to face them. "I hallucinated it. He said, 'Mab,' and the metal on his face split so I could see the wood underneath—" She felt ill thinking about it. "—and then he reached down his hand to help me up and I heard more metal tear. And then I screamed and he ran away."

"Hallucination," Ray said promptly. "It never happened. Put it out of your mind."

Glenda glared at him. "If she wants to talk about it, she can. You're upsetting her."

"I'm not upset. I don't get upset. Unless somebody is running around ruining my work, then I might get upset." Mab looked back at them, but nobody was paying attention to her. Ray scowled at Glenda, Glenda took a hard drag on her cigarette and stared at Ray, Delpha shook her head, and Frankie moved from foot to foot on Delpha's shoulder. "I'm missing something, aren't I?"

"No," Glenda said with finality. The kettle whistled and she put her cigarette on the side of the sink and picked up the teakettle, shutting off the awful screech.

Ray stood up. "I'm not happy about the lack of security in this park," he told Glenda. "Somebody coming in here, running around, knocking people down. We had a deal. I pay for the restoration, you run the place. If you can't do that, I'll have to take it over."

"Over my dead body," Glenda said.

Ray went very still, and Mab realized how really big he was, looming over Glenda, who was no waif herself. "If that's the way you want it," he said, smiling, and Glenda took a step forward, lowering her head, looking dangerously intent.

What the hell? Mab thought. "Hey," she said, and they both jerked around to look at her. "I don't know what's going on here, but knock it off."

Ray looked back at Glenda, and when he spoke again, it was very softly. "Don't cross me, Glenda. You have no idea how powerful I really am."

Then he turned and walked past Delpha and out the back door, and a moment later, they heard the outside door slam in the hall.

"Yeah, well, you have no idea how powerful *I* am, you dipstick,"

Glenda said to the doorway, and then she turned back to Mab and said brightly, "How about that tea?"

There was something bad going on here, Mab was sure of it, but she had a head injury and she was really tired, and her reality had been bent enough for one night.

"Wonderful," she said, and went back to sit down at the counter.

*****

The impact from the shot hitting his vest knocked Ethan backward and made the old bullet in his chest sear as he slammed into the ground. The shooter, dressed all in black and wearing a mask and night-vision goggles, watched him for a moment and then sprinted away toward the front of the park. Ethan tried to raise the pistol and fire, but the pain in his chest was too much. He let his head fall back and closed his eyes and waited to die.

After a few moments, when the pain receded and he was still breathing, he opened his eyes and saw Gus leaning over him, concerned. "You all right?"

"Who was that?" Ethan managed to get out.

"No idea."

"This happen often?"

"First time," Gus said, helping Ethan up to a sitting position.

"Great." Ethan tried taking a deeper breath. The pain was still bad but bearable now.

"We got other problems," Gus said. "Only four rattles. Means a demon is out." He shook his head. "If we're lucky, it's Fufluns and not Selvans or that devil Kharos."

Ethan rubbed his chest, still trying to breathe. "Gus, forget the demon stories. We got somebody in the park with a gun—"

"What stories?" Gus looked insulted. "What we got is a demon on the loose." He shook his head. "I shoulda guessed that when Mab got run down."

Gus believed there were demons. Ethan closed his eyes. He'd been away too long. Gus was losing more than his hearing, and Glenda had probably been trying to hold it together on her own. That impulse he'd had to come home, maybe it wasn't so insane after all.

Even if it did mean he'd gotten shot again.

"We gotta call the cops," Ethan said, trying to stand up on his own, his difficulty part pain and part alcohol.

"No cops," Gus said. "Cops can't fight demons."

"Forget the demons." Ethan levered himself to his feet using Gus's shoulder. "We got a shooter—*ouch*." He winced and put his hand over his chest. "*Damn* it."

"We should go to the first-aid station," Gus said, trying to support Ethan.

"Bullet didn't penetrate my Kevlar," Ethan said.

"We better go anyway." Gus slung an arm around Ethan. "You know how Glenda is."

Ethan was in too much pain to argue. He nodded and started down the midway, leaning on the old man.

"Real glad you're home," Gus said. "You got here just in time."

"Yeah," Ethan said, and kept walking.

*****

Glenda put a cup of hot water in front of Mab, dumping in a peppermint tea bag. "This'll make you feel better, honey."

Mab pulled the mug closer. "I'm sorry about Ray. Sometimes he's a little creepy."

Glenda nodded. "Your family's social skills could use some work."

Mab stirred her tea and thought of her grandmother, who had sold anti-evil charms and done exorcisms for the neighbors; and her mother, who had picketed Dreamland every Halloween, demanding the park be shut down with her sign that said THE DEVIL LIES WITHIN! thereby ensuring that Mab would never get a date or a friend without moving to a different town; and now her uncle, who had promised to fix the park and gotten himself elected mayor on that, in spite of his nonexistent charm. "We don't have any social skills. Thank you for the tea."

Glenda leaned against the counter. "So did the clown say anything else?"

"Uh, no." Mab blew on her tea, watching Glenda to see what was coming next.

Glenda nodded, noncommittal. "Did his eyes . . . flash or glow or . . . anything?"

"Of course not. They're painted turquoise. I painted them turquoise. I may have been hallucinating, but I was *accurate*."

"Of course you were." Glenda glanced at Delpha as if for support.

Delpha nodded.

"So," Glenda said, "there wasn't anything else . . . strange about him?"

"He was a robot clown. That was strange enough for me."

"Of course it was." Glenda patted her hand. "Don't you worry about it. We'll find the statue tomorrow. If it's banged up, you can just touch it up and it'll be good as new."

Mab looked at her in disbelief. Touch it up? That waistcoat had been *glazed*, ten coats to give it that depth. She'd painted the shadows in the folds of the coat, stroked individual hairs in those curls, put tiny glints of silver in the eyes to make them sparkle—

Touch it up?

She picked up her tea mug and slid off the stool before Glenda could say anything else insane. "Thank you very much for the tea and the nursing, but I need to go to bed—"

Delpha straightened and said, "Ethan is hurt," and Glenda stubbed out her cigarette in the sink and made a beeline for the front door.

"How do you know?" Mab said, but Delpha was already out the door, following Glenda.

Mab went to the window and saw Gus supporting Ethan as they staggered back from the Dragon, Ethan looking more drunk than injured. Glenda put her arms around them, and they made their way to the candy-colored first-aid station across from the Dream Cream. Clustered together like that, they looked like a family, a strange family, but still family, bonded and loving and supportive. Even

Frankie flying overhead was sort of Lassie-like, if Tim Burton had done Lassie.

Ray may have been all the family she had left, but at least he was normal.

Kind of.

She didn't need family anyway.

It was past midnight and her head hurt, and Ethan had his family propping him up, so she locked the front door and turned out the lights and carried her work bag upstairs. Tomorrow she'd find out what had happened to the FunFun at the gate, and if there was anything wrong with it, she'd take care of whoever had messed with her work.

That better have been a hallucination, she thought, and went to bed.

*****

Kharos had been drowsing, dreaming of conquering the park and the earth, when a surge of power had jolted him awake.

One had broken free.

He concentrated, searching for the miscreant, the one of four who had disobeyed him, but he already knew it was one of two. Vanth and Selvans would make no move without his order, but—

Another surge of power, another Untouchable free, two now, Fufluns and Tura. The damage they could do to his plan—

Ray walked up and sat down beside the Devil statue, lit up a cigar, and rapped on the metal. "Hey."

If Kharos had been out, he'd have swatted him like a fly.

"It's a good news, bad news thing," Ray said, leaning back and puffing away. "Fufluns is out."

HOW DID HE GET OUT?

Ray took the cigar out of his mouth. "Mab put the key in, and when I went to get the chalice, the statue was gone. College kids steal that damn statue all the time, so I'm guessing his chalice was broken and this time Fufluns got out and ran with it."

FIND HIM AND BRING HIM TO ME.

"How?" Ray said.

HE'LL POSSESS SOMEONE. THEN DRINK AND CHASE WOMEN.

"That's every guy in the park."

Kharos seethed for a moment. If he could have, he'd have smashed Ray's head like a clay pot. But he couldn't. Ray had power and skills. And he was on the outside of the prison in which Kharos was trapped, so he couldn't be reached anyway.

Although . . .

Fufluns' and Tura's escapes had strengthened Kharos. Straining against the confines of his chalice, he reached out with his mind and tweaked the back of Ray's head.

A clump of hair fell out.

Ray scratched the back of his head and then went on talking, oblivious. "It's not like I have time to go hunting down escaped demons. I'm the *mayor,* you know. I have things to do that don't involve you."

INSECT, Kharos thought. In two weeks, he was going to smash Ray's head like a clay pot.

"For example," Ray went on, "we have this Halloween merchant thing going on that's very popular—"

GO WHERE PEOPLE ARE LAUGHING. FIND THE HUMAN WHO IS THE CENTER OF ATTENTION. TOUCH HIM WITH IRON. IF HE FLINCHES, SAY, "KHAROS COMMANDS YOU TO GO TO HIM."

"You know," Ray said, "maybe we're rushing this. We don't have to do this right now. Another year wouldn't—"

NO, Kharos said. YOU HAVE DELAYED TOO MUCH ALREADY. FORTY YEARS.

"Hey, the first twenty were mine, that was the deal." Ray chomped his cigar gloomily. "I should have held out for fifty. When you're fifteen, thirty-five sounds ancient."

YOU'VE TAKEN FORTY.

"Yeah, but the last twenty have been working for you, making money for your big plan."

IT TOOK YOU TOO LONG.

"Even with your mojo, the markets are treacherous. I did the best I could." Ray looked mutinous. "And then I had to come back to this podunk town."

FORGET THAT. YOU HAVE MY WORK TO DO NOW.

"What I'm saying is that if you give me another year or two, maybe five, I'll own the whole town and the park, and then we won't have to go sneaking around like this. A little more time—"

YOU ARE TRYING MY PATIENCE.

"Wait. I have some good news." He put his cigar on the edge of the bench, reached under his long coat, and pulled out a wooden chalice. "I got Tura. One of two ain't bad."

THAT IS AN EMPTY VESSEL.

Ray looked at the wood in his hands. "But the lid is on. I swear, I haven't opened it."

FUFLUNS FREED HER.

"I didn't turn the key to open the statue. I told Mab to replace the flute key so I could get Fufluns' chalice out of his statue while she was up on the roof. She never suspected a thing." He looked away, frowning as he thought. "She must have found the dove key and put it on the Tunnel of Love on her own, thinking she was just putting back a missing bird." He shook his head. "That was not my fault—"

PUT TURA'S CHALICE BACK. FIND FUFLUNS. HE WILL DEAL WITH TURA.

"All right, although I still think waiting another five or ten years would be smarter." Ray stood up. "Oh, one other thing: Glenda's son came home. Ethan. He just got out of the Green Berets."

THAT IS NOTHING TO ME. FIND FUFLUNS.

"All right. I'll put off my own work to help you. But I can't keep dropping everything every time there's a glitch in your plan. It's taken me a long time to live down the Brannigan name. People are sucking up now, but they're just waiting for me to screw up, and then they'll be on me again."

Kharos could understand that. He'd been assuming Ray was going to screw up for forty years, but Ray had been smarter than expected. Which still wasn't very smart.

"Once I own the town and the park," Ray said, "I'll own them. Until then, I gotta keep busting myself here."

YOU WILL OWN THE PARK SOON.

"Can't be too soon for me." Ray turned and walked back down the midway, puffing on his cigar.

Kharos watched him go, thinking, *IT CAN'T BE TOO SOON FOR ME, EITHER.* He tried to go back to dreaming of all those hopeless souls coming to Dreamland, coming right to him, the way it had been at the very beginning, but there was too much power awakened in him now. Twenty-five hundred years was a long time to wait to rule again, but soon it would be time, time to escape, time to destroy the Guardia, time to take what was his. . . .

Two weeks . . .

CHAPTER 3

When Mab went down into the Dream Cream for breakfast, Cindy was already there, dressed in her pink-and-white-striped DC T-shirt and turquoise-and-blue-striped apron, her short curly black hair making her look like a very pretty, no-nonsense poodle as she beamed at the five customers who'd wandered in during a Thursday morning in the off-season: a mother and her two little kids at the table in front of the jukebox; a fair-haired guy in black-rimmed Coke-bottle glasses eating whole-wheat waffles and ice cream while he wrote in a notebook, his green trilby hat on the table beside him; and a younger guy with good shoulders at the end of the counter, staring at his bowl of waffles and cream in disbelief. Most people looked like that after their first taste of Cindy's ice cream, so Mab ignored him and sat down at the middle of the counter.

"Hey." Cindy flipped up the lid on one of the waffle-makers as its light began to blink, pried out two waffles, and dropped them on a plate. Then she opened the freezer case, scooped pale yellow ice cream on one waffle, and slapped the other one on top. She set it in front of Mab with a fork and a spoon. "Did I miss something last night? Because this morning, I found a bloody towel in the trash. You kill somebody?"

"No." Mab picked up the fork. "I got knocked down."

"Are you okay?"

"Yes. I can start on the Fortune-Telling Machine right away." Mab cut a piece of ice cream–filled waffle and bit into it, the cold high-fat cream flavored with something clean and fresh melting into the hot buttery crunch of the homemade whole-wheat pastry. Not maple nut ice cream this time. "Lemon?" she said to Cindy.

"Lemon balm, poppy seeds, and passionflower." Cindy put the ice cream back in the freezer case. "I call it The-Kids-Will-Go-Back-to-School-Soon Lemon because it's very calming. It was popular with mothers the last week the park was open full-time, so I brought it back for Halloween." She jerked her head to the mother with the two little kids in front of the jukebox. "I just double-dipped her. Two kids under four? Yowza. I double-dipped the guy with the hat, too. I think he comes here to get away from his wife; he's always getting naggy phone calls from somebody named Ursula. I don't know who the new guy is on the end, but he looks familiar. I'll find out before he goes."

"Yes, you will," Mab said, bemused again by Cindy's lust to acquire information about people. Things you could build or paint were so much more interesting than human beings. And so much safer.

Until they came to life and ran you down.

Mab scooped up more yellow ice cream. It did make her feel better.

"Now," Cindy said, "who knocked you down? Because whoever it is gets no ice cream here for life."

"A big metal-covered robot clown," Mab said around her mouthful of ice cream and waffle. "But I hallucinated that."

"You hit your head and hallucinated a robot clown? How did you hit your head?"

"The robot clown knocked me down."

Cindy frowned at her. "You got a chicken-and-egg thing going on there."

"I don't care," Mab said. "I'm going to work on the Fortune-Telling Machine." She thought about that while Cindy went over to refresh the coffee cup of the guy with the trilby hat and the glasses. The

Machine was going to be so beautiful when she'd restored it, once she'd studied it to get it right. Cindy came back, and Mab said, "I'm going to have to do rubbings of all four sides."

"Of the robot clown?" Cindy said.

"The Fortune-Telling Machine. Forget the robot clown."

"I don't want to forget the robot clown, the robot clown is exciting."

"That's because it didn't run into you."

Cindy shook her head. "Are you kidding? This is a great story to tell people. You can say, 'I got run down by a robot clown.' All I can say is, 'My roommate got run down by a robot clown.' It's not the same thing." She stopped and thought for a moment. "I'm thirty-two years old, and I've never been run down by a robot clown. That never bothered me before, but now—"

Mab put her fork down. "You know what was strange?"

"The robot clown."

"Besides that. Glenda wasn't surprised when I talked about it. She asked me questions about it like it was real."

"Did you ask her why?"

"She was busy selling me on the idea that it was a hallucination. Which, of course, it was. But if it wasn't, I'd swear she knew what it really was."

"Huh. I don't remember any park legends about robot clowns."

"There are park legends?" Mab frowned. "I researched this park and didn't find any legends." She thought about it. "Of course, I was looking for photographs of rides."

"Oh, yeah, we got legends. Like the Devil's Drop is haunted. And if you cheat on your honey here, you die of a heart attack with a mark on your chest. And if you throw a penny in the paddleboat lake, your wish will come true."

Mab blinked. "The last one's kind of an anticlimax."

"It doesn't work, either." Cindy looked around and then leaned across the counter to Mab. "But some stuff does work here. Like Delpha really can tell your fortune."

"Not mine, she can't," Mab said, digging into her waffles again.

"She's been after me ever since I got here, but I am not going into that booth. Going in there to repaint it was bad enough. She kept looking at me, like she was seeing something I didn't know about."

"She wants to tell your fortune and you won't let her?" Cindy said, pulling back. "Are you crazy? I'd kill to have her do mine."

"So go." Mab forked more waffle.

"I've tried. She won't do me. She says I'm a naturally happy person and I shouldn't mess with fate."

"Oh." Mab chewed a little slower as she considered that. "Then why is she so hot to get me in there? I'm a naturally happy person."

Cindy gave her a you're-kidding-me look.

"No, I am," Mab said. "I love my work."

"That's all you do," Cindy said. "You won't even take time out to smell the robot clown."

Mab screwed up her face. "Ew."

"Yeah, that wasn't good. But really, all this great stuff around you that you could be enjoying, and you go to work. I mean, this is probably the longest conversation we've ever had, and you've been living with me for nine months."

"I don't really have much interesting to say," Mab said. "Except about my work. Work is great stuff."

Cindy looked skeptical.

"And I'm not good with people," Mab said, trying to apologize. "It's not you. I've just found in general that it's better to shut up and work than try to . . . you know."

"Talk to people?" Cindy said, sounding appalled.

"People are—" *Pain.* "—strange," Mab said. "Work is safe. You know what's great? I get to start restoring the Fortune-Telling Machine today. I think it's going to be magnificent." She forked up more waffle. "My life is great."

"Your work is great," Cindy said, her cheeriness dialed down a notch to what might have been exasperation on a lesser woman. "You have no life."

"Hey," Mab said.

"Sorry," Cindy said. "I should talk. I live for my ice cream." She chewed her lip for a moment, looking thoughtful. "So what are you going to do about it?"

"About what?"

"About the *robot clown,*" Cindy said. "You're part of a new legend."

"Not if I don't tell anybody." Mab stabbed the last piece of waffle. "Glenda seemed like she wanted to keep it quiet."

"Glenda gets what she wants. I think she can . . ." Cindy stopped, letting her voice taper off.

"What?" Mab said.

"Nothing," Cindy said. "You wouldn't believe me anyway. Look, you have to open yourself to the possibilities in your life, or you won't have any."

"I wouldn't describe a robot clown I hallucinated as a life possibility." Mab stopped to think. "I'm not sure what I would describe as a life possibility."

Cindy leaned in close and whispered, "There's one at the end of the counter."

Mab turned to look. The guy with the good shoulders looked familiar, but she couldn't remember him. And she'd have remembered him. Not pretty but . . . Long nose, pointed chin, strong hand reaching for his coffee cup—

A yellow iron-gloved hand reaching down to her—

Not that. That was a hallucination.

This guy was not a hallucination. He looked down the counter and caught her watching him and grinned crookedly, the corners of his eyes crinkling up, and she thought, *Hello.*

"You okay?" Cindy said, and Mab tore her eyes away.

"Yeah. I'm just having a strange twenty-four hours. I'll be okay when I get back to work."

The door opened, and Ashley Willhoite came in, one of the few people Mab could recognize as a regular, mainly because avoiding her was impossible. Pretty, sunny Ashley was sure everybody wanted to talk to her, so she never met a stranger.

Wonder what that's like, Mab thought as Ashley plopped herself down on the next stool.

Cindy said, "Hi, Ashley! Breakfast?"

"Maple on waffle, please." Ashley smiled at Mab as Cindy opened the freezer and took out the maple ice cream. "Hi, Mab. Did you hear Ethan Wayne is back in town? I spent a lot of time in high school looking at his picture in the football trophy case. And now he's here for real." She beamed at them. "Tonight, I'm going to make my fantasies come true. You know, like Katie Holmes used to fantasize about Tom Cruise and then she married him?"

Mab looked at Ashley, perplexed at the idea of pursuing a guy she'd only seen in a photograph. What if he turned out to be boring? Or a serial killer? Or one of those guys who stuck around the next morning when you just wanted to work?

Ashley caught Mab frowning at her. "You're not dating him or anything, are you?" Then she took in Mab's paint-stained canvas coat and her yellow miner's hat on the counter. "No, you're not." She cheered up again. "I can't wait to meet him."

Cindy put Ashley's breakfast in front of her, and Mab got up and headed for the front window and craned her neck to get a sight line down to the park gate. "Oh."

"What?" Cindy said, coming to stand beside her.

"The FunFun at the gate is gone."

"Yes, he is," Cindy said, looking, too. "So he's the robot clown who knocked you down. Bastard."

"Yes," Mab said. "I spent a full week making him gorgeous and then he flattens me."

"What an ingrate," somebody said from behind them, and Mab turned and saw that the guy with the shoulders had come to look out the window with them.

Close up, he looked like Drunk Dave. Drunk Dave showered and shaved and possibly gainfully employed and dressed in a blue pin-striped shirt instead of something with BENGALS written on it, but still . . . "Dave?"

He grinned down at her, and she lost her breath. "I get that a lot." He held out his hand. "I'm Dave's cousin, Joe. Dave's out of town for a couple of weeks, so I'm house-sitting for him."

"Dave has a house?" Mab looked down and saw his outstretched hand and took it, trying to look calm, but there was still something about him that disoriented her, something besides his warm, firm grip and the fact that he held her hand a moment too long for just a handshake. She would have sworn he was Drunk Dave, except he was sentient and sober and attractive. And warm. And happy. And near. She felt stirrings. It had been a while since she'd felt stirrings. She'd given up stirrings because they never turned out well and they interfered with her work, but now here they were again.

He was definitely not Drunk Dave.

"So you're Dave's cousin," Cindy said. "Welcome to Dreamland. You should avoid the Beer Pavilion and just stay here with me where you'll be safe from robot clowns." She dimpled at him.

"Robot clowns?" he said to Cindy, laughing.

"Mab met one last night."

And there she was, a Batty Brannigan, her first seventeen years all over again. So much for stirrings. Well, she had work to do anyway.

"Tell me more," Joe said.

"Tragically, it's not my story," Cindy said. "It's Mab's."

He turned and looked at Mab again, and her heart beat faster. "A robot clown?"

"I was joking. He was a hallucination. I hit my head." *I'm not weird.*

"That's a shame."

"It's fine now."

"No, it's a shame it was a hallucination. How many people get run down by robot clowns?"

"Not many?" Mab guessed.

"It would be an experience," Joe said. "Instead of life as usual."

"Exactly," Cindy said.

Mab frowned at her. "I like life as usual."

"But you don't remember life as usual," Joe said, his smile warm on her. "At the end of your life, you're not going to remember all the life-as-usual days, but you're going to remember being run down by a robot clown."

"I wasn't run down by a robot clown."

"Are you sure?" Joe said, and Mab met his eyes and saw all the light and excitement there, and thought, *No, but I'm positive I'm stunned by you.*

"I like the way you think," Cindy told him.

"I don't," Mab said.

Joe smiled into Mab's eyes as if he knew her and spread out his arms. "Embrace the experience, honey."

Mab realized she wasn't breathing, which was absurd. She took a deep breath, trying to get oxygen back to her brain. Maybe it was the word *embrace* coupled with the stirrings. *I could embrace the experience if you were the experience.*

She picked up her work bag and her miner's hat before the stirrings got out of hand. "I have to go meet somebody."

"Who?" Cindy said.

"The Fortune-Telling Machine," Mab said, and went out the door, not looking back at Joe or anything else.

*****

Ethan woke late, smelling cigarette smoke and feeling hungover, like someone was standing on his chest, the old bullet aching inside him.

He cracked his eyes open and recognized the lines in the curved metal roof above him, lit by sunshine pouring in a narrow window behind him framed in green-and-yellow barkcloth curtains. He'd woken to that same roof, that same window, those same curtains for years, but not in a very long time.

He closed his eyes, put one foot on the floor to anchor himself, and then carefully sat up on the old U-shaped banquette in his mother's Airstream, holding the blanket around him. He rubbed his face, feeling the stubble of his beard, and then opened his eyes and recoiled as he saw Delpha sitting on the banquette on the other side of the table, staring right at him, with her raven on her shoulder, its little black eyes boring into him.

"Dang, Delpha."

The old woman smiled, and Ethan almost expected the lines on her face to explode, like ice cracking off the Antarctic shelf. "It's good you are back." The smile was gone so fast, he wondered if he had imagined it. Everyone was acting strange.

She put a beat-up deck of cards on the table. "Shuffle and cut," she said, and he'd have argued, but his head hurt, and his chest hurt, and she looked like she could take him. Hell, this morning anybody could take him.

He took the cards and shuffled them, wincing at the harsh flap on the table, and then cut them. Delpha put the deck back together and flipped over the first card. "Yes."

The card was old and worn, but it looked like a king on a throne holding a big sword. Ethan squinted at the writing on the bottom: KING OF SWORDS.

Glenda bustled in from the rear of the trailer, lit cigarette in hand. "How are you feeling, honey? That was a lousy welcome home you got."

Delpha said, "King of Swords," tapping the card. "He's finally come."

Glenda lost her smile. "Oh. Delpha, I don't think . . ."

Delpha scooped the card up and slid it into the pack. The deck disappeared into her cape pocket. She looked at Ethan. "You are ill."

No shit, Ethan thought.

"You will be better," Delpha said in that same voice he'd heard for years listening to her in the Oracle tent. She stood and said to Glenda, "You must tell him." Then she left, nodding good-bye to Ethan.

Frankie flew after her. He didn't nod good-bye.

"Tell me what?" Ethan said when the door had closed again

Glenda smiled tightly at him. "I'm so glad you're home. Gus needs you on night-security detail. You can move into Hank's trailer or Old Fred's, they're both empty—"

"I don't want a job or a trailer, Mom." Ethan tried to keep his voice polite. "I get a disability check from the government, and I can sleep in the woods. I just want to take it easy."

Glenda ground out her cigarette butt. "What disability?"

"This and that," Ethan said vaguely.

"Delpha said you were sick."

Ethan could feel the time bomb in his chest. He changed the subject. "You know Gus could—"

"I'm worried about you," Glenda said bluntly.

"I'm worried about all of you," Ethan said. "You're smoking like a chimney, Delpha looks like she's half dead, and Gus's raving about escaped demons."

Glenda stood up. "Fine. Don't tell your mother anything. That way she can just worry." She went to the fridge and began to rummage inside.

Great. He looked around the cleanly kept interior of the old Airstream trailer—the barkcloth curtains, the faded red banquette, the general air of having been decorated in 1935—and saw his own future, except for the cleanly kept part. Not that he had a future.

He shifted on the banquette and his chest throbbed. Whatever he'd been hit with had quite a punch, and he was surprised it hadn't jarred the old bullet into his heart. He picked up his Kevlar vest and saw a barbed metal circle, about the size of a bracelet, embedded in the front. He'd never seen ordnance like this, but it confirmed last night was not a bad dream. That and the ache in his chest. His butt kind of hurt, too, and he had to think for a moment before he recalled falling when trying to climb the gate.

"Hey, my rucksack—," he began, but Glenda was ahead of him, slamming the fridge door with her hip.

"Gus found it when he opened the gate this morning. It's on the floor under the window."

Ethan turned his attention back to the vest and pried the metal circle off. Some kind of shotgun round? The impact had been hard, but not too bad. He had a feeling if he hadn't been wearing the Kevlar, his chest would be hurting a lot worse, but the circle looked like it would have just torn up his skin with the barbs and been a bitch to pull off, not lethal.

He turned the circle over because it just wasn't right: it was too dark and not heavy enough for steel or lead. He held it up to the sunlight, squinting. The small barbs had flattened a considerable amount upon impact with the Kevlar.

Something bad was going on. "Have you been having problems with strangers in the park?"

"No," Glenda said, messing with something at the sink. "But we need more security. We're getting a lot more people since we've rehabbed the place, and Gus can't handle it by himself at night anymore."

"What wrong with Gus?" Ethan asked. "He's talking about demons. That's not good."

"Nothing's wrong with Gus."

"He can't hear."

"He can hear. Just not well. Stay on his left and it's easier for him." She came back to the table with a bowl, a bottle of milk, and a big orange box.

Ethan blinked. "Wheaties?"

"You love Wheaties," Glenda said. "It's your favorite."

Twenty years ago. "Uh, thanks." He put the strange round on the table, took the box, checking to make sure Mark Spitz wasn't still on it—Glenda saved everything—and poured a sufficient helping, his stomach rumbling dangerously as he topped it off with milk. He realized she had to have run into town before he woke up to get the cereal and he had to blink hard for a few seconds. "This is sweet of you, Mom."

Glenda rubbed a hand over his closely cropped hair and sat down on the other end of the banquette, firing up another cigarette. "Anything for you." She took a hard drag. "So who shot you?"

Ethan collected himself. "No idea. But if there are people in the park with guns, we should talk to the police."

"No police."

"Mom, if somebody else gets shot—"

"No." Glenda looked at her cigarette. "We just need better park security. We've got some people on during the day, but we need somebody on night detail with Gus. He doesn't want anybody. Says he can do it himself." She smiled at him. "He'd be real happy to have you, though."

Ethan closed his eyes. He knew they needed him, he'd known it since last night. He was stuck.

"Don't be like that, Ethan. It's an easy job. Our biggest problem is the frat kids coming here and stealing the FunFun at the entrance. We should have made him of solid iron. Give the little bastards hernias."

"I didn't get shot by a frat kid." More of the night before was coming back to him. The red dot, which meant laser sight. Night-vision goggles above a mask. Special round from a weird gun. Silencer. Professional. What the hell would a professional be doing here? Then he realized he was here and he was supposed to be a professional.

Glenda sighed as she exhaled smoke, and Ethan felt a stab of guilt at how exhausted she looked. He stood up, wrapping the blanket around him, and scooted past her and down the short hallway into the bathroom at the other end. The trailer was a lot smaller than he remembered it. His khaki pants and black turtleneck, still damp, were draped over the shower curtain. He put them on, bumping into the pink walls, and tried to be glad he was home.

He grabbed his boots and opened the door and looked down the hallway at his mother. She looked a million years old.

She took a final drag on her cigarette and stubbed it out. "We really need you, Ethan."

Ethan gave up. "I know. I'll help Gus with security." *I'll find out who shot me, too.*

Glenda nodded, still tense. "Thank you. We'll pay you, of course. We have money coming in again now that the park's fixed up. We should have a really good Halloween this year, too. We'll be okay." She sounded like she was talking to herself more than to Ethan.

He pulled on the Kevlar vest and checked his Mark 23, Special Operations modified pistol, making sure a bullet was in the chamber. Technically dangerous and not recommended for amateurs, but he wasn't an amateur.

"Before you go . . . ," Glenda began, and paused. "Sit down, Ethan. I have to tell you something. I'd wait until you were settled in, but we're running out of time and . . ." She looked upset. "Just sit down, please."

Oh, hell. He sat down and braced himself for whatever it was.

"Do you remember how, when you were a little boy, we used to have meetings here? Gus and Delpha and me and Old Fred and Hank?"

"Yeah," Ethan said. "I was sorry to hear about Hank. I know you were close."

"No, we weren't," Glenda said. "He was a drunk. That's how he died, ran his car into a tree." She watched Ethan. "On July twenty-ninth."

Ethan straightened. July 29 was the day of the firefight. July 29 was the day he'd gotten his bullet.

"Something happened to you on July twenty-ninth, didn't it?" Glenda said.

"I didn't die," Ethan said, his voice harsh. "What are you getting at?"

Glenda's expression had changed to worry. "What do you mean, you didn't die? You were in danger?"

"We got attacked high up in the mountains. Everybody on my team died." He swallowed. "I don't want to talk about it."

Glenda drew a deep breath. "Well, then, thank god Hank drove into that tree."

"Mom—"

"Ethan, the five of us weren't friends, we were the Guardia."

"A club?" Ethan said, just about ready to end the conversation.

"A team." Glenda smiled at him. "It's a good team, Ethan, we do good work—"

"Charity?"

"No," Glenda said. "Demons."

Oh, sweet Jesus, she's lost it, too. He should have come home sooner, the stress—

"Dreamland is a demon keep," Glenda went on. "A prison for five of the strongest demons in the history of the world. The Untouchables. They can't be killed, so they have to be held. Here. They're trapped in ancient chalices, wooden cups, and imprisoned in five statues around the park, and we watch over them." She paused. "I know that's probably hard to believe—"

"Did you . . . hit your head maybe?" Ethan said. He'd seen that in combat; head injuries were tricky things.

"No, Ethan," Glenda said patiently. "This is real."

"Any new medications?"

"Ethan."

He stood up. "Look, if you and Gus want to have this . . . club—"

"It's not a club, Ethan," Glenda said, her voice serious as death. "You don't join, you're called and the powers pass to you. Those powers saved you when the rest of your men died. You're the Hunter—"

"No, that is not what happened," Ethan said, and, grabbing his rucksack, turned and walked out of the trailer.

CHAPTER 4

It was chilly outside, and that felt good as Ethan walked down the path and out of sight of the trailers.

He didn't know why he was still alive, but it wasn't any damn mystical power. His mother was not going to take what had happened, the deaths of five brave men, and make it part of her fantasy, not now, not ever.

But she did need his help, there was a stranger in the park with a gun, and he was going to fix that for her. He stopped and opened his ruck and dug out the thigh holster rig he'd had custom-made before he shipped off to war for the first time and slid the Mark 23 into the holster with the ease of long practice. The gun rested comfortably on his upper thigh, right next to his hand. Then he walked down the narrow path to the midway, blinking in the bright sunlight, grateful there weren't any people around—

"Are you Ethan Wayne?" a voice to his right chirped.

Ethan tensed and then relaxed when he saw a pretty, wide-eyed blonde sitting on one of the picnic tables in front of the empty Beer Pavilion. She was bundled in a faded blue-green Parkersburg High letter jacket, but beneath that was a short skirt that showed off her long, lean legs, and her blond hair was gathered in some kind of cute fluffy thing on top of her head, and her smile almost hurt his eyes.

He'd come home to find solitude, but he wasn't going to be a hard-ass about it. Not unless she started talking about demons and asked him to join her club.

"I've heard about you," the girl said, sliding off the table. "You were, like, the best quarterback ever. The high school still has your picture up. At least it was there when I graduated two years ago."

Ethan winced. "Quarterback was a long time ago."

She didn't seem fazed. "Your picture was real nice." She came closer. "You're even better in person. I'm Ashley Willhoite. My uncle was on the team with you. I've heard all about you." Her eyes widened as she saw the ripped circle in the cloth covering the Kevlar, and she came closer to put her hand on it. "What happened here?"

"I got shot last night." *Brilliant,* he thought as soon as he said it, but he wasn't used to women coming up and putting their hands on his chest.

Ashley stepped closer. "Shot! Are you all right?"

Ethan nodded. "Kevlar took the brunt of it."

"Kevlar?"

"Body armor."

She pressed her hand harder against his chest. "You poor thing. You were lucky you weren't hurt."

"Nah. If the shooter had been any good, he'd have double-tapped me between the eyes, so—" He paused as he saw the disconcerted look on Ashley's face. *Got to work on the small talk.*

"You should come to the Dream Cream for breakfast." Ashley moved in closer, her big brown eyes gazing into his. "Cindy makes this wonderful waffle-and-maple-ice-cream thing, and she says—"

"I've got to search the park," Ethan said, but he didn't step back. "Find evidence. Track down the shooter." He had no idea what he was babbling about.

She batted her big brown eyes at him. "Are you sure?"

"Well—" The Wheaties weren't sitting too well in his stomach, so maybe some hot food would be nice. "What the heck."

"Great." She linked her arm in his and pulled him toward the front of the park.

Ethan tried not to enjoy her closeness too much. He concentrated on the Devil's Drop, the highest place in the park, a black Eiffel Tower–like structure with five arms stretching out from the top, ending in five tattered parachutes, still fenced off after all these years and looking really bad. He'd have thought that would be one of the first things to be redone. The seven-foot-high iron devil statue in front of the fence was in prime condition, though, leering and red and ugly as sin.

Ashley leaned in close, brushing her breast against his arm. "How long will you be staying?"

"Till I die," Ethan said, not moving away.

"That's good."

They went past the orange OK Corral booths—shooting gallery, fast-draw saloon, and roping range populated with assorted wood cowboys—and then rounded the bend to the next ride, the huge lump of pink concrete across from the Keep lake, known as the Tunnel of Love.

"We should try that," Ashley said.

Ethan had some fond memories of the Tunnel from high school. Perhaps he could make some new ones.

Beyond the Tunnel, the Worm ride leered at him, its ugly red face and bulging eyes a blight on the park, and beyond that, the seven-foot-tall double-D-cup blue-green mermaid statue pointed toward the Mermaid World Cruise, the tunnel there striped in blue and turquoise and plastered with flags of the world, or at least the twelve countries on the cruise.

Ashley stacked up pretty well against the statue.

"You know—," Ethan began as they passed it, but then he felt her stiffen. "What's wrong?"

Ashley shuddered for several seconds, then she pulled her hand out from his arm and turned to look at him. Her head tilted slightly as her gaze went from his head to his boots, then back to his eyes, her own eyes hard now, almost black in the midmorning sun.

"You all right?" Ethan asked.

She turned and walked back the way they'd come as if he didn't exist, her hips swaying and her skirt swishing around those strong legs.

"Great," Ethan said. He really had to work on his small talk.

He shook his throbbing head and headed back to the Dragon Coaster to look for evidence of his shooter.

*****

Mab walked through the park toward the Fortune-Telling Machine, admiring all the color and craftsmanship of the things she'd restored. Her work. It was all so much better without people climbing all over everything, just beautiful things . . .

That guy from the Dream Cream would look good here, she thought, and then frowned at herself. There was no point in attaching to people, she was going to be gone in two weeks anyway, and besides, he and Cindy were probably getting to know each other right now.

Back to work.

The Fortune-Telling Machine stood about seven feet tall and maybe thirty inches wide, made of cast iron, with cloudy glass windows on three sides under a peaked roof trimmed with metal scallops and iron tassels. The booth was dark, heavily molded in a wave pattern, and rusted in many spots, with most of its paint gone.

"Okay," Mab said. "Let's get you amazing again."

She took off her hat, put her bag down on the ground, and took out cleaning supplies. She moved around the box, taking off most of the surface grime, but barely made a dent in the cloudiness of the glass since most of the dust was on the inside, coming between her and the fortune-teller statue in there. Then she began on the deeper cleaning of the iron sides, using fine steel wool and a magnet to pick up the rust dust that generated. When she got to the fourth and most damaged side, the front, the carving was different. She squinted at the rubbing and realized there was a name there. *V . . . a . . . n . . .* Vanth? Vanth, the Fortune-Teller?

She pulled herself up by the corroded-in-place lever on the front of the case so she could peer at the face behind the cloudy glass. "Vanth?" she said, leaning hard on the lever as she stood, and then it moved and she almost fell as she heard the metallic grind of unoiled gears inside the machine, and a yellowed card spit out into the tray.

"I didn't put in a penny," she said.

The statue inside sat unmoving behind the clouded glass, so she picked up the card.

YOU HAVE GREAT ADVENTURES BEFORE YOU.

"Good to know," she told the statue, and put the card in her bag so that they could print new ones just like it. If she was lucky, the machine would be full of them and they could just copy those so she wouldn't have to make up fortunes for the next two weeks, which would be good, since her insights ran to *A job worth doing is worth doing meticulously and obsessively* and *Always floss.*

And maybe Embrace the experience.

"Oh, stop it," she told herself. "You don't even know that guy."

"What guy?" her uncle said, and she looked around to see Ray standing there, smiling in the sunshine, a cigar clamped in the corner of his mouth. The smile was about as believable as the robot clown.

"I hate it when you do that," she told him. "Moving around the park on little cat feet, startling people."

He walked around the booth. "Lot of work to do here."

"Yep," Mab said. "If you go away, I can do it."

Ray took the cigar out and tapped his ashes on the ground next to Mab's work bag. "I just came to see how my niece was feeling. It's just the two of us now, the only Brannigans left, so we have to look out for each other. How's your head?"

"Fine." Mab moved her bag and picked up her crayon, not sure what her uncle wanted, but positive it was good for him, not her. "What do you want?"

"I noticed the FunFun statue is missing. Damn college kids must have stolen it again and run into you with it." Ray tried to make his voice hearty, but there was tension there.

Mab hated tension. Another reason to avoid people, all that

emotion, gumming up her day. "I didn't see any kids, but I was hallucinating."

"So what did you see?"

"The big metal clown from the gate," Mab said patiently.

"You haven't seen him again, have you?"

"Ray, it was a hallucination."

"Right. Right." He seemed relieved as he gestured toward the box with the cigar. "Really looking forward to seeing what you do with this."

"Thank you," Mab said, still suspicious.

"If you see that clown again, you tell me, okay?"

"It was a *hallucination*, Ray."

"Right. Well, just in case, you tell me." He waved at her, stuck his cigar back in his mouth, and headed up the midway.

"I don't know him very well," she told the shadowy Vanth inside the box, "but I think he's up to something. My mother never trusted him." Then to be fair she added, "Of course, she didn't trust anybody, she used to call me demon spawn, so take that for what it's worth."

The Vanth didn't say anything, so she moved to the door in the back so she could clean the inside. The problem was the latch. She'd carved away as much grime as she could and scrubbed off the rust, but when she tugged on it, it wouldn't open.

She went around to the front of the box.

"I'll get this," she told the Vanth through the cloudy glass. "I just have to figure out how to open your box."

The machine whirred and a card spit out.

"Okay," Mab said. "I did not push that lever."

Inside the box, the figure sat unmoving.

Mab picked up the card.

FIND THE KEY AND ALL WILL BE ANSWERED.

"There's a key?" Mab said to the box. "There's no lock back there."

Then she realized she was having a conversation with a box.

Okay, the box was not talking to her. That was a standard . . . fortune. She patted the box. "I'm going to make you beautiful again."

The machine whirred and spit out a card:

THANK YOU.

"That's not funny," Mab said, and looked around to see if anybody was playing a trick on her.

Nothing. Just empty, dusty amusement park.

So maybe that was a joke, back in the old days you put in a penny for your fortune and got back a thank-you and everybody laughed. . . .

The box was not talking to her; the cards were just old fortunes.

"Sure, that's it," she said, and went back to her work, a little rattled this time.

*****

Ethan stood where the shooter had been and looked back toward the Dragon Coaster, the big ugly orange Strong Man statue in front of the ride giving him his approximate location from the night before. A long way at a tough angle. Hell of a shot in the dark, even with laser targeting, and given the depth perception problem when using night-vision goggles. He searched the ground for a spent shell casing, to no avail. So either the shooter had scooped it up or had used a round that left no casing. No signs of tracks in the loose gravel. The man in black was light on his feet or had learned the art of not leaving tracks. Or, most likely, had come back and cleaned up after himself.

Ethan sensed someone behind him and turned, hand twitching to go for his pistol.

A large-chested man wearing a sharp trench coat walked up like he owned the place. "Ethan Wayne?"

"Yeah."

"I'm Ray Brannigan." He didn't extend his hand, so Ethan didn't either.

Ethan noted a small black-and-gold Ranger crest pin on the man's lapel. "Winter or summer?"

Ray nodded. "Summer. Florida was hell." He reached into his pocket and pulled out a large coin. "Coin check."

"I don't do that," Ethan said, but Ray tossed the coin to him and he caught it. It was a Ranger coin with Ray's name inscribed on it, but a different color and weight from the standard coin, more like iron than bronze or brass. Ethan tossed it back to him. He'd never been impressed by the game some guys in elite units played, challenging with their coins because if the other guy didn't have his coin, they got a free drink.

Strangely, Ray nodded as if he'd passed some kind of test. He took out a cigar and lighter, tapped the cigar on the lighter, and lit it. "The FunFun statue from the park gate is missing. Need to find it. ASAP."

Ethan stiffened. He hadn't been issued orders in months. "I think you got bigger problems here than a missing statue."

"Find the statue," Ray barked, then chomped on the cigar, turned, and walked away.

"Asshole," Ethan muttered.

"Forget him. We gotta find the chalice," Gus rasped behind him.

Ethan turned. "Chalice?"

"The wood cup Fufluns was trapped in." Gus walked down the midway toward the entrance to the park, and Ethan followed him, making sure he was on the old man's left.

"Fufluns," Ethan said.

"Trickster demon," Gus said. "Untouchable. I told you this already."

Demons again. "Gus, look—"

"The chalice was in the FunFun statue that ran into Mab. We find that statue, we find the chalice."

"Gus, I think you and Glenda should see a doctor," Ethan said.

"Don't need to," Gus said.

"Ray wants me to find the statue, too," Ethan said.

That gave Gus pause; then he nodded. "Hurt his niece. Plus, first thing people see when they come in the park." He kept walking until they got to the front gate. "There, see?" He pointed to two patches of black in the shape of very large feet next to the gate.

Ethan knelt down and traced the outline of one of the dark patches with his finger. Clown feet. Great. He looked to the left and frowned. There was the faintest of imprints in the dirt scattered over the flagstones. He scooted over to it. Another big clown foot. Then another.

"This way, Gus." Ethan couldn't believe he was tracking a metal clown, but then he remembered those guys who did the Bigfoot scam, using dummy Bigfoot feet to leave tracks in the woods. Damn college kids.

Actually, pretty smart college kids. They'd managed to leave clown prints without leaving any of their own. Just like the shooter.

This wasn't college kids.

Ethan looked at Gus. "Maybe the guy who shot me took the clown?"

Gus looked exasperated. "Nobody took it. The demon was *inside* it. There weren't any people around to possess, so he possessed it."

Since it was looking more and more like finding the clown would lead to the shooter, Ethan decided to stop arguing about reality for the moment. "All right. Let's go find it."

Once Ethan focused, it wasn't hard to follow the tracks. They led to the carousel, where the grass was disturbed, then past the Roundabout to the Mermaid World Cruise, disappearing at the edge of the water the little cruise boats floated in. The taller-than-life-sized redheaded metal mermaid beside the ride held out her blue-green hand, beckoning to them, nothing small about her. Maybe the metal FunFun had stopped by and tried to pick her up. Ethan sure as hell would have, she was built like Ashley—

"He's in the tunnel," Gus said, and tried to climb over the side of the tank into the cold water.

"Wait a minute." That was all Gus needed, pneumonia at his age. "Let me do it." Ethan stepped into the tank, feeling the cold water soak into his boots. "You wait here," he told the old man and walked into the darkness of the long cavern, home to twelve dioramas of different countries, ignoring the happy little French dolls in berets in front of the Eiffel Tower, probably drunk on champagne, now frozen without power. Ditto for the Germans in their lederhosen, the Hawaiians in their leis, and the Russians doing that boot dance they always did, their little boots stuck in midair.

There were no clown footprints on the service ledge in the Mermaid Cruise, and the cars were undisturbed.

He went back out to Gus. "I don't think he went in there—"

"Around the back," Gus said, and took off again, and Ethan followed him, then drew his pistol as he saw somebody standing in the shadows in the back of the ride.

CHAPTER 5

"There it is." Gus stumbled into the shadows, and Ethan relaxed as he recognized the FunFun statue. Then he frowned. It looked . . . different. When they got up close to it, he realized why: The arms were down at its sides and the surface was mangled, the mouth torn at the corners, the neck stretched out of shape, gaping holes in the shoulders that exposed the wood beneath—

"Mab ain't gonna like this," Gus said.

He went to the rear of the statue as Ethan grabbed at it to gauge its weight. It was heavy but not impossibly so—thin sheet iron laminated over a wood frame—but it was bulky, too bulky to move by himself.

Gus was doing something on the back. "Damn it."

Ethan went around and looked over Gus's shoulder. He'd opened a door in the back of the statue and revealed a compartment with a large wooden cup, its heavily carved lid broken in several pieces.

"He wouldn't a gotten out if this lid hadn't been broke," Gus said, gathering up the pieces.

"Who?"

"I *tole* you. Fufluns. Trickster demon." Gus shook his head as he stowed the pieces of the lid in his jacket pockets. "Probably got cracked all the times the damn college kids stole the statue, knockin' around inside for forty years. Shoulda checked. Shoulda gotten the keys and checked them all. Shoulda—"

Ethan put his hand on Gus's shoulder, feeling sorry for the poor old guy, bedeviled by his illusions. "It's okay."

Gus shook his head. "Come on, we gotta get this back to the gate. Mab is gonna have to fix it for Halloween."

Ethan looked at the twisted statue. There was no way in hell anybody was fixing that ever again. "Sure," he said. "But we'll leave it here until we get a hand truck or something."

Gus nodded. "Yeah. A hand truck. Or maybe a golf cart."

"You go tell Glenda we found the statue," Ethan said. "I'll get a cart."

"Okay," Gus said, and began to amble toward the back of the park.

And then I'm going to ask some questions, Ethan thought. Somebody in the park had to know something. And if he stayed away from his mother and Gus, the chances were that whoever he asked wouldn't tell him about demons.

After his morning, that was a plus.

*****

By midafternoon, Mab had finished getting the booth ready to prime. Along the way, she had tripped the lever accidentally on purpose several times and gleaned much good advice:

SOMEONE CLOSE TO YOU HAS A SECRET TO SHARE.

IT'S GOING TO GET WORSE BEFORE IT GETS BETTER.

THAT'S NOT A GOOD LOOK FOR YOU.

But she hadn't found a way to open the box, and she was growing increasingly obsessed with getting in there to see Vanth's face.

She stood and scrubbed off her hands with a wipe, thinking, *I know you're in there, and I know you're beautiful.* Of course, just the box stripped to its basic iron was so gorgeous that she was tempted to leave it like that, but that wasn't her job. Her job was to put it back, and the way it had been was beautiful, too, those sea-greeny colors—

"You busy?" somebody said from behind her.

"Yes," Mab said.

The different swirls weren't just each painted different blues and greens; they had different blues and greens within them, she'd have to paint the undercoat and then—

"We found your clown."

Mab turned around. It was Ethan in camouflage and a lot of dust. *Bad colors*, she thought.

"He was behind the Mermaid Cruise," Ethan said. "He's pretty beat-up. Did you see who was carrying him when they hit you?"

"No," Mab said. "By the time I saw him, I was hallucinating. Will you be here long?"

Ethan looked around. "It's pretty empty here now."

Mab frowned. "It's October. The place is only open for the Dream Cream in the daytime and the Beer Pavilion at night during the week, so we don't charge admission until after four. We're busy on the weekends because we open the park as Screamland Friday and Saturday, but otherwise—don't you know this stuff?"

"I've been gone for a while," Ethan said, his blank face going blanker. "What I meant was, not a lot of people in the park to go running into you with some clown statue."

"Not some statue. The FunFun by the gate. And I hallucinated him."

"The evidence says it was him, not a hallucination." He rubbed his eyes, and she saw how red they were. "I tracked the clown's footprints. One set. Started at the gate, went through the park to the back of the Mermaid Cruise."

"He left *footprints?*"

"Have you ever seen anything here that struck you as . . . strange?"

Mab carefully did not look at the Fortune-Telling Machine. "Everything here is strange." When he looked exasperated, she said, "Look, it's an amusement park. Parks always have an unreal feeling about them because they're not real. Young Fred stands on the stage in a clown outfit and tells terrible jokes that nobody would laugh at, and people laugh because it's an amusement park. Delpha tells fortunes, and people come out of her tent amazed at how good she is because it's an amusement park. They drink awful beer and eat horrible food, and they think it's all fabulous because—"

"It's an amusement park," Ethan said.

"Although Cindy's ice cream really is fabulous."

"You don't have to explain the park to me. I grew up here."

"I know. I graduated with you."

"Okay," Ethan said, clearly not remembering her, which was not strange, considering what an outcast she'd been. "Uh, sure."

"I mostly stayed in the art room and the library. You didn't know me."

"Okay," Ethan said. "So you do this for a living, fix amusement parks? Or is this something you're just doing for Ray?"

He sounded suspicious, the way he said "Ray" sounded like "Batty Brannigan" to Mab, and she steeled herself for whatever insult was coming next.

"Because I'd think after growing up around here," he said, "the last thing you'd want to work on would be an amusement park. Didn't you get sick of this place as a kid?"

"I was never here as a kid," Mab said. "I wasn't allowed to come anywhere near here. I could hear the music at night during the summer, we didn't live that far away. And I could see the lights from our attic window." She swallowed, the yearning for lights coming back to her as if thirty years ago were yesterday, and then smiled tightly at him. "I never got to come here, but I did all my college art history work on carnivals and amusement parks and gypsy wagons, and I did my thesis on carnival art, so. . . . no, this is not something I'm doing for Ray."

"Oh," Ethan said. "So this means a lot to you, being in Dreamland."

"No, it's just a job," Mab lied.

"Right." Ethan looked uncomfortable, and Mab would have changed the subject, but he beat her to it. "What's it mean to your uncle?"

"What?"

"He's here a lot. What's he want with Dreamland?"

"I have no idea," Mab said. "Can I go back to work now?"

"Is there something here he wants?" Ethan said, not moving. "Or is he just coming here now because he couldn't when he was a kid?"

"He came all the time when he was a kid," Mab said. "He had his get-out-of-town epiphany here when he was fifteen."

"What?" Ethan scowled at her, as if she was being obscure.

"My mother said Ray came here one Halloween night and the next morning, he started doing everything he could to get out of Parkersburg." Of course, Mab thought, being a Brannigan in Parkersburg was enough reason to do everything you could to get out of Parkersburg.

"Fifteen," Ethan said. "What happened?"

"I don't know. He left the day after he graduated high school three years later and didn't come back, so I don't know him very well." The pause after that stretched out, so she added, "I was two when he left. We hadn't bonded."

"He's back now."

"Yes, he is. I have to work now."

"Have you ever seen guys dressed in black running around here at night? Black ops?"

"No. But I wouldn't, not unless they ran me down. I concentrate on my work. Which I should get back to."

"Somebody with high-tech equipment was in the park last night. That's who—"

"High tech?" Mab said, interested now. "High enough to animate an iron statue?"

"—shot me."

"Because that would be helpful. Frankly, the hallucination thing seems far-fetched, but I know what I saw, and I couldn't have seen that, so that left me with hallucinations, which is so unlike me, I'm a very calm person, and then you saw clown footprints, but if it's Men in Black animating statues . . ." Then the rest of what he'd said sank in. "You got shot?" She surveyed him doubtfully. "You look okay."

"It was a strange bullet." Ethan looked down at the base of the fortune-teller, frowning harder. "Can I borrow that magnet for a second?"

She picked up the magnet from the top of her bag and handed it over. “So you think it was a high-tech thing? Not the FunFun from the gate?”

“No, it was the statue from the gate. We found it behind the Mermaid Cruise.” Ethan dug in his pocket and brought out something that looked like a ring of barbed wire. It got sucked right to the magnet as soon as he brought it within a few inches.

“What’s that?”

“The round that hit me. But bullets are made of lead or steel. Not iron.”

“That’s a bullet?” Mab said, and then shook her head. “Never mind, I don’t care. So you found the gate FunFun. Thank you. Put it back where it belongs and I’ll fix it. I need to work on this now.”

“So who have you seen in the park at night?”

Mab sighed. Maybe if she cooperated, he’d leave faster. “Until eleven, anybody in the Beer Pavilion, but they make a beeline from the front gate to the Pavilion and back again, so they’re easy to avoid. After eleven, it’s just the people who live here.” When he waited, she elaborated. “Glenda, Gus, and Delpha back in the trailers. Young Fred in the apartment over the paddleboat dock. Cindy and me in her apartment over the Dream Cream.”

“What about Young Fred?”

Mab frowned. She had work to do. “What about him? He lives over the paddleboat dock. He’s a terrible comedian. He keeps an eye on the gate for Gus.” She thought about Young Fred. “He’s not a happy person. I don’t know why he doesn’t leave. He doesn’t like it here. Not the way the others like it.”

Ethan shook his head. “I saw him last night on the dock after you ran into the clown. He was watching you.”

“He watches everything. He’s bored.”

“Who inside the park would betray it?”

“Nobody,” Mab said. “Glenda and Gus and Delpha live for this park. Cindy runs the food concessions, and she plans on staying here forever. She told me that when she dies, she wants her ashes scattered in the Keep lake while the carousel plays ‘What Love Can Do.’ ” When Ethan frowned, she added, “It’s her favorite song, but it’s not going to happen because the carousel doesn't play 'What Love Can Do.' "

"Right," Ethan said. "The others, then, the help, somebody with a grudge—"

"You're wasting my time. The permanent help, the people who would know the park the way you're thinking, they're all local, and the park is what keeps Parkersburg going. My uncle is going to get named mayor for life because he's restoring it. Nobody in town would do anything to jeopardize this park—it's their lifeblood. Your Man in Black is not local."

"What about—?"

"I don't know anything else," Mab said, her patience exhausted. "Look, I only have two weeks left to finish this park before the big Halloween weekend, and if some moron is vandalizing it, I'd appreciate it if you'd find him and stop him, but other than that, I don't know what's going on."

"Okay," Ethan said. "Keep your eyes open. Tell me if you see anything strange."

Mab looked back at the Fortune-Telling Machine. "Right."

Ethan nodded and began to walk off and then turned back to her. "Anybody ever say anything to you about demons in the park?"

"Only my grandmother, who sold anti-demon charms, so she had a financial interest in the rumor. And my mother, who was nuts."

Ethan nodded. "How about Fufluns? Anybody ever say anything about somebody named Fufluns?"

"No," Mab said, frowning. "You mean FunFun?"

"No," Ethan said. "Thanks for your time."

He walked down the midway toward the back of the park, and Mab tried to put her mind back on her paint.

Demons.

The iron clown had said, "Mab" as it stretched out its hand to help her up. Maybe that week she'd been staring at it, leaning in close to put the details in the face, maybe something inside it had been staring back. She tried to look inside the box at Vanth, but the glass was too clouded. Maybe it was staring back, too, shuffling through its cards, getting ready to send her another message. Like STAY AWAY FROM THE CLOWN, HE'S MINE.

Well, that was crazy. *I am not crazy.*

Maybe she should tell somebody the machine was talking to her with cards. Of course, that on top of everything else could get her committed.

"I need help," she said out loud.

The machine whirred and spit out a card:

FIND THE KEY AND OPEN THE DOOR AND HELP WILL BE AT HAND.

Mab stared at it for a long time. That could be a fortune. It wasn't a *great* fortune, but it was . . . optimistic. Optimistic was good.

"Okay, then," she said, and went back to open her can of primer.

*****

At six-thirty, Mab straightened up, pushing at the small of her back to shove her spine into place, and looked at the Fortune-Telling Machine in the light from her miner's hat. She had the entire exterior cleaned, primed, and ready for the undercoat, as long as it didn't rain or drop below fifty degrees the next day. But she still hadn't found a way into the box.

"There's got to be a way," she told Vanth.

"There's always a way," a light voice said from behind her, and she turned to see the guy with the good shoulders from the Dream Cream there in the twilight, taller than she remembered, more curly-headed than she remembered, but just as cheerful as she remembered, his hands in his pockets, relaxed and smiling that crooked smile at her again. "I'm Joe. From this morning in the Dream Cream, remember?"

She pulled her paint coat closer around her. "Yes." She turned back to Vanth to get her bearings. It wasn't like he was drop-dead handsome. Or built like a wrestler. Or—

He came closer. "What's the problem?"

"The latch." Mab gestured to the box so she wouldn't have to look at him because her brain seemed to short out when she did that. "On the back, the latch that opens the door. It's . . . strange."

"Let's see it," Joe said, and walked around to the back.

"It's complicated." Mab went around the other side of the machine in time to see him pull the door open a couple of inches, using the tail of his shirt. "How did you do that?"

"You push it and lift it." Joe tugged on the door again to open it the rest of the way, and Mab heard metal complaining.

"Wait a minute." She went back to her paint bag to get her WD-40 and pumped oil into the hinges and then rocked the door gently back and forth so that it opened a little more. "This is *excellent*. Thank you."

"You're welcome."

She pumped in more oil and rocked the door again, and it gave up another couple of inches, enough that she could see inside.

It was a mess: dust and cobwebs and rust, all of it shrouding the back of the iron statue of Vanth—

Joe moved in closer to see, too, and she was so aware he was there and near that she stopped thinking about Vanth.

"Wouldn't it be better if you did this in daylight?" Joe said.

Mab swallowed. "I have the light on my hat. I can do it now. Thank you for helping. Good-bye."

"Or you could have dinner," Joe said. "With me."

She lost her breath again. It was ridiculous. She hadn't been this lame in junior high.

Of course, no boys had talked to her in junior high. And there hadn't been any boys like this in junior high, not even close.

"I just got this open, so I should keep working."

"Did you have lunch?" he said, his voice full of laughter.

"No. I was working."

"So it's been, what, nine hours since you had food?"

"Yes," Mab said, suddenly feeling hungry. "Could you show me how you opened this latch so I can do it, too?"

"If you'll have dinner with me."

Mab frowned, caught between exasperation and increasing stirrings. "This box is open *now*."

"Look, you have to eat," Joe said reasonably. "Starving yourself will not help you work. Show me the park between here and the Pavilion, and I'll feed you." He grinned at her. "They do have food, right?"

"Hot dogs. But this box is—"

"Dinner first. Then I'll show you the latch. And then tomorrow in the light of day, you can see what you're doing."

"I have my miner's hat," Mab said, pushing it back off her forehead.

His smile widened, and Mab remembered the Dream Cream that morning. How had he managed to pass by Cindy to come find her in her paint-stained canvas coat and yellow miner's hat? What kind of guy found that attractive? "What are you up to?"

"I'm hungry," Joe said. "I want to eat. With you. Soon. Are you always this difficult?"

"Yes," Mab said, and considered the situation. She did have to eat, in fact, she was starving now that she thought about it. And it was growing dark, and she did need daylight to see the entire inside of the machine; a miner's hat could only do so much.

And she really wanted to go with him.

"Okay, but we go dutch," she told him.

Joe sighed. "Fine. Which way do we go to get to the Pavilion?"

"Either way around the lake," Mab said. "Although it's shorter if we go to the right."

"The left it is." Joe closed the door to the Fortune-Telling Machine and then took her elbow and steered her toward the midway. She tried to look back, and he said, "Nope, keep your eyes ahead so you can see what's coming for you."

"What's coming for me?" Mab said, looking around.

"Me," Joe said, and she gave up and let him take her where he wanted to go.

*****

Ethan decided he'd more than earned his pay in the last twenty-four hours. Getting shot had not been in the job description, and when it had been in his previous job, he hadn't much cared for the experience.

And then there was his mother and Gus, losing their minds. He pulled his flask out and took a long swallow. *The hell with this.*

He looked up, searching in the fading daylight for the highest point in the park: the blinking lights on the star-shaped top of the Devil's Drop, conveniently located right in front of the Beer Pavilion and therefore his star to steer by in his quest for drink and Ashley. She'd acted weird this morning, but then again, so had everyone else in Dreamland. He walked around the lake that surrounded the Keep, being careful not to trip any more of the cheesecloth ghosts, past the Worm and the Tunnel of Love and the OK Corral games and the Devil's Drop, and on up to the Pavilion, where he heard voices raised in drunken revelry.

There wasn't much time could do to the Beer Pavilion. Long wooden tables that had been scarred and splintery before the Depression were scattered around an open fire pit in front of the newly repainted bar. Behind the bar was a row of kegs, a Coke cooler, a hot dog grill and bun steamer, and a girl dressed in Dreamland's version of German Oktoberfest, accepting the one-dollar per plastic cup and two-dollar hot dog fees along with whatever tips her cleavage drew. The place was packed with regulars from Parkersburg; even Ray was leaning on the bar, watching the crowd.

Gus waved Ethan over from a table near the back, but Ethan looked for Ashley, stopping when he found her sitting close to some balding guy he didn't recognize. She looked different—older, harder, not as bouncy. Ethan walked right past her table, and she didn't even give him a glance, although he slowed enough to give her plenty of time to see him, enough time for him to see the wedding ring on the guy's hand as it moved to Ashley's thigh. He felt stupid, then angry, then sad, like three blinks of the eye, and then he sank back into the hopelessness that had been ruling his life since Afghanistan and the bullet threatening his heart.

"Ethan!" Gus called, and Ethan stopped by the bar to grab a plastic cup of Ohio's finest, whatever the hell it was, and dropped two bucks on the table—one for the beer, one for the tip—which made the girl in the peasant top smile at him before she moved on to smile at the next guy. He stopped beside Ray, who now seemed to be coin-checking complete strangers—some guys couldn't leave the Army behind—and caught his eye.

"Found your statue," Ethan said.

Ray smiled, but it didn't reach his eyes. "Great." He went back to doing coin challenges with his ugly iron coin.

Ethan went to the back of the Pavilion and sat down. Gus acknowledged his presence with a nod, his sagging face even saggier.

Ethan's eyes slid back to Ashley. She was leaning on the guy now, whispering in his ear.

"Demons," Gus muttered.

"Women," Ethan said, and drank some of his beer.

*****

Mab had started down the midway with Joe, trying not to hyperventilate like a teenager on her first date. It was just so unlike her to be swamped with . . . well, feelings. *Maybe it's because I hit my head last night—*

"What's that?" Joe pointed to the blue-striped wooden Oracle booth to the left of the Fortune-Telling Machine, festooned with signs —CAREER PROSPECTS, TRUE LOVE, FAMILY AND FRIENDS— under a much bigger sign in gold that said DELPHA'S ORACLE: DREAMLAND PSYCHIC.

"That's where Delpha tells fortunes during the summer. It was built in '72, so it's got that hippie-dippie thing going for it, but I still like it. It wasn't too hard to restore except for a hole some delinquent had carved in the back." Mab nodded at the next ride on the left as they followed the curved flagstones around the lake. "The Double Ferris Wheel is from 1926. Incredible detail." She nodded to the right, at a black ship half in the waters of the Keep lake, its deck full of plastic pirates. "Pirate Ship. They put that in during the fifties." She scowled up at it. "I spent way too long on those pirates. Some idiot had beaten them with a board or something, and they were a mess." She pulled him into the center of the midway as they walked. "Stay away from the fence, that's where the triggers for the ghosts are. They're just cheesecloth and papier-mâché but they'll still scare the hell out of you." She smiled at the thought. "It's an old-fashioned way to make ghosts, but it's good."

"You like the old stuff," Joe said.

"I like the stuff with craftsmanship." Mab dismissed the Pirate Cove Games to their left in their boxy little striped orange buildings and pointed to the Dragon Coaster with its loading dock in the lake to the right. "Like that. Another ride from '26. That thing is a work of art. It took me and six interns three weeks just to paint the dragon tunnel and the cars. Gus worked for three days replacing lightbulbs." She pointed to the Test Your Strength machine next to it, an ugly orange Strong Man statue standing guard over it. "Then I spent a week on all the detail on the Strong Man statue. And then there's the wrought-iron fence that's all over the park. Took interns weeks to regild all the spear tips, but it was worth it."

"You really love this place," Joe said.

"Well, I did a good job on it, so I'm proud," Mab said. "I don't know that you can *love* a place—"

"You really love this place," Joe said again, stopping in the middle of the midway.

Mab blinked at him.

"Come on," Joe said. "How do you *feel* about it?"

"Uh . . ." Mab looked around at color and pattern, beautifully designed machinery and sturdy construction, and more than that, her work, her very good work, and realized that the park did make her feel . . . "I don't know. It's a good feeling."

"Happiness, maybe?" Joe said, laughter in his voice.

"Maybe," Mab said, and he shook his head and they walked on.

They passed under the tallest loop of the coaster, and she pointed to a row of three pink striped buildings to their left, closed now but emblazoned with signs for funnel cakes and french fries and sno-cones. "Anything painted pink in the park sells food and Cindy runs it. Anything painted orange is games, and different families in town run them, they're all hereditary." She gestured to one booth, full of fluorescent-furred teddy bears with a huge green velvet stuffed dragon at the top, hovering over a counter full of holes with padded hammers lined up in back of them. "Like Carl Jenkins runs the Whack-A-Mole because the Jenkinses have always run the Whack-A-Mole, so everybody calls him Carl Whack-A-Mole. And this," she added as they rounded the farthest curve and came up on a towering piece of tarnished black metalwork, "is the Devil's Drop." She looked up into darkening twilight, finding the top of the Drop by the lights pulsing up there to warn wayward aircraft, the tattered black and red parachutes on the ends of the five points fluttering in the wind. "It's a parachute ride, but Glenda won't run it. I think that's a bad idea. It's like having a dead body in the park. The rides were built to run."

"You didn't restore it," Joe said.

"Glenda didn't want it restored." Mab jerked her thumb at the seven-foot-tall statue of the glowering red devil in front of it. "I did him, though. Hate him. Ugly, ugly statue. Every minute of restoring him was awful." She gestured up the rise behind the Devil's Drop to a white open building with a pink pergola on top. "And that is the Beer Pavilion. If it gets really cold, they pull canvas curtains over the openings, but there's a big fire pit in the middle, so it's usually good in there through October. Then even Glenda gives up until April."

They walked up to the main opening of the Pavilion as she said, "That's your tour. The left half of it, anyway."

"So anything strange ever happen here?" Joe said, looking back at the park.

"A lot of people are asking me that lately." Mab tilted her head at him and realized what was going on. "You're a reporter."

"What?" Joe said.

"You're a reporter. You're here to get a jump on the big Halloween deal in two weeks. That's why you picked me up and tried to bribe me with dinner." It all made sense now.

"Because it's not possible that I'd want to feed you just to be with you?" Joe said.

"Well, it's unlikely," Mab said. "I have no charm. I'm no beauty. I dress like a tramp and not the slutty kind. What would draw you?"

"You," Joe said, and he made it sound like the truth.

She really wanted it to be the truth.

"Yeah, you're a reporter," Mab said, and went into the Pavilion.

*****

Ethan was not enjoying the Beer Pavilion.

Ashley was dividing her time between necking with the bald guy and watching the room, sizing up everybody as if making notes for later. She was nothing like he remembered her from his first meeting at the picnic table, but then he was lousy with women anyway. Maybe if he'd talked to her more that morning. He was trying to remember what he'd done or said to bring about the sudden change in her mood, but was drawing a blank. Several parts of his life since July 29 were blanks, so maybe . . .

Gus looked in the direction of Ethan's gaze. "Ashley? You can do better than that."

"Hell, I can't even do that," Ethan said.

Gus began to speak, but a woman sat down on the bench across from them and said, "May I join you?" and Gus stopped, his mouth open. Ethan understood his surprise. She looked to be in her late thirties, green eyes, sharp planes to her face, shoulder-length brown hair. She was beautiful, but more than that she was—

"Classy," Gus said.

"Thank you," she said, her voice pitched low with amusement. She handed Gus a five-dollar bill and said, "I'm buying," and Gus took the bill and left for the bar before she finished her two-word sentence.

She turned and smiled at Ethan and made him dizzy. Of course, he'd just had half a cup of warm beer on an empty stomach on top of the shots from the flask spaced throughout the day. That'd make any man dizzy. His eyes dropped to the neck of her white shirt, underneath an open leather jacket. A fringe of white lace was showing. That would make any man dizzy, too.

"Master Sergeant Wayne?" she asked.

Ethan snapped his eyes back up to her face. "Who's asking?"

"I'm Weaver," she said and held out her hand, slender and, Ethan was sure, soft.

"Just Weaver?" he said, but he couldn't stop himself from taking it. Her grip was warm, firm not soft; he felt calluses.

She pulled her hand back. "You're pretty famous around here, you know. Local hero."

Hero. Right. Ethan glanced back at Ashley. Her head swiveled and she looked right at Ethan and then through him as if he weren't there. "Yeah," Ethan said, harsher than he intended. "Big hero."

"So what brings you home, hero?" Weaver asked, smiling.

"My mother needed help." Ethan picked up his plastic cup and drained the rest of his beer in one long swallow.

"Glenda." Weaver nodded. "How's Glenda doing?"

Ethan focused on her, trying to figure out her angle. Did she know Glenda was losing her grip? "She's great."

"Good for her." Weaver smiled again as she said it, and Ethan felt himself drawn in.

He picked up his plastic cup to drink, but it was empty. He felt flustered putting it back down on the table, and his voice was sharper than he meant it to be when he spoke. "What are you doing here?"

She seemed taken aback. "Drinking with you."

"Yeah, I'm sure this is the best you can do." He looked her up and down again and shook his head. "What do you want?"

She leaned back, crossing her arms over her chest, and Ethan felt a slight disappointment.

"Well, I wanted to meet you, grumpy," she said, her smile fainter now, but still there. "You're Special Forces. Highly qualified. And now you're here in Dreamland doing . . . what?"

"Security guard," Ethan said.

Her smile vanished. "Security guard? Oh, come on."

She leaned forward again and Ethan thought, *Don't look*, and looked.

"What are you really doing here?" she asked. "You're on a mission, aren't you?"

Gus slapped a plastic cup in front of her, making the beer slop out and her jerk back, and Ethan accepted his cup gratefully. Then Gus put the tray he'd been carrying down in front of his seat, two more glasses on it for him. "I left the last buck for a tip. Shannon's a good girl."

"Of course," Weaver said, picking up her cup. She took a sip and winced at the taste. Then she looked up and caught him watching her and knocked back a good slug of it and slapped the cup down on the table.

Ethan smiled. He hadn't meant to, but there was something so good-natured in the way she knocked back the lousy beer, unguarded for the first time since she'd sat down, and then she grinned back and he thought, *Screw being careful, if she gets dangerous, I can take her.* That made him smile, too, and he leaned forward, only to catch sight of Mab in her miner's hat, talking to some stranger. Hell, maybe they'd all get laid tonight.

Mab caught him watching her just as Weaver turned around to see who he was looking at. He watched them size each other up across the room the way women always did, fast and thorough, pretending they weren't. Out of the corner of his eye, he also noticed Ashley watching the exchange between the two women as the bald guy chewed on her neck.

Women.

Weaver turned back to Ethan.

"So you come here often?" he said to her, and she smiled again.

"Do you?" she said. "Doesn't your boss mind you drinking on duty?"

Ethan looked at Gus. "You mind?"

"Hell no." Gus drank half of the first beer on the tray and wiped his mouth.

Weaver's smile faded, and she looked puzzled. "Gus is your boss?" she said to Ethan.

"Pretty much. Gus and Glenda. They're tough but fair." He tried smiling at her.

She still looked confused. "I thought Ray Brannigan bought the park."

"Ray don't own all of the park," Gus said, mustering some outrage. "He just got half."

Ethan turned to him, astounded. "What? How the hell did Ray get half the park?"

Gus moved his cup around on the table. "Park hasn't been doing that good. Ray said he'd buy half of our shares if we used the money to fix the park. We all sold him half, only Young Fred sold him all of his so now Ray's got half." Gus drained the rest of the first beer and moved on to the second.

"Your math's off, Gus," Weaver said, but Ethan was still dealing with the fact that his mother had let half the park be sold.

"It got that bad?" he said to Gus. "Why didn't you call me?"

"You know Glenda," Gus said. "She likes to do things herself."

"Crap," Ethan said. Ray with a 50 percent interest in the park could go a long way toward explaining why Glenda was deteriorating. Stress could screw with anybody's mind. He knew that one for sure.

He looked over at the bar, but Ray was gone, and then he caught sight of him in the middle of a group of people, all drunk and laughing except for him. He had his iron coin in his hand again. Loser.

"It's okay," Gus said, following Ethan's eyes to Ray. "He don't interfere much. And Mab's doin' a real good job; park looks like new. We had a real good summer, people coming to see it fixed up. Next year, we're gonna be fine again."

"Mab?" Weaver said, and Ethan realized that drinking had made him stupid; they'd been talking in front of her the whole time.

"Mab's the redhead you were checking out a minute ago," Ethan said, gesturing behind her.

Weaver turned around, but Mab and the guy were gone from the bar into the crowd. She turned back to Gus. "Right. I remember her. Nice hat. So Brannigan bought into the park but he's not interfering with anything." She looked at Ethan, still smiling but her eyes narrow now. "And you're just a security guard."

Ouch, Ethan thought, and drank the rest of his beer, still trying to figure out how Ray had muscled in and how bad it must have been for Glenda to let him.

Gus leaned toward her. "Who are you, lady?"

"Oh, I'm a big fan." Weaver got up and came around the picnic table to sit beside Ethan. She glanced down at the thigh rig. "Big gun."

"Mark 23 SOCOM," Ethan said, figuring that meant nothing to her.

"Can I see it?"

Ethan frowned. *Never give up your weapon* was a rule pounded into him in every training he'd had in the Army. He pulled the gun out of the rig, took the magazine out, ejected the round in the chamber, and handed it to her.

"Heavy," Weaver said, but she held it as if it were a feather. She hefted it in her hand. "Nice balance."

She moved fast, smoothly sliding the gun home into the holster before Ethan could react and buckling the keep on top, her fingers brushing over his thigh.

Ethan was trying to think of what to say when she stood up. She looked down at him while he looked at her formfitting jeans, and then she pulled a card out of her jacket pocket and handed it to him. "If anything . . . exciting happens, call me. I love a good Dreamland story. Or just call me. We can discuss your gun."

Ethan looked at the card. There was just a phone number on it. *At least I got her number,* he thought. "So," he began, but when he looked up, she was walking away.

She looked great walking away.

Ethan realized she'd put an unloaded gun back in his holster. "Damn." His life was a mess: robot clowns, black ops, crazy mother, hot cryptic women handling guns—

"She might be a demon," Gus said judiciously.

Ethan closed his eyes.

He really had hit bottom.

CHAPTER 6

Mab let Joe-the-reporter-on-an-expense-account buy the hot dogs, telling him, "Cindy has them shipped in from New York." The beer wasn't very good, but Mab was so tired and thirsty that she knocked back the whole first cup anyway while they were at the bar waiting for their hot dogs. She saw Ethan trying to be charming with a very attractive woman, and then Joe asked her about what she did when she wasn't working on the park, and he was so warm and so interested and so apparently happy to be listening to her that she followed him over to a table near the fire with her second beer and told him about the other things she'd restored, circus wagons and an old medicine wagon and lots of carousel horses in museum collections—"I've been doing this for twenty years, so pretty much anything old that has a carnival aspect to it, I'm your woman"—growing more relaxed as she talked about her work, so relaxed that she went on and told him about the paintings that she did for extra income, designed after vintage circus and amusement park posters, while he hung on every word, describing them all and then going back to talk about the different jobs she'd done, her heart lifting as she remembered all that beauty. She'd always been pleased with her work, but somehow, telling Joe about it now, she remembered it with real pleasure.

"There's not a lot of money in it," she finally finished, because that was what people always asked. "But I can run all my business stuff off my website, which is cheap, and I get room and board wherever I'm working, and I'm working all the time, and everything I own fits in two bags, so I do all right. And I love my work. That's important. Your work is always there for you, no matter what."

"You're amazing," he said, and she stopped, surprised. "What?"

"Men don't usually tell me I'm amazing." She felt tense again.

"Hey," he said, and put his hand over hers, and she didn't move it away although normally she would have.

It felt good there.

"I'm always the weird one," she told him. "When I was growing up here, it was because my family was the Batty Brannigans, and I really thought that once I got out of Parkersburg, I'd be okay, but then I went to art school, and I was *still* the weird one, so trust me, people do not tell me I'm amazing."

She stopped, appalled that she'd said that, and pulled back her hand.

Joe shook his head. "Normal is overrated. You are fascinating." He picked up her empty cup. "How about another beer?"

"That would be good," she said faintly, still wrapping her mind around *fascinating*, and he went back for more beer and dogs.

Okay, so he had called her fascinating, but that was because he was a reporter after a story. It wasn't—

Maybe he liked her. He *seemed* to like her. That was an unnerving thought, she could cope with being ignored or even ridiculed, but some guy *liking* her—

Two men sat down at the other end of their table and spread out their beers and hot dogs, the skinny one talking loudly in the middle of her nervous breakdown.

"Now, your basic hot dog is all well and good," Skinny said, "but it's the regional variations where you really get your bang for the buck. Like your Michigan hots and your Coneys, although putting meat sauce on a sausage? What's up with that?"

Up at the bar, Joe smiled at Shannon, who blushed and dimpled.

He leaned closer to talk to her—probably interviewing her, Mab told herself—and Shannon leaned forward, too.

Well, who wouldn't lean closer to Joe? He was charming. And funny. And—

"Now me," Skinny said loudly, "I'll take a good old kraut or slaw sauce, maybe a smear of mustard, nothing that gets in the way of the dog, if you know what I mean. You know what I think, Quentin? I think people just pile garbage on a good dog to be trendy. That's what I think."

Joe leaned in even more to whisper something in Shannon's ear, and Mab found herself annoyed with Skinny and his culinary opinions.

"Go with the classic," he was saying now, "that's what I say. In fact, you give me a choice, I'll go with a brat and kraut in a bun, any day of the week. That's good enough for me."

"Nathan's," his friend Quentin said.

"Okay," Skinny said.

Shut up, Mab thought.

Joe laughed with Shannon and then headed back to the table, stopping by the jukebox to punch up "What Love Can Do."

"So this is Cindy's favorite song," he said as he put her third beer in front of her and sat down.

"John Hiatt is a park favorite," Mab said, accepting another hot dog and forcing a smile. "He's on both park jukeboxes, the one at the Dream Cream and here."

Joe listened to the song. "Nice. Happy."

Mab listened to the jukebox. "I don't understand it."

"What's not to understand?" Joe bit into his next hot dog.

"Well, the part about love paying for the pie. Why would one of the things that love can do be pay for their pie? I know it's a metaphor, but I don't get it. Or the part about love can make you lose somebody you thought was you. That makes no sense."

"It means love changes everything," Joe said. "One day you're alone and starving, and the next day you're having dessert." He smiled at her again, that crooked, heart-lifting smile. "What do you want for dessert, Mab?"

Mab's treacherous heart beat faster, even though she was pretty sure it was the same smile he'd given Shannon, flawed and sweet. And there was sincere admiration in his eyes when he looked at her, and that was just wrong because she was wearing her canvas coat and miner's hat, and even without them, men did not look at her with sincere admiration.

No good can come of this, she thought.

On the other hand, he'd fed her three hot dogs and three beers and was clearly prepared to shell out more if she wanted it, so points there. And he'd opened up the Fortune-Telling Machine. And there were those stirrings, no doubt helped along by the three beers.

On the other hand, he hadn't told her anything about himself and he'd been whispering in Shannon's ear.

That was three hands.

"Mab?"

"I think I should stop drinking now."

"Sure."

The jukebox clicked over to the next song: Brad Paisley's "Alcohol," and Mab almost dropped her beer as people started to sing along. "It's ten thirty," she said, stunned. "The jukebox plays this song every night at ten thirty so people will know they have half an hour to closing. We've been here for almost four hours." She tried to remember what they'd done for four hours. Talked. Well, she'd talked. She still didn't know a damn thing about him except that he was a barmaid-whisperer. "I've been talking for four hours. You're a very generous conversationalist."

"Thank you," Joe said. "So you really know this park well. You must know the people pretty well, too. Have you heard any rumors—?"

"No. I wouldn't hear rumors." She smiled tightly at him. "I've been sleeping in Cindy's extra bedroom, and she's great, but otherwise, I don't see people much. I work a lot at night when no people are around, so I can focus. And I'm leaving the day after Halloween, so there's not much point in pursuing relationships. I'm temporary. I'm always temporary, but I like it that way—"

"You're not temporary," he said. "You're unforgettable."

There's something very wrong here, Mab thought, but then a big bald guy bumped into Joe's back and slopped some beer on his shirt.

"Hey," the guy said. "Sorry about that."

"No problem," Joe said, smiling at him. He held out his hand. "I'm Joe."

"Karl," the guy said, gesturing with a beer in each hand. "Glad to meet you. Can't stay. Got a hot one over there, and I think she's ready." He gestured toward the other side of the Pavilion toward Ashley, looking . . . different, sloe-eyed and slatternly, lounging against one of the Pavilion support posts.

Mab looked at Karl's left hand and the gold band there. "Aren't you married?"

Karl scowled. "What are you, the moral police? You can—"

"She's with me," Joe said, and when Mab looked at him, his smile was gone and he looked dangerous, his face hard and his eyes sharp.

"I don't ca—" Karl got a look at Joe and stopped. "Sure she is. Sorry about that." He detoured around Joe, giving him a wide berth, and went back to Ashley.

Mab looked at Ashley, trying to distract herself from feeling good that Joe had defended her. "You know, Ashley's a good-time girl, but I didn't think she'd fool around with a married man. She always seemed like a nice person. Open-minded, of course, but not . . . selfish." She looked up to see that Joe had stood and was gathering the beer cups and the hot dog wrappers.

"Time to go," he said. "Show me the rest of the park."

"Do you know Ashley?" Mab said, getting up, too.

"She was in the Dream Cream this morning, right?" Joe moved away from her toward one of the trash cans next to the Pavilion arches. "Not my type."

Mab looked back at Ashley, now in an all-hands lip lock with Karl. "Looks like she's anybody's type." She looked back at Joe and saw that he'd dumped the trash and was heading outside, and she took a step to join him.

"Miss?" somebody said from behind her, and she turned to see the fair-haired guy in Coke-bottle glasses and trilby hat from the Dream Cream holding out her work bag to her, one-handed, as if it didn't weigh anything.

"Don't forget this," he said.

"Thank you," she said, taking the bag with both hands. "You're a real lifesaver."

He smiled at her briefly, just a flash, and then turned back to his beer and his notebook, the antithesis of happy, attentive, always-smiling Joe.

Mab watched him for a moment; he was so still in the middle of all the chaos around him, his square shoulders hunched under his jacket, his hand moving with such certainty across the page, making strong neat marks in rapid succession. His concentration was so complete, his movement so sure, that it was almost erotic watching him.

Hard worker, she thought.

Then Joe called, "Mab!" from outside the Pavilion arch, and she shook her head to get the guy with the glasses out of her brain and went to Joe, thinking that somebody should tell that guy that work was not everything.

Almost everything, but not quite. Not tonight.

*****

"So this is the other half of the park," Mab told Joe when they were walking down the other side of the midway.

"Tell me everything."

He was very close to her, so she kept up a running patter about the park to distract herself. *I'm babbling,* she thought, and then he put his hand on her back and she talked faster. "This is the OK Corral, it's all games, it went in during the fifties and it looks it. This is the Tunnel of Love—" He slowed as they passed the hideous lump of pink stucco liberally festooned with doves and shells, its wrought-iron railing the only thing about it that was attractive. "—it's a dark ride that's been here from the beginning, but I couldn't find any pictures of it before the fifties."

"Is it running?"

"Only on the weekends."

"Good. I'll feed you hot dogs tomorrow and then we'll come here."

"No, we won't. My mother had an upsetting experience in there, and it makes me . . . I don't like it." Mab started walking again. "This is the Worm." She gestured to a creepy children's ride, a mini–roller coaster with a garish, bug-eyed, grinning worm's head, the cars behind it sections of its body. "That's from the fifties. I don't know what they were thinking, putting a worm beside the Tunnel of Love—"

"Upsetting experience?" Joe said, looking back at the Tunnel.

"What? Oh, my mother. Family legend. Not very interesting."

"I love family legends," Joe said.

Mab sighed. "When she was eighteen, she and her boyfriend took the slow evening ride, which takes twice as long as the day ride. Nine months later, there was me. She said that something just came over her." Actually what her mother had said was that she'd been possessed by a demon, but her mother had also been nuts.

"You were conceived in the Tunnel of Love?"

"Well, metaphorically, everybody is. But yes, I was. I started here as a zygote and now I'm back to fix up the place."

"We're definitely going in there," Joe said, but he let her pull him away from the Tunnel.

"This is the Roundabout, another old ride that's just beautiful," Mab said, dragging him past a tilted platform with shell-like cups, "and after that is the other dark ride in the park, the Mermaid World Cruise." She slowed in front of a seven-foot-tall blue-green mermaid that she'd spent a week repainting and that was now, for the first time, reminding her of Ashley. Same lungs anyway.

"World Cruise?"

"It has these awful little dolls from twelve different countries singing this horrible little song. I think they put it in during the fifties."

"I can do without that one," Joe said, and kept walking, but he stopped in front of the carousel.

"And this is where I leave you," Mab said. "I live there—" She pointed to the pink-striped Dream Cream with its mullioned windows, twenty yards away. "—so—"

"You didn't show me the carousel," Joe said, and caught her hand.

His hand was warm wrapped around hers, a shock to her system, but the urge to pull her hand away wasn't nearly as strong as the need to leave it there.

He interlaced his fingers with hers and tugged her gently toward the carousel.

"Okay," Mab said, following him just to keep his hand in hers. "This is the carousel. See?"

"Closer." He pulled her gently into the shadows and then up onto the carousel platform, out of the orange light on the midway and into the dark among the horses.

"This is a Dentzel carousel," Mab said, trying really hard to ignore how dark it was and how close he was and how good that was, "which you can tell because there's a lion and tiger on the outer ring. It has four rows of sixty-eight hand-carved basswood animals, eighteen fixed on the outer ring and fifty rising in the inner three rings, plus four mermaid chariots for people who just like to sit and watch the world go around." Her voice trailed off because he'd moved even closer and she couldn't talk with her heart pounding that hard. Maybe he was going to kiss her.

Maybe she should take off her miner's hat.

"Stay here," he said, and stepped off the carousel and into the control booth.

"That's shut down until tomorrow night," she called to him, trying not to be disappointed, but then the lights sprang to life and the carousel began to revolve, the calliope warming up into a vaguely recognizable melody.

Joe jumped onto the carousel.

"Obviously, you're a man of many talents," she said, taking a step back as he moved toward her. "There are fourteen hundred lightbulbs on here reflected in the cut-glass mirrors that line the center axis. And twelve polychrome FunFun faces on the outside of the canopy and a really beautiful basswood FunFun statue up there on the roof that I just finished restoring. This thing is a work of art."

"Yes, it is. Pick a horse."

Mab looked around as the carousel revolved and the dark park outside slid by them. "I don't ride the rides. I just restore them."

Joe looked extremely patient. "Pick a horse."

"Maybe the tiger," Mab said, trying to move past him to the stationary animals on the outer ring.

"The tiger doesn't move." Joe put his hands on her waist and made her breath go. "How about this blue one?"

She turned to look, and he boosted her up sidesaddle before she realized what he was doing. She grabbed on to the pole and looked down on him as it rose, and then straight at him as it fell. "This isn't blue. It's turquoise."

"Close enough," Joe said, and moved closer.

"Uh," Mab said, and then stopped, distracted by the music from the calliope, which was now recognizable. "This is 'What Love Can Do.' I told Cindy it wasn't on here—"

"What's your favorite song?"

Mab's head began to swim, maybe from the spinning of the carousel, maybe from the rise and fall of the horse, maybe from Joe. She leaned her head on the pole and let the horse take her up and down. "I don't do music. There's no place for it in my work."

"I bet you sing while you work," Joe said. "I bet you sing this song. And 'Child of the Wild Blue Yonder.' And—"

"How do you know?" Mab said, taken aback.

He smiled at her again, and her head reeled.

"I've had too much beer," she said, and slipped carefully off her horse to stand between it and him.

There wasn't much room.

"Good," Joe said, not moving, and the carousel turned, and the lights blinked, reflecting in the mirrors that lined the center, and the music from the calliope bounced as he leaned in closer.

He's going to kiss me, Mab thought, trying to breathe. He's really going to do it.

He stopped millimeters from her mouth and said, "Mab?"

"Yes?"

"You're supposed to close your eyes."

"Why?"

"It's what people do when they kiss."

"I never got that," Mab said. "It's like you said, I want to see what's coming for me—"

He kissed her and she closed her eyes, her head awash with alcohol and the carousel and the music and him, mostly him, tasting of beer and hot dogs and something different but familiar, something sharp and bright, something *like her*—

He smiled against her mouth and then kissed her cheek and the corner of her mouth, and then her mouth again, deeply, while she went dizzy, and then he slid his hand into her coat and under her T-shirt, and the touch of his warm hand on her skin woke her up.

"Hello," she said, grabbing his hand.

"Hello," he said against her mouth. "Let's go to your place."

Mab pulled back. "Just like that?" *Maybe.*

"We don't have much time," Joe said, moving to her neck. "I'm gone after Halloween, you're gone after Halloween, we're not looking at a long relationship here."

"True," Mab said, closing her eyes. His mouth felt great on her neck. And the idea that nothing was permanent was good—how big a mistake could this be?—so she pulled his face back to hers and kissed him again, all that warmth and light, drinking him in, wanting him, feeling her heart lift—

"C'mon," he whispered. "Let me drag you off to bed."

The demons will drag you down to hell, her mother had said.

"Are you going to drag me down to hell?" she asked Joe, her mouth close to his.

He looked startled. "*Bed,* I said bed. Lead you into sin, yes. Hell, no."

"Huh." Mab stepped out of his arms so she could get her bearings again. Her mother had been a fruitcake, but this really was moving too fast. "Thank you for the food and drink and the groping, but I think I am going to bed alone now because I have to work tomorrow." She moved back another step and he didn't follow, just smiled at her as the carousel revolved, which made her inexplicably and uncharacteristically happy.

"How about dinner tomorrow night?" he said, and she said, "Yes," without even thinking about it, and stepped backward off the carousel, stumbling a little as it spun away from her, and then her foot hit something and she really stumbled, falling onto her butt as Joe called, "Mab?" and then disappeared with the carousel's rotation.

"I'm all right," she began, and then realized what she'd fallen over was large and soft and . . . *"Joe!"*

The carousel came around again, and he jumped off and came to offer her his hand as she rolled to her knees. She let him pull her to her feet, fumbling to turn on the light on her hat.

"What's wrong?" Joe said, and then she got the light on and saw she'd fallen over somebody passed out on the flagstone, a big bald guy.

"Another drunk from the Beer Pavilion," she said, annoyed that their moment was ruined, and then Joe turned him over and she saw blank, staring eyes and a shirt ripped open to expose a black wavy mark on his flabby chest.

Mab screamed.

"That's Karl," Joe said.

*****

Ethan lay in the dark in his sleeping bag, alone, a rock poking him in the back, and stared up through the leafless trees at the red lights flashing at the top of the Devil's Drop. He could still hear voices from the last of the beer tent diehards, singing "Alcohol" as they stumbled home and the park closed, but it was mostly peaceful, a good place to—

A scream cut through the air, and he was up and running. He made it down the midway and past the Mermaid Cruise and saw people ahead, a couple of gawkers and somebody bent over something on the ground. He sped up as a man straightened and ran for the park gate.

Ethan skidded to a halt, recognizing Mab as she started CPR, pressing the chest of the guy on the ground like a pro. "What happened?"

"I don't know," Mab said, breathless as she kept on pulsing. "I just fell over him and called for help, then started CPR."

Ethan put a hand on the man's throat. No pulse, no breathing. "Damn." He shook his head, trying to clear the fog. "Stop for a minute," he told Mab, and she did. Keeping the head tilted back, he leaned over, pinched the man's nose, covered the mouth with his own, and gave two breaths. Straightening, he said, "Go," and Mab went back to compressing. "I need your cell to call 911."

"Already did," Mab said as she pushed. "Joe went to open the gate."

Ethan nodded, waited for her to stop, then leaned over and gave two quick breaths. Mab took up the beat again as he straightened, and then he saw a wavering light approaching. Gus with a flashlight, leading Glenda and Delpha as they pushed through the growing crowd of drunken gawkers.

"EMTs are coming," Ethan told Glenda.

Glenda's voice was ragged as she turned to Gus. "Go open the service gate on the bridge."

"Joe's on it." Mab kept pumping, but she was starting to flag.

"I'll take it," Ethan said, and Mab leaned back so he could finish the compressions.

Ethan became lost in the rhythm of two and thirty, staring at the man's unconscious face until his beer-fogged brain realized it was the guy from the Beer Pavilion, the one Ashley had left with.

Glenda knelt next to Mab, the light in her hand, shining it on the man's chest as Ethan took his hands away on the thirtieth push.

"It won't do any good," Glenda said. "He's gone."

Ethan heard a siren. "Keep up the compressions," he ordered Mab as he moved next to the man's head. Mab began again, and he could hear her counting under her breath. Then flashing lights reflected off the carousel mirrors as the ambulance skidded to a halt next to the small group. Two paramedics jumped out pulling a rolling stretcher with gear on it, and Ethan stumbled to his feet and out of the way, Mab with him, to stand next to his mother and Delpha, Frankie on her shoulder, unruffled by the chaos around them as the EMTs did their best to save what Ethan knew was a dead man.

"What the hell is going on?" Ray said from behind them, and Ethan turned to see him scowling at the EMTs as if it were their fault there was a body there. "What happened? Who is that?" He stepped forward and looked at Karl, first at his face and then at the mark on this chest, and stopped scowling. "What happened?"

"Somebody had a heart attack," Mab said. "Somebody named Karl. That's all we know."

"Who was he with?" Ray said, and Glenda looked at him sharply.

The EMTs were efficient, but they knew a waste of effort when they saw one. Within minutes, they had Karl loaded into the ambulance and were speeding off into the night, leaving an echoing silence.

Glenda turned to the crowd. "Nothing happened here," she said.

People looked at each other, confused.

"Nothing happened here," Glenda said again, and the crowd began to disperse, staggering off home.

"A tragedy," Ray said without expression, and turned and walked away.

"What was that mark on his chest?" Mab said.

Glenda looked into Mab's eyes. "Go back to the Dream Cream and go to sleep." Mab looked confused, and Glenda leaned closer and said, *"Sleep."*

Mab yawned. "Okay." She pulled her ugly canvas coat even tighter around her and yawned again. "If Joe comes back, tell him I went to bed." She looked around at the group. "I'm so sorry. I don't know who to say that to, but I am."

"Go sleep," Glenda said.

Mab nodded and walked toward the Dream Cream, the light from her miner's hat going before her.

Ethan dropped any pretense of normality. "What the hell is this?"

Glenda took out her cigarette pack and lighter. "He was killed by a demon."

"Okay, enough," Ethan said. "That's not funny—"

"I know," Glenda said. "I tried to tell you this morning, but you wouldn't listen—"

"Look, you want a secret society, good for you, but some guy just *died*—"

"We know, Ethan. Tura killed him. Her mark was on his chest. Gus's going to run the Dragon, but we already know there'll be only three rattles."

"Yeah, I better do that." Gus shambled off toward the roller coaster.

Ethan looked at his mother and little Delpha, older than God, nodding in agreement beside her. Crazy. And Gus, going off to listen to roller coaster rattles. Crazy. All of them. Crazy—

"We've been waiting for our new Hunter," Glenda said. "And now here you are. You've been called, Ethan, and you're going to have to answer because Tura will kill again if we don't put her back in her chalice."

"Have you had a checkup lately?" Ethan said, trying to keep his voice respectful.

Glenda looked more tired than he'd ever seen her. "Get Gus when he's done with the Dragon and come to the trailer. We need you, Ethan."

She turned and walked back down the midway, toward the Dragon and beyond that the trailers, Delpha by her side and Frankie flying overhead.

"Yeah, you do," Ethan said, and went to get Gus.

*****

When Ethan and Gus got to Glenda's trailer, she was seated on one side of the banquette beside Delpha, smoking as usual. She surveyed him with the acuity of a mother. "Hangover. There's coffee in the pot." She turned to Gus. "Three rattles?"

Gus was dejected. "Yeah."

Ethan poured himself a cup that was as thick as mud and sat down on the banquette across from her as Gus pushed in beside her, making Delpha slide around to the back of the banquette.

The door opened, and Young Fred came in.

Glenda lifted her chin and looked Ethan in the eye. "I will explain this to you once more, and then we will plan. Dreamland is prison for five dangerous demons, the Untouchables: Kharos, Vanth, Selvans, Tura, and Fufluns. Forget bell, book, and candle; forget holy water; forget anything that sends them screaming back to hell—the only thing that can be done with these demons is to hold them. That's why the park was built. On an island in a river because demons can't cross running water. With us to guard the cells, maintain the park, and keep the world safe. We hold the Untouchables here in their chalice cells, inside their iron statues, and hell is not opened up on earth."

"Hell," Ethan said, skeptical.

"They feed on emotional pain," Glenda said. "They create it and then harvest it, using humans like cattle, feasting on their hopelessness and depression and despair. The last time all five of them got out, an entire town in Italy was wiped out; some went mad and murdered their neighbors, others killed themselves. The Untouchables were moving on to other towns when the Guardia finally recaptured them. We can't let them get out again."

"When was this?" Ethan said.

"Eighteen ninety." Glenda nodded to the others. "There are five Untouchables and five Guardia. The Guardia are sworn to defeat the demons and support each other, bonded until death. Young Fred is the Trickster, I'm the Sorceress, Delpha's the Seer, and Gus is the Keeper. Hank was our Hunter until he ran his car into that tree. That's when you were called, Ethan. You're our Hunter now."

"Too bad." Young Fred looked at Ethan with a mixture of respect and pity. "Sorry, dude."

Ethan frowned at Young Fred. He was a wiseass, but he hadn't seemed nuts. "You believe this stuff?"

"It's true," Young Fred said. "We're as trapped as the demons. We're stuck here for eternity."

Ethan nodded. They were all crazy. "So you have this . . . club," he began carefully.

"The Guardia," Glenda said. "For twenty-five hundred years, the Guardia held the Untouchables in Italy until 1925 when a betrayer sold the five chalices that held them to an idiot American art collector. The Guardia followed the chalices here in time to save the collector from one of the demons. The collector built the park here on a place of power and gave it to the Guardia to keep the world safe, and we've been here ever since. When one of us dies, another is called to take his or her place. That's why you came home. You were called. On the twenty-ninth of July when Hank died."

Ethan took a deep breath. His headache was getting worse.

Glenda snapped her lighter and drew on the cigarette until the end glowed red. Then she shut the lighter. "The Untouchables will make their move on Halloween at midnight, All Saint's Eve, when the borders between the earth and the underworld grow thin and their powers grow stronger. If all five get out, they will have their full strength and can assume their true forms, and then . . ."

"We're fucked," Young Fred said. "I vote we all go somewhere else."

Ethan scowled at Young Fred. "Why are you helping them with this farce?"

"It's not a farce, it's real." He smiled without humor. "Welcome to the Guardia. It's a life sentence."

"It's a calling," Delpha said sharply, and Frankie fluttered his wings, evidently annoyed, too.

"Yeah, and how many of your ninety-odd years have you been called?" Young Fred said. "Do you even remember normal life? Because I do."

"Stop it," Glenda snapped at him. "There are demons in the park killing people. You can whine when the park is safe again."

Ethan stood up. "You're trying to tell me that Ashley's a demon and she killed that guy?"

"Not Ashley, but Tura possessing Ashley," Glenda said.

"Demons possess people," Gus said, sounding as if there was an *of course* attached. "Take over anybody close to them. They can't find a person, they'll take something else, like the FunFun statue. The clown's named after him. Fufluns. FunFun. See?"

"Yeah, that proves it," Ethan said. "Especially since it's iron and you said demons can't touch iron."

Glenda glared but kept her voice level. "All the statues are made of wood, it's just the outsides that are iron. When Mab put that flute in the carousel clown's hand, it opened the back of the FunFun statue down by the gate. I tried to stop her, but I couldn't get her off the roof in time. That wouldn't have been that bad, he'd still have been held in his chalice, but the lid had broken from all the times his statue had been knocked around, so he used the statue to find a host, got out through the open door in the back and possessed somebody, and then went to let Tura out. He always does."

"Why didn't he let them all out?" Ethan said, tired of humoring them. "Go ahead and take the town, get it over with?"

"The other keys weren't in place," Glenda said. "I think they're waiting for Halloween."

Halloween. "I get it," Ethan said, angry now. "This is some stunt you've cooked up for Screamland. Because the *media* will be here. Well, thanks a whole hell of a lot for screwing around with me—"

"Ethan," Glenda began, angry now, and Young Fred said, *"Hey,"* and Ethan looked down at him.

"Watch," Young Fred said, and changed into Gus. It wasn't a very good Gus, the edges wavered, but it was definitely not Young Fred. Then he changed back. "Like me to be something else? I take requests."

That was not real, Ethan told himself. "I'm tired, I have a hangover. I'm not trusting my eyes."

"Sure," Young Fred said. "Why believe what you can see? Especially since it's an illusion." Ethan glared at him and he added, "I don't change. You just think I do."

Ethan turned to look at Glenda. "So Fred does impressions. Good for him—"

Glenda held up her left hand and spread her fingers and flames appeared on the end of each one. She put her cigarette into the middle of one of them and drew on it, and the end glowed to life. Then she inhaled and sat back, shaking her fingers to put the flames out.

"What the hell?" Ethan said.

"Illusion," Glenda said, and showed him the end of her cigarette, unlit and unsinged. "I'm a sorceress. I can make you see things that aren't there, make you believe things that aren't real."

"No, you can't." Ethan looked at his hands. They were shaking. Damn alcohol. "These are all tricks, and it's not a good time for them. The black ops guy who shot me, he's dangerous. I think this woman I met tonight, Weaver, is up to something, so if you're hiding anything, watch out for her. And I'd bet money Ray's got a plan you're not going to like, buying into this place. You have to stop playing games, you have real problems, but they're human, not demon."

Glenda's face was hard. "Ethan, we've been patient but—"

"No." Ethan stood and turned for the door.

"Ethan, get back here—"

"I'll help you," he said to her. "But not with this fairy-tale stuff." And then he went out, leaving them to their collective insanity.

CHAPTER 7

Ray sat down beside Kharos's statue, lit a cigar, and said, "Your mermaid just killed somebody."

Kharos seethed. He was getting plenty of practice at seething.

"It's not my fault," Ray said. "And the Guardia aren't any happier than you are. You should have seen their faces."

Kharos stopped seething. ARE THEY DESPAIRING?

"They looked . . . tired, I guess. Well, they're old. Gus is pushing eighty, and Delpha's in her nineties. Even Glenda's almost sixty."

Kharos considered that. They were old, but they had experience and they knew that Fufluns and Tura were out. They were on guard now. But not resilient, they were tired, Ray said. That meant they were losing faith, the first step on the road to despair.

Ray took another drag on his cigar. "I couldn't find Fufluns, either. I touched iron to as many people as I could and got nothing. He could be anywhere in anyone. Who the hell knows?"

If Tura was exhausting the Guardia, that was good. But it could be better. More trauma meant more exhaustion, confusion, mistakes.

BRING IN MINIONS.

"What? Oh, hell." Ray exhaled. "I don't like them, little rabid animals, always chattering and ganging up on things that are smaller than they are. It's like herding pit bulls on meth. Where do I get them this time?"

I WILL CALL THEM AND THEY WILL COME TO YOU. BRING THEM ACROSS THE RIVER IN A BOAT. DON'T LET THEM TOUCH THE MOVING WATER.

Ray nodded. "You know, if we gave ourselves some more time, a couple years maybe, we could really—"

NO.

Ray sighed and said, "Fine," and then stood up and left, striding down the midway as if he owned it, or thought he would shortly.

Kharos forgot him to concentrate on thoughts of the old Guardia wearing themselves out dealing with Tura and an infestation of minion demons, falling into hopelessness before he escaped and killed them. He could almost taste their despair. It had been so long, too long, since he'd fed, too long since he'd felt anything.

SOON, he told himself, and began to call the minions.

*****

When Mab came down for breakfast, Cindy was waiting for her, hands on her hips.

"There was an ambulance down here last night," she said as Mab sat down at the counter.

"I know." Mab put her hat on the counter and her bag on the floor and tried to look normal after a night of almost no sleep.

"You look awful," Cindy said. "What *happened*?"

"A guy named Karl had a heart attack and died in front of the carousel."

"Carl who runs the Whack-A-Mole?" Cindy said, horrified.

"No," Mab said. "Big guy. Bald. Married. Fooling around with Ashley."

"Oh, Karl the Cheater." Cindy relaxed. "Well, may he rest in peace, the son of a bitch. Carl Whack-A-Mole is a good guy, but Karl the Cheater we can spare."

"What?" Mab said, appalled. A man had died, right there at her feet—

"Wife-beater," Cindy said, looking almost angry. "Sleeps with anything that will say yes, then goes home and hits her. Awful, awful man."

"Oh." Mab felt the weight that had kept her from sleeping the night before lift a little as she considered it. It would be so much tidier if she didn't have to feel bad about Karl's death. If she hadn't seen the body, it would even be feasible.

"Once I found out he was scum, I wouldn't sell him ice cream," Cindy said. "He got nasty, tried to grab me."

"What?" Mab said, outraged.

"So I stabbed him with a fork, and then Gus took him out."

"Gus?"

"Gus has his moments." Cindy looked at her sympathetically. "That must have been awful for you, finding him dead."

"It was," Mab said. "I was so tired when I got home, I could barely walk, but then I couldn't sleep. I should have talked to you."

Cindy nodded. "Always talk to me. Tell me you weren't alone when you found him."

"No, I was with—"

The door opened, bell jingling, and Cindy beamed past Mab at the newcomer. "Well, hello and welcome back."

Mab turned and there was Joe, sliding onto the seat beside her, and her heart kicked up a beat, which was just foolish of it, and then he leaned in and kissed her, and she kissed him back because who wouldn't?

When she stopped to breathe, she rested her forehead against his, so glad he was there that it worried her, but then he brushed back her hair with his finger and said softly, "You okay?" and she felt so much better that she smiled.

"It turns out Karl was a cheater and a wife-beater. And not Carl from the Whack-A-Mole, so we can spare him." *Kiss me again.*

"Good to know," Joe said, and kissed her again.

It was the best breakfast she'd had in years.

"I can't stay," he said when she pulled back again to breathe. "I just wanted to make sure you were all right. By the time I came back, they'd locked the gate to the bridge. I didn't want you to be alone." He grinned at Cindy. "But then I remembered who you roomed with."

Cindy grinned back.

"I'm fine," Mab said, amazed that he'd tried to come back.

He looked back from Cindy to her, as if he'd forgotten for a moment that she was there, and put his hand on her back and rubbed a little. Friendly. Warm. "So, can I talk you into hot dogs and beer tonight?"

He smiled at her, that glorious, crooked, sunny smile that melted her toes, and she smiled back, helpless.

"Yes. I'll be at the Fortune-Telling Machine."

"Then that's where I'll come get you." He kissed her again, and something unfamiliar welled up inside her, *bubbled* up inside her, and she realized it was happiness, not contentment, not satisfaction, *happiness*. She kissed him again, and then he got up, waved to Cindy, swooped in for a final kiss, and left.

Mab blinked a couple of times to get her bearings, and then turned back to Cindy, who looked delighted. And avid.

"I want to know *everything*," she said, leaning over the counter. "This is so *good* for you."

Mab took a deep breath just to get her lungs back to normal. "He took me to dinner at the Beer Pavilion, and then we frenched on the carousel, and then I fell over Karl. Dead Karl, not Whack-A-Mole Carl."

"Whoa," Cindy said. "That's some first date."

"I don't think it was actually a date," Mab said, trying to evaluate things calmly.

"You got tongue on a carousel. That's a date."

"It ended with a dead body," Mab pointed out.

"Yes, but it was Karl's," Cindy said. "You said heart attack, right?"

"I think so, but . . ." She hesitated, knowing what was coming. ". . . he had this wavy mark on his chest . . ."

Cindy straightened. "He had *the mark?*" She shook her head, marveling. "*My god*, you have a great life."

"Because I fell over Dead Karl?"

"You got a robot clown, you got a hot guy, and now you're part of the legend. Mary Alice Brannigan, this is your week." Cindy beamed at her. "I'd give you ice cream on the house, but you get that anyway." Then she got serious. "So what does this mark look like?"

"Just a black wavy line."

"Oh." Cindy pulled back, disappointed. "I was hoping for a skull or at least a big black *X*. Just a wavy line . . ." She shrugged.

"On *a dead guy*," Mab pointed out.

"Okay, points for that. You want waffles? I've got a new flavor, but it's a love potion and you clearly are past that."

"Past what?" Mab said. "Joe? He's just—"

"Don't even try to pretend," Cindy said. "He's probably carving your initials inside a heart on something right now. And I hope for his sake it isn't anything you painted."

Mab laughed and Cindy looked surprised.

"What now?" Mab said.

"I've never heard you laugh before." Cindy looked amazed. "Wow. I made Mab Brannigan laugh."

"I laugh," Mab said, and then realized she couldn't remember when. She certainly *had* laughed. Some time. In her life. "I'm not . . . emotional. My mother used to get upset when I'd cry or get angry, so I stopped. It makes life a lot easier if you just don't react to things."

"Like Joe," Cindy said.

"Well," Mab said, and found herself smiling again.

"Dreamland is very good for you," Cindy said smugly. "So waffles? With a little What-Love-Can-Do strawberry ice cream in between them?"

"What's in . . ." Mab began and then thought, *What the hell*, and said, "Yes. That's what I want."

Cindy went down the counter and started the waffles, and Mab put her mind back where it belonged, on the Fortune-Telling Machine. But this time, instead of thinking about colors, she thought about Vanth. Vanth was new information, a name she could look up. There might be pictures. . . .

Cindy came back, and Mab said, "Do you still have your laptop under the counter?"

"Yep." Cindy pulled it out and handed it over.

Mab opened Cindy's browser and typed in *Vanth,* hit the URL for Wikipedia, and read out loud, " 'Vanth is a female demon in the Etruscan underworld.' "

"Good to know," Cindy said, looking confused.

"Vanth is the name on the Fortune-Telling Machine," Mab told her, and read the rest of the entry while Cindy slapped her waffles and love potion together. Then she pushed the laptop around so Cindy could read for herself. She picked up her spoon and tasted the pink ice cream, momentarily distracted from demon lore. "Strawberries, passion fruit, and . . . ?"

"Honey, vanilla, and cinnamon," Cindy said, squinting at the screen as she skimmed the article. "Maybe she's an oracle. Oh. No, she's not. But this says she's benevolent. She even has a boyfriend. A demon named Kharos." Her face changed.

"What?" Mab said around a mouthful of waffle.

"He's a bastard. The Etruscan Devil."

"I'll tell her he's no good for her." Mab cut into her waffle again.

"You talk to her?"

Mab nodded, swiveling the computer back around to her with one hand while she scooped waffle and cream with the other. "She talks back. With cards."

"Cards," Cindy said. "The machine talks to you with cards."

"Old fortunes. Like these." Mab reached in the side pocket of her bag where she'd stashed the cards, but they weren't there. "I had cards." She put down her fork and went through the other pockets, but still no cards. "Who took my cards?"

"I didn't see any cards," Cindy said, clearly trying to follow.

Mab dropped her bag to the floor. "Am I losing my mind?"

"No, but something's going on." Cindy leaned against the back counter. "Cards, heart attacks, robot clowns. Maybe we're being haunted by Etruscan demons."

"In southern Ohio," Mab said. "I don't think so." She forked another piece of waffle and then stopped. "Wait a minute. Glenda's son mentioned somebody. . . ."

She pulled the laptop closer and typed *Fufluns* into the browser, hit the first URL, and read, " 'In Etruscan mythology, Fufluns was a god of happiness and growth in all things. He later appears as an underworld demon, supplanted in the pantheon by Bacchus.' Fun guy. Except for the demon part."

"FunFun?"

"Fufluns."

Cindy frowned. "He starts out as a god and ends up a demon?"

Mab shrugged. "It says 'supplanted by Bacchus.' He's the Roman god of drunken revelry and general good times. Maybe two was a crowd, so Fufluns got moved to the basement."

"Pink-slipped into hell." Cindy shook her head. "Poor guy."

Mab closed her browser. "Don't feel too bad. He's not real. But this whole Etruscan thing . . ." She shook her head. "I'm confused."

"You should go ask Delpha," Cindy said. "She knows everything. And she's never wrong."

Mab was tempted, which was insane. She looked around the shop, looking for normal life. There were two mothers with little kids there, and a retired couple oohing and aahing over their ice cream, and two seats down the counter, the fair-haired guy with the big black-rimmed Coke-bottle glasses, finished with his waffles and ice cream, his green trilby on the seat beside him, his notebook open in front of him. What would it be like to be them, not dealing with Dead Karl and Etruscan demons?

She shook her head. "I think I should go to work."

"That will be soothing for you," Cindy said.

"It will," Mab said, and picked up her work bag.

"And after that there's Joe," Cindy said happily. "You are one lucky woman."

"Yes," Mab said, surprised to realize that she was.

In fact, if somebody would explain all the craziness to her so she could stop wondering about it, her life would be just about perfect.

"Delpha, huh?" she said to Cindy.

"Oh, yeah," Cindy said. "Delpha."

"Okay, then," Mab said, and headed out the door.

She was halfway down the midway to the Fortune-Telling Machine and the Delpha's Oracle booth when she heard someone say, "Miss?"

She turned around.

It was the fair-haired guy with glasses from the Dream Cream, his trilby hat squarely on his head.

"You forgot this," he said, and handed over her yellow miner's cap, his gray eyes steady on hers behind those ridiculous glasses.

"Thank you," she said, and he nodded and turned back to the Dream Cream.

She frowned as she watched him walk away. For some reason she'd assumed he was retired, the thick glasses, the old-fashioned hat, but he moved like a young guy, sure and strong, and his face had been unlined, his eyes sharp.

So what was he doing spending most of his life at the Dream Cream?

"Huh," she said, and went to ask Delpha about Etruscan demons.

*****

When Mab got to the Fortune-Telling Machine, she hesitated. The Delpha's Oracle booth was right next door, but the chances that Delpha was in there on a weekday were slim and—

She heard a cawing sound and looked up to see Frankie perched on the peak of the tent-shaped wooden booth.

The Oracle was in.

She walked over and went through the opening in the wrought-iron fence, hesitating before the sliding wood doors painted to look like tent flaps, and then lifted her fist to knock.

"Come in, Mab," Delpha said, and Mab looked at her fist, shrugged, pushed the doors apart, and went in, Frankie swooping in behind her.

Delpha sat behind an old table with a pile of stuff in front of her. Frankie landed on the table and began to pick through the pile daintily, using his beak and one claw to sort through the stuff. Probably looking for an eyeball.

"I'm sorry," Mab said. "Are you busy? I can come back."

"No." Delpha picked up a paper fan with a clawlike hand and dropped it in the trash bag beside her table. "Sit down." She picked up her dark blue shawl and folded it and put it on top of a box on the other side of the table. "Have you come to let me read your cards?" She picked up something else from the pile and then dropped that in the trash, too.

"No, I have a question." Mab frowned at the box. "Are you packing up? I thought you were working next weekend, too."

"Someone else will be here next weekend." Delpha nodded to a blue chair Mab had painted when she'd done the table. "Sit down." She crooked her finger, and Frankie left his scavenging to flap off the table and onto her shoulder.

Mab hesitated and then sat down. "Someone died last night. Cindy said there was a legend, and then I heard . . ." She was not going to say *demons.* She leaned forward. "Do we have a killer in the park? A human serial killer who's striking again after forty years?"

"No," Delpha said.

"That's it? No?"

Delpha studied her for a moment, then put a pack of tarot cards on the table.

"You turn over a card, I will answer a question. Ten cards. Ten questions."

"You've been trying to get me to do this ever since I got here. Admit it."

"Yes." Delpha smiled, startling Mab with the transformation. "And now you are here. Shuffle the cards."

"Fine." Mab shuffled and tried to hand the deck to Delpha, but the old lady shook her head. "Cut them," she said, and Mab did. "Now turn up the first one."

Mab did and saw a pale-faced woman dressed in black holding a sword almost as tall as she was with a crown floating above her head. The writing at the bottom said REGINA DI SPADE, translated at the top into QUEEN OF SWORDS.

"That is your card," Delpha said, looking very satisfied. "You are the Queen of Swords, a solitary woman of much intelligence and strength." She looked at Mab pointedly. "Ethan is the King of Swords."

"Do not matchmake," Mab said.

"No, he is not your mate. He is your brother in a great, never-ending battle."

"Brother is fine. The rest of it, no. What's happening in this park?"

"Many things," Delpha said. "Next card."

"Oh, come on," Mab said, "play fair."

"Then ask good questions," Delpha said.

Mab thought about it. "Okay, let's start at the beginning. Did the FunFun statue from the park entrance run into me two nights ago?"

"Yes," Delpha said.

Mab nodded. "And how is that possible?"

"Put the next card across your card," Delpha said, and Mab did.

This one looked like the Keep, a big stone tower that appeared to be blowing up. Mab looked closer. Bodies were falling from the tower.

"This is what crosses you," Delpha said. "Change. It is difficult, but it is good."

"Yeah, it looks good. How is it possible that the statue ran into me?"

"It was possessed by a demon. Put the next card to the left of the first two."

"A demon," Mab said, somehow not surprised.

"A card," Delpha said, putting her finger down to the left of the first two cards.

Mab put the next card down while she thought fast. This one was some guy on a horse in the snow, three swords on his banner, looking depressed as all hell.

"You must have been very lonely," Delpha said, looking at the card.

"When? No, wait, that's not my question. A demon knocked me down with the statue. Is that like a figure of speech, a guy so bad, he's demonic—"

"Fufluns," Delpha said. "He's a demon. The next card goes beneath the others."

Mab turned over the next card, a man looking at a far-off city, five cups at his feet. "So Fufluns. Is he dangerous?"

"Sometimes," Delpha said, studying the cards. "He plays tricks and seduces and lies and betrays. That can be dangerous. The next card goes above."

Mab flipped the next card over. She put it above the first two, in the place that Delpha pointed to. This one was somebody in goggles wearing a hat and holding a painter's palette, flanked by paintings of two naked women holding coins. "But he doesn't kill, right? Tricks and seduction and lies, but not death? He didn't kill Karl?"

"You have had much isolation and betrayal in your past. . . ." Delpha tapped the card below the others. "And now, you carry loneliness within you, you're locked inside yourself, trapped by your own dem—"

"Actually, I'm fine," Mab said, "except for the dead body and the robot clown."

"Achievement," Delpha said, tapping the card above. "You find your meaning in artistic ability. You hide in your work like a little girl."

"Hey," Mab said.

Delpha gestured to the cards and Mab flipped the next one and paused. It was obscene, a huge, leering, naked devil looming over two equally naked blue people.

Frankie cawed, and Delpha said, "And now you face great evil."

"That I knew when I saw Dead Karl," Mab said. "You didn't answer my question. Did Fufluns kill Karl?"

"No. Put the last four in a vertical row to the right, starting at the bottom."

"Then who did?"

"A card."

Mab flipped up a woman crouching in a gray, desolate landscape, eight swords thrust into the ground around her. "Who killed Dead Karl?"

"Tura."

Mab flipped up the next card and put it above the last one, a guy in front of a blast furnace, evidently making money, since there were eight coins lined up along the bottom. "Who's Tura? And don't tell me she's an Etruscan demon."

"She's an Etruscan demon," Delpha said, almost absentmindedly, as she studied the cards.

Mab flipped up the next one, and stopped. It was a picture of a couple, him with a ridiculous hat, her with red hair, staring into each other's eyes while a child poked a turtle with a stick behind them, ten gold cups floating in the air above them.

So not me, she thought. "Who is Vanth?"

"An Etruscan demon," Delpha said. "Turn the last card."

Mab flipped it over.

A naked woman sat on a rock at daybreak, pouring water from a pitcher into a stream. Her hair was dark red, and she looked cold but not unhappy.

"That is your future," Delpha said, sitting back, satisfied.

"Pouring water naked into a pond?" Mab said. "Well, it's within my skill set. Enough with this demon stuff. What's going on in this park?"

Delpha looked at her steadily for a moment and then nodded. "You have shown me what I need to see; I will tell you. When you put the pipes back in the hand of the carousel FunFun, they opened the iron FunFun statue at the gate, and he escaped. Karl was killed by a second demon, Tura, imprisoned in the mermaid statue, who punishes betrayers."

"Betrayers? That's why she killed Karl last night?"

Delpha nodded.

"The mermaid killed Dead Karl." Mab rubbed her head. "Look, I don't believe in demons. Is it possible that some human person is doing this and using the demon legends as a cover? Is it possible Dead Karl just had a plain old heart attack? Is it possible—?"

"No," Delpha said. "It is the demons. They possess people, spread pain and hopelessness, break hearts and poison minds and kill from within. They—"

"No," Mab said, losing patience. "No more fantasy, this is real. We need to stop this—"

"We try." Delpha sat back, looking even more tired than usual. "The Guardia fight the demon. But we are few and mostly old. New Guardia must be called if we are to win this time." She looked at Mab fixedly. "Young, strong Guardia."

"So you've got a secret demon-fighting society." Mab gave up. "Great. Look, I need to call the police. Or something."

"You would be a good Guardia," Delpha said.

"I'm really not a joiner," Mab said, trying to figure her next move.

Delpha picked up the Devil card. "You are facing great evil, and you will have to change, to fight. There will be darkness. The Devil will try to enslave you, so you must struggle to see—"

"I have to go now." Mab pushed her chair back, but Delpha's hand shot out and grabbed her arm as Frankie lowered his head and stared into her eyes.

"Your strength is the way you *see* things. You must remember to *look* on all things with an open heart and mind. Ignore the illusion. *See the truth.*"

"I do that anyway," Mab said. "In my work, you have to."

"The last four cards hold the truth," Delpha said, as if Mab hadn't spoken. "The first is how you see yourself, trapped and alone."

"I do not—"

"The second is how people see you, taking great pride and success in your work. The third is your hopes and dreams—"

Mab looked at the happy couple on that card. *I hardly even know Joe.*

"—part of a family, not alone anymore. And the last . . ." Delpha let go of her arm and picked up the card. "The last is your future, Mary Alice Brannigan. Hope. Balance. Harmony after the storm."

"Oh." Mab took a breath. "Well, that's good. No demons."

"But only if you defeat the Devil," Delpha said, dropping the card back on the table.

"Right, defeat the Devil, save the world." Mab got up.

"You have another question," Delpha said. "A personal question. About a man."

Joe. "No—"

Delpha picked up the card with the couple on it. "You want to know if he is your true love. Give me your hand."

Mab hesitated and then sat down again and put her right hand in Delpha's.

"Other one," Delpha said, and Mab put her left hand in Delpha's.

Delpha drew her finger across Mab's palm with one perfectly manicured nail, painted in royal blue with tiny gold stars stuck on it. Then she gazed into Mab's eyes until her own unfocused. After a minute, she let Mab's hand drop and sat back. "Your true love is here, the one you will love forever. You have met him."

"Well, good for me," Mab said, trying to stay calm. "Anything else I should know? Because I really—"

"His name is Joe."

Mab tried to ignore the leap her heart took. "You're kidding. You can see *names*?"

"No, I heard you say it in the future," Delpha said. "You will be standing in the sunlight in front of the Dream Cream, and you'll say his name and laugh. But he is not what you think he is."

"They never are," Mab said, standing up again. "Well, thank you very much—"

"You are very strong," Delpha said. "The Guardia will need you to fight the demons."

"I don't believe in demons," Mab said.

"You will believe." Delpha hesitated. "There is something else. I think . . ."

Frankie hopped off her shoulder and onto the table, and she sorted through the pile of stuff there.

"I don't really need anything," Mab began, and then Delpha held up a long loop of blue-green ribbon with a small green rock dangling from it.

"You will need this," Delpha said, handing it to her.

Mab looked at the rock. It was an inch-long chunk of dark green stone, crudely carved to look like a rabbit.

"It's a malachite bunny," Delpha said.

"A bunny," Mab said, trying to sound appreciative.

"Malachite wards off evil." Delpha nodded. "You'll need that later. For when she comes."

"She," Mab said, lost.

Delpha nodded and went back to her work, and Mab pushed the sliding doors apart and went out into the brisk October day.

The sun was shining, and the whole fortune-telling-demons-on-the-loose bit should have seemed even more ridiculous in the bright light, especially given the weirdness of the malachite bunny she now clutched that she was evidently supposed to use to ward off some female demon but . . .

His name is Joe, Delpha had said, and that had made her treacherously happy. Hell, Joe made her happy. Well, Joe made everybody happy, he was just that kind of guy, but . . .

Demons.

"That was a complete waste of time," she told herself sternly, and went back to the Fortune-Telling Machine.

CHAPTER 8

Later, after an afternoon of particularly heavy drinking in the woods, Ethan went looking for Gus to tell the old man he'd be passing on the evening patrol and found him behind the mermaid statue.

"What're you doin'?" Ethan said, knowing he was slurring his words and not caring.

Gus jerked his head back, banging it on the top of the hatch on the rear of the statue and letting loose a string of curses that would have done a drill sergeant proud.

Ethan looked over Gus's shoulder. A carved wooden cup similar to the one inside the FunFun statue was crammed in there. "Wha's wi' the wood cups?"

"Chalices." Gus carefully retrieved the cup and lid. "This one's not broken. Means we can put Tura back. But Fufluns—" He shook his head. "Gotta get Mab to fix it."

"You gonna tell Mab she has to fix a demon prison?"

Gus looked at him, shaking his head in exasperation. "Dreamland's the prison. The chalices are just the cells."

"Right." Ethan took out his flask and drank and then stopped.

Ashley was passing by.

She looked sharp-eyed and hot, like she owned the place, exuding sex so strongly that the men who were opening up the rides and the games stopped to look at her as she went past. She owned them, too. Hell, she owned Ethan. He couldn't even hear what Gus was saying anymore.

Gus slammed his hand into Ethan's chest, making the old bullet sear, although it felt funny this time, the pain was duller, probably because of all the booze—

Gus got in his face. "You're not listening—"

"Not the chest," Ethan said, pronouncing each word as carefully and distinctly as he could. "And I am tired of this demon bullshit."

He walked away, staggering a little, heading for Ashley, although he could sense he wasn't exactly following a straight trajectory. Ashley was passing the Worm when she suddenly stopped and turned. Her eyes bore into Ethan's, and her smile heated him.

"Well, hey there," she said softly. There was something about Ashley—Ethan strained his alcohol-fogged brain to remember.

"Hey," he managed.

"You were awfully friendly with that woman in the Beer Pavilion," she said, moving closer. "I saw her sitting next to you. You were sitting close."

"Weaver?" Ethan shook his head and felt dizzy.

"She had her hand on your leg. I saw you. You're with her, aren't you? I could see the connection between you. She's the one for you."

Ethan shook his head again. *Stop that.* "She's nothin' to me." He couldn't focus his mind. No blood there, too much alcohol, too much Ashley.

Ashley smiled slowly and then looped her arm into his and tugged. "Then let's go into the Tunnel of Love."

Ethan followed her to the Tunnel, bumping once into the fence and biting back a curse when a ghost flew at him—fucking ghosts were everywhere—and then Ashley pulled him over and got into the lead swan boat. He tried stepping in and fell, doing a face-plant into her lap. *Slower,* he thought, and pulled himself up and back into his seat, the narrowness of the boat forcing him against her.

"I don't think this is runnin' yet," he told her, squinting at the empty ticket booth, and then, with a clang, the hook on the underwater cable engaged, and they were propelled forward into the yawning dark mouth of the Tunnel.

Ashley's arm slid around Ethan's shoulder, and he wanted to sink into her, all that softness, all that comfort, all that normal human biology. Then they came to the first diorama, and he saw Adam staring down Eve, who was offering up an apple.

Don' take it, Ethan thought, and then Ashley leaned in and kissed him, and he thought, *Take it.* She put a hand on the side of his face and pulled his head so that he was looking directly into her eyes as they moved past the diorama and into the blackness before the next one. She kissed him again, hard this time, with tongue, and he put his hand on her breast and squeezed the fullness just as she put her hand on his chest and pressed. He winced, but then she slid her hand lower and he forgot about the pain. Another diorama slid by, and then another, and then out of the corner of his eye, he saw Antony and Cleopatra.

Ashley pulled her tongue out of his mouth. "Do you want me?"

"Yeah. *Yes.*"

Ashley smiled, and despite the fog of alcohol and lust, the hairs on the back of Ethan's neck tingled. Then she gripped his head with surprising strength, and her eyes flashed blue-green, *glowed* blue-green.

Ethan froze. He couldn't move; he couldn't shake his attention from those glowing eyes.

"Betrayer," Ashley whispered as she put her hand on his chest. *"Die,* betrayer."

Blue-green light flowed from her into him, blue-green fog filled his chest, squeezing his heart, the pain from the bullet cutting through the middle of his chest as she possessed him, suffocating him, her laughter echoing inside him.

"No," he said, and wrenched back, and then a man in black stood up from behind Cleopatra and fired at Ashley, who jerked away, screaming, blue-green smoke spewing everywhere as she leapt out to disappear into the darkness of the tunnel, leaving Ethan free.

Damn demons, Ethan thought, and slumped into darkness.

*****

Mab had run out of cleaner for her brushes about an hour before dark and headed to the Dream Cream for a refill. On the way, she glanced out at the gate to the causeway and saw the FunFun statue was back.

Kind of.

She walked toward the statue, her horror growing, until she was standing in front of it. "Sweet baby Jesus," she said in despair, "what happened to you?"

He'd been so bright and beautiful, that orange-and-gold-checked waistcoat gleaming, the hand with the flute flung above his head in delight, his other hand gesturing the way into Dreamland, his big yellow glove like a beacon—

Both arms were down at his sides, the metal at his shoulders torn and gaping over the broken wood. The layers of paint and glazes that she'd slaved over were scraped down to the metal in places, pieces of his coat broken off entirely. He was missing a finger. Worst of all was his beautiful face: torn, dented, scraped . . .

"No," she said, close to crying. "I can't fix you. Nobody can fix you."

"Looks pretty bad," a voice said from behind her, and she turned and saw one of the college kids who maintained the park—the turquoise-and-blue-striped shirt gave him away—smiling at the ruined statue.

"Pretty bad?" she said. "Somebody *killed* him."

He came to stand beside her, and she saw the name embroidered on his pocket: *Sam.* "Got a spare?"

"Sure," Mab said. "We always keep extra iron-clad statues from a hundred years ago around. *Got a spare?* Are you crazy?"

"Sorry," Sam said hastily. "Wasn't thinking."

Mab felt lousy. "No, no, I'm sorry. This isn't your fault."

"Well, you're upset. You worked hard on this."

"How do you know?"

"Everybody knows." Sam looked down into her eyes, smiling crookedly at her. "You saved the park."

His eyes were brown, nothing remarkable, but Mab felt stirrings. . . .

Stirrings? Was she insane? She was in love with Joe—

No, she wasn't.

"Do I know you?" she said. "You seem really familiar."

"I've been working here all year," he said, hitting her with that crooked grin again.

"And I've been oblivious." Mab sighed. "Well, it's good to finally meet you, Sam."

She stuck out her hand and he took it, holding it for a second too long.

"Well," she said again, a little rattled. "We have to get this out of here. Can you get Gus or Young Fred or Ethan or . . ." She looked at the seven-foot statue doubtfully. ". . . all of them to put this in the Keep basement?"

"I could help," Sam offered. "We could do it together."

He smiled down at her, and his smile was familiar, and she thought, *He's not talking about the statue*, and the stirrings came back.

Jesus, she was getting turned on by college kids.

"I have to go to work," she told him. "Just call Gus."

"You bet," Sam said. "I'll go get him now. You have a good day."

"Thank you," Mab said, and felt a little disappointed when he walked off.

She really was losing it.

She looked back at the FunFun, broken and somehow *not there*, not the way he'd been when she'd been restoring him, when just working on him had made her happy. Maybe when they'd mangled him, they really had killed him.

"I'm so sorry," she said, and patted him for the last time and then went on to the Dream Cream.

*****

Ethan first became aware of pain. Everywhere. Then the memories flooded back: Ashley's eyes flashing blue-green. The suffocating blue-green pressure in his chest. The man in black shooting her. Demons.

He reached down and felt the scar on his chest, surprised to still be alive, since Tura had squeezed his heart so tightly. Even weirder, the pain wasn't as bad as usual. He heard the murmur of voices, felt softness underneath, saw shiny metal overhead, and knew he was back in Glenda's trailer on the banquette. He opened his eyes and waited for the world to stop spinning. It was futile. He stuck one foot out and placed it on the floor to anchor himself to reality, then slowly sat up. The murmuring stopped.

Glenda, Gus, Delpha, and Frankie stared at him from across the banquette. Young Fred, sitting slouched against the trailer near the fridge, toasted him with a beer bottle.

Glenda leaned forward. "You all right?"

"Where's the man in black?"

"Who?"

Ethan shook his head, a mistake as he winced in pain. "The man in black. Saved me. Ashley attacked me. She's a demon. She tried to possess me—"

"Really?" Glenda said. *"Who knew?"*

"What?" Ethan said, taken aback.

"I have been trying to tell you this and you would not listen and now you almost died and I could just *kill* you!" Glenda got up and went to the refrigerator.

"What man in black?" Young Fred said from the floor.

"This guy who's been in the park," Ethan said, watching Glenda slam the refrigerator door. "He shot her and there was all this blue-green fog everywhere—"

"Tura," Delpha said. "If Ashley bled Tura's spirit, she was hit with iron. Your man in black had an iron bullet." She nodded. "I like that."

Ethan remembered the round iron bullet in his Kevlar, and the pieces clicked into place: that first night, the man in black had thought he was a demon and shot him. And then he shot Ashley when . . . "Where's Ashley?"

"She wasn't there." Glenda still looked mad enough to bite nails.

"Tura must still have her. And now we have to go find her and put Tura back before she kills again. I know you're hurt and I know you're *drunk*—"

Ethan winced.

"—but the park is full of people who are in danger. We have to go *now*."

"I got her chalice," Gus said, pulling the carved wooden cup out of his coat. "We can take her."

Ethan saw that the old man's eyes were clear, eager even, spoiling for action. "How?"

"Oh, good, *now* you'll listen." Glenda leaned forward. "Demons are fast, but if we can make them feel emotion, there's a flash in their eyes. When Young Fred shape-changes or throws his voice, he startles the demon into dropping its guard so that Delpha can see the flash. He says, 'Frustro,' when the demon reacts; and Delpha sees the spirit and says, 'Specto,' and holds it; and you say, 'Capio,' and take the son of a bitch; and I say, 'Redimio,' and bind it, and then Gus says, 'Servo,' and shuts it back in its chalice to rot until the end of days."

"Capio," Ethan said. "And what happens after I say that?"

"It forces the demon to possess you," Glenda said. "But you have the power to hold it without dying. You have a strong heart, and you can hold on to the demon long enough for the capture."

Long enough for it to drive that bullet into my heart.

"We can't do it without you, Ethan."

Her voice was serious, and Ethan knew she was telling the truth. There was a demon killing people, and if he died capturing it, well, he'd die in battle instead of sitting around waiting for a piece of lead to move a couple of millimeters.

"I'm in," Ethan said. "At least this way I'll know if I'm crazy, too."

"You're not crazy," Glenda snapped. "You're *gifted*."

Lucky me, Ethan thought, and got up to go demon-hunting.

*****

Up at the Beer Pavilion, working on her second beer, Mab was telling Joe, "It was just a really bad day."

"How bad?" he said around his hot dog.

"The gate FunFun is *destroyed.* After I saw that I didn't get any work done." Mab rubbed her forehead. "Nothing. I couldn't see anything, I couldn't think anything, I didn't even get any cards from the machine. All I could think of was the FunFun and what Delpha had said. See, this is why emotion is bad. You can't *work.*"

"What did Delpha say?"

"That there were demons in the park."

"You need another beer," Joe said, and went to get her one.

She drank the rest of her second beer while he was gone, trying to anesthetize herself, but it didn't work. She looked to see where he was and saw him talking to Ashley, scowling at her as she leaned close, and then he came back to the table.

He put the beer in front of her, and she said, "Look, I know it's crazy, I don't think there are demons, but it's still screwing up my work. I'm distracted. I mean, you showed up to get me, and I forgot to bring *my hat.*" She touched her bare head, feeling naked. "That's the second time today I've left it behind. I don't have any *light* without my hat."

"Drink," Joe said, and she did and achieved that Zen state that three beers took her to. "Now, listen to me," he said. "You are staring so hard at so many problems that you can't see any answers. You have to let go, and the answers will appear."

"If you call me grasshopper, I'm hitting you with my fourth beer," Mab said.

"You don't have a fourth beer," Joe said.

"I know," Mab said. "It's tragic."

Joe got her another beer while she knocked back her third, surveying the Pavilion, seeing familiar faces there, people like Ray, showing people some kind of coin, and Carl Whack-A-Mole talking seriously with Harold Ferris Wheel, and at the next table, Skinny and Quentin working their way through hot dogs again, Skinny getting vehement about condiments—"I don't care if salsa sells more than ketchup, ketchup is the king of condiments, that's what I think"—and two tables down, the guy in the Coke-bottle glasses writing in his notebook, endearingly dorky, his beer untouched in front of him.

People, Mab thought, and somehow found them less annoying than usual.

Joe came back, handed over her beer, and when she'd made good inroads into it, he said, "You need to let go of your problem and relax."

"Relax," Mab said. "I should relax, that's what you think."

"Yep," Joe said. "Let's go ride the Tunnel of Love."

He smiled at her, and she lost her breath again. Whatever it was that he had—charm, charisma—he had it in spades.

And she wanted it, wanted to feel the way he made her feel, wanted to be part of that glow. . . .

"Okay," Mab said, then knocked back the rest of her beer and followed him out of the Pavilion.

*****

Once in the Tunnel, Ethan looked at the people clustered around him and didn't feel particularly confident. An old psychic, a young comedian, an almost deaf ride pusher, and his mother. Not exactly the "tip of the spear," as his teams in Special Operations had been called.

"There's Ashley," Young Fred said, sounding excited now as he spotted her outside, waiting in line for the ride.

Action. Ethan felt his own blood stir. He peered at Ashley. She had a coat on that she hadn't been wearing before. *Covering the wound,* he thought.

"And of course the sap is wearing a wedding ring," Glenda said, looking at the guy who had his hand on Ashley's butt.

Ethan spotted Mab and Joe in line in front of Ashley and her sap, waiting for the car that had just pulled up to the platform. Just what he needed: an audience. "What now?"

Glenda nodded to Young Fred. "You're up."

Young Fred nodded and sauntered out to the line, walking by everyone waiting as if they couldn't see him.

Evidently, they couldn't.

"When it's your turn, Ethan," Glenda said, "when Delpha shows you the spirit flash, you say, 'Capio!' Can you remember that?"

"Capio," Ethan said, watching Young Fred. "Got it."

Delpha spoke up, Frankie moving from foot to foot on her shoulder. "When the demon is getting ready to jump, her eyes will change. If the demon is Tura, the flash will be blue-green."

Ethan nodded, his brain still muddled from the alcohol. If it hadn't been for that blue-green light in Ashley's eyes just before he blacked out, and the dead guy with the mark on his chest the other night, he'd have told them they were all crazy and headed for the Beer Pavilion. He pulled out his flask and unscrewed the top but stopped when Glenda said in a low voice only he could hear: *"Ethan.* You're *demon-hunting."*

With a sigh, Ethan slid the flask back into his combat vest. He noted that Ashley and her sap were next to get on the ride, and Young Fred was right behind them. "We better get moving."

"Wait," Glenda said, and watched Young Fred step up as his features shifted, turning into the image of the sap as he shoved the guy away. It all happened so fast, Ethan wasn't sure he could trust his eyes, and neither could the sap when he turned to yell and saw himself. Or whatever it was he saw that made him back away horrified. *Young Fred can be anything,* Ethan remembered.

Ashley and Young-Fred-as-the-Sap got in the boat behind Mab and Joe, and began to float into the tunnel.

"Now," Glenda said, and led them behind the tunnel and into a service door.

The dioramas had some kind of scrim mesh behind them, newly repainted as backdrops, that let them see what was happening beyond the brightly lit scenes. When they were behind Adam and Eve, the prow of the next boat appeared and Ethan spotted Ashley and Young Fred lip-locked. She was all over him, one hand behind his head, the other on his chest. *How the hell is he supposed to see when her eyes change?* Ethan thought. He moved on, faster than the boats, the rest trailing him until they reached Antony and Cleopatra, where he moved through a break in the scrim and into the diorama, ducking behind the Antony statue as the next swan boat came round the bend. He saw Mab and Joe, her finally without her miner's hat, him holding her close as he whispered in her ear. She laughed, her hand on his cheek, and leaned in to kiss him, and Ethan thought, *Must be love,* and poked his head out to see better, bumping into Antony and making him rock dangerously over Cleo. Mab turned at the sound and then her eyes widened as she spotted him and Ethan gave her a thumbs-up. She pulled away from Joe, craning to see him, and then their boat went around the curve and they were out of sight.

Ethan turned his attention the other way. The next swan boat appeared. This time it was Ashley, one hand in Young Fred's crotch, the other tight behind his head. She was kissing him, and it was a good thing she had her eyes closed, because Fred kept losing his morph, flickering between his real face and that of the sap. He saw Ethan in the diorama and looked disappointed, but he said, "Hey," and Ashley looked surprised, and then he turned back into Young Fred and she pulled back, shocked, her eyes glinting blue-green.

"Frustro," Young Fred said sadly, and then her eyes really lit up, glowing like a demon, as Delpha moved to the front of the diorama.

"Specto!" Delpha said, throwing her fist toward Ashley, and Tura's spirit leapt into the air, a blue-green mermaid, as Ethan stepped into the boat and said, "Uh, capio?"

*****

Joe pulled Mab out of the boat at the next diorama and onto the narrow walkway beside the water.

"What are you doing?" she said, flushed from fooling around. "What's Ethan doing—?"

"Come on." He pulled her through the tunnel, and she shut up so she could concentrate on moving fast without falling into the water—*Dark ride,* she thought, *they weren't kidding*— and then they were out into the orange-lit night, the midway now obscured by orange clouds from the fog machines and crowded with local people dressed up like the undead, offering plastic brains on plates to shrieking teenagers. The music from the carousel piped out over the laughter, and the lights from the rides glittered green and yellow and orange in the navy blue sky, and Mab looked back at the Tunnel and said, "What was that about?"

Joe led her around the bend in the midway to the front of the carousel, and stopped by one of the steel-drum fires set to take the chill off the night. "I want you," he said, the light from the fire flickering in his eyes.

"I saw Ethan," Mab said, stepping closer. "I think something bad is happening—"

"Something bad is always happening," Joe said. "Do you want tonight with me?" He stared at her, and she saw how much he wanted her, and she lost her breath.

"Yes," Mab said.

"Then take me home," Joe said.

She led him down the midway, around to the back of the Dream Cream, past Ray's RV office and up the back stairs to her bedroom, making a detour to the bathroom to hit Cindy's condom stash. When she shut her bedroom door, Joe let out his breath, as if he'd been waiting for somebody to stop them.

She took off her paint coat, and he put his arms around her and said, "I didn't think I'd ever get you alone," and she laughed and said, "You only waited two days," and he said, "It felt like months," and kissed her, and her heart lifted, the way it always did when she was with him, and she laughed again because she was so glad he was there. "Come here," he said, and pulled her down onto the bed with him, and she rolled close to him, wanting to be part of him and yet. . . .

"What?" He pushed up her T-shirt, tickling her stomach and making her laugh again, and then he stripped off her clothes—she tried to help, but he said, "Let me"—and took off his. When he was close against her again, he pushed her hair back and kissed her, and she put her arms around him, feeling happy and yet vaguely . . . not hot. "Laugh for me," he said, and then kissed her neck, making her shiver and smile, and then her shoulder, and then he moved down her body with more tickling kisses that made her laugh again, and she fell into all his brightness as his hands and mouth moved over her, expertly building that missing heat in her. She tried to touch him, and he said, "No, let me do it all, I want you happy," and she lay back, feeling a little rejected and then lost herself in him until he came back to her again.

Then, suffused with heat, she opened her eyes, and he pulled back, staring at her.

"What?" she said, trying to sit up, dizzy and confused. *"What?"*

He laughed and said, "You are an amazing woman, Mary Alice Brannigan," and pushed her back onto the bed, spreading her thighs with his as she arched up to meet him, and then he was inside her, and she let her head fall back, smiling because he felt so good, as he whispered in her ear, "Tell me you're happy, *tell me,*" and she said, "I'm *happy.*" Then he rocked her to her finish and left her gasping and satisfied, laughing as she held him close.

*****

The blue-green spirit slammed into Ethan, the same blue-green light in his head as before, the same tentacles around his heart, but this time instead of fighting it, he grabbed on to the demon inside him. Ashley collapsed into the boat, dispossessed and unconscious, and Ethan slid away from her, holding that writhing, fluid, fighting turquoise weight in his chest, her furious screams tearing his mind.

He held on to her, the screaming almost unbearable as he crawled out of the boat and fell toward the emergency exit. Then he looked up and saw his mother standing over him and felt her voice echo with power inside his head: *"Redimio."*

The blue-green exploded from him, and Glenda caught it and bound it and forced it into the chalice, and Ethan's head was quiet again and his heart was free.

But Gus wasn't in place; he was kneeling next to Delpha, who had collapsed on the walkway.

"Gus!" Glenda screamed, but Ethan could tell Gus couldn't hear.

Glenda slapped the lid on, but it wouldn't seal, and when Gus finally turned and tried to reach for it, it was too late: the blue-green slithered out from under the chalice lid, spiraled down the tunnel, and disappeared into the darkness.

"Delpha," Glenda said, and dropped to her knees beside her.

"I thought it was my time," Delpha said, her voice faint.

"Not yet it isn't," Glenda said, putting her arm around her. "We can't lose you yet." She looked down the tunnel after Tura, her face grim.

"Tura—"

"We'll get her the next time." Glenda stood up. "Ethan, you'll have to carry Delpha home."

"Sure," Ethan said, looking after Gus, who was staring down the tunnel, too.

"I'm sorry," Gus said, turning back to Glenda. "I—"

"We'll get her next time," Glenda told him, staring into his eyes. "It's all right. We'll win. We're the Guardia."

Gus seemed caught for a moment, and then he nodded back, relieved.

We are so screwed, Ethan thought, and stood up to carry Delpha home.

*****

"This isn't my fault." Ray spoke fast as he stood before Kharos's statue. "The Guardia just tried to capture Tura, but they couldn't get her. Ethan was with them. I think Ethan is Guardia. I think their Hunter finally showed up."

Kharos ran through every Etruscan curse he knew. It took a while, but then he was calm enough to think. So now the Guardia had a strong Hunter. But not a very good one if Tura escaped.

"It took him long enough to get here," Ray was saying. "The last one died in July. Three months. He must have walked from—"

THE MINIONS HAVE ARRIVED.

"Yeah," Ray said without enthusiasm.

SEND THEM TO KILL DELPHA AND THE OLD MAN.

"Gus? Why?"

THEY ARE THE MOST EXPERIENCED GUARDIA. AND THEIR DEATHS WILL DEMORALIZE THE REST. Kharos smiled, just thinking about the Guardia's grief, the taste of it. So much more delicious than that of regular human cattle.

"Should I send them after Glenda, too?"

GLENDA. Kharos grew warmer inside his chalice. Glenda had been—

"Might as well," Ray said. "Get 'em all at once."

NO, Kharos said. she . . . WEAKENS THEM WITH HER AGE.

Ray looked up at him strangely, but didn't argue. "Okay," he said. "I'll send the minions after Delpha and Gus. But there'll be new Guardia to take their places."

IT WILL NOT MATTER. THEY WILL NOT ARRIVE IN TIME.

"Unless the old Guardia get organized and go looking for them."

THEY WILL NOT. THEY WILL GRIEVE, ESPECIALLY GLENDA. AND SUFFER GREATLY. Inside his prison, Kharos smiled again. Glenda's grief was a fine thing, rich and deep. Even after forty years, he could remember the taste of it—

"So it's a diversionary tactic," Ray said. "Okay. Got it. I'll send the minions after them tonight."

THEN COME AND TELL ME OF THEIR SUFFERING.

"Uh, sure," Ray said.

Kharos considered the fact that the Guardia now had a Hunter. HAVE THE MINIONS ATTACK THE OLD MAN WHEN HE RUNS THE COASTER. FREE SELVANS THEN.

"Look, I lost most of today getting the minions, and I can't afford another wasted day right now. I have things to do. I'm the *mayor.*"

Kharos sent images into Ray's mind, his investments disappearing along with his fortune, his mayoral office lost to impeachment, his body returning to its hollow-chested weakness, his hair falling out . . .

"No," Ray said, his face ashen. "Don't take this away from me."

THEN DO NOT FORGET WHO IS THE MASTER HERE.

"Okay, okay, just . . . don't do that again."

Ray got up and walked away, clearly shaken, leaving Kharos to his memories.

Of the Guardia, who should suffer the agony of failure for eternity for imprisoning him before he obliterated them.

Of Glenda, so young and so lovely and so possessed . . .

And of Vanth, round and warm and yielding to him.

To be out again. To touch Vanth, take Glenda, to feel warm flesh under his hands, to *feed* again—

Kharos strained against his chalice, needing to get at the fools who had imprisoned him, the fools he'd destroy in two weeks.

HALLOWEEN, he thought, but without satisfaction. It was so far away.

TWO WEEKS, he thought. TWO WEEKS.

*****

Mab lay awake, staring at the ceiling while Joe snored beside her. She felt weird. The sex had been good, Joe had obviously been practicing for years, and she'd come just fine, so why was she still awake? It was like eating Chinese food, an hour later you were hungry again, except that wasn't it, because she didn't want more sex, she really was satisfied, but there was something missing—

Somebody pounded on the door downstairs. Mab sighed and slid naked out of bed. She picked up her paint coat and shrugged it on, then pulled on her jeans and went to see what was going on.

Ashley was standing outside the Dream Cream door, looking like hell.

Mab unlocked the door and said, "What happened?" and Ashley pushed her way in.

"It was awful. Somebody *hit* me." She pulled open her coat and looked down at her stomach. There was a bloody red ring there, as if somebody had shoved the sharpened top of a can into her.

"My god, is that deep?" Mab said, trying to pull the fabric away.

"Not very," Ashley said. "You're with somebody right now, aren't you?"

"What?"

"You've just had sex. You're cheating on that guy with the glasses."

"What guy with the glasses?" Mab took a step back. "What are you talking about?"

"I saw you with him—he handed you your bag," Ashley said, and leaned closer. "He watches you, he takes care of you, he's your soul mate. *Betrayer!*"

She put her hand on Mab's coat over her breast, and there was bright blue-green light, and Mab felt bitter, despairing blue-green fog flood into her. She staggered back against a table as Ashley slumped unconscious to the ground and the blue-green fog tightened like a fist around her heart and lungs, squeezing the life out of her—

"No," she choked out, and fought back, pushing against the fog until she could breathe again, rejecting the despair that told her to give up, forcing her heart to beat until the bitter blue-green turned to fury, fighting inside her. She staggered for the door, but the blue-green dragged her down. "No," she whispered, breathless as she sank to her knees. "No, no, *no*—" She fought hard, keeping a space so her heart could beat, her lungs could move—

And then Joe was there, yelling, *"Get the hell out of her!"* and the blue-green writhed and was gone, and Mab was left gasping on the floor as he dropped to his knees and pulled her into his arms.

Across the shop, Ashley stirred and sat up.

"Get out," Joe said, his face hard, and Ashley got to her feet, shook her hair out, and smiled at him.

"Later," she said, and walked out of the shop.

"That was a demon," Mab said, breathless. "She possessed me." She struggled to stand up. *"She's possessing Ashley."*

"I know," Joe said, holding on to her.

Mab looked at him, incredulous. "How do you know?"

"I'm a demon hunter," Joe said.

CHAPTER 9

An hour after they left Delpha at her trailer, Ethan was still trapped on Glenda's banquette, listening to the history of the Guardia and famous Hunters past. He was so tired, he was almost unconscious, and he needed a drink, bad, but she would not shut up. Finally, he gave up and reached for his flask.

"No," Glenda said.

"Just one," Ethan said. "It'll clear my head." If there ever was a time for a drink, this was it.

"I've got something better." Glenda took the flask from him before he could react. "You sit."

She went to the cupboard and took down a mug, and Ethan put his head in his hands. "I'm sorry we missed Tura, Mom."

"You did fine. We're just out of practice." She dumped whatever it was into the mug, topped it up with water from the sink, stirred it, put it in the microwave, punched the button, and leaned against the counter. "We have to get back into shape, all of us. And you have to take this seriously—"

"I do," Ethan said. "After tonight, you bet your ass I do. We need organization, a plan. We can't just go wandering around the park—"

The microwave dinged. Glenda opened the door and took the mug out.

"—hoping to trip over a demon so we can shout Latin at it."

"Drink this." Glenda gave it another quick stir, first clockwise, then counter, then tapped the spoon five times on the rim and handed the steaming mug to him.

He cradled his hands around it, feeling the warmth sink into his skin.

"Drink it," Glenda said.

Ethan put the mug to his lips. Whatever was in it smelled enticing. He took a deep swallow, feeling the warmth coil down his throat, into his guts. Then he bolted for the door as the liquid savagely uncoiled and came roaring back up. He made it outside and bent over, retching so hard he expected to see his internal organs come spewing out.

He was aware that Glenda was next to him, the mug in her hand as he slowly straightened. She held it out once more. "Drink."

"What the hell is that crap?" Ethan demanded, staring at his mother.

"We need you, Ethan. We need you at full strength and sober. We don't have time for the poison in your body to work its way out naturally. This will take the alcohol from your system." She pushed the mug toward him. "Drink it."

Ethan knocked the mug from her hand, spilling it over the ground. "Don't tell me what to do. Not when cocktail hour for you starts at noon and goes till midnight." He saw her flinch and felt like hell. He straightened slowly. "I'm sorry. I'm sorry. Look, I'm with you now, I understand about the demons, I'll make a plan, we'll get the two that are out back inside, and then I'll review everything, the security system, the rides, the statues, I'll go over every inch. But don't tell me I'm a drunk the same night I'm almost killed by something I don't even believe in."

Glenda went back into the trailer, and he followed her and slumped onto the banquette, exhausted.

"Okay," he said, trying to focus. "I don't want any more history. Where's Ashley?"

"I sent Gus and Young Fred to look for her hours ago." Glenda put the kettle on the stove and lit the fire under it, keeping her back to him. "It's late. Everybody's left the park. There isn't anybody for Tura to possess. She'll probably just let Ashley go."

"Ashley's wounded," Ethan said. "She's going to wonder how that happened."

"She'll think she had a blackout," Glenda said, and moved to the sink. "Ashley is not our problem."

"Okay," Ethan said, not wanting to start another argument, "then Tura and Fufluns. We have Tura's chalice. Gus was going to have Mab fix Fufluns' chalice lid."

Glenda nodded, her back still to him. "Take it to her tomorrow. There's a mold for the chalice in the Keep that'll help her get it right. Go with Gus to get it so he doesn't kill himself on those stairs."

"Okay," Ethan said. "Are you ever going to look at me again?"

She turned around, tears in her eyes, her face angry. "I have been Guardia for forty years. I have stayed in this park, I have patrolled it, I have checked the statues, I have made sure that everything was secure *for forty years*. I'm sick of it, but it's not a job you can quit. I'll be Guardia until I die."

"Mom—"

"I held it together while Delpha and Gus grew older and I took over more of their work, I held it together when Old Fred died and Young Fred threw a fit because he had to serve, I held it together for forty years after your father died and that drunken asshole Hank was called to take his place. And then he drove into that tree and we didn't have a Hunter and I still kept things together."

Ethan waited, knowing she had to get this out.

"And now you're called and how do you handle that news? You attack me. You think I don't know that potion wouldn't have solved your problems? Whatever the reason you drink yourself into a stupor every damn night, some magic tea is not going to fix it. But it would have cleared your body and your mind, and then maybe serving the Guardia would have given you something to help whatever it is you're trying to drink away. I had to hope so because as a drunk, Ethan, you are just one more body I have to carry, right along with Delpha and Gus and Young Fred. So don't come in here and think you're going to take over. I can't let you if I don't know if you're going to be sober when it's time for you to lead. Until you dry out or I die, I'm in charge."

"I'm not a drunk," Ethan said, really wanting a drink.

Glenda looked at him tiredly. "What happened, Ethan? You were never like this before."

Ethan shook his head. "It doesn't matter—"

"Yes, it does." Glenda crossed her arms in front of her. "It matters because you're Guardia now and it matters because I'm your mother. Stop shutting me out. *What the hell happened?*"

Ethan hesitated and then let go. "We were on a recon patrol. Half a team. Just six of us. High in the mountains. We weren't supposed to make contact. But no one told the Taliban. They hit us in the perfect spot. Three guys went down right away, torn apart by an RPG round —a rocket—" He took a deep breath. "My team leader—" He stopped again as the scene played out in his mind again, the darkness coming down on him. "—my team leader was caught in the open, wounded. They kept shooting at him, shooting his legs up, playing with him. I took my Kevlar off and threw it over his legs."

"Ethan," Glenda said. "I—"

"Then I got hit. Here." Ethan touched his chest over his heart. "I woke up in the field hospital. I was the only survivor, and they were amazed I was alive because the bullet had hit so close to my heart and then lodged there. The surgeons said it was impossible to remove it without killing me, that it will probably work its way farther in and kill me before the year is out. So . . ."

Glenda had gone pale as he'd talked, and she sat down now, hard, and looked at him, tears in her eyes. "The bullet is still in you?"

"In my chest. Where everybody keeps hitting me, for some reason." He reached out for her hand and patted it. "It doesn't hurt. I just know I don't have much time. So we should get Tura and this other jerk captured fast."

Glenda swallowed back tears and patted his hand. "It's okay. Your heart is stronger than a normal person's. You're not going to die from that bullet, Ethan. You're Guardia."

Ethan nodded. He wasn't sure if she was saying that to reassure him or herself, but either way, it was Glenda being Glenda, and he was grateful.

She went back to business. "But you're right, we have to capture Tura quickly before she kills someone else, and that means before next weekend when we have to open the Tunnel of Love again."

"Okay," Ethan said, glad to be back on strategy. "I'll make sure the Tunnel of Love can't run this week."

The kettle started to whine, and Glenda took down two cups, opened a box and took out two tea bags, put the bags into the cups, and poured the hot water over them.

"Think Tura will go back into Ashley?" Ethan asked, trying to keep the conversation on the park's demons and not his.

Glenda shrugged. "It's risky for a demon to keep taking the same host, because eventually the host catches on. But if she likes Ashley's body, she might not care about that." She brought the teacups over and put one in front of him. "Chamomile. No potion."

She looked like she was gearing herself up to change the subject back to him, so he said, "Why'd she come after me? I wasn't unfaithful." He paused. "No, wait. She said something about seeing me with Weaver. Maybe she thought—"

"Demons don't think, Ethan. They act, based on their drives." She stared at him meaningfully. "Like a lot of humans. We just have to capture the two that are out and put them back and everything will be fine. I know how to do this."

"Okay, but this black-ops guy who shot me, he knows something about demons. He could have killed me that first night and he didn't, and he saved me from Tura. If I can find him, can get him to work with us—"

"Only the Guardia can defeat the Untouchables," Glenda said.

"The Guardia didn't do too good tonight," Ethan said.

"With your help, we'll be strong again," Glenda said.

"We'd be even stronger with the man in black. He has weapons, knowledge we don't have. If he can help us—"

"We can't trust anyone but the Guardia," Glenda said. "That why we need you strong and sober—"

"All right." Ethan felt exhaustion pressing down on his eyelids. "Let's talk about it in the morning." He stretched out on the banquette, closing his eyes to shut her out, and he heard her get up and then a minute later felt her cover him with the blanket from her bed, tucking it gently in around him.

Afghan insurgents couldn't kill him, but his mother was probably going to.

Gotta get the demons put back, gotta get a fighting team. . . . He drifted off to sleep, but his last thoughts were of how he could make contact with the man in black.

And how much he wanted a drink.

*****

Mab yanked back from Joe. "You're a what?"

"Demon hunter," Joe said. "It's a hobby." He opened his arms to her. "Come here."

"Wait a minute." Mab pulled her coat around her tighter. "You knew there were demons in the park? *And you didn't tell me?*"

"Everybody knows there are demons in the park. The legends have been around for years."

"Yeah. *Legends.* Not real blue-green fog that tries to kill you." Mab wrapped her arms tighter around herself. "My mother told me there were demons in the park, hell, she told *everybody* there were demons in the park, it's why the Brannigans have always been outcasts in Parkersburg, it's why I left home and didn't come back until now, because my mother was a freaking nutcase. Except now I find out that she wasn't." Mab thought about it. "Well, yeah she was, just not about the demons. The demons are real. My mother was right. Which means everything I believed about my life here, growing up, about . . . *reality*, it's all wrong. There really are demons." Her lungs still hurt from trying to breathe, and her heart ached. "*There really are demons.* My god, *my god*."

Joe sighed and moved closer to her. "You're okay, Mab. Hell, you should be proud. You just stood off a demon possession. How many people can say that?"

"Okay," Mab said. "Okay. Just let me get my head around this. Demons are real, and you knew about it and didn't tell me, and oh yeah, I almost died. Crap." She jerked her head up. "Ashley—the demon has her—"

"Ashley will be all right."

"I'm not all right."

"You're fine." Joe pulled her back to him again and she let him, really needing something to hold on to. "You even stayed conscious. Most people don't. They wake up later and think they've had a blackout."

Mab pulled back. "That bitch was trying to kill me!"

Joe shrugged. "Or they don't wake up later."

"Is that what killed Karl?" Mab had a thought and pulled open her coat to look at her chest. A faint wavy mark curved over her left breast. "Damn it. Does this wash off?"

"Well, we could certainly try," Joe said, staring.

Mab pulled her coat closed. "Okay. Okay. So. You hunt them? Here? They come here? To Dreamland?"

"Sure, they come here," Joe said. "They eat funnel cake, ride the Dragon, possess people. Why don't we talk about this later?" He looked around the Dream Cream. "Is there anything to eat? I'm starving." He stood up and went behind the counter. "You want anything?"

I want this not to have happened. I want it to be an hour ago when I was all warm and happy.

Should have known that wasn't going to last.

He opened the freezer. "There's chocolate and something pink and something yellow. What do you want?"

"The pink is a love potion and the yellow is an antidepressant." She put her hand over her breast and rubbed at the mark, hating it.

"How about if I put all three in?"

"Whatever." *Stop feeling sorry for yourself,* Mab thought. *Get organized. FIX this.* "Okay, first things first. Is anybody else in the park in danger right now?"

"The park is closed, so I'm guessing no." Joe found a bowl and put it on the counter. "My guess is that the demon gave up and Ashley's probably on her way home now, really tired. She'll sleep for hours and wake up fine." He rummaged in a drawer and pulled out an ice cream scoop and started dishing ice cream.

"No, she won't," Mab said, remembering. "She was hurt. There was a cut on her stomach, like a circle. Her shirt was cut and there was blood." She looked up to see Joe had stopped scooping and turned around. "Do you know what that was?"

"No," he said. "Tura doesn't wound people. Somebody else must have done that."

"It was a circle about this big. . . ." She held up her hands to show him, making a circle that was about bracelet size, and then she remembered. "Ethan got hit by the same thing. It was a circle with barbs on it, made of iron."

Joe looked even more uneasy as he shut the freezer case. He dropped the ice cream scoop in the sink, put two spoons in the bowl, and brought it around the counter to her. "Iron is bad for demons. So if somebody shot something iron at Ashley—"

"They were trying to get the demon." Mab picked up a spoon. "So that means somebody else is here hunting demons besides you and the Guardia. The Guardia are the park's demon hunters." She dipped her spoon into the lemon and let the cold tangy cream melt on her tongue. It did make her feel better. "Whoever shot that thing, they're high tech." She stopped again. "Wait. High tech. Ethan said there was a man in black in the park. I bet it's him."

"Man in black?"

"He called him black ops. Like, super-secret government . . . demon hunters." Mab felt the edges of reality evaporating again and put down her spoon. It was one thing to hold on to reality by getting practical and organizing her information; it was another thing entirely to get practical and organize information about *demons.*

"So the Guardia is hunting demons," Joe said, "the government is hunting demons, and I'm hunting demons. Almost makes you feel sorry for the demons."

"Are you *crazy*? That bitch killed Dead Karl—"

"I am not going to mourn Dead Karl."

"—and I think the other bastard ran me down inside the FunFun statue. Ethan mentioned him and so did Delpha. Fufluns." She frowned. "Fufluns. FunFun. Whoever named that clown FunFun knew about the demon Fufluns." She ate more lemon ice cream, needing it now. "Which means these demons were around when the park was built in 1926. They've been here forever."

Joe kept eating ice cream.

"Doesn't this *bother* you?" Mab asked him.

"No. But I've known about it for a while. Try the pink love potion stuff, it's really good."

"I'm not in a loving mood."

"That's why you should try the pink stuff."

"So you hunt demons," Mab said, her thoughts finally organized. "How does that work?"

Joe shook his head. "Eat your ice cream. We can talk demons later if you still want to, but right now you're just revving yourself up."

Mab rubbed her forehead, and he dropped his spoon in the bowl and put his arm around her. She put her head on his shoulder and said, "I don't want to believe in demons."

"I know, baby."

"But now I have to."

"I know."

"My world is so fucked."

"Not really. It's a whole new world. The old one is gone. You haven't had time to fuck this one up yet."

"I liked the old one," Mab said miserably. "Did you?"

"Yeah. I had plenty of work and it was interesting and . . ."

"You didn't have Dreamland."

"I don't have Dreamland now. I leave the day after Halloween."

"You didn't have me."

"You're leaving the day after Halloween, too."

"Mab," he said, and she looked up to see him staring down at her, serious for once. "Do you have something *against* happiness?"

"Yes," she said. "It doesn't last."

"Well, of course not. If it lasted, you'd be happy all the time and then you wouldn't know you were happy."

Mab frowned, trying to follow that.

"Live in the moment, babe," Joe said, smiling down at her with immense affection. "It's all you've got."

"My moment has *demons* in it," Mab said. "So frankly, I'd like to move on."

"Good idea." Joe put his arms around her. "Play your cards right and you'll get possessed again. By me." He kissed her on the neck. "Come on, lighten up."

"I have to call somebody. Delpha. I have to tell Delpha there's a demon." Mab pushed his arms away and got up and went behind the counter to the phone. She punched in Delpha's extension, written on the list on the wall. Then she turned and watched Joe while she let it ring, thinking, *I trusted him and he lied to me,* but really, if he'd said, "I'm a demon hunter," would she have believed him?

The phone rang on and finally Mab hung up. "She's not answering. She must be with Glenda." Joe got up as she picked up the receiver again to call Glenda and came around the counter and took it from her.

"Nothing happens in this park that Glenda doesn't know about," he told her. "She knows the demons are out. It's way past midnight. You can talk to her in the morning."

He hung up the phone and she hesitated.

"Do you want me to go?" he said. She started to say yes because he'd lied to her, and then he added, "Do you want to be alone tonight?" and she said, *"No."*

He put his arms around her again. "We'll work this out. Tomorrow, you can talk to people and organize meetings and do research and make a plan for the future. Now you need sleep. And somebody to watch over you and make you smile again."

"Okay," she said, because that sounded good.

"Then let's go to bed," he said, and kissed her again, and she let him, and after a minute she kissed him back.

I wouldn't have believed him if he' d told me he was a demon hunter, she thought. I probably wouldn't have told me, either.

Maybe that doesn't count as a lie.

"Come on," he said, and she followed him up to bed.

*****

Mab woke up late the next morning and found Joe gone, which was a relief. The people she wanted to talk to were Cindy and Delpha, not him. Common sense and supernatural sense—that's what she needed, not somebody trying to get her to laugh about a demon infestation.

She got dressed and went downstairs, but the Dream Cream was full of the early lunch crowd, including Ashley telling everybody about the enormous blackout she'd had the night before—two nights in a row, could you believe it?—and how she really had to stop drinking. Skinny and Quentin from the Pavilion were there, too, Skinny still talking—"Now, the most popular ice cream flavor is vanilla, second is chocolate, but vanilla beats it by a mile. Then strawberry is third, but it's tied with butter pecan, and what's up with that?"—and the guy in the Coke-bottle glasses was sitting at the counter again, on his cell phone this time. There was one seat left on the end next to him, and he had his trilby hat on it, but when he saw Mab, he moved it.

"Thank you," she said, and sat down, dropping her work bag on the floor between them as Skinny moved into high gear behind her.

"But the fifth flavor is really a killer: Neapolitan. You know what I think, Quentin? I think it's for people who can't make up their minds about the first three. That's what I think. Go with vanilla, that's what I say. Twenty-nine percent of Americans go with vanilla, and that's good enough for me."

"Chocolate," Quentin said.

"Okay," Skinny said.

Cindy came down the counter to Mab, looking almost annoyed. "Those guys are driving me crazy. Tell me about last night and talk loud so you drown out the skinny one."

"Can we go in the storeroom?" Mab said, not wanting to share her bad news with Quentin and Skinny or the guy with the glasses and the hat, who was getting out his notebook.

"That good?" Cindy turned and called down the counter to her college help, "Emily, yell if you need me."

Emily looked at the packed shop wide-eyed, and Mab detoured around the Coke-bottle glasses guy to follow Cindy into the storeroom. She turned to close the door and found the guy with the glasses watching her, his eyes cool behind the thick lenses.

Demon?

He smiled at her. It was a brief smile, disappearing as fast as it came, but still a good smile, straightforward and nondemonic. . . .

"Mab?" Cindy said.

She closed the door and said, "What do you know about that guy with the glasses?"

"He comes in every day. His wife, Ursula, calls a lot. He doesn't like her." Cindy put her hands on her hips. "So, young lady. I saw I was down some condoms. You weren't making water balloons, were you?"

Mab took a deep breath. "I was possessed by a demon."

She pulled back. "Whoa, he's that good?"

"No," Mab said. "Well, yes, but—"

Cindy threw her hands up. "You've, like, won the life lottery. Robot clowns and legends coming true and now a guy who's a demon in the sack. I've been making ice cream here for fifteen years, and nothing like that has ever happened to me."

Mab stopped. "Fifteen years?"

Cindy nodded. "I've worked in Dreamland longer than that, but I started making ice cream when I was eighteen. And in fifteen years, I never had anything like you've had in the past three days."

"You've been here for fifteen years? And you never noticed the demons?"

"Well, I got married once and moved to Columbus. But the only place I could find work was Baskin-Robbins, and it just wasn't the same. So I came back here. And then about five years ago, this fancy restaurant in Cincinnati offered me some big bucks to make ice cream just for them, so I went for it, but two months later I had to come back. They liked the ice cream just fine, but I knew it wasn't right. This is the only place I can make truly great ice cream. Like you restoring amusement parks. Once you find what you're meant to do, you have to do that."

"Okay," Mab said. "Did you miss the part about the demon?"

"Joe as a demon in the sack?" Cindy said, refocusing.

"No, real demons. There are real demons in the park."

Cindy blinked at her.

"They're real. Demons. They're real. One possessed me last night. It had Ashley and she knocked on the door and I let her in and then the demon flowed out of her and into me and tried to stop my heart and lungs. They're real. Joe knows about it. He came here to hunt them. And Delpha and Glenda and Gus, they're the Guardia, they—"

Cindy pulled over a step stool and sat down. "Demons."

"They're real. I swear, they're real. They possess people. They can be *anybody*. Maybe that guy with the glasses out at the counter. *Anybody*."

Her voice rose at the end, and Cindy got up and shoved the step stool over to her.

"I'm still a little upset," Mab said, sitting down.

"I . . . yeah," Cindy said. "Demons. Okay."

"You believe me?"

"I think you're the only person I would believe. You're not . . . fanciful. You don't joke around. If you say there are demons, there are demons. Wow. So now what?"

"I go talk to Delpha." Mab nodded, even surer now that she'd said it out loud. "She tried to tell me about them, but I wouldn't listen. Now I'll listen."

"Good." Cindy nodded. "Delpha's good. Go talk to her. And take notes and then come back and tell me because this is really . . ."

"Unbelievable?"

"Kind of exciting," Cindy said. "Assuming, you know, nobody dies or anything."

"Dead Karl," Mab said.

"Nobody else." Cindy straightened. "And look on the bright side. You're sleeping with a demon hunter."

"Yeah," Mab said.

"And what's wrong with that?"

"He lied to me. Well, he didn't lie to me, he just didn't tell me he was a demon hunter. That's kind of big."

Cindy frowned. "I don't think that's the kind of thing you drop on a woman you're trying to get into bed."

Mab thought about it. "That's a good point. But—"

"Did he say 'I'm not a demon hunter'?"

"No."

"Did he say he was something else?"

"No."

"And he's good in bed."

"Yeah," Mab said.

"Might want to lower your standards there," Cindy said.

Emily knocked on the door of the storeroom and said, "Cindy?" in a high voice that meant *Help*, and Cindy opened the door and then turned back to Mab.

"I'll help all I can. Can you defeat demons with ice cream?"

"If anybody can, you can," Mab said, and followed her back out to the counter.

The guy in the Coke-bottle glasses had his notebook open in front of him, but he was looking into his empty coffee cup.

"I'll get that for you." Mab went behind the counter to get the pot, and when she filled his cup, he looked up and said, "Thank you."

She looked into his sharp gray eyes, sharp even behind those thick glasses, trying to see if there was a demon in there—

"Something wrong?" he said, and she realized she'd been staring.

"No." She put the coffeepot back. "Sorry, I just—"

His eyes were really sharp behind those glasses. Glasses that thick shouldn't be that clear; glasses that thick almost always distorted what was behind them—

"Are those just plain glass?" she said.

"No." He picked up his coffee cup.

"Oh." She hesitated, but he went back to his notebook, so she went back around the counter and waved to Cindy, heading for the door and Delpha for some answers.

A whistle, sharp and short, made her turn around.

He was holding out her work bag to her with one hand, not even looking at her while he drank his coffee and read his notebook.

She went and got her bag. "Thank you," she said, and he nodded, his eyes still on his notebook, but she saw that grin flash again.

So he's probably not a demon, she thought, and went out to find Delpha.

*****

Mab dropped her bag at the Fortune-Telling Machine and headed down the midway to the back of the park and Delpha's trailer. She ignored everything on the way except for Sam the maintenance guy, who returned her wave with a polite hello as if he'd never met her before—so much for her deathless allure—and Carl Whack-A-Mole, who was standing in front of his booth, looking annoyed.

"What's wrong?" she said, slowing.

"Somebody broke in here last night," he said, disgust in his voice. "Didn't take nothing, but some of the bears are dirty. Don't make no sense to do that."

"There's a lot of that going around," Mab said. "I have to go see Delpha, but I can come back and help you if—"

"Nah," Carl said. "Can't give out dirty bears. I'll get some new ones. But thank you just the same."

"You're welcome," Mab said, and picked up speed, moving past the Dragon and the hulking orange Strong Man statue, and then through the woods, between Old Fred's and Hank's empty trailers on the left and Gus's and Glenda's trailers on the right and down the path to the edge of the island and Delpha's Airstream.

When she got there, the door was ajar, which was odd since it was cold.

Too cold.

That's not right, Mab thought, and even though the door was in her way, she suddenly saw Delpha lying on the floor, her eyes staring up at the ceiling, her hands clenched into fists—

"No, no, *no.*" Mab ran to the trailer and yanked the door wide open.

Delpha was lying on the floor, her eyes staring up at the ceiling, her hands clenched into fists. . . .

"Glenda!" Mab screamed, and turned and ran for Glenda's trailer.

CHAPTER 10

Ethan had woken slowly with a hangover, easing up on the banquette, his hand over his chest to press down the pain from the old bullet, which seemed not so bad these days. Probably because of all the other pain he'd been feeling. Given the number of hits he'd taken in the past few days, he was grateful to be alive.

Then he heard Mab scream, and he was out the door before Glenda made it out of her bedroom.

He ran down the steps and looked down the path to the park, and Mab hit him from behind, pulling at him, crying, *"Delpha,"* and he pushed her aside and ran back to Delpha's trailer.

She was on the floor, and he knelt down beside her, but it was obvious she was gone, had been gone since the night before. Probably not too long after he'd left her to go back to his mother's and find his flask.

He should have stayed.

He touched her and she was icy cold, beyond death cold, and he looked up and saw that the window over her couch was open. It didn't matter, she hadn't frozen to death, but he still hated that she'd lain there all night in the cold. . . .

"What is it?" Glenda said from behind him, and then drew in her breath. *"No."*

"I'm sorry, Mom," Ethan said, not turning around. "I should have stayed with her."

"Oh, no," Glenda said, coming in to kneel down beside him. "Not like this. She knew it was her time, but not like this."

Ethan frowned at her, but she was crying now, picking up Delpha's hand to hold it, so he went outside to see what in hell had murdered his mother's best friend.

It had to be demons, but somehow, this didn't seem like Tura's style. Maybe Fufluns wasn't as harmless as they thought.

He walked around to the side of the trailer to look at the open window. The hitch was there with a cigar butt beneath it, and an old, rotting lawn chair had been dragged over beside it, under the window, but it was one with strips of plastic for a seat, ancient strips of plastic at that; it could never have held a human being.

Something bright blue was caught in the window, between the casement and the frame. He stood on the hitch to reach it, tugging it free, and then couldn't figure out what it was: something kind of . . . fluffy.

"I need to make some calls," Glenda said from behind him, and when he turned, her face was tearstained even though her voice had been sure.

"A human being was here," Ethan said. "Somebody who knew Delpha was alone and lived clear back here, somebody who knew the park. Could even be another Guardia—"

"No," Glenda said. "A Guardia cannot physically harm another Guardia. We're bound together. But other people besides the Guardia know this park. How do you know there was a human here?"

"Cigar butt," Ethan said pointing to it.

Glenda stiffened. "Ray." Then she shook her head. "He waited outside. Demons killed Delpha. He just . . . waited."

"I need to go ask some questions," Ethan said, his anger rising.

"Don't do anything to him," Glenda said, looking with loathing at the cigar butt. “Don’t give away that we know he’s involved. We need to find out how involved.”

“I can ask him,” Ethan said grimly.

“No,” Glenda said. “We need to be smart. Delpha . . .” Her voice cracked. “. . . would want us to be smart.” She shook her head, blinking hard, and then went down the path, and Mab put her arm around her and went back to her trailer with her.

Ethan walked around to the path and looked through the doorway to Delpha’s body, covered by a dark blue blanket now.

He shouldn’t have left her the night before. He should have been there to take out the demons and that animal Ray, who’d smoked while she suffered.

He could ask questions later. He sat down on the step to stay with Delpha until the ambulance came to take her away.

*****

When Delpha was gone, Ethan went to find Gus.

The old man took the bad news pretty well, shaking a bit as he sat down after Ethan told him, but calmer than Ethan had thought he’d be.

“She was a good woman,” he said. “She knew it was her time. She told us that before we went to find Tura. But I thought when she was all right after that . . .”

“I’m sorry, Gus,” Ethan said.

Gus nodded and then took a deep breath. “Now we gotta get that chalice to Mab to fix, there’s a mold for it in the Keep, and there’s . . .” Tears brightened his eyes. “Delpha, she was a real good woman.”

Ethan put his hand on the old man’s shoulder. “Then let’s get the bastards who killed her.”

“Right.” Gus blinked his eyes back to normal. “Let’s go get those bastards. Put ’em back in their damn chalices. We’ll go do that.” He set off down the midway, toward the front of the park.

Ethan followed him to one of the clown-topped garbage bins, this one behind the carousel. Gus put his shoulder to it, and Ethan joined him, and together they rolled the metal container out of the way, revealing a trapdoor.

Ethan pulled it open, and a shaft beckoned. Gus climbed down as Ethan put a mini-Maglite between his teeth and brought up the rear, closing the trapdoor behind.

He paused for a second to get oriented. They were in one of the tunnels that ran under Dreamland, tunnels Ethan had been expressly forbidden to explore as a boy, which was why he knew most of them. Gus was heading toward the center of the park, into a descending tunnel that Ethan was pretty sure went under the Keep lake and then up to an old wooden door with a large iron handle in the center and an oddly shaped keyhole above it. When they reached the door, Gus produced a large ring of keys. He fumbled through them until he found an ornately crafted iron key, which he slid into the hole and turned.

There was a screech, and Gus stumbled as the key did a quarter turn. The door swung open, and Ethan felt a whoosh of stale, dry air blow over him. He followed Gus inside, his hand hovering over the grip of the pistol strapped to his thigh.

"There's a switch in here somewhere," Gus muttered, shining his light around.

Ethan felt a chill as the wavering beam lit up the rusting, rotting odds and ends of the old amusement park, all tumbled together in the huge circular stone basement of the Keep, a place he hadn't seen for over twenty years. Faded signs, broken statues, weather-beaten trunks: Glenda never could throw anything out. He didn't shut the door behind him, afraid they might not be able to get it open again.

Gus headed in the direction of the narrow stone staircase that circled up to a wooden door one level above. He reached the bottom of it, flipped a switch, and a row of naked lightbulbs around the wall flickered to life.

Ethan followed him to the base of the stairs and climbed. The door at the top was locked.

"Gus, you got the key for this?" Ethan called out. "If the stuff's in here, I'll get it."

"Yeah. The chalice mold's up there. And the weapons. Hold on a minute."

He slowly climbed the stairs, and Ethan winced with him as he climbed. No wonder Glenda didn't want him in here alone. Gus produced another iron key and opened the door and went in.

Ethan started to follow and then paused, sensing something. He turned on the landing and knelt, pulling his gun out and pointing it at the open door below. The door behind him swung shut with a click, Gus on the other side.

Down below, the man in black slid in the open door, holding a large, strange gun, like an oversized shotgun with a large round drum magazine. He had hard black body armor on the upper body, goggles, and a mask over his mouth as he looked around the room, coming to stand directly beneath Ethan.

It wasn't demons, but it was something real he could fight.

Got you, Ethan thought, and jumped.

*****

When the ambulance had taken Delpha away, Glenda said, "I have to talk to you," and led Mab into Delpha's Airstream.

Mab's only two previous experiences of Airstreams had been Glenda's retro green-and-yellow barkcloth with red Formica, and Gus's camouflage with industrial shelving, but Delpha had taken trailer living to a new level. The walls were painted blue with tiny gold stars, the couch was purple velvet scattered with heavily embroidered velvet pillows, the tabletop was a huge cracked slab of malachite, and the crown molding was branches, twined around the living area for Frankie, who was roosting up there now, in a nest over the entry to the kitchen, where Delpha had hung a dark blue bead curtain. The place looked like a seraglio with an aviary.

She must have loved living here, Mab thought, and stroked her fingers over the malachite. Even cracked, the table had to be worth thousands; it was beautifully made and very old, but then Delpha had been very old. Maybe she'd gotten it for a steal because it was cracked, at some secondhand shop back in the forties. Maybe . . .

I should have talked to her more, Mab thought with real regret. She knew so much, and I just ignored her.

Of course, she ignored everybody. She didn't do people; she did work. Suddenly, Joe made a lot more sense. Seize the moment, be happy, *connect—*

"Sit down, Mab," Glenda said, taking a seat on the velvet couch, and Mab sat down opposite her in a beautifully carved, wide-seated ebony chair, determined to listen this time. To connect, goddamn it.

"I'm so sorry about Delpha," she said, leaning forward a little over the beautiful table. "I know how close you were. She really was an amazing woman—"

"Thank you," Glenda said, red-eyed but calm. "She left you everything."

Mab blinked at her, stunned.

"She wrote out a will, so we have that if anybody makes trouble, but nobody will."

She left you everything. The ebony chair, the malachite table, the Airstream, *a home—*

"She told me last night before we went to catch Tura," Glenda went on.

"She said that she wanted you to have everything, so I'm handing it over."

"No, no," Mab said, wanting it all and knowing it wasn't hers; everything she owned fit in two suitcases, that was best, no ties. . . . "It should go to you," she said to Glenda. "I didn't even know her. You were her best friend."

"I have everything I need. She knew that—"

"Glenda, this table alone is worth thousands of dollars—"

"—you would be called to succeed her."

Mab blinked again. "Uh—"

"She had this all planned," Glenda went on. "She cleaned the trailer out. The trash cans are full, and there's a box on her bed labeled 'Goodwill.' " Her face began to crumple, but then she got control of herself again. "She knew. She was a Seer. And she said the next Seer is you."

Mab sat back as far as she could. Taking the trailer, staying in the park, surrounded by people—"I can't."

"You have to." Glenda was the one leaning forward now. "There's nobody else. She left you everything you need to take over for her, this trailer and its contents, like this malachite table. It wards off evil, you know." She looked down at it sadly, running her finger along the crack in its surface. "This crack is new. Too much evil to ward off last night."

"Maybe you didn't hear her right. You know, Delpha wasn't always clear when she said things."

"It's the curse of the Oracle," Glenda said. "They get obscure messages. Like 'There will be a great victory.' "

"Huh?" Mab said.

"This famous general asked an oracle once who would win the battle he was going to fight, and the oracle said, 'There will be a great victory,' and—"

"And the general assumed that meant him and he went out and got his ass kicked."

"You know the story."

"No, but it sounds like something a military guy would do," Mab said, and then remembered Ethan was Glenda's son. "No offense."

Glenda shook her head. "Besides the trailer, you get the Delpha's Oracle booth, a ten percent share in the park, and Frankie."

Mab looked up at the raven perched over the kitchen archway.

Frankie looked back down.

"I don't think so," Mab said.

"You need Frankie," Glenda said. "Once your power hits full strength—"

"Power?" Mab said, startled again.

"Well, of course, you get her sight, too." Mab must have looked confused, because Glenda prompted her. "Her visions." Mab still frowned, so Glenda said, "Oh, for heaven's sake, you're the one who painted the Oracle booth. Did you miss the sign that said 'Psychic'?"

"No," Mab said. "But I didn't miss the sign that said 'OK Corral,' either, and I don't think those are real cowboys. Look, Glenda—"

"She had real powers, and now they're yours. You're the Oracle now. And . . ." Glenda began speaking very slowly. "You're part of the Guardia now, too. The Guardia is—"

"A bunch of people who fight demons," Mab said. "No, I can't."

For the first time since Mab had come into the trailer, Glenda looked at a loss for words.

"Nothing personal," Mab said. "It's just not something I'd be good at. As I told Delpha, I'm not a joiner. People . . . I don't do people. So this inheritance should go to whoever does join—"

"You don't understand," Glenda said. "The Guardia isn't a club, it's the world's only defense against the worst demons. Demons are *real*, Mab—"

"I know. I was possessed by one last night." Mab wrapped her arms around herself, remembering all that murderous blue-green pressing down on her heart.

"Tura possessed you?" Glenda said, definitely off balance now.

"Tried to kill me." Mab shook her head, back on safer ground now. Reality was demons who tried to kill you, not supernatural powers. "Dumb bitch said I was cheating on the guy with the glasses in the Dream Cream. Where she got the idea that he and I ever said boo to each other, I don't know. I don't even know his name. So go, Guardia—that's what I say. Just not with me."

"We can't." Glenda looked upset now. "We need all five to capture, and you're refusing. If you're not with us, the demons win."

That was annoying, a flashback to her mother, threatening her with demons. "Why do you sound like the Department of Homeland Security?"

"Because we are, in a way." Glenda leaned forward, intense. "The five demons here are special, the Untouchables, they can't be exorcised or cast out, so we guard them—"

"Wait a minute, *five*?"

"Kharos, Vanth, Selvans, Tura, and Fufluns." Glenda smiled encouragingly. "They're imprisoned in wooden chalices that are locked in the five iron statues in the park with their keys kept in hard-to-get-to places. All we have to do is put them back in their chalices if they get out. You're our new Seer, so you'll see them, of course. Kharos is a red spirit, Vanth blue, Selvans orange, Tura blue-green, and Fufluns—"

Mab put up her hand. "Okay, hold it. I'm having problems with this because I'm not used to believing in demons, although I do now, of course, and five, that's not good news, but why in the name of god would you put all of them in the same place?"

Glenda opened her mouth and then closed it again.

"Why didn't you each take one and bury it in an ocean far from the others? What idiot thought it was a good idea to bring them here, all together, and lock them in *statues*, for Christ's sake? And then put the keys to the statues on rides? Was this person insane?"

"Possibly," Glenda said, taken aback. "It was before my time. They have to be together because the Guardia have to be together to watch them and capture them if they escape. And it has to be here, because this is a place where our powers are the strongest. And—"

"You never questioned it? You just accepted that you were as trapped in this park as they are?"

"We're not trapped. That's what Young Fred says. Neither one of you understand, this is a *calling.*"

"I'm not accepting the call," Mab said. "I've restored the park, there's nothing left for me here, and I'm not the kind of person who hunts things. You want an amusement park demon repainted, I'm your girl, but hunting them down? Me? Look at me. Do I strike you as anybody you'd send to beat somebody up? Look, I want to be *normal.* Or at least in a position where I can fake it—"

"You have to accept." Glenda began to look put out. "You have no choice—"

"I always have a choice." Mab stood up. "I really appreciate Delpha leaving me all of this—" She looked around. "—especially the mint vintage Airstream, which makes my heart beat faster, and I truly regret that I didn't spend time with her, talk with her more, she was an amazing woman, but I can't take her legacy. I'm not a Seer. I'm *normal.*"

"But, Mab . . ."

"No," Mab said, "thank you, but no."

She left the trailer trying to be calm but then she hit the midway and realized she was shaking. Nobody was going to make her weird again; sure as hell nobody was going to trap her here with demon talk. Yes, demons were real. But she was free—

She heard a caw, like a cheese grater on a fire escape, and looked up to see Frankie flying above her.

She stopped, looking up. "Okay, look, nothing personal, but—"

He swooped down and landed on the shoulder of her paint coat, digging his claws into the canvas enough to hold on but not enough to hurt, and she found herself looking into dark, bright, wise, dangerous eyes. They stared at each other for a long moment, and she could have sworn he was evaluating her.

"I don't think—" she began, and then he put his head against her cheek, his feathers softer than down, and she closed her eyes and stopped shaking and thought, *Mine,* and heard an echo, *Mine.*

She didn't want a bird, but this one was hers.

"All right, I'll accept you, but not the rest of it," she told him, and walked back to the Fortune-Telling Machine with him on her shoulder, wondering what had happened to her life and what the hell ravens ate.

*****

The man in black tried bringing the gun up, but was too late; Ethan landed on top of him and they crashed to the floor. Ethan levered his forearm underneath the mask's mouthpiece, while he jammed hard with his knee into the guy's midsection, shoving the bulky gun out of arm's reach. That gave him the time to draw his own gun and push the muzzle into the man in black's right ear.

Which was a mistake. The man in black rolled, knocking the gun away with a forearm swipe and hitting Ethan in the center of the chest with an open-hand strike. Ethan winced as the bullet stabbed inside him but went with the blow, rolled, and came to his feet, hands at the ready for combat. He blocked a snap kick toward his midsection, followed by a spinning back-fist, giving ground until he was backed up against an old wooden statue. He feinted a punch to the head and then snapped a blow for the neck. It missed as the man in black stepped back and whipped out a short wand, pressed the base, and expanded the thing to a three-foot-long baton.

Ethan stopped. "Could we talk?"

The guy jabbed the baton toward his face, and he jerked back.

"That's not the appropriate way to wield a baton," Ethan said as he backed up. "I'll show you how to use that if you—"

The man in black jabbed again for the face and Ethan ducked, rolled away, grabbed his pistol, and came to his feet, gun at the ready. "Drop the baton."

The man in black hesitated, then dropped it to the ground with a clatter.

"Thank you. Take your goggles and mask off."

The man in black took a step toward him. "You won't shoot me." The voice was a whisper.

Ethan shrugged. "I'm in a bad mood. Too many people hitting me in the chest."

"You won't." The man in black took another step closer. "That's not who you are."

"Sure it is." Ethan pulled the trigger. The round hit center of mass into the body armor, and the man in black let out a surprised yell as he slammed back to the ground.

Ethan walked forward, put his knee right where the round was embedded, and ripped off the goggles.

And stared right into Weaver's electric green eyes.

"Oh, crap," Ethan said.

*****

When they got to the Fortune-Telling Machine, Frankie flew up to sit on the peaked roof, and Mab peered through the dusty glass to see if there was a demon loose in there. She was not joining the Guardia, she was not going to mortgage the rest of her life to a bunch of crazy people and demons, but that didn't mean she wasn't going to be careful. There was too much dirt to really see anything, so she gave up and went around to the back, trying to remember what Joe had told her about opening it. Something about pushing and lifting . . .

She put her hand on the latch and thought, *Of course, it's like this,* and pushed the latch in, lifting it at the same time, as if she could see how to do it.

The door swung open, squeaking, its hinges loose again.

The dust was thick inside, coating everything in a gray blanket. The back of the Vanth statue was a single sheet of it, and Mab realized that was because she had some kind of scarf or shawl that fell from the top of her head. She reached up gingerly and found two clips welded to the top of the statue. When she flipped those open, the scarf fell, the dust sheeting off as Mab caught it before it hit the ground and shook it out.

It was blue, sky blue, madonna blue, made of something so slippery, so finely woven, that the dust didn't stick at all. Mab shook it again, marveling at how beautiful it was and then folded it carefully and put it into her work bag.

"Okay, then." She put her hands on the waist of the Vanth statue and tugged on it to gauge the weight, and it rolled out of the box, almost knocking her down before she stopped it. She got a clean, soft cloth from her bag and began to wipe the dust from the back, uncovering beautiful paintwork in the statue's blue drapery, untouched by sun or weather, making her way around to the front of the statue, where she gently brushed the dust from the delicately painted face. When she was done, she stood back to see what she had.

Vanth was serenely beautiful, thick auburn hair and big sky-blue eyes, looking almost maternal in her round benevolence, her arms out and her hands cupped. She looked like she was reaching for something, her hands grasping, and as Mab watched, the statue began to roll toward her.

"Whoa," Mab said, and caught it, her hands on Vanth's arms. "Hang on there. . . ."

Her voice died as she stared into those painted blue eyes. There was something behind there.

"Vanth?" she said. "You're in there, aren't you? This is where they keep you. In your . . . chalice . . . cup cell thing." She waited, but nothing happened except a growing conviction on her part that she was right and that Vanth should go back inside her booth. Soon.

"Wait here," she said to the statue. "I have to clean that booth out. It's a mess."

She waited a moment and then stepped back, and the statue didn't roll.

"Okay. Just give me half an hour to clean out that booth. Don't *go* anywhere."

She picked up her cleaner and more rags and moved into the booth, doing a fast but thorough basic house cleaning in there, since none of the colors needed retouching, protected by the dust and out of the weather.

So if Vanth was inside the statue, could she get away? Fufluns had taken his statue and run when she'd put the key in, so apparently Vanth could, too. No, wait, Vanth couldn't get out; her statue hadn't been unlocked. Fufluns hadn't run until she'd put the panpipes in and wiggled them. So as long as she didn't put anything in anywhere . . . She finished cleaning the glass and wiped down the surface of the counter and the glass ball glued to the counter. Then she backed out of the box and turned to the Vanth statue. "There. It's beautiful for you."

Vanth sat there, unmoving.

Well, good. That meant she was still locked up.

Mab pushed the statue back into the booth, feeling it roll into grooves in the floor that kept it stable. She got the blue shawl out of her bag, clipped it back onto Vanth's head, and settled it around her shoulders and over her arms. Then she closed and latched the door and went around to the front, marveling at the beauty of it all: the delicate figure, the detailed sides of the box that she'd be painting soon, the arched roof with the raven on the top . . .

"What do you think, Frankie?" she called up.

He moved from foot to foot, not happy but not flying away, either.

"That's what I think, too. Don't worry, but be careful." She went closer to the box and looked inside. "It's you, isn't it? Vanth?"

The gears moved and a card shot into the tray.

Mab picked it up.

HELLO, MAB.

CHAPTER 11

Mab swallowed hard. "Hello. You, uh, you look beautiful." Another card:

LET ME OUT.

Mab took a step back, looking at the cards in her hands. "No. No, absolutely not, never. You—" She looked closer at the cards. They looked . . . fuzzy around the edges. The more she stared at them, the flimsier they got until she could see through them, they were dissolving, and then they were gone and she was looking at her empty hands. "They're not cards," she said to Vanth. "They're an illusion. You made me think they were cards." She took another step back. "I don't like it. Don't do that anymore." She brushed her hands off, as if the illusion had left dust, and then she said, "I'm going to do the undercoat on your box now. You sit tight."

She opened the first bottle of paint she'd mixed and looked at the primed booth.

As if by magic, she saw where that color went, where it blended with the other two underpaint colors, how the entire underpainting had been done.

Seer, she thought. Delpha gave me the power to see things.

That was a good power. If she'd had it from the beginning of the park restoration, things would have gone a lot faster.

Of course, it was probably supposed to be used for other things. Like . . .

She put down the paint and stepped closer to the box, looking into Vanth's flat painted eyes, and then, with effort, beyond, to what at first was a faint blue cloud that became upon concentration a pulsing form inside the statue.

"I'm sorry," she said. "You look like a really nice demon. But I'll never let you out."

The blue pulsed harder, sad and angry and alone.

"I'm *really* sorry," Mab said, and went back to her paint, thinking hard.

A couple of hours ago, she had offered to give Delpha's legacy to someone else. But now if she could keep the power and the Airstream—

Frankie cawed above her.

—and Frankie, without getting swept up in some demon vigilante group, that could be wonderful. A home of her own with a magic table that warded off evil, her own instincts supernaturally enhanced—

Frankie cawed above her.

—and a bird to live with and talk to, these were good things.

"I just don't want to be a demon cop," she told Frankie. "And it's not fair to cherry-pick the good stuff and dump the bad on somebody else."

Frankie cawed again. It sounded like *coward* this time.

"You're probably right," she said, and began to paint the Fortune-Telling Machine.

*****

Ethan had thought about having Weaver under him, but not like this.

"Who the hell are you?" Ethan demanded.

"Weaver. We've met, remember?" She looked up at him and he felt himself drawn into those eyes. "Could you get your knee off my chest? Kind of hurts."

Ethan removed his knee. "Kind of hurts to get shot by that thing you carry."

Weaver grunted in pain as she sat up. "The D-gun. I invented it."

"D-gun?"

"Demon gun." She unbuckled the black bulletproof vest she'd been wearing and pulled it off, revealing a thin black turtleneck underneath.

It was chilly in the basement of the Keep.

"Oh, grow up," Weaver snapped as she rubbed through her shirt between her breasts and he stared. "What are you, fourteen? And did you have to shoot me?"

"Did *you* have to shoot *me*?"

"Yes."

"Why?"

That brought a long silence.

"You thought I was a demon, didn't you?" Ethan asked. "Do you just go around shooting people you think look demonic?"

"Well, so far it's working." She looked around the room. "So this is what, where amusement parks go to die?"

"Storeroom," Ethan said. "So how did you find out about the demons?"

"We're under the Keep, right?"

Ethan didn't like being questioned, and he especially didn't like having his questions ignored. "Who are you? Who do you work for? And how the hell did you know there were demons in Dreamland?"

Weaver considered him, her green eyes narrowed. "Okay, that's fair." She lifted her tight turtleneck slightly, revealing a sliver of smooth skin and a platinum badge that Ethan didn't recognize.

Ethan blinked. "You're a cop?"

"Homeland Security. Department 51."

Great. The government. "You search demons at airports?"

"Oh, funny." Weaver picked up her vest and slid it back on, disappointing Ethan as she buckled up. "Department 51 is a secret department detailed to study, among other things, whether demons exist and if they do, to evaluate their possible threats and . . ."

Her voice trailed off.

"And uses," Ethan said. "Somebody in the government is insane enough to think that demons could be used as weapons?"

"That would be my boss," Weaver said. "Fortunately, she doesn't believe in demons, so that threat isn't great right now."

"She doesn't believe in demons and she's your boss?"

Weaver pushed herself up off the floor, wincing a little. "She's the boss of a lot of little departments that deal in odd things. I think she screwed up and got the assignment as a punishment. She puts up with us on the off chance that we'll actually find something she can use to get back to the top."

"And have you?"

"Isn't it my turn to ask a question?" she said, smiling at him.

"No. What are you doing in Dreamland?"

"We're just checking out the place, eating funnel cakes, the usual."

"Who's we?"

"Department 51. My partner and me. We don't have a large department." She began to walk around the room, looking into boxes, frowning.

"How large is it?"

"My partner and me"

"Like The X-Files."

"Only we're real and we don't banter."

"So what are you doing here?"

"Staying at this really annoying B and B in town. There are teddy bears on the bed and my partner doesn't like teddy bears—"

"What are you doing in Dreamland?"

Weaver stopped poking into junk and frowned harder. "My turn to ask questions. What are you doing down here? There's nothing here. You had a man die two nights ago, and you're cleaning the basement?"

"You were asking questions about Ray that night in the Beer Pavilion. Are you here watching him? Were you watching him last night?"

She crossed her arms. "So it seems we both need information. And I've been giving up a lot more than you have." She smiled at him again, and he thought, *Play your cards right, I'll tell you anything.* "How about a deal? I tell you exactly what we're doing, what we've found—well, some of it—and you agree to tell us what you're doing and to let us give you a physical. Normal stuff, vital signs, draw a little blood . . ."

Ethan tried not to think about Weaver giving him a physical. "Why? And who would do the examining?"

"My partner. He's a doctor."

"Good for him," Ethan said, disappointed. "Why do you want my blood?"

Weaver smiled at him without a trace of sincerity. "Just a general checkup. I'd be really grateful if you'd let us—"

"How grateful?" Ethan said. "Because I could use half a dozen of those demon guns. What are the goggles for?"

"Oh, you'd really like the goggles," Weaver said. "You'd give me your blood for the goggles alone."

"No, I wouldn't," Ethan said. "What do they do?"

"They highlight francium," Weaver said, watching him.

"Francium."

"The most unstable element in the universe. Evil is drawn to instability, so francium is the only concrete thing it can bind to. That's what demons are made of, evil and francium. And some trace elements, of course, but francium is the key. And these—" She dangled the goggles in front of him. "—see francium, so they see demons. Wherever demons are, these goggles can find them."

Ethan nodded. "Good, I'll take a half dozen of those, too. Plus everything you know about Ray. Basically, you tell me everything about your mission, and the real reason you want my blood, and hand over the equipment, and I'll let you do a physical. If you do the physical. Here in Dreamland."

"I don't think so," Weaver said.

"Then you can't poke at me," Ethan said, and she smiled, this time with that glint in her eye, and he thought, *Oh, sure you can.*

"What the hell is she doing here?" Gus asked from the top of the stairs, and they both turned in surprise. He had a dusty leather bag slung over one shoulder, the tips of several swords and lances poking out the top.

Weaver waved. "Hey, Gus. How you doing?"

"This is Weaver, you met her at the Pavilion," Ethan said.

"I bought you beer," Weaver called up to him.

Gus nodded and came down the stairs balancing the bag on his back, and they both watched him, holding their breaths. At least Ethan did. Weaver's chest wasn't moving so he assumed—

"I got the mold," Gus said to Ethan when he got to the bottom.

"What mold?" Weaver asked.

"Hobby of Gus's," Ethan said.

"We'll take it to Mab with—"

"Good job, Gus," Ethan said, clapping him on the shoulder before Gus could say *the chalice*. "You take that to Mab. Weaver and I have some trading to do."

"So tell me about the mold, Gus," Weaver said, turning all her wattage on the old man.

"No," Gus said.

Evidently beer could only buy so much.

Weaver picked up the D-gun from where it had fallen to the floor. "Okay, then. I will consult with my partner and get back to you. In the meantime, you might reconsider your terms. You've got big problems here. I can help you solve them."

"Maybe," Ethan said. "So were you watching Ray Brannigan last night?"

She hesitated and then shook her head. "No. My partner and I went back to town when the park closed. What happened?" She waited, and when he didn't say anything, she said, "Right. Information only goes one way. Call me when it's a two-way street," and walked out the door, which was just as well, Ethan thought. He had things to find out, and she wasn't going anywhere far; there was something in Dreamland she wanted.

Too bad it wasn't him.

"How'd she get down here?" Gus said.

"She followed us."

"That's no good."

"So I shot her."

Gus patted his arm. "That's my boy."

Yeah, but I can't keep shooting her. Whether Glenda liked it or not, he was going to find a way to work with Weaver.

As closely as possible.

*****

Mab had just finished the underpainting on the front of the box when Frankie cawed down from the scalloped roof, and she looked up to see Gus heading up the midway toward her.

She stood, wiping her hands on a paint rag, and when he reached her, she said, "Hey, Gus. How are you doing?" because she knew how much he'd cared about Delpha.

"I'm okay." He held out some pieces of wood to her. "Wonderin' if you could fix this."

She took one of the pieces and looked at it closely. It was heavily carved but primitive, not like the sophisticated swirls on the Fortune-Telling Machine. "This is really old, Gus."

"Yeah." He held out the rest to her.

"Really old," she said as she took them. "Like . . ."

"Twenty-five hundred years," he said, and her eyebrows went up.

"That much." She stooped down to the flagstones and laid the pieces out, rearranging them until they were in the right pattern, constructing a 3-D model in her imagination, the way she'd done with other things a thousand times before—

The pieces rose up under her eyes and fitted themselves together.

"Whoa," she said, sitting back.

"What?" Gus said.

"Didn't you *see* that?" she said, and then realized that he hadn't. "Never mind."

She looked more closely at the lid as it hovered before her. It was missing a piece—no, as she crawled around to the other side, she saw it was two very small pieces. "You're missing two little wood pieces. One's kind of a triangle and the other one's more of a square. About a quarter inch across. Get me those and I'll put this back together for you."

"Okay. I got you this to help," Gus said, and handed her a wood bowl.

She took it, saying, "Thank you," confused, but then the illusion of the wood pieces inverted itself and slid into the bowl, and she realized it was a template for fixing the lid. "Thank you, this will be a big help."

"Two pieces, huh?" Gus said.

"Yeah. Where did you find these pieces?"

"Inside the FunFun statue."

"Oh." Mab looked at the pieces in front of her again. "So this is the lid that keeps him trapped in the chalice, right?"

"Right."

"Well, hurry up and find me those pieces and I'll fix this, and you can put him back."

"Not without you," Gus said, and Mab winced. "Delpha knew you'd be called, she knew you were our Seer. We need you."

She stood and put the pieces in her paint bag, the wood template bowl on top. "Gus, I'm not a fighter. You ever need anybody to fix things, I'll be here for you—" She stopped, startled that she'd said that, but it was true. "The rest of it . . ." She shook her head. "You get me the missing pieces to this, I'll fix it right away."

His face fell. "Did you take the dove key out of the Tunnel of Love?"

"The dove key? No. I didn't take any dove away. I put one back on the Tunnel before I put the pipes in the carousel FunFun's hand, but I didn't take anything away."

"Someone took it." Gus shook his head. "That's no good. When we get Tura back in her chalice, we won't be able to put her back in the mermaid without the key." He shuffled off, looking glum, and she felt lousy for not promising to help him.

"I'll keep my eyes open for that dove," she called after him, and he waved without turning around.

"I'd really make a lousy demon hunter," she said, keeping her voice low that time, but Frankie cawed at her from the top of the booth anyway.

"You stay out of this," she told him.

Then she went back to work.

*****

When Mab finished the underpainting, it was getting dark, but it didn't matter, she knew where the paint went even without the light from her miner's hat; she could probably have seen it without any light at all. The sight Delpha had given her was an incredible gift, priceless, and it had only one big string attached, more of a rope really, she thought, enough rope to tie her to this place forever—

Frankie cawed, a shrill edge to his cry this time, and she looked up to see Ray, stepping off the flagstone of the midway and coming toward her.

"Mary Alice," Ray said, smiling approvingly at her as he came to stand beside her, the end of his cigar glowing orange in the gloom. "Now that's starting to look like a Fortune-Telling Machine."

"It's just the underpainting," she began, but he was peering at the Vanth inside.

"Beautiful. That's a piece of art. Why are you out here so late?"

"Working."

He shook her head. "You shouldn't be out here alone. Come on, I'll walk you to the Dream Cream."

He reached for her arm, and Frankie cawed down at him.

"What the hell is that?" Ray took his cigar out of his mouth as he looked up.

"That's my bird," Mab said. Ray was perfectly capable of pulling out a gun and blowing a raven away, so she wanted to stake her claim.

"Isn't that Delpha's bird?" Ray said, looking suspicious.

"Yes. She left him to me."

"Left it to you?"

"She died last night. I have to get back to work now—"

"She left you her bird," Ray said, staring at her. "I didn't know you were close. Did she leave you anything else?"

"Everything," Mab said, suddenly feeling uneasy. "I *really* have to—"

"She left you her share of the park?" Ray said sharply, moving closer.

"Yes."

He smiled at her. "Mary Alice, this is your lucky day. I'll give you two hundred and fifty thousand dollars for your ten percent of the park."

Mab blinked at him. A quarter of a million for ten percent of Dreamland? Was he nuts?

"Think of what you could do with that money."

Mab was way ahead of him. She'd be free. She could invest it and live on the interest and what she made on her paintings. She wouldn't be rich, but she'd be secure—

Frankie cawed above her, and she looked up and saw him staring at her. He swooped down around them and then settled on Mab's shoulder and looked into her eyes.

No.

"Yeah," she said to Frankie. "I know." If Ray wanted to pay her a quarter of a million for a tenth of Dreamland, something was very wrong. "No, thank you," she said to Ray. "I think I'm just going to give it to Glenda."

"Are you crazy?"

Frankie cawed and flapped his wings as Mab stepped back from the sudden rage in Ray's voice. "No. It's not my park, it's hers."

"No, it isn't." Ray came closer. "Mary Alice, I am looking out for your best interests here. I'm your only living relative." He hesitated, and then he said, "I've left you everything, you know. In my will. You'll inherit it all. You can trust me."

"I bet she's heard that before," Joe said from behind him, and they both turned to see him standing there, a grocery bag in one hand and two champagne flutes in the other. The stems on the flutes were bony hands holding the flute part of the glass.

"You've been to the Dreamland gift store," Mab said, still not sure how she felt about him being a lying demon hunter, but delighted that he was there now that Ray was acting weird.

Joe grinned as he came closer. "Dave got me the wine and steaks, but he forgot the glasses and these made me laugh, so . . ." He bent and kissed her.

"Hello," Ray said, no smile. "I'm Mary Alice's uncle."

"Good to meet you," Joe said, no smile either.

Ray stared at Joe for a couple of long seconds while Joe stared back, Ray threatening and Joe with a you've-got-to-be-kidding look on his face. Then Ray nodded to Mab. "You think about my offer. Don't be a fool." He gave Joe one last fuck-you stare, stuck his cigar back in his mouth, and went down the midway.

Mab let her breath out.

"What a guy," Joe said. "Let's try this again. Hello to you." He kissed her, long and slow this time, no hands because his were full.

"Hello," she said, coming up for air. Lying demon hunter or not, she was glad he was there. She peeked into the grocery bag and saw a bottle of wine beside white butcher-wrapped packages. "Wine?"

"I thought we'd stay in tonight," Joe said. "Make dinner at your place. Go to bed early . . ." His voice trailed off as he looked at the Fortune-Telling Machine.

"Isn't she beautiful?" Mab said.

"Very. So what do you say about dinner?" Joe said, hoisting the bag again.

"Oh, yeah." Mab took the bony-hand-stemmed glasses from him.

Joe turned to look at Vanth again as Mab tucked the glasses into her work bag.

"Don't stare," she said. "There's a demon in there. Vanth."

"You sure?"

Mab picked up her bag and turned back to Vanth. She could see the blue pulsing inside easily now. No effort at all. "I'm sure." She walked over to the glass. "I'll be back tomorrow to start the final over-painting on the outside of your booth. You look beautiful. Have a good night."

The gears ground and a card shot out.

BE CAREFUL.

"Careful?" Mab said, frowning at it. "Careful of what? You?"

More gears and another card:

HE LOVES YOU ALL HE CAN, BUT HE CANNOT LOVE YOU VERY MUCH.

Mab caught her breath and looked at Joe.

"What's wrong?" he said, coming closer, and she handed him the card.

When he took it, it dissolved, turning into nothingness.

"Nice trick," he said to the box, and then turned back to Mab. "You ready?"

"Nice trick?" she said to him.

"You said there's a demon in there, right?"

"Yes," Mab said.

"Well, then, 'nice trick, demon.' " He looked down at her, for once not smiling. "I'm starving. You ready?"

"Yes," she said, not looking at Vanth. She'd have to be crazy to take advice from a demon. Especially about a demon hunter.

"Then let's go," he said, his voice easy again.

He put his arm around her, and Frankie launched himself off her shoulder to fly ahead, and they walked up the midway toward the Dream Cream, and Mab did not look back at all.

*****

That night at quarter to twelve, Ethan sat in the control booth for the Double Ferris Wheel, across the midway from Gus, who was in the Dragon Coaster booth, oblivious to the fact that he had a bodyguard nearby.

Ethan settled in and considered his day's work. He'd looked at the weapons Gus had brought from the Keep in his pack: all iron, which was brittle and could easily break; all thin and pointed; and all in need of a good cleaning. The only thing worth keeping in the whole batch had been a knife with a long thin blade and a design on the handle—a crude arrow shape—that Gus told him to keep when he picked it up. "That's your dad's knife," Gus had said. "It's a good Hunter's knife. Hank never carried it. He was lazy. And drunk most of the time."

Ethan had taken his razor-sharp commando knife from its sheath on his combat vest and replaced it with his dad's knife. They'd patrolled the park but hadn't found any more evidence of the Untouchables, and through it all, Ethan stuck close to the old man. Glenda was back home after making arrangements for Delpha's cremation, safe in her own trailer now with the doors and windows locked, and Young Fred could defend himself, but Gus was getting slower by the minute and couldn't. So Ethan stood close by. No more demonic murders on his watch, not if he could help it—

Something moved in the dark, outside Ethan's booth. He stepped back into the shadows, and when it slipped inside the booth, he grabbed it by the throat and drew his dad's knife.

"Aaargh," Weaver said.

He let go of her and put his knife away. "What the hell are you doing here?"

She rubbed her throat. "I told you I'd be in touch, although getting strangled wasn't what I had in mind. What are you doing here? Something's happening, isn't it?"

"How did you find me?"

She hesitated. "I bugged you."

"What?" he said, outraged. "How . . ." Then he remembered, that light hand on his thigh, taking his gun.

He pulled out his gun and looked at the holster closely until he found the bug.

"Okay, I'm sorry about that," she said, not sounding sorry at all. She held something up in the darkness, big and bulky, like a bag. "But I brought guns. Demon guns. Is that what we're here for?"

"Just stay behind me and do what I tell you to do."

"Sure, that's gonna happen." She peered out the booth window. "Gus is just getting ready to run the Dragon. What's up?"

"Demons killed Delpha last night. Glenda's back at her trailer with a crossbow with iron-tipped bolts and the doors locked, but I don't want them to get Gus while he does the Dragon run."

She moved closer to him to see better, her shoulder touching his. "I'm sorry about Delpha. She told my fortune once. She seemed like the real deal."

"She was." Ethan thought about that for a second. "What did she tell you?"

Weaver shook her head. "So the plan is we wait for demons to attack Gus and then shoot them? Works for me. I hate the evil bastards." She shrugged off her bag and opened it, and pulled out a demon gun with a folding stock. She snapped the stock open and handed it to Ethan, along with two drum magazines.

"Now *this* is a gun," Ethan said, hefting it with pleasure.

"That's a loaner just for tonight," Weaver said. "Think of it as a taste before buying. I can't give it to you permanently, because Ursula will miss it sooner or later. Although since it's Ursula, most likely later."

"Ursula?"

"Our boss."

"We just have to make it through Halloween," Ethan said.

The Dragon Coaster came alive with light, and Ethan put his eyes back on Gus. "Is Ray Brannigan a demon?"

She shook her head. "Nope. But he's an asshole. I tried to track his money, and he's played hard and fast on a lot of shady deals, insider information. Screwed a lot of people over." Her voice changed in the dark, lighter with puzzlement. "The thing is, he doesn't seem to have ties to anybody who could give him inside information. He just . . . *knows*."

With a rattle, the Dragon began its run.

Weaver shifted in the dark beside him, brushing against his arm, and he took a deep breath. He was feeling really alive for the first time in a very long time.

"Uh-oh," Weaver said.

Ethan looked out. Something small was crawling along the ground, and then he saw another, and another, lumpy little things coming from behind the closed Whack-A-Mole, creeping across the flagstones, at least a dozen of them, more coming all the time—

"Teddy bears?" Weaver said.

"Don't laugh," Ethan said, scanning the park, trying to judge how many there were. Maybe two dozen now. "There are demons in them."

Weaver stared and he heard her whisper, "Their name is Legion, for they are many."

"What?" he said.

"I've never seen that many before. Swarming evil." She took a deep breath. "Let's go kill them."

Over at the Dragon, Gus came out of the control booth and grabbed the railing over the water, getting ready to lean down and put his ear against the rail—

"They're going to push him over," Ethan said, and shoved out of the booth to run toward Gus.

The little bastards were moving fast. Ethan saw one crawl up on the platform, and he raised the demon gun and fired, the silencer dampening the sound of the blast. The iron round hit the bear in the butt, and it exploded silently in a mixture of cheap stuffing and some kind of demon goo, splashing purple so dark it was almost nothingness, antimatter, onto the flagstone, where it sizzled like acid. Weaver fired from behind him, and another blew apart. Ethan fired again, shredding another bear and spattering more goo on the walkway while Gus leaned over the rail, oblivious to the silenced conflict behind him, his good ear on the rattles. Ethan hit another bear just as it began to climb the railing, but even as he did, one landed on his shoulder. He looked up and saw four in the tree above him, their eyes dark with purple demon malevolence. He ignored the one on his shoulder, which was trying to work its way up to his head, and fired up into the tree, but a second teddy bear jumped, hitting him in the chest and hanging on, scaling his Kevlar vest, going for his face.

Weaver was still firing at the bears heading for Gus as a third bear hit Ethan in the legs. He shot a second one in the tree, spattering goo as another jumped down, aiming straight for his face, and he fired, blowing it apart in midair in a shower of acid purple that hit his arms and burned through his jacket, but missing the one behind it that landed directly on his head. He dropped the demon gun and clawed at it, grabbing big chunks of teddy bear fur to pull it off as it stuffed its paws into his mouth, the other two piling on, smothering him with demonic strength, making little chittering sounds as they dragged him down.

Weaver blasted one off him, which was enough to make the other two let go, and then another half dozen of the little bastards converged on him instead of Gus, their shoe-button eyes glowing with purple hate.

"Shoot them off me!" he yelled, and Weaver did, angling her shots perfectly, taking them all out with fast practiced shots as demon goo went everywhere, burning spatter spots into the flagstone.

When she was done, Ethan lay on his back, staring at the night sky, spitting polyester fur out of his mouth and breathing hard. The stuff was stuck to the sweat on his hands, too, and he realized that this was how Delpha had died.

"You okay?" Weaver asked, bending over him.

"Yeah." Ethan got to his feet and dusted the fur off his hands. He walked over to Gus, who was listening for the rattles now. "Gus?" he said to the old man's left side, tapping him on the shoulder.

Gus waved him away so he could hear, so Ethan figured he was fine and went back to Weaver.

"They came from over there," she said, pointing to the Whack-A-Mole, and he followed her over and helped her open the front of the stand.

It was full of innocent teddy bears, none of them radiating hate, their shoe-button eyes just shoe buttons.

"Jesus," Weaver said, staring at them all. "I don't ever want to see a teddy bear again." She took a deep breath. "I've never seen that many demons at once. And they were fast."

"Yeah." Ethan looked at her. "What was that legion stuff you were talking about?"

Weaver tore her eyes from the bears. "What? Oh. 'My name is

Legion.' Mark 5:9. The demon says his name is Legion for he is many in one. These don't seem to work on one mind, though—"

"The *Bible*?"

"Good source for demon research," Weaver said. "Also my daddy was a preacher."

"You're a preacher's daughter?" Ethan said.

"Don't believe everything you hear about preachers' daughters," Weaver said, her voice getting lighter again. "So." She looked back at the litter of bright fur and dark purple goo. "We did good work tonight."

"Yes, we did, especially you, Sureshot."

She grinned at him, and Ethan felt an overpowering urge to give her something to keep that grin going, anything—he looked into the Whack-A-Mole booth—anything except a teddy bear. But high up above all the bears was a huge stuffed velvet dragon, its wings and chest glittering under the orange light. He vaulted over the counter, reached up, pulled it down, dusted it off, and handed it to her. "You win the grand prize."

"Gee." Weaver took it, trying to look cool and failing. "Does this mean we're going steady?"

"Yes," Ethan said, "so we shouldn't keep secrets. Tell me everything you know about demons. You can leave out the Bible parts."

"The Bible parts are the best parts." She held the big dragon out to see it better in the awful orange light. "I'll call him Behemoth. 'His limbs are as strong as copper, his bones as a load of iron.' Iron limbs. He can protect me from demons."

"Copper?" Ethan said.

"Well, something's glittering on him. Looks copper in this orange light. I'll switch him out for the teddy bear on the bed at the B and B. Much better." She put the dragon under one arm, all business again. "I have to report this demon attack. I'll let you keep the D-gun overnight so you can take it apart and look at it, but if you want it permanently, you volunteer blood and information, buddy." Then she hesitated. "You and Gus okay now?"

"Yep," Ethan said. "Thank you for saving both our asses."

"Just doing my job," Weaver said, and walked back to the Ferris Wheel booth to pick up her bag, her big velvet dragon under her arm.

Ethan watched her go and then went to join Gus. "I think we can call it a night," he began, and then he saw Gus's face. "What?"

"Only two rattles," he said. "There's another Untouchable out there."

CHAPTER 12

"Okay, what's so important that I had to come back down here?" Glenda said when she met them at the Dragon, and Ethan pointed up to the gaping-mouthed Dragon's head that, for the first time in his life, had two glittering eyes.

"Somebody put the eye in," he told her. "Gus says it's the key to the orange Strong Man statue."

"Yeah, it's Selvans' key." Glenda went around to the back of the massive rust-colored Strong Man and looked in the open panel. "Where's the chalice?"

"Gus has it and the demon isn't in it. He went to get Young Fred. How are we going to do this without a Seer?"

Glenda rubbed her forehead. "Okay, it's Selvans. He's not the sharpest knife in the drawer and he moves slow, but he's very strong. If Young Fred can startle him, you might be able to get to him without a Seer holding him. You'll have to move fast, though. . . ."

She kept talking, but Ethan stopped listening.

Something was moving out from behind the Dragon.

"Mom," Ethan said, and then relaxed. "Never mind. It's just Carl Whack-A-Mole."

Glenda jerked around. "Not this late, it isn't."

Carl lumbered toward them, the massive hammer from the Test Your Strength machine in his hand.

"Oh, *crap,*" Ethan said, and stepped in front of his mother. He tried to think fast, and then realized he had time: Carl was moving at the speed of mud.

"Just capio him when Young Fred startles him and he drops his guard," Glenda was saying behind him as Carl staggered closer.

"Right." He was more than willing to take Selvans inside him; he just didn't know how to get him out of Carl, since Young Fred was missing at the moment. "Uh, *boo,*" he said as Carl stumbled closer.

Carl responded by swinging the large hammer with tremendous force, the blunt face of it whistling by, narrowly missing Ethan's head.

"I thought you said he was slow?" Ethan said, pushing Glenda back as he got out of range.

"Well, momentum," Glenda said as Carl followed the hammer around in a circle.

Ethan drew his pistol.

"You can't shoot Carl!" Glenda said.

Ethan shoved the pistol back in the holster, trying to think as they backed away.

They were next to the Dragon control booth now. Carl swung the hammer again, and Ethan ducked low to let it go by as it smashed into the wall of the booth. Chunks of wood went flying.

"Hey, Carl!" Young Fred yelled from behind Ethan, and Carl swung his head around as if it was too heavy to hold up, looking like a poleaxed bull as Young Fred reached his side.

Young Fred morphed into a huge ten-foot-tall teddy bear—with fangs.

Carl screamed and jerked back, and Young Fred yelled, "Frustro!" and a huge orange demon erupted from Carl, who collapsed to the ground.

The demon moved in slow motion as if to flee, but Ethan shouted, "Capio!" reaching after him, pulling him in. . . .

It was like being filled with orange mud. Heavy orange mud, smothering him, pulling him under, he was going to lose this battle.

The world became a Tang-colored slow-motion movie as Ethan felt a heaviness on his heart, heard his mother's voice at a slower, deeper speed, "Ri . . . deeeeeeee . . . meeeeeeeee . . . ohhhhhhhhhh—"

And then Selvans was pulled out of him, into the chalice, and the world went back to normal speed as Gus slapped the chalice lid on and said, "Servo!"

"What the hell *was* that?" Ethan said, grabbing the broken wall of the booth to support himself.

"Selvans," Glenda said. "Kharos's right-hand man."

"Kharos's dog," Gus said, looking at the chalice with loathing.

"Who let him out?" Glenda said as if it had all been business as usual. "It wasn't Mab—she knows about this now."

"It wasn't just Selvans, either," Ethan said. "We were attacked tonight by possessed teddy bears. A couple dozen of them."

"We?" Glenda said.

"Gus and me," Ethan said, not interested in discussing Weaver with his mother.

Gus ignored him to stick to the problem at hand. "There's only five Untouchables, and they won't possess teddy bears, they got too much pride for that. Even Selvans wouldn't possess a teddy bear." He stopped as if caught by a thought.

"What?" Ethan said.

"Wait a minute," Glenda said. "You were attacked by possessed teddy bears?"

Ethan waved her off, trying to listen to Gus.

"Untouchables wouldn't possess teddy bears," Gus was saying. "But your minion demons, now, they're like animals, they'll take anything. Nasty little critters. Mean as snot. You can always tell when they possess somebody, the human always acts like a mean drunk. That's why they like to take smaller things and run in packs."

"Minion demons." Ethan took a deep breath. "There's more than one kind of demon in this park?"

"Minions," Glenda said, her voice grim. "Just what we needed."

"They shouldn't be in the park," Gus said. "The iron fence around the perimeter should keep 'em out. It looks like plain old chain link, but it's got a lotta iron in it. Had it made special in '26. And the river. Running water keeps 'em out. Unless somebody brings 'em over in a boat." Gus stood up as if he wanted something to do. "We gotta check the fence—"

"Tomorrow," Ethan said. "We'll check it tomorrow. You go back to the trailer and lock the door and the windows and get some sleep. We'll figure it all out tomorrow."

Gus nodded and turned to go down the path behind the Dragon to the trailers. "Oh, hell," he said, and stooped to pat Carl Whack-A-Mole's cheek.

"That's what killed Delpha, isn't it?" Glenda said quietly. "Minion-possessed teddy bears."

"I think so," Ethan said. "There was blue fur caught in the window."

"It's part of a plan." Glenda drew a deep breath. "Kharos has a plan, and somebody's putting it into practice for him."

"Ray," Ethan said.

"What happened?" Carl Whack-A-Mole said, trying to sit up.

"I'll take care of him," Glenda said to Ethan. "You do a fast patrol around the midway. Make sure you didn't miss any minions."

"Right," Ethan said. "Teddy bear patrol."

He left Glenda and Gus to deal with Carl and did a final patrol around the park. No bears. Then he sat down in the bright lights of the closed Dream Cream and took the D-gun apart and put it back together several times, marveling at Weaver's design. Finally as the Dream Cream clock chimed 2 A.M., he walked by the trailers to make sure Gus and Glenda were locked in and safe, and then went back to his sleeping bag behind the Devil's Drop. He lay there, alone, a rock poking him in the back, and stared up at the five red lights flashing at the top of the Drop through the leafless trees that surrounded him, considering his new life or what was left of it. Okay, so he was under a death sentence, but tonight he'd felt alive again, fighting teddy bears, taking down an orange demon. He hadn't even wanted a drink. What he wanted was—

Something was moving through the trees. He sat up, grabbing the D-gun, prepared to waste more teddy bear ass.

Weaver stepped over some brush and into his clearing. "Why are you sleeping in the woods?"

"It's soothing," Ethan said, lowering the gun.

"You're a strange man." She came closer. "Thank you for not shooting me. Again." She broke a green chem light and hung it from a nearby branch, then pulled her goggles off and shook out her hair in the dim glow. She took a small black case from a pocket on her vest. "I gave my report. Ursula isn't happy that you have a D-gun. Turns out this afternoon was monthly inventory. Bad luck." She opened the case and a needle glinted in the chem light. "I'm going to need some of your blood to placate her."

Ethan sighed. "I thought you were coming here to see me."

"I did. I came to see you to get the D-gun and your blood so Ursula will quit yapping at me. Sit down. Lie down if losing blood makes you woozy."

Losing blood didn't bother him, but he lay down anyway.

"So," she said, kneeling beside him. "Which arm?"

"This one," he said, and reached up and pulled her to him and kissed her, and she kissed him back, hard, the way she did everything, which was good because he liked everything she did.

"Exactly what am I going to have to do to get this blood?" she said as she pulled back, breathless.

He took the needle from her and threw it into the woods. "How about if I show you?" he said, and rolled to trap her beneath him, and she said, "Ouch, there's a rock," and then laughed, and then they didn't say anything at all.

*****

It was after 3 A.M. when Ray sat down beside the Devil statue, lit up his cigar, and said, "Look, it's been a bad weekend, and I don't want to hear any complaining."

YOU'LL COMPLAIN, Kharos thought. ONCE I AM FREE—

"We're batting fifty percent, which ain't bad in the majors. The minions got Delpha last night, although she put up a fight. I had to wait outside that trailer a good ten minutes before they finished her. It was damn cold, too—"

WHAT ABOUT SELVANS?

"Look," Ray said, blustering now. "I did what you said, I set him free. But Ethan was there and Glenda and then Gus and Young Fred. All of them. They got Selvans."

DID THE MINIONS KILL THE KEEPER?

"Gus? Uh, no."

WHY?

"Ethan saved him. Ethan and his girlfriend who has a gun that blows them to pieces. Which is the rest of the bad news. The minion demons I brought in? They're all gone. I don't know where the hell Selvans went for the fight, he was probably lost in the Dragon struts somewhere, but the minions are now two dozen puddles of purple demon splat. What is that stuff? Antimatter?"

Kharos had a moment where he thought about telling Ray to put in the key to the Devil statue and let him out just so he could kill him. But it was too soon, and the Guardia were on alert now. . . .

Still, Delpha was dead. The Guardia would be grieving. That was good. And if they were harried and hunted, that would be even better.

BRING IN MORE MINIONS.

"Listen, I told you, I don't like them, and I'm not a demon chauffeur. I have—*hey*!" Ray looked down at the large clump of hair that had fallen into his lap. "You have a sick sense of humor." He brushed off his lap. "All right, I get the message, I'll bring them in."

SET THEM ON THE GUARDIA.

"Should I warn them about the gun?"

NO.

"Okay, then. You want the rest of the Guardia killed. Got it." Ray got up.

WAIT.

Ray waited.

NOT GLENDA.

Ray raised his eyebrows. "You and Glenda got something going on? Because I have to tell you, it's been forty years since the last time you were out. She's changed."

I GROW IMPATIENT WITH YOU.

"Yeah, yeah," Ray said. "I don't think you appreciate what I do for you. The risks I take. My position in this town is not solid yet. They find out I'm bringing in demons, I don't think they're gonna let the fact that I'm mayor stop them from hunting me down."

THEY KNOW THERE ARE DEMONS?

"They will if they catch me with a boatload of minions." He shook his head. "I'm taking a lot of chances for you, and do you appreciate it? No." He chomped on his cigar and walked down the midway, feeling his hair.

YOU'RE GOING TO DIE, Kharos thought.

Then he thought about the Guardia overrun by packs of minion demons, opening the hell-gate, the pleasure of having fresh souls to torment—a buffet of despair, each one different—and felt better.

But Ray was still going to die.

*****

Mab came down to breakfast with Frankie the next morning semi-reassured about Joe, who had made her dinner, made her laugh, and made her come the night before. At least, there didn't seem to be anything to object to. She found Cindy slammed with a breakfast crowd again and frowned. A crowd on Sunday wasn't unusual; a crowd on a Monday in October was.

"What is this?" she said, going around behind the counter to help pour coffee and make change while Frankie flew out the door in search of his own breakfast.

"I think it's because of the new love potion flavor," Cindy said, plates with waffles with pink ice cream in each hand. "Evidently What-Love-Can-Do works."

"Really." Mab looked out over the counter and noticed that everybody was in couples eating pink ice cream except for the guy in Coke-bottle glasses, if you counted Skinny and Quentin as a couple. Skinny was lecturing on the art of the sundae today: "You know what I think, Quentin? I think the tin roof has it all over the banana split. That's what I think." Meanwhile, the guy in the glasses sat alone at the counter, reading his notebook as usual with his back to the crowd, but, Mab realized suddenly, with his eyes on the mirror behind the counter, not on the notebook. He was watching the room.

"It must be the cinnamon," Cindy said, surveying the crowd. "Could you get that lady on the end a refill? And spill something on the loud-mouthed skinny guy, he's driving me crazy."

By the time the crowd dwindled, it was after noon, so Mab made sure she had her work bag, waved to Cindy, and took off to spend the last hours of afternoon daylight painting the Fortune-Telling Machine, an absolute pleasure because the colors were so lovely and she could see so clearly where they went. That set up her rhythm for the next four days. Help Cindy sling What-Love-Can-Do waffles in the morning, paint the Fortune-Telling Machine in the afternoon while talking to Frankie, make dinner and love with Joe at night. Mab had never laughed so much in bed, and the more she laughed, the happier Joe got. "You are a real clown," she said, and he said, "Oh, yeah," and tickled her and made her laugh again. He still wouldn't talk about demon-hunting, but he wanted to know everything about her life, her work, her dreams, and that was flattering. And disconcertingly illuminating.

The night before he'd smiled at her, holding the bony-hand stem of one of the champagne flutes he'd brought her earlier in the week. "So after this you're going to . . ."

"There's a little museum I do work for," Mab said. "They were donated a dozen damaged carousel horses they want me to fix when I'm done here. That should be fun. And the gallery that takes my paintings said they'll take a couple more, which is—"

"What about people?"

"What about them?"

"Don't you miss them when you're gone?"

"No," Mab said. "I'm not much with people."

"You're not going to miss Cindy?" Joe said. "Glenda? *Me?*"

And Mab had thought about Cindy, smiling at her over waffles, and Glenda, flicking that cigarette as she told Mab to put a coat on because it was cold, and that guy with the Coke-bottle glasses handing her her bag, and Joe. . . .

If I joined the Guardia, I could live in Delpha's Airstream with Frankie, I could do paintings of Dreamland and work on the park and have breakfast with Cindy every day and make love every night with Joe. . . .

And she'd be a Batty Brannigan again, her whole life about demons, a credit to her whack-job family.

"Yeah," she said. "You guys I'll miss. But I'm still leaving."

She wasn't going to miss Ray, who stopped by to show her his will. "See," he said, shoving the papers at her. "You're my sole heir."

"This is dated yesterday," Mab pointed out, and Ray looked annoyed and said, "The point is, *you're my heir.*" Then he handed her a sheet of paper. "Now just to be safe, you should have a will, too. I had my lawyer draw this one up." Mab looked at it. "This says I leave everything to you. Ray, I don't have anything. You want to inherit two suitcases and a raven?" and then she remembered: a tenth of Dreamland. "I don't think so," she said, trying to hand the papers back, but he said, "You keep them and think about it," and walked off, his cigar clamped between his teeth, not so much mad as determined. "I don't know about him," she said to Frankie, and stuck the papers in her bag and went back to work.

Then there was Ethan and his new buddy, Army Barbie, who at least was making him something approaching cheerful. Ethan tried to talk Mab into joining the Guardia, just as Glenda had been trying to all week, but he did it with blunt force, which was a nice change. "How about if I give my power to your new girlfriend?" she said finally when he came by the Fortune-Telling Machine Thursday afternoon, and then hated the idea, but Ethan said, "No," and Mab didn't offer again.

And of course, there was Vanth, who'd given up spitting cards at her and just talked to her telepathically now, asking random questions about almost anything: if all women dressed like Mab ("No, I'm an original"), if Mab had children ("No, and I don't want any"), if Mab had restored the rest of the statues ("Yes, but I'm not putting in any more keys"), and dozens of other miscellaneous topics. It was clear that Vanth was not a deep thinker, nor did she have much focus. But she was kind and interested in many things, and aside from a daily request to be let out, she was pleasant to have around, a kind of Mother-in-the-Box, popping up to tell Mab to dress warmer or be careful of strangers.

Even with all the interruptions, by Friday morning, the day the media arrived, Mab had the Fortune-Telling Machine mostly painted, only a few detailed touches of silver on the tiny fish remaining. "Do you need help this morning?" she asked Cindy when she got downstairs with Frankie. "Because I'm almost done, and the media—"

She broke off, seeing half a dozen strangers in the shop with notebooks and cell phones.

"—are here," Cindy finished for her. "Not a lot of them, but enough. We're not busy, because I took What-Love-Can-Do off the menu. The crowds were making me crazy. Sit down and I'll get your breakfast."

Mab took a stool at the end of the counter, the only stool where nobody would be sitting beside her, one seat down from the guy in the Coke-bottle glasses, who was writing in his notebook again.

"You must really like Cindy's ice cream," she said to him.

He looked over, his eyes sharp behind the thick glass. "She constantly amazes."

"Yes, she does," Mab said. "So, do you live around here?"

"No," he said, and went back to his work.

Okay, she thought, and then Glenda came and sat down between them.

"No," Mab said. "Do not harass me today. I am almost done with the park and I want to savor my accomplishment."

Glenda put a bronze vase on the counter in front of Mab. It was about a foot tall, heavily detailed with bronze appliquéd decorations, with two writhing dragons for handles and a phoenix carved on the smooth round side. "This is yours."

"What is it?" Mab said, taken by how beautiful it was, but pretty sure there was a catch.

"It's Delpha. She picked out the urn a long time ago."

"Delpha." Mab drew back a little. "Delpha's *ashes?*"

"Just take it," Glenda said, looking into her eyes. "You got her sight, you can take her ashes."

Mab hesitated, and Glenda picked up the urn and put Delpha in Mab's work bag.

Mab looked at Frankie, who seemed fine with it.

"Okay," she said.

"And now I need a favor," Glenda said. "I need you to open the Oracle tent this afternoon. We need a fortune-teller for the last two weeks of Screamland. Just today and tomorrow and then next Friday and Saturday. That's all I ask."

Mab frowned at her. "I don't know how to tell fortunes."

"They're not hard," Glenda said. "Most people ask the same questions. Love or business. You can guess the answers."

"That doesn't seem fair."

"You'll be better at it than you think," Glenda said. "Will you do it? For me? And for Delpha?" She looked down at the urn in Mab's work bag, pointedly.

"Yes," Mab said, grateful that it wasn't about killing demons. And besides, she owed Delpha.

"Good," Glenda said, and got up and walked out.

"I should have asked if she wanted the ashes scattered," Mab said to Frankie.

Frankie shook out his feathers.

"I guess that's a no," Mab said as Cindy came down the counter to her.

"What's Glenda on you about?"

"She wants me to open the Oracle for the weekend." Mab frowned after Glenda. "You know, she's really hard to say no to."

"Tell me about it," Cindy said as the door opened and two families came in, the kids crowding up to the counter, so Mab said, "I'll fill you in later," and rolled off the stool. She bent to pick up her work bag and hesitated, seeing the dragon-handled urn in there. She pulled the work bag up and put it on the stool and looked at the urn, undecided.

When she glanced at the guy with the glasses beside her, he was looking at the urn, too.

"Nice dragons," he said.

"Oh." Mab nodded. "So what do I do with it?"

"Did you like her?"

"Her?"

"The lady in the urn."

"Yes," Mab said, realizing that she had. "I didn't know her long, but I liked her a lot."

"Then put her somewhere she'd like and you can see her and remember her," the guy said, and went back to his notebook.

"Okay, then," Mab said to his profile, and put the bag over her shoulder and headed for the Fortune-Telling Machine to paint the last of the tiny silver fish before she opened the Oracle tent at noon. And then the park would be finished. And she would be, too. Done with Dreamland.

She hesitated, not happy about that.

Just finish it, she told herself, and left the Dream Cream with Frankie and Delpha no more sure of her future after the past four days than she had been before.

*****

Those same four days had Ethan trying to build a fighting team out of the Guardia and losing.

Glenda was adamant about sticking to the way things had always been done. Gus had put Selvans' chalice back in the rust orange Strong Man statue and had given Glenda the Dragon's eye key to keep, and was now focusing on the big day coming up on Friday, checking to make sure all the golf carts were running smoothly, since the media didn't like to walk, he said, and running the Dragon Coaster every night, still two rattles short. Young Fred didn't give a damn about any of it. And Mab wanted nothing to do with the Guardia, which reinforced Ethan's desire to go for a techno-natural solution to capturing the demons, rather than a supernatural one. He also had his hands full with Weaver, demanding his knowledge of demons every day and his body every night, not the worst situation he'd ever been in, although Carl Whack-A-Mole had not been happy about the loss of his big plush dragon and demanded a new one to the tune of seventy-five dollars, not mentioning that he'd been inhabited by a demon the night before, which confirmed for Ethan that people couldn't remember being possessed. Ethan winced at the seventy-five bucks but paid, figuring it was more than worth it for those nights with Weaver.

Then Carl said, "And who did you give two dozen bears to, big spender?" and Ethan hesitated and said, "They were possessed by minion demons." "Oh, crap," Carl said, "did you get them all?" "Uh, yeah," Ethan said, and Carl clapped him on the shoulder and said, "Good work. Tell Glenda the Guardia owes me some bears," and went back to work, leaving Ethan with the feeling that he had a lot to learn about Dreamland.

He and Weaver locked down and secured the Tunnel of Love: chains around the lead car and motion sensors covering every way into it. If Tura somehow found a cheater to drag into the Tunnel, she was going to have a hell of a time getting anywhere, and Ethan would know right away. And Weaver had come across with a lot more information during their times in the dark, the key piece being that Ray Brannigan had been seen bringing minion demons across the water and, presumably, into the park. "And you didn't think to stop him?" Ethan said, exasperated, and Weaver said, "My partner doesn't believe in evil, he thinks everybody and everything can be rehabilitated or at least studied, so I promised him I'd only observe, not interfere unless human life is in danger." "That must be hard for you, not being able to shoot on sight," Ethan said, but he was grateful for the information, just the same. It was one more reason to take Ray out permanently as soon as they made it through Halloween.

But that was the only bright side, Ethan thought as he patrolled the tunnels with Weaver on Friday afternoon, his Mark 23 in one hand, a flashlight in the other. Gus had wanted to do it, but Ethan had sent him back to watch the park, in the safety of daylight, promising him to check the Keep while they were at it.

"I hate patrolling," Weaver said conversationally as they drew near the Keep door. "I know it's necessary but—"

Ethan sensed a presence ahead, dropped to one knee, and drew his pistol with a practiced move, the light in his other hand pointing toward the Keep door.

The door banged open and a plastic pirate ran toward him, cutlass raised, toxic purple eyes glaring, and Ethan fired twice, the rounds hitting right between the glowing purple eyes, both bullets punching a single black hole. *Nice,* Ethan thought, but it kept coming straight for him.

Then a muzzle flash blinded him as Weaver fired her D-gun. He blinked, and saw the pirate on its back, the circular round of the demon gun embedded in its center, the plastic pieces dissolving around a puddle of dark, empty demon ooze, sizzling as it ate into the stone.

"There are more," Ethan said, standing up, not seeing any more coming from the Keep, but sure they were there.

Something moved inside the Keep basement.

"Cover!" Ethan yelled, grabbing up his gun. He fired and so did Weaver, his bullets slowing the oncoming pirate, hers exploding it, and several pirates behind that one turned and scrambled for the stairs. Ethan pulled the clip out of the Mark 23 and slammed a fresh one home. "Okay, *you get me a damn D-gun.*"

"Yeah, yeah, yeah." Weaver stepped into the Keep basement over the plastic pieces and demon goo and headed for the stairs. "Ursula counts them every day now, and you know the deal, you tell me things and you let my partner examine you."

Ethan followed her up the stairs and paused just before the door. There was no noise on the other side, but he had no doubt there was something waiting for them there. He could feel it.

He looked at Weaver. He held up three fingers and pointed at the door. She nodded.

They hit the door exactly the same way.

Ethan barely ducked the hook that slashed at him, firing as fast as he could pull the trigger, the muzzle of the pistol inches from the pirate. The big .45-caliber rounds slammed into the plastic, blowing chunks out the back. The pirate swung the hook past Ethan toward Weaver and then the entire arm—and pirate—disintegrated as she fired.

Acid purple goo splattered Ethan's Kevlar vest and etched itself into the surface as Weaver kept firing, blowing two more pirates away before the rest scrambled for the stone steps circling the wall, making chittering sounds that were probably demon for "They're not supposed to be doing that."

They didn't seem to be expecting the demon gun.

Ethan scanned the big room, once the Keep Dining Hall, full of old restaurant tables and bentwood chairs but not, as far as he could see, any more demons.

"Only three?" Weaver said, sounding disappointed.

"With the two in the tunnel, that's five," Ethan said. "There are twelve pirates on the pirate ride, so you're probably gonna shoot seven more any minute now."

She reloaded.

They were on the first floor of the Keep, the drawbridge level. He looked around to see the massive wood-and-iron door taking up a good part of the outer wall, the side he knew that faced the boathouse and dock, with its smaller door in the center of the drawbridge, no other way out. "They're all gonna be up there," Ethan said, and reloaded. "Ready?"

Weaver nodded.

They climbed the stairs, and Ethan paused once more, leaning close to the door. Once more he heard nothing, and didn't sense anything on the other side.

"Not here," he told Weaver. "They must have retreated to the top level. Be careful anyway."

They went through the door, covering each other, but there was nothing there except the old restaurant kitchen, its stainless shelving dulled with dust. Ethan didn't pause, climbing the next set of stone stairs to the top level of the Keep with Weaver right behind him.

He stopped at the door and pulled back. "They're on the other side."

"How do you know? I don't hear anything."

"I know."

Ethan kicked the door open and began shooting as the minion pirates charged at him, their eyes glowing with rage. His bullets slammed them, slowing their assault as Weaver fired the demon gun as fast as she could, but there were too many and they were too fast—

Ethan spotted movement to his left and spun to see the one-eyed pirate captain running toward him.

"That's their leader, take him out!" Ethan yelled to Weaver, and raised his gun to fire, but before he could, the other pirates turned on the captain, piling on him, bringing him down, tearing at the plastic that encased him as Weaver picked them off, rapid fire, spattering demon goo everywhere.

When the last one was a mess of plastic and sizzling spatter, Weaver lowered her gun. "What the hell?"

"I don't know," Ethan said. "Maybe they don't like authority."

"I've thought about doing that to Ursula," Weaver said. "But they didn't even stop to defend themselves from me. I know they're evil, but you'd think they'd have some survival instincts."

"They're demons. Not deep thinkers."

Ethan turned and looked around, ignoring the oozing demon goo eating through the plastic remains and doing a light etch on the stone.

A five-sided wood table dominated the center of the room, five chairs circling it. Stairs went around the back of the room to the roof, and stacked under those were old trunks and boxes. A big armoire was to the right, and beyond that a weapons rack piled high with lances, spears, pikes, swords, and axes.

Weaver picked up a sword. "Nice."

"Iron. So they didn't come for the weapons." Ethan looked around the room. "Were they waiting for us?"

Weaver slashed the sword through the air. "Nice balance. I do like a classic weapon. Aren't you going to take one?"

"I have a knife," Ethan said, and headed for the door. The pirate attack hadn't been random. They'd been lying in wait, which meant something. He just didn't know what.

But Glenda might know. Or Ray, if Ethan stepped on his neck. Somebody was going to start giving up answers. Now.

*****

The park was filling up as Mab headed for the Oracle tent, media all over the place taking pictures of people in costumes screaming on the repainted rides, eating Cindy's ice cream cones, and laughing at the park staff, who were slathered in gray-green makeup and playing undead all over the midway. It was all going to be wonderful advertising as long as nobody tried to interview a demon. Mab opened the sliding doors of the Delpha's Oracle tent and went in, Frankie almost cooing on her shoulder, he was so pleased to be there.

He flew up to the rafters, and she put her bag down on the table, prepared to clean up, and found that Delpha had done it already. The only thing there was the cardboard box that Delpha had been packing the day she'd told Mab's fortune. Mab took her bag off the table and went around to the other side—*Delpha's side,* she thought—and dropped her bag on the floor, making Delpha's urn clink. She hesitated, but thinking of the guy with the Coke-bottle glasses in the Dream Cream, she put the urn on the table.

Delpha's shawl was folded neatly on top of her box, dark blue chenille shot with silver threads, with little silver stars sewn onto the ends. Mab hesitated, then shrugged off her paint coat—that would not inspire faith in the customers—and wrapped the shawl around her instead.

It was warm, deeply warm, like a chenille embrace. She tried a couple of different ways of wrapping it and finally settled for putting it over her head and shoulders and wrapping it in front of her because that provided the most warmth. She was considering whether to go back to the Dream Cream for a hot tea when two people came through the open doors, a young blonde and her boyfriend, her giggling, him rolling his eyes.

"Hi," Mab said, sitting down. "I'm Mab." *I tell fortunes. No, really.*

"It says 'Delpha' on the tent," the guy said, holding out one of the chairs for the girl.

Mab glanced at the urn where Delpha was ensconced in bronze and dragons. "Yeah, she's here, too."

"Stop it, Bill," the woman said, giving him a little push as she sat down. "He's a reporter," she told Mab, "so he's kinda skeptical."

"Yeah, Bill," Mab said, feeling a little nervous now. "Knock it off. So, what's your question?"

"We have to ask a question?" Bill said, sitting down. "You don't just see our futures?"

Don't make this any harder than it already is, Bill. "Do you have any idea how much crap there is in your future? Hours, days, months, years, full of stuff. How much time do you have and how much money?"

"I have a question," the woman said.

"Of course you do, Honey," Bill said, rolling his eyes again.

Mab looked up at Frankie, sharing the experience of what a dick Bill was. "You know, Bill, you should see an optometrist about that rolling-eye problem. Makes you look rude and patronizing."

"Well, I'm sorry," Bill said, clearly not. "But I don't believe in this stuff."

"Now there we share an experience. However, your beloved does believe, and it's just mean to keep patronizing her like that, so stop it."

"Yeah," Honey said.

"You don't believe in this, either?" Bill laughed. "That's a good one. That'll be great for my article."

"I didn't believe," Mab said, "until I got hit with the magic stick and now I see a whole lot more. Ten bucks, please."

"Ten bucks," Honey said. "It used to be five."

"And you used to be a brunette," Mab said. "Things change."

"Wow, you could see that?"

"Anybody can see that," Bill said. "Your roots are showing." He nodded at Mab. "You're on." He got out his wallet and slapped a ten on the table. "You get this if I believe you're really seeing the future."

"It's not always the future," Mab said, remembering Delpha's reading for her. "Sometimes it's just deeper into the present. It's not much fun."

"You need to work on your patter," Honey said. "You're kind of a downer."

"You want happy, go see a clown," Mab said. "What's your question?"

Honey beamed at Bill. "I want to know that we're going to live happily ever after."

"I want to lose ten pounds," Mab said. "Give me your hand."

Honey put her right hand out, and Mab remembered Delpha and said, "The other one."

Honey put her left hand out, and Mab took it gingerly, not sure what she was going to see or if she was going to see, pressing her palm down on Honey's—

At first there was nothing there, and Mab thought, *I knew this wouldn't work*. And then there was something, not visions, not voices, just a feeling, love and longing and fear—*Terror*, she thought, and tried to figure out what that was about. Honey was radiating not physical fear, but abandonment, loss, something beyond the need for love, although that was overwhelming. . . .

Mab dropped her hand, stunned. The psychic thing worked. Now what was she going to do with it?

"What?" Honey said, alarmed.

"You love him so much," Mab said.

"Yes, I do," Honey said.

"But you're afraid there's something wrong, you're so terribly afraid—"

"No," Honey said, losing her smile. "No, I'm not, I'm *not*—"

"Give me your hand, Bill," Mab said, and when he hesitated, she said, "You don't believe in this crap anyway," and he put out his hand.

She took it and put her palm on his, determined to find out what Honey already knew, subconsciously. If this jerk was . . .

Love, good steady love, and guilt, and fear . . .

"Oh, hell," Mab said, "you love her, too."

"Of course I do," Bill said, and Honey began to smile again.

"But you're going to hurt her, you're going to leave her." Mab looked at Honey with sympathy. "He loves you all he can, but he cannot love you very much."

"What?" Honey said. *"Why?"*

"Honey, she's just yanking your chain," Bill said, trying to get his hand back from Mab.

He's terrified, she thought, getting a word for the first time, *terrified . . . no, that's not it.* "Terry," she said, and Bill looked at her, appalled. "Terry, do you know a Terry?"

"Of course we know a Terry," Honey said. "He's Bill's best friend. They play basketball every Sunday."

They don't play basketball. "You have to tell her," she said to him. "It's not fair. She loves you very much, but she knows something is wrong and it's making her miserable."

Bill looked at Honey, who still looked mystified. "I don't—"

"Don't be a bastard, Bill," Mab said, letting go of his hand. "People don't lie to people they love, they lie to people they're using because they think their needs are more important than anybody else's." She thought of Joe for a minute and then thought, *No, he's different.* "Look at her, Bill. She doesn't deserve to be lied to. *Nobody* deserves to be lied to."

"Bill?" Honey said.

Bill stood up. "Come on. Let's go."

Honey stood up. "We're all right. You love me. She said so."

"You want your money back, Bill?" Mab said.

"No," he said, and left the tent, Honey hurrying to catch up with him.

Mab looked at Frankie, perched up in the rafters. "This job sucks."

Except I really can tell fortunes.

Another woman, a brunette in her forties this time, came through the open doors and sat down. "I want to know about my boyfriend."

"Of course you do," Mab said. "Ten bucks."

It was going to be a long day.

CHAPTER 13

Ethan led Weaver to the trailers and said, "My mother lives here."

Weaver frowned at the neat grouping of Airstreams, two on each side of the path. "Who lives in the others?"

"Gus next to Glenda. The other two used to be Old Fred and Hank, but they're gone now. Delpha's is down that path next to the river."

"So there are two empty trailers, but you're sleeping in the woods."

"I like the woods—you never know who might show up there." Ethan knocked on the door of Glenda's trailer. When she opened it, he said, "Remember how you always wanted me to bring home a nice girl?"

Glenda looked past him to Weaver, dressed all in black with her gun under her arm.

"This isn't her," Ethan said. "This is Weaver. The man in black."

Glenda looked at Weaver again and nodded. "Mab mentioned you."

He turned to Weaver. "Come on in and tell Glenda everything."

"Ursula will be upset," Weaver said.

"How badly do you want me to do that medical exam?" Ethan said.

Weaver pressed her lips together for a minute and then walked up the trailer steps, and pushed past Glenda to go in.

Glenda lowered her voice. "So this is the infamous Army Barbie. I hear you gave her Carl's dragon."

"Weaver has a gun that kills minion demons," Ethan told Glenda. "And glasses that can see them in the dark."

"We don't need that," Glenda said, "we have *powers.*"

"And if we play our cards right, we'll have both," Ethan said, and gently pushed her into the trailer.

When they were all inside, he said, "Okay, let me start. Weaver, my mother and I are part of the Guardia, a hereditary anti-demon peace-keeping force with supernatural powers stationed here in Dreamland to watch over five super-demons called the Untouchables."

"Ethan!" Glenda said, outraged.

"Supernatural powers?" Weaver said, sounding skeptical.

"Mom, Weaver is part of an elite secret government demon research group investigating Dreamland because of its high demon population."

"So much for 'secret,' " Weaver said.

"Elite?" Glenda said, looking Weaver up and down.

He looked from one to the other. "Play nice."

Glenda's chin went up and she pressed her lips firmly together, so Weaver said, "Fine. I'll go first. The government is interested in demons the same way it's interested in any force, as a possible threat and a possible weapon. My partner feels strongly that using demons as weapons is a bad idea because he thinks exploiting living things for government ends is wrong, and I think using them is a bad idea because they're evil little suckers and they'll turn on us in a heartbeat."

"She's also blown a hell of a lot of them away for us," Ethan said, hoping that would soften Glenda.

Glenda didn't say anything, so Weaver moved on. "My boss, however, is torn. She doesn't really believe in demons, thinks they're like UFOs and my partner and I are crazy, but if they turn out to be real, then finding a way to use them could considerably up her status in the Defense Department."

"Particularly after the demons kill everybody above her," Glenda said, taking out a cigarette, which Ethan saw as a good sign.

Weaver nodded. "The problem is, she's becoming more convinced they're real with every report we turn in. And she's talking about coming here herself, and if she decides that the demons are real and of use to her, she'll try to commandeer the park for the government."

"Over my dead body," Glenda said. "She has no idea what she's messing with."

"I agree," Weaver said. "Especially since I have no idea what we're messing with. Which is why I need information." She sat back, waiting politely.

"She saved my life, Mom," Ethan said. "More than once. Talk to her."

"So there are minion demons in the park," Glenda said. "How are they getting in?"

"Ray Brannigan is bringing them in," Weaver said.

"Why?" Glenda said, looking taken aback for the first time. "He wants to run the park, not destroy it. I know he wants us all out of here, but he doesn't want the park wrecked."

"He's bringing them in to kill us, Mom," Ethan said. "They killed Delpha, they tried to kill Gus earlier this week, and they tried to kill Weaver and me today."

Glenda jerked her head up. "What good does it do Ray to have you two dead? I can see him going after Mab, he'll inherit her ten percent, but it's not like he's going to get any richer killing you and Weaver. He's all about money, he'd sell his soul for . . ." Her voice broke off.

"Sell his soul for . . . ," Ethan prompted.

Glenda sat back. "My god. It was right there and I never saw it."

"What?" Ethan asked.

"He made a deal with Kharos to take over the park."

"Who is Kharos?" Weaver said.

"The Devil," Glenda said. "Ray's traded his soul for money and power. He made the deal forty years ago, why didn't I see it?"

"I don't see how you could have seen it," Ethan said, not following. "I don't see how you see it now."

"Wait a minute," Weaver said, straightening in her chair. *"The Devil?"*

Glenda ignored her to talk to Ethan. "Forty years ago, Ray Brannigan was a skinny, stupid teenager. Sometime after the weekend that the Untouchables escaped, he began to change. He filled out, got smarter, hell, his *hair* got thicker, almost overnight. Everything came his way. West Point, the Army Rangers, great investments, mayor . . ." Glenda tapped her cigarette, upset now. "And I didn't pay any attention back then because your father had just died and you were on the way and . . . Oh, god, Ethan, he's been planning on handing the park to Kharos for forty years."

"Why wait so long?" Ethan said.

"I don't know, go ask Ray." Glenda stubbed out her unlit cigarette. "This is bad. Ray has access everywhere. He—"

"Okay, about *the Devil*," Weaver said, her self-possession gone. "The real Devil? He *exists*?"

"A devil," Glenda said. "A big one. And yes, he's real, the son of a bitch." She shivered a little bit as if someone had walked over her grave. Or was digging it. "Kharos wants out, he wants all the Untouchables out, and once they're all free, they'll take their real forms, they'll be so powerful that we can't—"

"We need Weaver with us on this, Mom," Ethan said, cutting her off as her voice began to rise in panic.

Glenda swallowed. "All right." She nodded at Weaver. "All right, you can help. But you do not interfere with the capture of an Untouchable. You can do whatever you want with the minions, but you have to leave the Untouchables to us."

"And this devil is one of the Untouchables?" Weaver asked.

"Yes," Glenda said. "There are five: the Devil, his wife, his right-hand man, a sex-crazed mermaid, and a trickster."

Weaver nodded, a little wide-eyed. "Okay, then."

"And you have to keep the government out of this," Glenda said.

"I'll keep Ursula out of it," Weaver said. "My partner needs to know. And then we'll decide together what we report. He's against killing, but I think even he would have to admit the Devil needs to be put down. We still have a mission to complete, we can't stop our work, but we can help you fight evil."

"I have a mission, too," Glenda said. "And I'll cut you off at the knees if you get in the way of my duty."

"That's fair," Weaver said. "Especially if we're dealing with, you know, *the Devil.*" She shook her head, a little pale.

Glenda looked at her, puzzled, and Ethan said, "Her dad was a preacher. Now our first problem. We got attacked by pirates—"

"Pirates?" Glenda said, lost.

"From the Pirate Ship," Ethan said. "They were possessed. We destroyed them all, but I'm pretty sure there'll be more attacks because I think Kharos is trying to kill us all. So—"

"You destroyed them?" Glenda said. "But then we have no Pirate Ship ride."

Ethan looked at her, dumbfounded. "They were trying to kill us."

"I know, but now we're down a ride," Glenda said. "That's going to hurt the park receipts."

"So would a dozen minion-possessed pirates," Weaver pointed out.

"Right, right," Glenda said, frowning. "Okay, forget the pirates, we'll just have to close the ride. Now we have to get Tura back in her chalice."

"Tura?" Weaver said, trying to follow.

"The sex-crazed mermaid, kills cheaters," Ethan said.

Glenda nodded. "Then get Fufluns' chalice repaired and get him back."

"Chalice?" Weaver said.

"Ancient wood cup that traps Untouchables," Ethan said. "Fufluns is the trickster."

"Okay," Weaver said.

Glenda went on. "And stop Ray, whatever he's doing, but don't let him know we know he's in league with Kharos. Once Kharos knows we're on to Ray, he'll get another flunky and we won't know who he is." She thought over what she'd just said and then nodded. "Those are the big fixes. After that, we can mop up the minion demons." She stood up. "I'll go warn Gus that the minions are after him; he's probably at the Dragon. You warn Mab. She's in Delpha's tent telling fortunes, so she's probably okay for the moment, but let her know."

Ethan nodded. "So I say, 'Mab, your uncle's made a deal with a devil, and he's trying to kill you'?"

"Yes."

"Mab is Ray's niece?" Weaver said. "Can we trust her?"

"Yes," Ethan said. "She's Guardia, so she can't hurt us. Guardia can't harm other Guardia."

"Can't harm them," Weaver said. "Is that just physically, or does that mean she can't betray you, either?"

"Mab wouldn't," Glenda said firmly. "Delpha trusted her. Delpha never made mistakes."

"So we go warn Mab." Weaver stood up. "Thank you very much for accepting me, Mrs. Wayne."

She held out her hand, and Glenda looked at it for a moment, and then she took it.

"Stop Ray," she said, and they left the trailer to go warn Mab.

"I say we just shoot him," Weaver said. "Evil bastard, trying to unleash the Devil on earth."

"You heard Mom. Ray's the Devil we know. We go after the demons first. Which reminds me. Can I have a D-gun now?"

"Maybe," Weaver said.

Well, the good news was that his mother and Weaver were now talking, Ethan thought as he followed her.

Then he stopped.

That was good news depending on what they talked about.

"You didn't like my mother that much, right?" he said, and followed Weaver down the path to the midway.

*****

Four hours after her first customer, Mab's skills were sharpening enough that she was getting pictures and words, as if somebody were whispering in her head, along with all the emotions her clients were feeling. And they were all seething with emotion, usually about relationships. At first she thought she'd just gotten a lot of excitable people, but as the day wore on, she realized it was part of being human, emotions zinging around inside you like pinballs even if you thought you were calm. And going to a psychic didn't calm people down any; a lot of them were thinking *Don't think that*, hoping she wouldn't pick up on their loudest needs.

It was exhausting.

"I don't know how you stood this," she said to the urn, and then the next customer came in, a guy who had his tie on in the middle of an amusement park. "I have a business question," he said, sitting down.

"No kidding," Mab said. "Ten bucks."

"That's a lot of money."

"You can take it back if you don't think what I say is true," Mab said, and watched a greedy light appear in his eyes.

In the rafters above, Frankie cawed and spread his wings.

"That's fair enough," he said, and put two fives on the table. "What can you tell me about my business dealings?"

"I can tell you that you're planning on telling me that you don't believe me even if you do so that you can take your ten bucks back."

The guy pulled back a little. "Your psychic abilities tell you that?" he said, a sneer in his voice.

"No, my vast experience with human nature tells me that." Mab reached out. "Give me your hand."

He gave her his right hand, and she said, "Other one," so he switched hands.

She pressed her palm to his and saw . . . nothing. A great yawning void. "Huh, you may be getting that ten back legitimately. Let me try the other one after all."

The guy rolled his eyes and gave her his right hand, and this time when she pressed her palm to his, feelings rolled over her, seething needs, slithering little intents, and oppressive greed, and then a vision of him shaking hands with three other men. . . . "You're cheating your business partners." She looked up at him. "Wouldn't you think people would be smarter about that stuff now?"

"You don't know that," the guy said, trying to take his hand back.

Mab held on. "No, but you know it and that's what I hear, what you know. What was your question?"

The man stopped struggling. "I just want to know if my *business dealings* will be successful."

"The future," Mab said. "Well, the future is iffy. Lots of choices to be made. But if things continue the way they are now . . ." She got a flash of him in a Mercedes, confident and proud. ". . . you'll be driving a Mercedes."

The man relaxed. "Well, that's good to know, not that I believe in this stuff."

The self-satisfaction rolled off him, no guilt at all, and Mab said, "Of course, that's in this lifetime."

"What?"

"After you die, you're going to hell for being a dishonest bastard, and you'll burn for eternity."

The guy snatched his hand back. "I don't believe in hell."

"Most people don't until they get there." Mab smiled at him. "Of course, if you stop lying and cheating, you can probably redeem yourself. If not, have them put marshmallows in your coffin. There's a bright side to everything, I always say."

"That's the most ridiculous thing I've ever heard," the man said, and turned to go. Then he turned back and reached for the two fives on the table.

"You really don't believe a word I've said?" Mab said, looking at him with cool eyes. "Remember where lying's going to get you, Snowball."

The man really wanted to pick up those two fives, Mab could tell he wanted to, but he pulled his hand back and walked out.

"I made up the part about hell," Mab said to Frankie after the guy had closed the sliding doors. "But I'm pretty sure I was right anyway."

The doors slid open, and Ray came in carrying a Styrofoam cup with a lid on it, a cigar chomped between his teeth. Frankie cawed again.

"Speak of the Devil," Mab said, taken aback. "You want your fortune read?"

"No." He smiled down at her. "So, I don't suppose you've changed your mind about selling?"

"No." Mab squinted at him. "Are you losing your hair?"

"No," Ray said, sounding surly. "The light in here is bad. Did you sign that will yet?"

"Ray, I'm not accepting Delpha's legacy, so I have nothing to leave anybody. There's no point in my making a will."

He nodded as if he wasn't surprised, and then glanced at his hand and seemed to remember he was holding a cup. "Almost forgot. Cindy sent you some tea."

"Thank you," Mab said, taking the cup. She cracked the lid and sniffed it. Odd. She made a face.

"It's some kind of herbal gunk," Ray said around his cigar. "She said it was full of vitamins, keep you from getting sick out here in the cold."

"Okay." Mab put the lid back on the cup and set it to one side. "Sit down, I'll read your palm. Tell you how your business is going to do."

"Very funny. Drink your tea."

"No, trust me, it turns out I really can do this." Mab held out her hand. "Give me your hand, I'll tell your future."

"No." He hesitated, and then he took the cigar out of his mouth and added, "You're a good girl, Mab," and walked out.

"What are you talking about?" Mab called after him, and then a woman came through the open doors, a ten-dollar bill in her hand, leaving the sliding doors open behind her.

"I want to know about my boyfriend," she said as she sat down.

"Imagine my surprise," Mab said, and pulled the cup of tea in front of her. "Sit down and—"

Ethan knocked on the side of the tent and came in, and Frankie gave a caw from his roost in the rafters, startling the woman, who hadn't noticed him.

"I'm kind of in the middle of something here," Mab said.

"We need to talk to you," he said as Weaver followed him in.

"Oh," Mab said. "Hi, Weaver."

Weaver folded her arms. "Army Barbie?"

Mab returned the smile. "I'm sure you've thought of worse for me. Now as you see, this lovely woman would like her fortune told—"

Ethan nodded at the woman. "Park security, ma'am. If you could give us a minute."

The woman looked at Mab. "It's drugs, isn't it?"

"No, she just acts like she's on drugs," Ethan said, and the woman got up and left, not happy.

"Good thing I don't make my living doing this," Mab said, reaching for her tea. "I'd be *annoyed.*"

Frankie swooped down low across the table and grabbed at the cup with his claws, spilling hot liquid everywhere.

"Frankie!" Mab said, yanking her shawl away from the spill. "Damn."

"Where'd you get the tea?" Ethan said.

"Ray brought it. . . ." Mab's voice trailed off at the look on his face.

"Your uncle's trying to kill you," Ethan said. "Did he bring you anything else? What's in the jug?"

"Jug?" Mab looked at the urn. "That's Delpha. Why is Ray trying to kill me?"

Ethan frowned at the urn and then evidently decided to let that one ride. "He's trying to kill all of us. He's made a deal with the Devil, Kharos, and that's part of it."

"I see," Mab said, and pushed herself past *Are you out of your mind?* to genuinely consider it, since most of what she considered rational had gone by the wayside in the past week. "The Devil. Huh." She looked at the cup on the ground where Frankie had dropped it.

"That bird is smarter than you are," Weaver said.

"Probably." Mab looked up to the rafters. "Sorry I yelled. Thanks for saving my life."

Frankie spread his wings and moved from foot to foot, then settled back down to sleep.

"Be careful," Ethan told Mab. "Don't wander around outside after dark. Don't go anywhere alone. Lock your doors and windows—"

"It's that bad?" Mab said, realizing that he was serious. "He's stalking us all? You know, he was an Army Ranger, he probably knows how to kill people with his little finger or something."

"He'll send minion demons," Weaver said. "They're evil little bastards that can possess anything, so watch your surroundings at all times."

"There's more than one kind of demon?" Mab said.

"Oh, yeah," Weaver said. "Incubi, succubi, marching hordes—"

"You're a demon *expert?*" Mab said, incredulous.

"I've done my research."

"Research?" Mab lost her breath for a moment at the idea of having demon research already done for her. "Can I look at this research?"

Weaver looked at Ethan, who nodded. "Well, sure. My partner is the real researcher, though. I'll introduce you."

"I apologize for 'Army Barbie,' " Mab said.

"Just be *careful,*" Ethan said, and then they left and she wanted to say, *Wait, come back, don't leave me,* which was a new thing for her to want from Ethan, let alone Weaver.

Another woman came in and sat down.

"Hi," Mab said, still distracted by the news that she was marked for death by demons and her uncle. "Uh, you want to know about your boyfriend?"

"Yes," the woman said, startled. "How did you know?"

"I'm psychic," Mab said. "Give me your hand."

*****

When Weaver came back at six, she brought Ethan a D-gun.

"Thank you," he said. "Ammo?"

She passed over a heavy bag, and he took it.

"That's yours to keep. Screw Ursula."

"Thank you," Ethan said.

"I want to go with you tonight on the capture," she went on. "I won't interfere, but I want to see what happens with the Untouchables."

Ethan hesitated—Glenda wouldn't be happy—and then hefted the bag of ammo. She'd set him up well, but . . . "No goggles?"

She shook her head.

"Okay." He felt the balance of the gun in his hand. It was a good one. "Come on, I'll show you the plan."

After unlocking the cars, he took her into the Tunnel behind the scrim until they reached the Antony and Cleopatra diorama, then waited until the last boat had gone past and showed her the way into the diorama through a split in the backdrop.

"I've been here before, you know," she said when she was through the scrim. "Saving your ass."

"Right," Ethan said. "We'll wait here. Young Fred will have replaced whatever cheating idiot Tura has zeroed in on. They'll float by here, and that's when Fred will change back into Fred and say, 'Frustro,' and the spirit will leap."

"Frustro?" Weaver frowned. "I disappoint?"

"Never," Ethan said.

"I deceive, I trick—"

"That's it, trick. Then Mab is supposed to freeze the spirit by saying, 'Specto'—"

"I spy?" Weaver said, snorting.

"But since she's not with us, I'm going to have to try to grab Tura without that. I did it with Selvans, but he moves slow. Tura is fast." He remembered the last time she'd possessed him, slamming into him and grabbing his heart. "Then Glenda puts her into the chalice and Gus seals it, and we're done."

"No shooting?" Weaver said.

"No. We're classier than that. We just say a lot of Latin and sock their asses into wood cups."

"Why not just shoot them?"

"Because you can't kill an Untouchable."

"Have you *tried*?"

Ethan looked at the woman he was fairly sure was his soul mate. "No. But you did. You shot Tura when you were saving my ass. It didn't work. She just left her host."

"Let me try again," Weaver said grimly.

"Not tonight, honey," Ethan said, and led her down the tunnel to the entrance.

The park was crowded as they came out onto the midway, not as many as would come for the big Halloween blast next week, but enough that the Dreamland bank account was going to be a lot fatter come midnight. They got some startled looks from park-goers who weren't expecting anybody in body armor carrying bulky demon guns. "Park security," Ethan told anyone who looked really alarmed, and then they looked impressed. "On Halloween, they'll just think we're in costume," he told Weaver. "Even easier."

"For the demons, too," she said.

They walked up the midway near the Devil's Drop, and Ethan slowed. Ray was seated on the bench next to the Devil statue, smoking a cigar and looking none too happy. When he saw them, he looked startled, but so did everybody else who saw them, so Ethan ignored that.

Weaver unslung her demon gun from over her shoulder, tense with anger. "So you're just sitting here, Ray? Chatting? *With the Devil?*"

Ray smiled. "What? I'm alone."

Weaver gestured to the statue beside him. *"Him."*

"Oh." Ray shrugged, folding his arms over his chest. "He's good company. Doesn't say much. My kind of guy."

"Evidently," Weaver said, and walked closer to the statue, as if she were daring herself to do it.

Ray's face darkened at her tone and he straightened. "What are you doing here anyway?"

"Park security," Ethan said. He looked past Ray to the seven-foot-high Devil statue. The red eyes seemed alive with energy, and for the first time he felt some misgivings about his plan.

Ray glared at Weaver. "I don't remember hiring any women for park security."

"Glenda hired me," Weaver said, staring at the Devil statue. "Affirmative action."

"You're fired," Ray said.

Weaver ignored him. She was pale now, fixated on the statue, and just as Ethan was going to say something, she turned and walked away, up the path to the Beer Pavilion and his campsite beyond that.

"Disrespectful," Ray said to Ethan, staring after Weaver. "Doesn't know who's boss. Get rid of her. She looks unstable."

"Meanwhile you're talking to a Devil statue," Ethan said, and walked up the path to the trailers, lengthening his stride to catch up to Weaver.

"I want to shoot him," she said.

"So do I," Ethan said. "Believe me, I've thought about it."

She stepped off the path, and he followed her through the trees and over the last of the brush to arrive at his campsite. "So," he began, not sure where to go next, although he knew where he wanted to go.

"I've fought a lot of demons," Weaver said.

"Yes, you have," Ethan said, trying to be supportive.

"But nothing like the thing that's in that statue."

"Weaver—"

She started to shake. "My father used to tell me, every damn morning before I went to school, 'Be sober, be vigilant because your adversary the Devil walks about like a roaring lion, seeking whom he may devour.' And now, the Devil is *here,* I could *feel* it, Ethan, it's *evil* and it's *in there,* it's not a lion, it's pain and death and despair, and that asshole Ray wants to set it *free*—"

He put his arms around her, meaning to comfort her, but she pulled back.

"I don't like being afraid," she said, her voice close to breaking. "This is every nightmare my father ever gave me. He used to scream at the congregation about the Devil being everywhere, ready to take them down to *the flames of hell*—"

"Weaver—"

"And now it's *real.*" She shook. "I hate fucking demons, little evil bastards, but that thing in the statue, that's not just evil, it's . . . vile. It's apocalyptic."

"Yeah, but you're with the Guardia," Ethan said, trying to keep his voice light. "We've kicked his ass before, and we'll do it again."

"Yeah?" she said, and let him pull her close. "Okay, then. I'm sorry. I didn't mean to go all girly on you. Make me forget I did that, will you?"

"You bet," he said, and pulled her down onto his sleeping bag and held her because she was still shaking.

"Ouch," she said, trying to make her voice light. "Will you get rid of that damn rock?"

"Sorry." He pulled it out and threw it into the bushes.

"From now on, we're doing this in one of those trailers. No rocks."

Her voice was still high, still tight, so Ethan pushed himself up on one arm. "Glenda fixed up Hank's trailer for me. We can go now if you'll feel safer there."

"No," she said, looking into his eyes. "I want to be right here with you."

"You're safe with me," he said. "I swear it. The Devil comes near you, I will send him back to hell."

"All right, then," she said, and pulled him down to her, and he did everything he could to make her forget that she'd been afraid.

*****

"That bitch," Ray said when Ethan and Weaver were gone. "Talking to me like I'm nothing. Calling me Ray like she has a right. That's *Mayor Brannigan* to you, bitch."

SHE IS INSIGNIFICANT.

"Yeah, well, she may be insignificant, but she knows I'm talking to you. My cover is blown."

THE MINION DEMONS WILL KILL THEM.

"There's some bad news there," Ray said. "They're supposed to already be dead. I heard Ethan talking about going into the Keep, so I sent the minions there to wait for them, and now here they are, still alive. So I'm assuming we're down another dozen of the little bastards."

Kharos thought of several ways to make Ray suffer slowly. YOU ARE NOT DOING WELL.

"It's not me, it's the minions," Ray said. "I tried to organize them. Took them to the Keep, told them the plan, put one of them in charge—"

NEVER PUT ONE OVER THE OTHERS. THEY DESPISE THOSE THEY THINK ARE ABOVE THEM.

"Hell, everybody's above them," Ray said, and then stopped. "That's probably why they're so mad all the time. That kind of crap can get to you. Okay, no more organizing minions. I'll just . . . point them at the targets. I'll tell them you're issuing the orders. They're terrified of you." Ray sounded a little petulant about that.

IS YOUR NIECE DEAD?

"Probably. I just poisoned her." Ray stubbed out his cigar on the bench. "It's not easy at the top. I'm not going to sleep well tonight." He stood up. "I can't wait until Halloween is over."

FIND FUFLUNS AND TURA. HE'LL BE WITH LAUGHING PEOPLE. SHE'LL BE SURROUNDED BY MEN.

"I told you, *I looked*," Ray said.

The end of his cigar fell off.

Ray brushed the ash off his pants and looked at his truncated, limp cigar. "Sure," he said. "I'll go find your bimbo and your joker for you. I have nothing *better to do*."

He threw his cigar down in disgust and walked off down the midway.

Kharos realized he had one thing in common with Ray.

He couldn't wait until Halloween was over, either.

CHAPTER 14

By the time the twentieth woman had come into the tent and asked to know about her true love, Mab was cranky. It wasn't so much that they all wanted to know about the same thing; she sympathized with that. She wanted to know about that, too. It was just that they were so depressingly similar, full of doubt about being in love, if they were loved, did they want *this* love, some of them full of longing for a baby more than a man, some of them afraid they were having a baby, terrified and exhilarated and desperate for answers.

It was like watching the same movie over and over with an open ending because, as she kept telling most of them, it depended on what they wanted and what they did. Except for three of them. To those women, she said, "He's a bastard. Run away."

"How can you tell?" the last of the women said, indignant.

"I don't have to tell, you already know," Mab told her. "I heard it in your head, that's how I know."

The woman stood up furious and left the tent, but she didn't take her ten bucks back.

The next woman who came in was Glenda.

"You've got quite a line out there," she said, sitting down as Frankie cawed his welcome from up in the rafters.

"I don't know why," Mab said. "I'm just telling them what they already know. It's not like I can see the future."

Glenda smiled faintly. "Of course not."

"So give me your hand," Mab said.

"We have to capture Tura tonight, Mab. The Guardia needs you."

Mab felt exasperation rise. "We've had this conversation already. No. A thousand times, *no*."

Glenda hesitated, and then reached in her jeans pocket and pulled out some bills. She sorted out a ten and put it on the table and crammed the rest of the bills back in her pocket. "Okay." She held out her hand.

"I don't need the ten," Mab said pushing it back to her. "Professional courtesy, you get a free one."

Glenda pushed it across the table again. "I want a real reading, not a pro bono."

"What's the difference?"

"You have to tell me the truth if I pay."

"I'd tell you the truth anyway," Mab said.

Glenda put her right hand across the table, palm up.

"Other hand."

"The left's for love," Glenda said. "My question is about business. Right hand."

"That I didn't know," Mab said. "You want to know about the park?" She put her palm down on Glenda's right hand and then almost pulled it back, Glenda's palm held so much energy. And then—

Images this time: darkness, the park in ruins, the Devil's Drop fallen, the Dragon splintered into the lake, the carousel collapsed, shattered wooden horses everywhere—

Mab snatched her hand back.

"What?" Glenda said.

"What's your question?" Mab said, trying to shut out the carnage. "I know what you're worried about, but that's not going to happen. Nobody would do that to the park."

Glenda blinked. "Do what to the park?"

"What's your question?" Mab said, her heart pounding now.

"This Weaver," Glenda began.

"I know. Camouflage and spike heels." Mab relaxed a little. "For what it's worth, she seems to be on his side. And she knows demons."

"She's the black-ops person who shot him," Glenda said.

"For Ethan, that's true love."

"He wants her along on the capture tonight. She has a demon gun and demon goggles—"

"Demon goggles?"

"—and he wants all this high-tech stuff on the capture. He thinks it's better than the old ways. I told him no, but I know Ethan. She'll be there."

"If she shot Ethan, she's probably going to be useful. What are you afraid of?"

"The captures aren't high tech; they're magic, Mab. I don't think mixing the two . . . I know you won't come with us, but we'll be down in magic force already and then adding this stuff . . . I think things are going to go terribly wrong. And you can see the future, you know. Just glimpses of it and then you have to figure out what it means. It used to drive Delpha crazy. But I can change the future if I alter the course. I want to know what's going to happen tonight so I can change course if I have to."

"I don't read the future," Mab said.

Glenda stuck out her right hand again. "Then just read my palm."

Mab hesitated, and then she put her palm on Glenda's again.

Emotions this time: confusion, fear, a fair amount of anger toward Mab, a lot more toward Weaver, a terrified sense of things spiraling out of control, a paralyzing sense of responsibility . . .

"You're in hell," Mab said, feeling guilty.

"Tell me something I don't know," Glenda said. "Go deeper."

Mab closed her eyes and tried harder, reaching for places she hadn't before. The emotion was terrible, aching lost love, terror for a child in battle, grinding concern for the park and its people—

Mab pulled her hand back. "Jesus. You need a vacation."

"It's not working, is it?" Glenda said. "You can't see tonight?"

"No." Mab considered it. "Maybe I'm trying too hard." She looked up at Frankie in the rafters and his calm drifted down to her. "Maybe . . ."

She put her hand back on Glenda's without thought or pressure, open to whatever happened, and images hit her like bullets, Weaver with a gun, Glenda falling, a black helicopter, Gus screaming, blue-green vapor everywhere, Glenda again, sightless eyes staring up at the top of a tunnel—

Mab pulled her hand back. "Oh my god."

"What?" Glenda said.

Mab pushed the ten across the table to her. "You win. I'm going with you tonight."

Frankie cawed his approval.

Glenda swallowed. "It's that bad?"

"Not if I can help it," Mab said.

*****

At six, Mab let her last customer out and called out, "That's it for today, folks. Sorry!" and then stopped when Joe stepped out of the line and said, "How about me?"

"You, I'll take," Mab said, smiling.

"Hey," the first person in line said, and Joe said, "Chill, I'm the boyfriend," and pulled Mab inside the tent.

"The boyfriend?" Mab said, trying not to giggle. She was not a giggler, but around Joe, everything seemed to be funny.

"Lover seemed like too much information," Joe said, and kissed her, and she leaned against him and kissed him back. "So tonight—"

"Can I meet you later?" she said, cursing Glenda for having gotten to her. "Like at midnight? I promised Glenda I'd help her with something."

"Sure." He smiled down at her. "What are you helping her with?"

"Catching a demon." Mab shook her head, still not quite sure she believed it all.

"Catching demons, huh? You need help?"

"I think Glenda likes to do it her way."

"Don't we all?" Joe said, and kissed her again, and she laughed and said, "Come on, you can walk me to the Dream Cream," and caught his hand, holding tightly—

—yellow light, a handsome man with curly hair and little horns, goat's legs, and a crooked smile, kissing a mermaid, tumbling in a sea of turquoise, shouting, a chalice, darkness—

"What?" Joe said, and Mab looked deeper and saw someone sleeping inside him, two spirits in there, one a human being and the other a yellow flame—

Frankie flew down to sit on her shoulder, as if he'd seen through her eyes what she'd just seen, and she dropped Joe's hand and stepped back, breathless. "You lied to me."

"Is this about the demon hunter thing?" Joe said. "Look, you wouldn't have believed me—"

"You're not a demon hunter."

"Well," Joe began.

She backed away until she was behind her chair. "You're a demon. You're Fufluns."

"Mab," he said, and took a step toward her. "I can explain."

"Really?" Mab said. "How?"

"Well," he said, and frowned. "Yeah, I can't explain. You've got me."

"I don't want you," Mab said. "Get out. Get out *now*!"

Frankie cawed and flapped his wings, lowering his head to stare balefully at Joe.

No, at Fufluns.

"You don't understand," he said. "I'm different with you. You're the only person I've slept with in this body since I got out."

Mab lost her breath. "In that body."

"Well, you know," Fufluns said. "Dave."

"Oh my god." Mab sat down. "I've been sleeping with Drunk Dave."

"No, no," Fufluns said, coming closer to the table that separated them. "He's been out cold. He has no idea. Well, he has some idea, but only what I've told him."

"You told him . . ." Mab looked up at the man she loved, dumbstruck. "My god."

"He was all for it. His life has improved a lot since I started possessing him." He began to move around the table to her.

She got up and moved, keeping the table between them.

"He's not drinking himself into a stupor every night, he wakes up relaxed, he's dressing better, he's doing great at work—"

"I can't believe this," she said, keeping the table between them, and Frankie cawed his agreement.

"—women like him more, his hair is curlier, he's a lot happier, really, he's fine with it."

"I'm not." She looked at him, trying to separate the demon from the man, revolted by both of them and still wanting the combination. "Oh, god," she said again. *"Go away."*

"Mab, I love you," he said, switching directions to come around the table to her, and she backed toward the door, Frankie sending up a racket now that Fufluns was moving.

"You've slept with other women," she said louder, over Frankie's anger, feeling for the edge of the sliding door.

"Not in this body—"

"That doesn't matter," Mab snapped. "Although it's also irrelevant *because you're a demon."*

"Don't be a bigot."

"I need to go now." She slid the door open, and he tried to reach her, and Frankie let loose with a spine-rending caw, spreading his wings, ready to launch. "Don't piss off my bird, or Dave's gonna lose an eye."

She backed out onto the midway, and he watched her from the doorway, looking truly sad for the first time since she'd met him.

"No," she said, and turned and ran, Frankie flying behind her.

*****

Mab walked through the Dream Cream past Cindy, slinging ice cream to a full house, and upstairs to Cindy's living room. She sat down on the couch, shaking, while Frankie did his version of a comforting coo from her shoulder. Okay, so Joe was a demon and since he was

Fufluns, the trickster, he'd probably been playing her and didn't love her at all, *duh,* and . . .

That was the part where she started to cry.

"You okay?" Cindy said, closing the door behind her. "You look like hell."

Mab swallowed her tears. "Bad day."

Cindy leaned against the window. "Want to talk about it?"

Mab frowned at her, trying to find irritation instead of grief. "Aren't you slammed downstairs?"

"That's what the student help is for. And you look like your dog died."

"He did," Mab said, her lip quivering. "The son of a bitch."

Cindy sat down next to her. "Spill it."

"Joe turned out to be Dave possessed by a demon, so I've been sleeping with a drunk all week. Joe, who is really a demon named Fufluns, has been possessing other people and sleeping with other people the whole time, so there goes my great love affair. Delpha passed on her second sight to me—it was real—along with her bird, only I can't control it—the sight, not the bird—so I see things I shouldn't see, don't want to see. Half the time it's awful, the things I know, the things I have to tell them. That's how I found out about Joe. He came in to get me for dinner and I took his hand and saw . . . all of it. And I still love the dumb son of a bitch, so how pathetic am I?" She swallowed a sob. "Oh, and I think my uncle tried to poison me today, unless you sent me herbal tea."

"No, I didn't," Cindy said.

Mab nodded. "It's been a bad day."

"Wow."

"I know, I don't believe it, either."

"I believe it."

Mab turned to look at her in the dim light. "What?"

"Well, Joe did look an awful lot like Drunk Dave, but it wasn't Drunk Dave, so demon possession is a good explanation. And Delpha did have second sight, and she left everything to you, so it makes sense the sight would go to you, too. Joe cheating sucks, I thought he was better than that, but he's a demon, so the odds were always against you on that one. What else was there? Oh, Ray. Well, I always thought he was kind of creepy, but I never thought he was murderer."

"Ray wants to inherit my share of the park," Mab said. "Although to be fair, he tried to buy it first. You know, he's right, I should make a will. I'll leave everything to you. Then maybe he'll stop trying to kill me. Did you know the park was a demon keep?"

"A what?"

"A prison for demons. There are five of them imprisoned here. Were imprisoned. Two are out."

"No, I didn't know," Cindy said, looking a little stunned. "How did I miss that?"

"They haven't escaped in forty years. There was nothing for you to see." She frowned. "Although I think Fufluns gets out more. He would." She shook her head. "And Tura's out now, too. Plus the park is full of these little ratty minion demons. You know what they call the five big demons? The Untouchables. *And I touched one.*"

Frankie cawed and stepped from foot to foot, digging lightly into her shoulder.

"Okay, let's be calm," Cindy said. "You're starting to sound like that nut job who used to picket the park."

"That was my mother."

"Okay, so moving past that." Cindy nodded. "Delpha's gone. That puts them down a demon fighter, right?"

"Yeah, and I'm supposed to step up."

"And you don't want to?"

Mab started to say *I just want to be normal,* and then stopped. Maybe she didn't. Today had been awful, the whole week had been awful, but if somebody said, "Okay, you can hand it all over to somebody else now," would she give up Frankie and the sight?

Give up Dreamland?

"I don't know."

"Yeah, you do." Cindy put her arm around her. "If you don't know, then you know. Because if you didn't want to, you'd say, 'I don't want it.' You're always sure. So if you're not sure—"

"Oh, hell." Mab put her face in her hands. "There's more stuff out there, Joe knows something he's not telling me. No, Fufluns knows stuff he's not telling me. I ran away from him, but . . . I should have stayed. I should have gotten some answers." She sniffed. "Of course, he's a *liar*."

"Makes sense. He's a demon."

"Yeah, but he's *my* demon, the son of a bitch. And he owes me some answers."

"So go get them." Cindy drew back. "Unless you're afraid of him. I mean, you know, *demon*."

"I'm not afraid of him," Mab said. "I'm afraid of what he'll tell me. People have been telling me a lot of stuff lately, and none of it has been good."

"Yeah," Cindy said. "I'm not envying you so much anymore. Normal is looking good right now."

Mab nodded. "Now that I've found out what love really can do, I'm not envying me, either."

"So what are you going to do?"

"I'm gonna go ask him what he's not telling me," Mab said, and headed for the door, Frankie protesting on her shoulder.

*****

Since the chances were excellent that Fufluns had gone where the easy people were, Mab headed to the Beer Pavilion and looked around until she saw Joe talking with Laura Ferris Wheel. Frankie flew up to sit on the edge of the roof, and she started toward Joe and then realized just from the way he moved that he wasn't Joe, he was Drunk Dave, dispossessed.

You've had some of the best times you'll never remember with me, Dave, Mab thought, and then Dave looked up and saw her watching him and waved at her tentatively, and she realized he was sober, the glass in front of him just soda water.

Good for you, Mab thought, and looked around the rest of the crowd. It was impossible, she'd never find Fufluns—

And then there he was, in a dark-haired guy in a blue-striped park shirt this time, leaning toward a dark-haired girl who was giggling. Mab wasn't sure how she knew it was him, but she did—maybe the crooked grin, the angle of his head, the way his body moved, maybe it was just because it was *him*—and she crossed the floor to stand in front of him and recognized the guy he was possessing: Sam, the maintenance guy from the front gate.

He looked up, that crooked smile on his face, and then he saw that it was her, and his face lit up.

"Mab!"

"I need to talk to you," Mab said, tamping down any impulse to be glad that he was glad to see her. "Alone."

He stood up so fast, the girl with him rocked back a little.

"Hey," she said, losing her giggle to glare at Mab.

"Keep smiling, he'll be back," Mab said, and turned and walked across the room and out through the archway Frankie was perched on, Joe—not Joe—following her. As he went past the jukebox, "What Love Can Do" started to play.

Funny, Mab thought. Real fucking funny.

When she got outside, the temperature dropped twenty degrees. *Good*, she thought, and turned around to find him right behind her.

"Let me buy you a beer," he said, "and we'll—"

"No. This is not a social call. Hell, I don't even know what to call you."

" 'Joe' works for me."

He moved closer and she wanted to back away, but he was warm and the night was cold, so she stood her ground, even though Frankie cawed down a warning. "It doesn't work for me. You're not Joe. Joe was a lie. You're not even Sam. That was you that day at the gate with the statue, wasn't it? That wasn't Sam, that was you possessing Sam."

"Okay, fine, go with Fun. That's what you called me when I first met you, when you came to fix my statue." He smiled down at her. "That was when I—"

"Fun," Mab said. "Wonderful. Listen, you demon bastard, you let Tura out, Glenda told me you let her out."

He laughed. "All Tura wants is a good time."

"She killed Dead Karl."

"So? Nobody misses Karl. He was a liar and a cheat."

"So are you."

"Yes," Fun said patiently. "But people would miss me."

Mab bit back the impulse to say, *I wouldn't.* That would be a lie and there had been enough lies. People *would* miss him; the bastard radiated joy and happiness and . . .

"I don't want to lose you, Mab," he said, and his voice sounded honest even though he wasn't. "I think—"

"What did you think you were doing?" she asked, hating it that there was so much hurt in her voice. "How could you tell me all those lies?"

He sighed. "Because saying 'Hi, I'm a demon and I've been crazy about you since you spent a week painting every part of my body' didn't seem like a good approach."

"But 'Hi, I'm Dave's cousin, Joe, the demon hunter' did?"

"It worked."

"Not for long."

"I wasn't looking for long," Fun said. "Although I didn't expect you to figure it out this fast."

"I'm going to have to catch you—," Mab said, her voice breaking.

"Honey, I'm not running," Fun said, opening his arms.

Frankie sent up a rant as Mab finished, "—and put you in that damn chalice, I have to fix your chalice and put you back in it."

"We should talk about that."

He tried to put his arm around her, and Frankie flew down to her shoulder as she stepped away, hating how hard it was to step away.

"You're a demon," she said. "I've seen the flash in your eyes, I thought it was firelight, but I can see it now, and I know, you're a *demon.*"

He crossed his arms, looking annoyed. "Well, I've seen the flash in yours, too, honey, and I'm not passing judgment."

Mab scowled at him. "What are you talking about?"

He hesitated, and then he uncrossed his arms and smiled at her, and she thought, *Here comes a lie.*

"I looked in your eyes and I saw the flash of love," Fun said, and underneath it she could hear him thinking, *Don't tell her, don't tell her.*

Mab stepped closer, fury rising, as Frankie flapped up off her shoulder to sit on the roof line above them, screaming his head off. "If you want me to loathe you forever, just keep lying to me. Liars are selfish, arrogant, cowardly bastards who think that they can deceive and use people to get what they want. They hurt people."

"I'm a *demon*," Fun said.

"You were also my friend and lover and I deserved better." She sniffed and hated herself for it.

"Oh, hell, Mab," Fun said, sliding down the side of the Pavilion to sit on the cold, hard ground. "Does everything have to be so serious?"

"Yes," Mab said. "My whole world is inside out, I don't know what's real anymore, and I need to find solid ground to stand on. The only way I can do that is to find out the truth, all the truths, and if you know something, then you're a selfish pig not to tell me. I don't want anything from you but the truth. I don't even want to put you back in your box, although I will help Ethan do it if you let any of the others loose, I swear to god, I will."

"I don't want anybody else out," Fun said. "Vanth and Selvans will free that psychopath Kharos and all the good times will be over."

"What makes you think Tura won't set Kharos free?" Mab said, exasperated.

"Tura has her own plans." Fun looked up at her. "You know, you and Tura should get along. She hates liars and cheats, too."

"She *kills* them," Mab said. "And she's not too damn careful about her selection process. She tried to kill Ethan, and he wasn't even with anybody. She has to go back in the box."

"I'm not stopping you." Fun held up his hand as Mab opened her mouth again. "And I won't let her out again. She's getting crazier every century."

"Well, thank you for noticing," Mab said. "Now what the hell are you talking about, this flash you saw?"

"Let it go, Mab," Fun said, serious now.

Mab swallowed. "Why are you stalling? What was so bad?"

Fun sat silent for a moment and then said, "I saw a demon flash." When she frowned, he said, "The thing you see in the eyes of the possessed that tells you one of us is in there. I saw a glow in your eyes."

Mab drew back. "I was *possessed*?"

"No, I'd have known that." Fun got up. "Just the glow, that's all. Don't worry about it. You're not a demon and you're not possessed, so what difference does it make?" His voice softened. "I'm sorry I lied, although I can't promise you it won't happen again. But I'll do my damnedest not to hurt you again. Let's have a beer and talk this out—"

"And then have makeup sex? No," Mab said, although it sounded damn good. "If I wasn't possessed, why were my eyes glowing?"

"I don't know," Fun said. "My guess is, you're a little bit human and a little bit rock and roll."

"What?"

"Human and demon. Remember what you told me, that you felt you'd finally found your kind with me? Well, maybe you did, demon girl." He grinned at her again. "Welcome to the dark side."

"I don't believe it," Mab said, but she didn't step back. *Demon girl. Demon spawn.*

"Yeah, you do," Fun said, and there was sympathy in his voice. "You just don't want to. It doesn't make any difference, Mab. You're still you. If that's what it is, you've been part demon all your life. The only difference is, now you know."

"Oh god," Mab said, as the truth sank in. "Everybody was right. I really am weird."

"You're an amazing woman, Mary Alice." Fun took a step closer, and then after a moment, put his arms around her. "You just didn't know how amazing."

"What kind of flash was it?" Mab said into his chest, really needing him, even if Frankie was cawing like crazy above. "I know they're different colors, what was it?"

"Blue, I think. I don't know, there wasn't any blood in Drunk Dave's brain, so it was hard to focus."

"Blue," Mab said.

"It goes red when you're mad," Fun said.

Mab pulled away. "Red. This is *not happening*."

"Sure it is," Fun said. "Might as well accept it and learn to use it. You've got a lot of power there, you know. Be dumb to ignore it because you don't like where it came from."

"From demons?"

"Just like you, honey. And now, if you're not going to cheer up, I have a brunette to make happy."

Ouch, she thought, but it didn't matter, she was done with him, it had all been a lie, none of it meant anything.

Ouch, ouch. OUCH.

He paused. "Tell you what. As a makeup gift. You see that platinum blonde over there?" He pointed.

Laura Ferris Wheel was standing in the archway, inside a circle of appreciative men, one of whom was Ray. She didn't seem to be appreciating what he was telling her.

"That's Tura's ride for the night. Don't worry, she won't do anything until the park is empty and as close to midnight as she can make it. She likes the bodies found when she's far away." He kissed her cheek. "Give me a call if you need a laugh."

"Hell will freeze over."

"I'd like that," he said, and went back inside the Pavilion to the brunette, and Mab stood outside in the cold and the dark and thought, *No, no, no,* as the tears filled her eyes again.

He was going to make love to another woman, her great love affair was over, she was part demon, and her mother had been right.

I need a drink, she thought, and went back in the Pavilion and headed for the bar. She could watch Tura and get tanked at the same time. Efficient.

I don't care what he does. And I am not a demon.

She ordered a beer.

*****

Weaver had left the park, mollified by sex and a vial of Ethan's blood, one of which Ethan had been glad to give her, the other not so much. "Now I know you trust me," she said and went off as happy as he'd ever seen her, so it was a small price to pay, depending on what she did with it. He patrolled the park after that until ten, when he got a call from Glenda. When he went to her trailer, she handed him a flask and said, "Go get Mab. Gus just called and said she's drunk in the Pavilion." By the time he got to the bar, Mab had five empty cups lined up in front of her and was finishing her sixth.

"Gimme another," Mab said, and Shannon looked past her to Ethan, who shook his head.

Shannon moved away.

"Hey!" Mab said, craning to see where she was going.

Ethan sat down beside her.

"So," he said, looking at the empty cups in exasperation. "This isn't good."

"I am drowning my sorrows," Mab said, enunciating clearly.

"How's that going?"

"Not too well." She gazed at the empty cups sadly. "The little suckers are buoyant as all hell."

"That's a shame," Ethan said. "Glenda said you're going to join us tonight. Sober would be good for that."

Mab narrowed her eyes. "You have a flask, right?"

Ethan stood up. "Come with me."

"Okay." Mab stood up but her knees didn't, and Ethan caught her before she hit the floor. "You're right, this is not good."

"Yep." Ethan steered her past the mostly oblivious crowd—only one guy in black-rimmed glasses watching them go—through one of the Pavilion arches and out into the chilly darkness, and then around the corner to the blue-painted cement-block men's restroom. Frankie flew down to sit on the edge of the roof, cawing at them in reproof, probably mad at Mab for being drunk.

"Come into my office," Ethan said, opening the blue door.

"This is your office? This is the men's room." Mab let him steer her inside and looked around, bleary-eyed. "You know, no matter what I did to this place, it still looked like a men's room."

"That's because it's a men's room." Ethan took a wood sign that said CLOSED off the wall and put it on the outside of the door and then shut it and locked the door. "Now. What happened that made you—" He looked at her in distaste. "—do this? Talk."

"Flask," Mab said, holding out her hand.

Ethan pulled out Glenda's flask and extended it. "It's Glenda's. You might want to go slow."

Mab snapped her fingers at him. "I can handle anything Glenda can drink."

"Go for it," Ethan said, and she unscrewed the top and tilted it to her lips, taking a good long slug of it.

She barely made it inside one of the stalls before she lost it, and he winced as he heard her heave again and again.

Then she came back out, looking like crap, her red hair sticking to the sweat on her forehead, and handed him back the flask, wiping her mouth on the back of her hand. "What the hell was that?"

"Glenda's anti-drunk recipe." Ethan screwed the top back on the flask and put it away. "So talk."

Mab went over to the sink and cupped her hand under the faucet. She drank several times and spit it out, and then she turned the faucet off, putting her hand on the wall to steady herself. "Jesus." She looked around the room. "There's no place to sit. Well, except for . . ." She frowned at him. "Why are we here?"

"It's lined with iron. No demons. Found that out today from Gus. I figure they made this as a demon bunker in case someone needed to escape if demons were rampaging in the park. Pretty smart."

"Oh." Mab sniffed. "You're wrong about the no demons in here, though."

Her lip quivered, and he could see her eyes go bright with tears.

"No crying," Ethan said, alarmed. "Just talk."

"Okay, wait a minute. I'll have to get emotional to show you." Mab shut her eyes and screwed up her face. "I'm mad," she said, talking to herself. "I'm really, really mad."

Then her face crumpled and tears started, and Ethan thought, *Oh, great.* Every minute with Mab made him appreciate Weaver more.

He should probably tell Weaver that.

"I love him," Mab said, trying to wipe the tears away and crying harder. "I know it's ridiculous to love somebody you've only known a week, I didn't really know him at all, but I love him and I ache for him even though I wouldn't have him back as a gift—"

"So this is about Joe," Ethan said helpfully, thinking *Kill me now.*

"I was just so *happy* with him," Mab said, just letting the tears go now. "I finally belonged with somebody, he understood me, you know? And then . . ." She threw her hands up and cried on, an emotional mess. "And now it's *gone*—"

"Uh, sorry," Ethan said. "Look, kid—"

"No," she said, gulping in air around her tears. "*I'm* sorry." She leaned against the mirror and cried harder. "I'm sorry I've been a fool, and now I'm in trouble, and I wanted to be angry so you could see, but I'm no good at emotions and that's all his fault, too, I never even *had* emotions until I met him, and now I'm just so *miserable*. . . ."

She opened her eyes, blubbering, and Ethan stepped back.

They were glowing blue, unnatural blue, *Children of the Damned* blue.

"What's wrong?" Mab said, blinking back tears.

Fuck, he thought, and knew what he had to do.

CHAPTER 15

"What?" Mab said.

Ethan pointed to the mirror, and she turned and saw the same thing he did: thick, straight red hair, tearstained cheeks, glowing blue eyes . . .

"Huh," she said and tilted her head, her tears stopping.

It was the irises, Ethan realized. It would have been really freaky if the white had been blue, too, but with the radioactive glowing, it all came down to the same thing.

"You're possessed," he told her, his voice preternaturally calm. "Don't panic. We can fix this."

"No, I'm not," Mab said, sniffing again.

Ethan came closer, hoping he could catch her when the demon jumped into him. *"Capio!"*

"I'm not possessed."

"Capio!"

"No, really."

"Capio, damn it!"

She blinked at him, annoyed, practically back to normal except for the dirty tear tracks on her scowling face. "Ethan, I'm the only one in here. It's just me. Stop yelling Latin at me, I'm having a bad day."

"What the hell is that in your eyes?"

"That is the question." She swallowed hard. "I might be part demon."

Part demon. Right. "No, you're not. But you're right, you're not possessed, either, since you're inside an iron men's room. Sorry about the capio. Had to try it." He frowned at her, trying to think what it could be. "Stop crying. You're not a demon."

"Well, then, what's that?" She turned to look in the mirror as her eyes faded back to brown. "What was that? I think it's demon spirit, and it's mine. I'm a demon." She sniffed. "My mother always said I was demon spawn."

"Your mother was a whack job. When did this happen?"

"I don't know." Mab sniffed again. "I just found out about it, but other people have noticed."

"What other people?"

"Joe."

"Joe." Ethan nodded. "And he didn't think that was strange." *Maybe that's why he left?*

"Joe isn't Joe. Joe is Drunk Dave possessed by Fufluns. Or was. He's in Sam now."

"What?" Ethan turned for the door, thinking fast. "Where is he?"

"In the Pavilion flirting with some bimbo. Tura's out there, too. She's in that bimbo blonde Laura Ferris Wheel." Mab sniffed again. "You know, for a small town, we have a high percentage of bimbos."

"Forget the bimbos," Ethan said, exasperated. "We have to get the demons. Starting with Fufluns."

"How?" Mab said. "Don't you need his chalice repaired first?"

"Yes," Ethan said, feeling annoyed.

"Well, Gus hasn't given me the missing pieces yet. So Fun's out for a while." Mab wiped the last of the tears from her cheeks. "He's not killing anybody, he's just having a lot of sex." The tears started again. *"Bastard."*

Stop crying, for the love of god. "So you slept with the demon and got this flash thing?"

Mab jerked her head up, red light flashing in her eyes. "It's not an STD, Ethan. I didn't get demon cooties. It's part of *me*."

Red light. That couldn't be good. "Do you feel different?"

"What do you mean, *different*?" Mab said. "My eyes glow blue. That makes me feel creepy."

"I mean, do you have any . . . urges?"

"Urges?" Mab looked at him incredulous, the red light flickering stronger in her eyes. "Like what? Do I want to eat your brains? No, no urges." She exhaled in exasperation. "Although I wouldn't mind slapping the shit out of you right now for asking such *dumbass questions*."

Ethan nodded. This was better than crying. A little. He could do without the red light. "So you're not feeling evil at the moment?"

Her irises went solid red. "Of course not. What is wrong with you?"

"When you get really mad, the light in your eyes changes to red," Ethan said. "It looks like the same kind of flash I saw in Tura's eyes. Different color. Why do you have two different colors?"

"I don't know, Ethan," Mab snapped. "Maybe I'm a human mood ring. And now my mood is *pissed off*!"

"That would be my guess," Ethan said. "Red for anger. Not very original."

"Are you saying that to make me mad, or because you're terminally tactless?"

"So what is it?" Ethan said. "If there's not somebody in there with you, and you're not a demon, what the hell is it?"

"I don't know," Mab said, her face crumpling again.

"It's okay," Ethan said, and then, not sure what to do, he put his arm around her tentatively and patted her. "We'll figure it out. You're not a demon. You passed the men's room test. You're just . . . special."

"Special," Mab said, holding on to his shirt, which was getting damper by the minute. "That's the nice name for weird, isn't it?"

Ethan patted her some more. "We'll figure it out, and we'll fix it. Glenda might have an idea."

"Glenda will put me in a box," Mab wailed.

"Nobody's putting you in a box," Ethan said, trying to keep the exasperation out of his voice. "Although that asshole you've been sleeping with is going down."

"Bad choice of words," Mab said. "I feel sick."

"You want to throw up again, this is the place," Ethan said, still patting.

"I really love him." Her lip quivered. "This is what love can do, it makes you want to throw up."

"You'll get over him," Ethan said. "There'll be somebody better. Can't you see the future?"

"Not like that," Mab said. "I can see a couple of guys headed over this way to use the john, but I can't see my Second True Love coming for me. Besides, Delpha told me that Joe was my one true love and she was never wrong. I'm doomed to love him *forever*."

"Yeah, sure." Ethan gave her shoulder one last pat and edged her toward the door. "Come on. Let's go capture Tura; that'll make you feel better. And if you see that bastard Fufluns on the way, let me know and I'll capio his ass."

"You don't have any place to put him," Mab said as he opened the door.

"Glenda's got some Tupperware," Ethan said. "He can share space with some tuna until Gus finds the pieces to his box."

"He likes fish," Mab said. "At least he likes that damn mermaid. I hate fish. Fish are killer sluts."

"Good to know," Ethan said, rolling his eyes behind her, and motioned her out the door.

*****

Ethan gathered his team behind the Roundabout, not sure they were all going to make it. Weaver was geared up and alert; Glenda was tense; Gus was excited and worried, fumbling with the chalice; Young Fred was drinking from a beer hidden underneath his coat; and Mab, dry-eyed and half-sober now, was watching everybody and everything, reminding him of Delpha, since she was wrapped in that blue shawl with Frankie on her shoulder.

An hour later, Weaver was still alert, Glenda was more relaxed, Gus was asleep, and Young Fred was mournful about his empty beer bottle.

Mab was still watching everybody.

"You okay?" he said to her.

"No," she said. "Are you?"

"No."

"Well, there you are."

He was about ready to call it a night. The park had closed, so it was almost empty of people, the Tunnel of Love had shut down twenty minutes ago with no sign of Tura in the blonde, and his team was less than ready. Maybe they'd gotten a break and could get in a day of training—

A woman's laugh echoed out of the darkness as two figures passed underneath an orange glowing light coming from the direction of the Devil's Drop.

"Got anything?" he asked Weaver, and she nodded.

"I see a francium trace," she said.

"What?" Mab said.

"Francium." Weaver smiled at her, not warmly. "Demons are made of it. The goggles select for francium, which means I can see demons with them."

"How nice for you," Mab said, shifting a little so that she was standing behind Glenda.

"Tura's an Untouchable," Glenda said. "Does your technology work on them?"

"In our experience, all demons are essentially the same," Weaver said. "Francium and evil form their base structure, which is why hitting them with iron, the most stable element, destroys them—"

"Shhh," Ethan said.

The figures were passing them now, leaning on each other. The tall blonde and a shorter, frumpy guy.

"Recognize her?" Ethan whispered to Glenda.

"Crap," Glenda said, worry in her voice. "That's Laura Ferris Wheel."

Weaver frowned at Ethan. "Laura Ferris Wheel?"

"Her people run the Ferris Wheel."

"She's a good girl," Glenda said.

"She isn't now," Ethan said as he saw Laura Ferris Wheel lead the man toward the Tunnel of Love.

"Recognize the guy?" Ethan asked.

"Some cheating schmuck," Glenda said tiredly. "They always are."

The lights outside the Tunnel went on without anyone entering the control booth. The schmuck didn't appear to notice as Tura led him up the ramp to the first swan boat.

"All right," Ethan said. "Just as we planned. We're going in."

"Not with Weaver." Glenda stepped in front of him. "Ethan, it's wrong to bring non-Guardia on a capture. It's *dangerous*."

Weaver hefted her demon gun. "Just give me a chance. I'll stay out of the way until I'm needed, but you're better off with me as backup."

Glenda and Mab looked at each other, and Weaver rolled her eyes and turned back to Ethan.

Oh, good, Ethan thought. Catfight.

Tura and the schmuck got into the boat, and Ethan heard the loud, echoing clang as the hook engaged and the boat began to move.

"Let's go," he said, and they headed out, around the right side of the heap of ugly pink concrete housing the Tunnel. Ethan pulled open the access door and led them all behind the dioramas to Antony and Cleopatra, where Frankie flew into the diorama and tried to eat a grape on Cleo's table.

"That's not an eyeball," Mab whispered to him.

Gus held up Tura's chalice and said, "I'm ready," and Young Fred nodded as his face began to shiver and change.

The swan appeared around the first bend, Tura leaning into the man, her hands all over him, whispering into his ear.

Young Fred's face solidified into Dead Karl's, and he stepped to the edge of the waterway. Tura looked up and saw him, shock crossing her face, blue-green flashing in her eyes.

"Frustro!" Young Fred called out and Mab said, "Uh, specto."

Ethan thought, *Oh, for fuck's sake,* as the blue-green glowed stronger in Tura's eyes.

"What the hell?" the guy with her said, looking from the diorama to his date as the swan floated by.

"Specto!" Mab said louder, and threw her fist toward the glow, and Tura laughed an unearthly laugh.

The guy with her drew back as the boat floated on. "What the *hell?*"

"I know you," Tura said, looking back at Mab, contempt thick in her voice. "Demon-lover."

Mab ran after the boat, catching up to it, her face furious as she snarled, "I said *Specto! you bitch,*" and flung her hand, pointed like a spear directly at the light in Tura, just as Weaver fired, the light writhing out of Laura a fraction of a second before Weaver's round hit her. The light expanded and crystallized into a mermaid, full-lipped, long-haired, and voluptuous, frozen in surprise against the wall as the swan boat floated on, taking an unconscious, wounded Laura and a terrified schmuck around the bend.

"What the hell are you doing?" Mab yelled at Weaver as Ethan stepped in front of them and said, *"Capio,"* and sucked the blue-green mermaid into him, sure this time of how to capture. He felt Tura grab his heart, shrieking, and the pain was terrible, but he caught her, held her, conquered her, not even feeling the bullet inside him anymore, and then he turned as if in slow motion toward Gus, who held out the chalice.

Glenda put her hand on his shoulder and said, *"Redimio,"* and he felt Tura flow out of him, blessed relief, and toward the chalice.

Gus stepped forward with the lid, but the demon shifted and rushed into Glenda, the force of the possession slamming her off the walkway and into the water to the bottom of the tank.

Then the blue-green shot up from the water again and Mab yelled, *"SPECTO!"* and the mermaid took form, squirming furiously, and Ethan yelled, "Capio!" and took her, and this time, he grabbed on to Gus, and tried to expel the demon himself as she went for his heart.

*****

"Glenda!" Mab said, but Weaver already had her body out of the water and was starting CPR. Mab looked back at Ethan, seeing the furious spirit struggling inside him, along with something else wrapped around it, something red and hot and strong, and then Weaver stopped compressing, and Mab bent and breathed into Glenda's mouth twice, trying to put more than just breath in there.

"I think she's gone," Weaver said, her voice sick.

"No," Mab said. *"Glenda!"* She shook her, and Glenda's head rolled back, her eyes staring sightlessly at the roof of the tunnel. "No, no, *no.*" Mab began to pump, and Weaver said, "Let me," and went back to doing a professional job while Mab bent over Glenda and said, "You are not dead. You. Are. Not. *Dead.*"

Frankie flew down to land on a fake tree branch above her, and for a moment Mab had double vision, staring at Glenda and staring at herself staring at Glenda. She shook her head to clear it, and thought, *Delpha said you can see things, that you had to look hard.* She stared into Glenda's dead eyes, reaching inside her instinctively, searching for a spark, a memory, anything that was alive, and found it, a small point of tension, as if Glenda's spirit was holding on by just that thread even though her body had died.

Mab latched on to that spark. Come on, Glenda, come on, you don't want to die, you're not ready to die, come on, you have so much to live for—

And then Ethan was there beside them, breathing two breaths into his mother's mouth, taking over the chest compressions as Weaver moved back, but he looked sick.

Maybe because he knew she was dead.

Mab leaned down to Glenda's ear. "You get your ass back here," she whispered. "If you don't, Weaver is going to fuck up the Guardia forever."

The point of tension seemed to grow a little tighter, as if Glenda's spirit was clenching its fist.

Ethan kept pumping.

Mab whispered again. "She's going to drag Ethan back to the military, do demon experiments on him."

The point turned into a knot, glowing now.

"And she's probably gonna be the mother of your grandchildren. Think how badly she's going to fuck *them* up."

The knot exploded, and Glenda gasped and sat up, wide-eyed and shaking, as Ethan fell back.

"Don't do that again," Mab said as she held on to her, tears in her eyes. "You scared *the hell* out of us."

"Medevac chopper is on the way," Weaver said from behind them, and then her voice changed. "She's *alive*?"

"Chopper?" Mab said.

"Thank *god,*" Weaver said. "We'll get her to the hospital at Wright Pat. Top priority—"

"No!" Glenda said, and Ethan put his arm around her and said, "Easy, Mom, you need—"

She pushed him away. "I am not going to a hospital, and I am sure as hell not going to a military hospital." She glared at Weaver. "I know what you're doing, the same thing you want to do with Ethan. You're not getting me into some Area 52 experimental lab."

"Department 51," Weaver said, taken aback. "And I wasn't—"

"No," Glenda said, and Mab could feel her spirit trembling as she said it.

"Okay, that's it." Mab stood up. "Glenda, you calm down. Weaver worked like crazy to save your life, she's on our side. Weaver, stand down. Glenda's not going anywhere in any helicopter." She looked at Weaver. "It's a black helicopter, isn't it?"

"Yes," Weaver said, annoyed now. "What the hell does that have to do with anything?"

"Just checking my work." Mab held out her hand to Glenda and helped her to her feet. "You really should let me call 911. You just *died,* for Christ's sake."

Glenda leaned on her, white-faced and shaking. "No helicopter. No military." She looked at Ethan. "Tura?"

"We got her," Ethan said, and behind him Gus held up the chalice, looking like hell. "I don't know how, but it's over, she didn't kill the schmuck. We need to make sure Laura's all right."

"I'll go see." Gus shoved the chalice into Ethan's hand and hurried out of the tunnel.

Glenda slumped against Mab.

"Okay," Mab said, holding her up. "We're going back to the trailers. Fred?"

Young Fred appeared from behind Weaver, looking shaken.

"Go get a golf cart. We have to get Glenda back home."

"You bet," he said, and ran down the tunnel to the opening, only to come back right away. "There's a helicopter out there."

"Tell it to go away," Mab said, and Weaver said, "You prefer a golf cart to a medevac? What's wrong with you people?" and strode down the tunnel.

"Lovely woman," Mab said to Ethan.

"She has a point," Ethan said, looking at his mother with concern, the chalice tucked under his arm. "You should be in a hospital," he told her. "You should—"

"I want Mab," Glenda said. "She'll know." She pulled away and held out her right hand. "Tell me. Am I going to die?"

"Eventually," Mab said. "Stop being such a drama queen. One near-death experience and you're acting like a diva."

Glenda gave her the old don't-fuck-with-me look.

"Welcome back, Glenda," Mab said, feeling a little teary about getting glared at again. "Left hand. This is about the heart, remember?"

Glenda held out her left hand, and Mab put her palm down on it.

A fluttery heartbeat growing stronger, sun shining, Glenda laughing in front of the Statue of Liberty.

"Huh," Mab said.

"Am I going to make it?" Glenda said.

"Unless Heaven has a Statue of Liberty, yes."

"Then I'm going back to my trailer," Glenda said, just as Young Fred came back and said, "I've got the golf cart."

Glenda took an unsteady step toward him, and he put his arm around her for support. "Come on, old lady, you ain't dead yet."

"Call me an old lady again and you will be," Glenda said, but she leaned on him just the same.

"I'll stay the night with her," Mab told Ethan. "But then we have to talk. There are so many things wrong here—"

"*I'll* stay the night with her," Ethan said, and after a moment, she nodded. "The high-tech stuff will work, we just have to figure out how."

"The tech is crap," Mab said, and went out into the cool night air.

A helicopter lifted off as she hit the midway, and Weaver stood looking after it, mad as hell, as Glenda got into the golf cart.

Ethan walked over to Weaver and put a hand on her shoulder, and she turned to him, furious. "I'm going with Glenda," he said. "I'll talk to you later."

Then he got into the golf cart with his mother and set off down the midway, Weaver watching him in stony silence.

"I don't know him very well," Mab said to her. "But I think he's a good guy. Tonight was just a mess all around, but he's doing his best—"

"He wants me to give everything while he gives nothing," Weaver said. "My job is on the line here, he needs this equipment, but—"

"Just give him a chance," Mab said. "We have to figure this out, but the two of you seem really good together—"

Weaver turned away, and Mab watched her walk off into the darkness, carrying her stupid gun.

"Don't blow this," she called after her. "He's a good guy."

Unlike the cheating bastard demon I had to go and fall for.

On the other hand, Glenda was alive. And now that she'd stopped fighting it, living the rest of her life in Dreamland didn't sound that bad. It wasn't like she'd *married* Fun or done anything irrevocable, she'd only known him a week, how bad could it be—?

Frankie flew down to rest on Mab's shoulder.

"I'd take him back," she told the raven. "If he wasn't a demon, I'd take him back."

Frankie did the closest thing to an eye roll she'd ever seen in a bird.

"Right. So tomorrow we move to Delpha's trailer so we can keep an eye on Gus and Glenda. You'll be back in your nest by this time tomorrow night."

Frankie cawed, a cheese grater on a fire escape, and Mab smiled at the beautiful sound, full of approval and love.

"Yeah, that seems right to me, too," she said, and headed for the Dream Cream.

*****

Ray sat down on the bench and said, "I found Tura and told her what you said, and she wasn't happy about it, but she let the Guardia take her. She's back in her chalice."

TAKE THE CHALICE TO THE KEEP BEFORE SHE ESCAPES AGAIN.

"Tura killed Glenda."

GLENDA.

"But then Mab brought her back."

MAB IS YOUR NIECE.

"Yeah. She's not dead, either. I think she's Delpha's replacement."

Too many young Guardia now. Too resilient. Not enough despair. BRING MORE MINIONS.

"Okay, maybe you didn't notice this, but the minions are not effective."

SEND THEM TO HARASS THE GUARDIA UNTIL HALLOWEEN. THEN AT ONE MINUTE AFTER MIDNIGHT ON HALLOWEEN, DIVIDE THEM INTO FIVE GROUPS AND SEND THEM TO KILL EACH OF THE GUARDIA SEPARATELY AND SIMULTANEOUSLY.

"That's a lot of minions."

The front section of Ray's hair fell out, leaving him with a very high forehead.

"Right," Ray said tiredly. "Minions harrying all week, killing all five at once after midnight Friday. So we're not protecting Glenda anymore?"

GLENDA IS NO LONGER GUARDIA. Kharos paused for a moment, regretting the loss of all that beautiful power. She'd been . . . delicious.

"So okay," Ray said. "The demons go after the Guardia on Saturday—"

THROW THEM INTO CHAOS. GRIND THEM WITH GRIEF AT THEIR LOSSES SO THEY ARE AS DUST.

"Sure. Oh, I found out that Mab's going to repair Fufluns' chalice so they can recapture him. It's not a high priority, though. Ethan's a lot more worried about Glenda dying than he is about Fufluns."

Kharos stared down at Ray. He was getting a lot of very good information about the Guardia very quickly.

How was Ray getting such good information?

Ray stood up. "So I'll go get the minions—"

CALL YOUR PARTNER TO ME.

"What?" Ray said, cautious now.

I WISH TO MEET THE TRAITOR WHO IS HELPING YOU. SOMEONE IS TELLING YOU THINGS ONLY THE GUARDIA COULD KNOW. YOU HAVE SUBORNED SOMEONE WITHIN.

"Well," Ray said.

CALL THIS TRAITOR TO ME.

"He's not going to be happy. He's doing this because he wants to retire, not because he hates the Guardia. And frankly, he's not of my quality. You're going to be disappointed when you meet him—"

CALL HIM.

"Right," Ray said, and dialed his cell phone.

Ten minutes later, Kharos stared out at a stripling.

YOU WISH TO RETIRE?

"I just want out," Young Fred said, looking unsure. "You need to be free, we need to be free, it's a no-brainer. I set you free and nobody gets hurt, right?"

YOU'RE ALL GOING TO DIE, Kharos thought, but he said, RIGHT.

Behind Young Fred, Ray rolled his eyes.

HERE'S WHAT I NEED YOU TO DO, Kharos said.

CHAPTER 16

"You rest," Ethan said to Glenda as soon as they were in her trailer. "Just . . . sit down."

Glenda sank down onto the red banquette, still a little rocky, and Ethan got the scotch from the cupboard, poured out a good slug, and drank it.

Then he looked at his mother. "You scared the hell out of me." Glenda nodded jerkily. "I scared the hell out of me." She found her cigarette pack and took one out, and then stared at it. "Death. That'll make you think."

Ethan sat across from her with the bottle and his glass. "That was too close, too close to losing you, too close to not getting Tura. We have to do better." He poured himself another slug.

"Not 'we,' " Glenda said. "I don't think I'm Guardia anymore."

Ethan's hand paused with the glass halfway to his mouth. "What?"

Glenda spread her fingers out, concentrating—"Come on, burn," she said—but they stayed just fingers, no little flames sprouting from the tips, and she folded her hand again, looking disconcerted but not unhappy. "I think I died and somebody else was called." She smiled, and she suddenly looked twenty years younger, if still a little shaky. "I feel . . . different. Lighter." She pointed to Ethan's glass. "Except for that, which depresses the hell out of me."

Ethan closed his eyes.

"You have to stop drinking," she said, and when he pulled back, she said, "Ethan, life is too short to waste. You have to stop taking the easy way out. That's why you brought Weaver in, big gun, big helicopter—because that's what we need here, more goddamn *metal*—you went with what was easy for you because your life is so damn hard. That's why you drink, so you don't feel life, feeling sorry for yourself. The lone survivor." Her voice grew harsh. "Well, better to be the survivor than the dead."

She stopped, and Ethan realized she was breathing hard.

"Hey, slow down," he said.

Glenda shook her head. "Gus is the only Guardia left with experience. And his hearing is going and he's old. It's amazing he can walk the tracks every morning and run the Dragon every night. You have an untrained team that you haven't even tried to bring together, and you don't know a damned thing about hunting Untouchables because you don't want to think about it, it's *unpleasant*."

Ethan pushed the glass away. She was wrong, but she'd almost died and he was grateful to have her there, even if she was bitching at him.

She stood up, her hand on the table for support. "It's all up to you now, so you can do whatever you want, and if it doesn't work, well, you can just have a drink and forget it. The rest of the world will be in hell, but you'll be safe in the bottle."

Ethan held up the wooden chalice. It was still warm, and he could sense Tura's seething presence inside. "Hey, we got her, we did that right. And we got Selvans, too." He put the chalice down on the table with a thud. "And Fufluns is not going to kill anyone, right?"

"Just him being loose makes us vulnerable. The more Untouchables that are out of their chalices, the greater Kharos's powers. They strengthen him. And if Fufluns gets a chance, he'll let Tura out again. If all five get out, they can take their own shapes, they won't have to possess anybody, and then they'll be in full possession of their powers. We can't let that happen."

"See, you didn't tell me that," Ethan said, picking up his glass again.

"You wouldn't listen." Glenda took a deep shuddery breath, and Ethan felt like hell.

She went over to the cupboard above the fridge, pulled out a small wooden box, opened the lid, retrieved a small steel key and handed it to Ethan. "The key to Hank's trailer. I made it ready for you whenever you decide to rejoin the human race." She leaned over and kissed the top of his head and put a shaky hand on his shoulder. "Thank you for saving my life. Now sober up and save the world."

She went down the short hall and shut the door, and Ethan was left alone at the banquette with the bottle, the chalice, and the key in front of him.

Save the world.

Well, not tonight.

He drank the rest of his scotch and then went out to the woods and got his sleeping bag. When he came back, he listened at Glenda's door. Snoring. Alive.

He wedged the bedding in the hall in front of her door and stretched out.

He couldn't save the world tonight, but he could protect his mother.

*****

Ethan woke before dawn. He hadn't slept well, dreaming about being shot again, a searing pain in his chest, the screams of his team leader, so it took him a few seconds to get oriented. He almost knocked over Tura's chalice, which was right next to his head as he sat up and reached for his pistol.

His chest was killing him. He reached inside his vest and shirt to the scar where the bullet had entered and felt a hard lump. *What now?* He sat up and peeled off the vest, then removed his shirt. He could see the lump, right below the scar, and for a moment thought it was old stitches working their way out but realized it was too big and too hard for that.

Much too big. More the size of . . . a bullet.

Ethan slid his dad's knife out. Probing with the point, he dug into the skin and extracted a spent AK-47 round. *The* round. Looking at the bloody piece of lead in his hand, Ethan barely registered the trickle of blood on his chest. It had been so close to his heart, the surgeons didn't dare go after it. So how . . .

He'd felt the pain changing, lessening, the longer he stayed in the park, the more he'd joined with his mother and her team. Something had made the bullet move away from his heart, something that wanted him strong to fight demons. Glenda was right, the Guardia had given him his life back.

Abruptly, he turned his head, listening. Someone was coming, even though it was an hour or so before dawn. Not a demon. *How the hell did he know that?* He looked at his chest. The bleeding had stopped. The scar looked as it always had. Shaking his head, he pulled on his shirt and combat vest and slid the pistol in its holster. He pocketed the AK-47 bullet, then tucked the chalice under his arm.

He went outside and spotted a slender figure coming from the direction of the Beer Pavilion. Weaver. She had her demon gun slung over her shoulder and was wearing her goggles.

"You get any sleep?" Ethan asked, trying to keep from laughing. He wasn't going to die. His whole life was back in front of him again, with another mission to accomplish. One he could feel good about. One that saved people.

"No." She pulled the goggles up and looked at him without warmth. "How did you know it was me?"

"Saw you under the trees." A mission with Weaver by his side. Ethan smiled.

Weaver looked over her shoulder. "No way you could see me there."

"I think it's part of being the Hunter."

"Great," Weaver said. "Now Ursula's really going to want me to bring you in."

Ethan stopped thinking about the rest of his life—he had a rest-of-his-life, that was enough—long enough to notice that she was upset. "What's going on?"

"She was not happy requesting a covert ops Nighthawk and having it waved off. She was not happy learning I took an extra D-gun. She was not happy that I didn't bring her back anything more than your blood, which you'll be unhappy to know has francium in it."

"You don't look so happy, either," Ethan said.

Weaver smiled at him tightly. "How's Glenda?"

That wasn't good. "Still sleeping. What's wrong?"

Weaver lifted her chin. "Nothing's wrong, Ethan. I just put my career on the line for you last night and got it handed back to me with a 'No, thanks, we'll use magic.' If you weren't going to use me, why was I there?"

"Because you asked to be," Ethan said, exasperated that she was dwelling on the past when there was all this future before them. "Because I thought the D-gun might be useful. I was wrong."

"Not a problem," Weaver said, clearly lying. "Your problem is Ursula. She's coming to the park today. Wants to meet you."

"No," Ethan said, having enough women on his hands at the moment.

"She thinks the whole thing is a crock, but she's not sure. So she's going to find out."

"Screw Ursula." He shifted the chalice in his arms and hit the old wound and winced from habit but there was no pain. The bullet was gone, and he had his future back, and he did not want to talk about Ursula. "I'm sorry if I wasn't appreciative last night."

"If?"

"I'm sorry I wasn't appreciative last night." He hefted the chalice to balance it under his arm. "I have to lock this up in the Keep. Want to go with me, protect me from whatever is walking around out there?"

She looked at him as if she wanted to say something—probably *Up yours*—and then she sighed and said, "Sure."

That wasn't good. He wanted her happy. Looking forward to the future. Maybe with him.

I have a future, he thought, still amazed at the idea. So maybe it was time to start thinking about what he wanted to do with it.

"Glenda's got Hank's trailer all set up, ready to move into." He took a deep breath. "I think you should move out here. Easier for you to watch the park if you're staying out here instead of in town."

Weaver looked skeptical. "Does Glenda want that?"

"I want that," Ethan said.

She shrugged. "Okay. Sure. It will be better for the mission to be out here."

"And then after you're moved in, we'll . . . talk," Ethan said, praying she wouldn't want to.

"Whatever you want," Weaver said, and started down the path to the midway without him.

"Oh, great," Ethan said, wondering how long she was going to be mad, and then he remembered he had a future. She could be mad for a while and it was okay because he wasn't going to die at any minute, he had a future. It was still a shock every time he realized it, it was going to take some getting used to, but it was there. "Great," he said again, and took off to catch up with Weaver.

*****

Mab's plan to get up early and move out to Delpha's trailer that morning ended when she woke up and immediately rolled over and threw up into her wastebasket. "Oh *god,*" she said, and stumbled into the bathroom, where she threw up again.

Frankie did his raspy raven coo, which was a comfort but not a help.

"Flu," she told Cindy when she got downstairs with Frankie on her shoulder. "Or maybe I'm still barfing from that stuff Ethan made me drink last night. Whatever, I feel like hell."

"Yeah," Cindy said, looking down the counter to where Coke-bottle-glasses guy was sitting next to a middle-aged woman with tightly waved dark hair wearing an expensive powder blue suit and an unpleasant expression. Except for a mother and a couple of kids, they were the only ones in the place.

"What's wrong?" Mab said. "Why aren't there more people here?"

Even as she spoke, somebody rattled the doorknob, and Mab saw that Cindy had put the CLOSED sign on the door.

"Cindy, it's Saturday, you need to . . . ," she began and then got a good look at her roommate.

She looked panic-stricken.

"Are you okay?" Mab whispered to her.

"That's a *bird*," the woman called down the counter to Mab. "Birds are unsanitary."

"Thank you for sharing," Mab called back while Frankie glared at the woman from her shoulder. Then she turned to Cindy. "Okay, I had a bad night, and now I'm sick, and I need a big dose of cheer and whatever ice cream you've got that cures flu, but first, what's wrong?"

"I said," the woman at the end of the counter said more loudly, "that bird is unsanitary!"

Cindy's gaze wandered toward the ceiling again, as if she were concentrating very hard on not paying attention.

Mab leaned toward Cindy and whispered, "Who is that woman?"

"She's something to do with the government," Cindy said, still staring at the ceiling. "She was asking me questions about the park."

"Government," Mab said, thinking of black helicopters. "That's not good." She looked down the counter at them. The woman was exactly the kind of person who would think a black helicopter was a good idea.

"You have to get that bird out of here," the woman said to her. "That bird is a violation of health department regulations." She transferred her attention to Cindy. "You're in charge here. It's your responsibility."

Cindy looked at the woman without speaking, her whole body tense.

"Are you okay?" Mab said to her.

"Yes." Cindy refocused on her. "Did you say you had a bad night?"

"Yeah, Glenda died."

"What?"

"And then we brought her back. It was not fun."

Cindy was really focused now. "Is she okay?"

"She was a little shaky the last time I saw her, but I think she's going to be fine. Can I have breakfast or do we have to do something to the government first?"

The woman straightened on her stool, probably so she could threaten louder. "I'm going to make a formal complaint to the health department about that bird."

Frankie cawed at her, which did not help, and Cindy stared at the ceiling again, clenching her jaw, as if she were holding back a scream.

"Okay, now you're creeping me out," Mab said. "And given my life lately, that is not easy to do. What's wrong with you?"

"I woke up funny," Cindy said tightly.

"Funny how?" Mab said.

"Stuff has been happening."

"What kind of stuff?"

"Are you listening to me?" the woman demanded. She turned to the guy in the Coke-bottle glasses. "Stop eating that damn waffle and do something about that disease-carrying bird."

The man lifted his head from his ice cream and said, "The bird is fine." Then his glasses became round shiny eyes and his body began to elongate, looming over her, muscles rippling as his pin-striped suit turned to scales, his coattails shooting out to become a long, thick, lashing—

"Dragon," Mab said, fascinated.

—tail spiked with green trilby hats, just as he opened his mouth, filled with rows of serrated teeth.

"You, on the other hand, are a pain in the ass," the dragon said calmly.

The woman froze, staring at him, and then toppled off her stool onto the tile floor, out cold.

"I can't stop doing that," Cindy whispered to Mab.

"Uh-huh," Mab said, still staring at the dragon, the muscles moving under its beautiful scales, the grace in the way it turned its head on its long strong neck to look at her, the heat in its sharp gray eyes.

Then it disappeared and the guy with the glasses was back. He looked away from Mab and down at the woman.

"Now what's wrong?" he said to her unconscious body.

"I think I'm losing my mind," Cindy whispered to Mab. "Those two little kids were whining while their mother talked on her cell. The marshmallows in their hot chocolate turned into little white dragons and sang 'You've Got a Friend in Me.' Off-key. Marshmallows are evidently tone deaf."

"Who knew?" Mab said, trying not to stare at the guy. He'd been such a great dragon.

"Exactly. Their mother couldn't see them at all. Just me and the kids. I think the only people who can see them are me and the ones I'm annoyed with."

"*I* saw them," Mab said, wishing the dragon would come back.

"Well, yeah, you're a *Seer*," Cindy said.

"Right." Mab gave up on the dragon and turned back to her.

There was panic in Cindy's eyes. "Mab, what's happening to me?"

"You're creating illusions for people," Mab said as things clicked into place. "Like Young Fred. No, wait, that's not right, you're not becoming somebody else but . . ." She thought for a minute. "It's like your ice cream. It really is good ice cream, but when people eat it here in Dreamland in front of you, it's a religious experience. You create the illusion that it's otherworldly."

Cindy blinked at her and Mab tried again.

"You make people believe what you want them to believe. Like Glenda." Mab stopped. "*Oh.* That's it. You got a bump up the ladder in sorcery at midnight last night when Glenda died." Mab looked back at the unconscious woman, still dumbfounded. "Wow."

"I was in bed at midnight," Cindy said. "I did not bump."

"Yes, you did. Glenda died, and a new Sorceress was called. You. You've been practicing to be her successor all your life, and now she's passed the baton to you, and you're casting illusions. Beyond the ice cream. Only dragons. Wow. This is very cool." Mab took out her cell phone and punched in Glenda's number.

Down the counter, the woman stirred on the floor and tried to sit up. *"I saw a dragon."*

The guy took off his glasses and helped her up. "Sure you did, Ursula."

He always looked so different without the glasses, Mab thought. It surprised her every time, sharper planes to his face, sharper eyes, sharper everything. Plus, he'd been a *great* dragon.

He put the awful glasses back on again as Ursula said, *"There was a dragon."*

"I don't want a baton," Cindy whispered to Mab. "Glenda's not dead anymore. She can have the baton back."

Mab heard Glenda's "Hello?" on her cell phone and said, "This is Mab. How are you feeling?"

"Alive, thanks to you," Glenda said. "What can I do for you?"

Mab lowered her voice. "Get down to the Dream Cream and talk your replacement off the ledge. She's making dragons instead of ice cream."

"It's Cindy?" Glenda laughed, the lightest sound that Mab had ever heard her make. "Of course it's Cindy. I'm on my way."

"Thank you very much for the ice cream," the guy with the glasses said as he guided a shaken Ursula toward the door. "I'll be back."

"No, no," Cindy called after him. "We're closing for the season. Try us next May."

"And miss Halloween?" the guy said, and Mab met his sharp eyes and realized Ursula hadn't been the biggest danger after all.

"I thought I saw a dragon," Ursula said, still sounding dazed, and he guided her out the door.

"That's not good," Mab said, sitting back down.

"Make the dragon not come back," Cindy said, holding on to the edge of the counter.

"And the little singing marshmallows," Mab said, nodding.

"I like the marshmallows," Cindy said. "But that dragon is dangerous."

"I know," Mab said, thinking about all the power that had been there. "I know."

*****

Ethan caught up to Weaver, Tura's chalice still under his arm. "Look, I know you're mad about last night, but we did what had to be done."

"I know."

"I think the D-gun has its place here, we're going to need it. And you. Your expertise."

"Thank you."

Okay, it was good he had a future, but he'd prefer not to spend it all trying to coax Weaver out of a snit. "How long are you going to be mad at me?"

Weaver stopped and turned to face him. "You think you know it all. You don't. You don't even know what you are."

Ethan held up a hand. "No, I'm learning that. The Hunter thing, what I can do, I'm still finding that out. This morning—"

"Not the Hunter thing." Weaver bit her lip, as if she was trying to decide something. "You don't show a lot of emotion, but when we have sex—"

I'm gonna hate this, Ethan thought.

"—your eyes glow. Red. The first time I was startled but we were in the middle of things, and I thought maybe I imagined it, and then it happened again but by then I knew you weren't a demon, but . . . that's not normal."

"Great," Ethan said, trying to wrap his head around that one. His eyes glowed red. Probably should keep his eyes closed during sex in the future.

Weaver frowned at him, annoyed again. "You don't seem surprised."

"I'm surprised. But I've seen Mab's eyes glow, so—"

"You had sex with Mab?"

"No. *No.*" Women. He watched her narrowed eyes and said, "No, no. *Never*. Her eyes flash when she gets angry. Almost like a person possessed by a demon. But she's not a demon. And neither am I." *But I am different,* he thought.

"So what are you?" Weaver demanded. "And by the way, this is another thing I haven't told Ursula, so you're welcome. But you have to admit, sensing demons behind doors, seeing in the dark, francium in the blood, eyes glowing . . . You're not scoring high on the 'not demon' chart. I believe in you, but I don't see anybody else giving you a pass on this."

They came out onto the midway near the Keep lake. "It's okay," Ethan said. "I figure it's like my ability to sense demons, to see better in the dark—part of being Guardia. Maybe Guardia are anti-demons. Yin and yang. You know. A little outside the bell curve."

"A little? Do Glenda's eyes glow? You must have seen her mad plenty of times."

That gave Ethan pause. "Never saw them do it."

"Gus's? Delpha's? Young Fred's?"

"No, but . . . Okay, so maybe it's not a Guardia thing."

A long silence played out, and Ethan kept walking.

"I've got to take you in," Weaver finally said.

"No."

"Look, Ursula plays dirty. She's talking about erasing your identity if you don't cooperate. Your disability pay will be gone. No record of your service in the Army at all. No record of you. You won't exist anymore."

"Does she have that kind of power?"

"She wants that kind of power," Weaver said. "Whether she has it remains to be seen. I just don't want to see it when you disappear."

"I don't care. I'm Guardia. Nothing else matters. Look." He slowed and reached into his pocket and pulled out the AK-47 round. "This is the bullet they couldn't take out because it was too close to my heart, the bullet that was going to kill me any time. I was doomed. This morning it was right under my skin. Popped it out. And the wound healed right away. I have my life back. You think I care about your Ursula?"

Weaver stared at the bullet. "You've had that inside you? Pressing on your heart? *And you didn't tell me?*"

"Uh," Ethan said, not expecting that.

"You . . . *idiot*," Weaver said, fuming. "You could have *died*!"

"I know," Ethan said, cautious now. "But it's out. I'm okay now—"

"No, you're *not*. That's what I'm trying to tell you. Ursula's dangerous. She's ambitious as all hell and if she can prove demons are real—and whatever powers you Guardia have are real—she'll use it to get more power. She's already brought in muscle to grab you if she decides she wants to. And if you defy her, if you get in her way . . ." She swallowed. "The life you just got back could be over pretty fast."

Ethan shrugged. "Let her try." He slowed as they reached the garbage can beside the carousel. "Last night my mother died and we brought her back. Today, I carved my death sentence out of my chest. Somebody up there likes us, and I'm going to keep working to keep it that way. The hell with Ursula and her muscle." He shoved the can aside and opened the trap door to the tunnels. "You with me?"

Weaver hesitated.

"It's okay," Ethan said. "I never expected you to risk your career for this."

"I'm with you," she said, and climbed down into the tunnel.

*****

"And then Ethan took Glenda home, and Frankie and I came here and packed," Mab said over her waffles as Frankie crunched pistachios on the floor. She was eating cautiously, and so far her stomach was being edgy but cooperative. "We're moving out to the trailers today so you get your guest room back."

"Oh," Cindy said. "Well, that'll be . . . nice. So the Guardia thing, it's not hard?"

"We had some problems," Mab said, and then saw Cindy get tense again. "Nothing we couldn't fix, everything was fine, you can do this.

Things got a little screwed up because Ethan insisted on bringing Weaver along—"

"He took a date to a demon battle?" Cindy said. "Oh, wait, it's Ethan. Of course he took a date to a demon battle."

"Not a date. Remember the man in black who kept shooting him? The man in black was Weaver."

"I thought it was Johnny Cash."

"No—"

Glenda rattled the door and Mab went to let her in.

"You have to open up," Glenda said to Cindy. "People need ice cream."

"I will," Cindy said, "as soon as you tell me how to stop making dragons."

Glenda looked at Mab.

Mab smiled, ignoring her queasy stomach. "Ethan told me that you cast illusions as the Sorceress. Well, when Cindy gets annoyed, she casts an illusion to pay off the person annoying her. Apparently her subconscious communicates in dragons."

Glenda looked at Cindy. "I didn't know you ever got annoyed. You always seemed so . . . cheery."

"I repress a lot," Cindy said.

"Oh." Glenda sat down on a counter stool. "So, let's start at the beginning. You're part of the Guardia now. The Guardia is—"

"Yeah, Mab told me. I'm the Sorceress, I yell 'Redimio,' and demons go into chalices, we save the world. She did not mention dragons, though, or what else these powers do, or how I control them."

"Control them." Glenda looked confused. "I don't remember them ever getting out of control. I want something to happen, I concentrate on it happening, it happens. It doesn't just happen on its own."

"Not when you got angry?" Mab said. "I remember you getting pretty angry a couple of times. You must have had . . . thoughts."

"Yeah," Glenda said. "But they never became dragons. That's new."

"Oh, well, that's wonderful," Cindy snapped, and Mab pulled back a little, surprised.

"I can see why you're . . . upset," Glenda began.

"Upset?" Cindy said, and the napkin holder on the counter morphed into a silver dragon about two feet tall and began spitting napkins.

"Oh," Glenda said, watching it. "That's a problem. Possibly you just need to, uh, control yourself—"

"Don't you people have a handbook or something?" Cindy said. "With a troubleshooting section in the back? Somebody you can *call*?"

"There are old books in the Keep," Glenda said. "Mab could look around."

"Sure," Mab said, and took an incautious bite of her waffle. "I could—"

Her stomach revolted and she ran for the bathroom and lost everything. She splashed water on her face, rinsed her mouth out, and thought, *Just what I needed, flu.* Then she went back to the counter, only to meet two women who were looking at her appraisingly.

"What?" she said.

"Cindy says you have the flu," Glenda said. "There's no flu going around."

"Well, I've got something," Mab said. "Maybe it's from that stuff in the flask you made Ethan give me last night. That was awful."

Cindy nodded, for the moment back to her old cheerful self. "So I know you've been using condoms, but . . . did anything go wrong?"

"No," Mab said. "What? *No.* Listen, I'm *careful.*"

"Put your hand on your stomach," Glenda said.

Mab looked at her warily. "Why?"

"Put your hand on your stomach and see what you see," Glenda said patiently.

Mab took a deep breath and put her hand on her stomach. Nothing. "I don't think the sight thing works like that—"

A toddler with curly red hair stood there, grinning crookedly up at her, a wicked little baby glint in her green eyes and a green malachite bunny clutched in her fat little hand.

Mab stopped breathing, but Frankie did his rasping coo, and the baby laughed.

"Yeah," Glenda said, evidently reading the expression on her face. "Girl or boy?"

"Girl," Mab said faintly, as the baby toddled across the floor, through the door, and out onto the flagstones. Still laughing.

Very happy baby with her malachite bunny warding off evil, the gift of her far-seeing aunt Delpha.

Mab watched her until she was out of sight, her mind folding in on itself. Baby. She was going to have a baby. Baby. Baby, baby, baby.

"Who's the father?" Glenda said.

"Fun. Oh, *god*. My kid's got a demon for a father." Mab sat down, still floored from the idea that she was going to have a kid, let alone a part-demon kid. "This isn't happening to me."

Cindy put a cup of tea in front of her. "Peppermint. No caffeine. No dragons."

Mab looked at the cup. "I got drunk last night. And then Ethan gave me that stuff that made me throw it all up. That could have hurt—"

"Did she look hurt?" Glenda said.

"No, but . . ."

"So back to the problem at hand," Glenda said, turning back to Cindy. "Maybe if you tried meditation—"

"Hey," Mab said. "I'm *pregnant*. I'm gonna have a *baby*."

"In nine months," Glenda told her. "Cindy has dragons right now. Get in line." She smiled at Cindy. "So Mab will go to the Keep and find the books and . . . we'll go from there. After she tells fortunes this afternoon."

"Fortunes?" Mab said. "Oh, hell, the Oracle tent. I forgot." *What with the baby and all.*

"And after you sell ice cream," Glenda said to Cindy. "This is a park, too, you know. Both of you, get to work." She looked up at the menu. "I want something that says 'I almost died and now I'm free.' What have you got?"

"Chocolate," Cindy said, and went to get her breakfast.

"Was what I saw real?" Mab asked Glenda. "That little girl?"

"Hard telling," Glenda said. "Maybe it's just what you wish for."

"Yeah, because I'm so the maternal type," Mab said, and picked up her tea and walked out the door, her raven on her shoulder and a baby on board.

"So," she said to Frankie as they hit the midway. "You ever do any babysitting?"

She turned her head and met him eye to eye. He didn't seem enthusiastic.

"Well, you can learn," she said, and headed for the Oracle booth.

CHAPTER 17

Once Ethan and Weaver were in the Keep, they made their way up to the restaurant level, where Ethan paused. The small door built into the drawbridge was open. Looking out, he saw one of the paddleboats tied to the ledge outside.

He drew his gun and led Weaver to the top room of the Keep. He picked up no sense of demon, but that didn't put him at ease. The trapdoor at the top of the stairs leading to the battlement roof was open. He put Tura's chalice on the pentagonal table, indicated for Weaver to cover him, then climbed the stairs, pistol leading.

He popped his head up over the threshold and saw Ray Brannigan, smoking a cigar and staring out at Dreamland, looking like the king of the Keep.

Ethan climbed onto the battlement, and Ray spun about, hand flashing inside his expensive coat. He saw that Ethan had already beaten him to the draw and raised both hands very slightly.

Somehow having a future made Ethan dislike Ray even more. He raised his gun higher.

"Hey, it's just me," Ray said. "Owner of half the park, remember? I'm allowed to be up here." He smiled, just pals.

Remember he's the Devil you know, Ethan told himself. Don't shoot him.

"Which reminds me," Ray said. "You have twenty percent of the park. I'll give you half a million for it." He looked past Ethan at Weaver as she climbed out onto the roof and lost his smile. "I thought I told you to get rid of her."

"You'll give me your share of the park," Ethan said. "And then you'll go. I know you were outside Delpha's trailer while she was dying, I know you sent the demons after Gus, I know you made a deal with the Devil, which just shows how dumb you really are."

"Listen, you punk, I'm the mayor of this town and half owner of this park, and you do *not* talk to me like that." Ray took a menacing step forward, and then there was the *thuft* of the D-gun firing, and he staggered back, hit by a demon round slamming into the left side of his coat. Ethan charged forward and did a leg sweep, knocking Ray to the ground. He ripped the demon round off the coat and pulled it back. The round had hit the outside of a leather holster housing a massive Desert Eagle pistol. Ethan pulled it out and handed it to Weaver.

"A little compensation going on there, Ray?" Weaver asked, hefting the massive gun. "Chambered for fifty caliber? Are you nuts?"

Ray tried to get up, and Ethan pushed him back, patted him down, extracted a set of iron rings from an inner pocket, and slid them into one of his own pockets.

Ray got to his feet cursing. "You're the one who's crazy. You had that Nighthawk land here last night, didn't you? You're government? Well, this is private property. You got a warrant?"

"I don't need a warrant," Weaver said calmly, tucking the Desert Eagle into her vest and filling the empty chamber on her D-gun. "I'm with Ethan. This is his Keep. And you were advancing in a threatening manner."

"Give me my gun and my keys," Ray snarled to Ethan. *"And get rid of that bitch!"*

"I could throw you off this roof," Ethan said, thinking seriously about it. "You've been depressed lately. We've all noticed it."

Weaver took out Ray's gun and leveled it at him. "Let me just shoot him. You never let me shoot anybody." Ethan detected sincerity in her voice.

A vein pulsed in Ray's forehead. "I'm the *mayor.* I own *half of this park—"*

"And I have all of your gun," Weaver said brightly.

"Fuck you," Ray said, and headed for the door and stairs.

Ethan followed him down, Weaver covering his back.

Ray paused before the next set of stairs, staring at Tura's chalice on the pentagonal table. "What is that?"

"Get out," Ethan said. "You're done here."

Ray glared at him. "This isn't the end of this. You don't treat a Brannigan like this and get away with it."

"That's the best you've got?" Weaver said. "Didn't making a deal with the Devil give you snappier patter than that?"

Ray clenched his jaw and then disappeared down the stairs. Ethan went over to one of the narrow windows and watched. A minute later Ray appeared, looking mad as hell and just as foolish, pedaling away in the boat toward shore.

"How did you know the gun would take the impact of the demon round?" Ethan asked Weaver.

"I didn't," she said, looking at Ray's gun with admiration. "I don't like guys who try to bully me."

"Good to know."

"Okay, I lost my temper. I'm sorry. Well, not really . . ."

"Try not to do that again." Ethan surveyed the room once more and nodded. "This is it."

"This is what?" Weaver asked.

"Our fallback position. It's the safest place in the park from demons. Surrounded by water."

"Not running water," Weaver said.

"Maybe we could do something about that," Ethan said. "And it's lined with iron. We have the keys to the two doors. And they're covered in iron. Everything outside of here is vulnerable, but this tower, this room, is where we can make a stand if we have to. This is our Alamo."

"Everybody died at the Alamo. What's the midway, the Little Big Horn?"

Ethan looked at her, exasperated.

She shrugged. "I'm just saying that if you want to rally the troops, avoid the *A* word."

"Fine," Ethan said. "We've got a week to get ready and this is going to be the center of our defensive position, our command central. I'll call the Guardia to meet here Sunday, after the park closes. We'll get all the chalices in here for safekeeping, make our plans, train for Halloween."

"That won't keep Ursula out," Weaver said.

"Ursula is the least of our problems," Ethan said, and went to shut Tura's chalice in the armoire.

"That may be, but she's still a problem," Weaver said.

Ethan latched the armoire door. "I can handle her." *I can handle anything now.*

"I'm glad you're not going to die," Weaver said. "I mean . . . congratulations. On your bullet."

"Thank you," Ethan said. "Do they have a card for that?"

"I don't send cards," Weaver said, and went out the door, sounding a little unsettled.

"There are other ways we can celebrate," Ethan said, and followed her down the stairs.

*****

Mab moved her two bags into Delpha's trailer and put Delpha's urn up on the ledge beside Frankie's nest. He seemed pleased. Then she went back to the park, crossing Weaver's path as she carried her duffel bag into Hank's trailer. She spent the afternoon reading the hearts and palms of Parkersburg's romantically crossed until six, when she put up her CLOSED sign and went to look for a Guardia handbook in the Keep. She took her good heavy flashlight, used a paddleboat to cross the Keep lake, let herself in with the key Glenda had given her, ignored the basement because she knew what was down there and it wasn't books, and went up to the top room, where she stopped inside the door.

It was pretty much the same as she remembered from the first time she'd gone through it in April. There was a five-sided table with five beat-up wooden chairs around it, a wall full of weapons that looked like an Ethan-Weaver wet dream, and a big, battered, heavy wood armoire that was full of books and ledgers and tied bundles of papers. New was a wooden chalice that she recognized.

"Hey, Tura," she said, and moved the chalice to one side. "Okay," she said to Frankie. "This is going to be boring. No drawings."

She found a light switch in the room and turned it on, which helped since the light through the windows was growing dim, and then she started going through the stuff in the armoire, pulling a notebook out of her work bag to catalog things as she sorted them on the floor. When she was done, she had a lot of stacks but only four things laid out on the table that looked like a good bet for figuring out the Guardia. She was starting to put the rest back into the armoire when the door opened.

She spun around, her heart in her throat, and saw Ethan pointing a gun at her.

"Hey!" she said, and he lowered the gun.

"Sorry," he said. "We saw a light in the window." He frowned at the mess on the floor. "What are you doing?"

"Looking for the Guardia instruction manual." She picked up a stack of books and shelved them on the bottom of the armoire.

"Find one?" he said, moving to the window. He opened the casement and leaned out and waved, presumably to stop Weaver from coming up to blow her away. Then he shut the window again and came over to the table. "What's this stuff?"

Mab picked up a leather-bound notebook. "This is a Sorceress's diary from the eighteenth century. It has recipes and what I assume is good advice, the little I can make out. It's in Italian, and my Italian is not good."

"So how is Cindy going to read it?"

"To get recipes and advice on how to stop the dragons, Cindy will learn Italian."

"Dragons?"

Mab picked up the second book, bound in black leather. "This is a thirteenth-century armory book. It's full of hand drawings and handwritten notations—"

Ethan took it from her.

"—and it's in Latin, but I'm assuming the drawings will do the trick for you."

"Weaver's gonna love this," Ethan said, turning the pages in fascination.

"Yeah, it'll be like a pillow book for you two," Mab said. "Now that you're going to have pillows."

Ethan frowned at her.

"I saw Weaver move into Hank's trailer," Mab said. "Never mind. I also found this."

She held up a satin-bound book. "It's a history of the Guardia written by the first American Seer. In English. I'm taking that one."

"Yeah," Ethan said, still paging through weapons.

"And *this* . . . ," she said a little louder, trying to get his attention. When he finally looked up, she unrolled a map. "This is the first map of Dreamland. The original drawing. I haven't had time to look at it closely, but it has—"

He took it out of her hands and looked at it closer. "This is detailed."

"Yes," Mab said. "It was stuck in with a bunch of ledger sheets, or I'd have found it on my first pass through here last April. It even has drawings of the wrought-iron fencing, and I think those really faint dotted lines are the tunnels—"

"Damn," Ethan said. "We can use this."

"You're welcome," Mab said.

"What? Oh, sorry." He rolled the map up and put it with the armory book. "Here. Let me carry all of these down for you. You're lugging that bag—"

"That's okay, I can carry—"

Frankie cawed from on top of the armoire and she stopped, wondering what his problem was.

Ethan frowned up at Frankie. "He doesn't want you carrying things?"

"Oh," Mab said. "Chill, bird, we got eight and three-quarters months to go yet."

"Until what?" Ethan said, looking confused.

"Until I give birth to demon spawn," Mab said, only half joking.

"You're *pregnant*?"

"Yes, Ethan, I'm pregnant."

"With Joe's . . ."

"Yes," Mab said. "I was impregnated by a demon in the body of the local drunk. Go ahead, try to make me feel worse than I already do."

"How do you know the baby's not human? I mean, fully human. You know what I mean."

"What are the chances?" Mab said.

"I don't know. I don't even know how we ended up . . . demon spawn."

"We?" Mab said. "We who, Batman?"

"You and me. With the red in the eyes."

"Your eyes do it, too?"

"So says Weaver."

"Well, she should know," Mab said. "What does Glenda say? Any memories of demon possession?"

"I haven't asked her yet."

"Why not?"

Ethan gave her the dead eye. "It's not an easy thing to ask your mother."

"Sure it is. You say, 'While you were making me, was there anybody else inside you? . . .' Oh. Never mind, I'll ask her."

"I'll do it. You just . . ." He gestured helplessly. "You're not having any cravings for raw meat, are you?"

"No," Mab said. "I don't want to drink anybody's blood, either. I do, as usual, want to kill you."

"Get in line," Ethan said. Outside, the end-of-the-night fireworks started to crack, and he picked up the books. "I'll go down and finish the last patrol with Weaver, cover Gus at the Dragon, then we'll walk you back to the trailer. Don't go alone. We still don't know what's out there."

"That's until *midnight.*"

"It's eleven now," Ethan said, looking mystified. "Can't you read your diary thing until then?"

"Oh," Mab said. "I spent five hours going through this stuff? Okay, fine, I'll wait for you on the paddleboat dock. At midnight."

He nodded and then hesitated. "About the baby."

Mab steeled herself for whatever clueless comment was coming.

"You know I've got your back, right?"

She blinked at him. He'd been odd ever since he'd come into the room, lighter somehow, not so much like the Grim Reaper in camo. But this—

"You're not alone. Anything you need . . ." He stopped, clearly miserable at having to be sensitive and supportive. "Just because Joe isn't gonna be there, doesn't mean you're on your own."

Mab swallowed. "Thank you."

He started to say something else, then nodded and left.

"Damn," Mab said to Frankie, and blinked back tears. Her baby was going to have backup. Ethan said so.

I'm going to have a baby.

So, okay, she'd learn to be a mother. Better than her mother. None of that crap about demons . . .

Oh, hell.

But Glenda would be a good grandmother. And Ethan would make a good, dependable, protective surly uncle. And Cindy would make wonderful ice cream for the little demon spawn. . . .

Gotta get a name for this kid.

She put the papers back in the armoire and closed the doors and shut off the light. The room fell into darkness, but the brightness outside drew her to the window, and she leaned on the sill and stared out at all the color as the last of the fireworks burst in the sky, the way they had thirty years ago when she'd leaned on the attic windowsill and wondered what Dreamland was like. Gold sparks exploded in the air, and blue and white and red, and the orange and yellow lights on the Double Ferris Wheel revolved in front of her, and she heard the fat, chuckly sound of the carousel, its gold and turquoise lights gleaming below, and the Dragon swooped its green lights up the last incline and then down into the orange smoky depths of the fog-machine-clouded midway.

It was so beautiful, it made her throat ache. And it was hers, she was inside the park now, a part of it. Even better, this was what her baby would grow up seeing, light and color and laughter and love.

She had to keep her baby safe. She'd never felt like that before, but now she had to keep somebody safe. And there'd be people to help her with that. Ethan would beat up any kid who was mean to her demon spawn on the playground. Weaver would shoot any boy who broke her heart. Her kid was covered.

One by one, the lights went out, the Dragon powering down, the carousel music slowing to a stop, the twin circles of the Ferris Wheel disappearing into the night. When the park was darkened, only the orange cellophane streetlights left on to illuminate the rapidly disappearing cotton candy fog, she closed the window and went down the stairs, Frankie swooping down in a circle in front of her, Delpha's malachite bunny bouncing from the ribbon tied to her bag.

"I think I'll call the baby Delphie," Mab called out to Frankie, and he rasped back his approval.

Mab and Delphie and Frankie. And Glenda and Ethan. And Cindy. And Gus. And Weaver. That was a family.

She put her flashlight back into her bag and went out to paddle back to the dock.

*****

"A peace offering," Ethan said, holding out the Latin weapons book to Weaver when he met her on the midway, the cold night air biting at them.

She had her D-gun slung at the ready, her goggles up on her forehead for the moment, but she took the book from him and flipped through it. "Neat. We can get ready to fight the Crusades."

"It's weaponry to use against demons," Ethan said. "Probably tactics, too, once we translate it. People still study Sun Tzu, you know." He nodded toward the Dragon Coaster. "We need to cover Gus for the midnight run in an hour. Then we have to meet Mab back at the paddleboat dock and escort her to her trailer. And then we can, uh . . ."

"Talk in Hank's trailer."

"Sure," Ethan said, thinking, *Talk?*

They patrolled the park until the lights on the Dragon Coaster came alive. "Anything?" Ethan asked as Weaver's head turned back and forth, scanning the area around Gus.

"Nope."

"There's someone over by the Pirate Ship."

Weaver swiveled her head in that direction. "A person. Not a demon. Fuck."

"What?"

"It's Ursula."

Ursula stepped out of the shadows of the Pirate Ship, a set of demon goggles askew on her head and a D-gun held awkwardly in her hands. They clashed with the finely tailored powder blue business suit, which was clearly not warm enough. She was shivering, which might have been why she looked so bitchy.

"Master Sergeant Wayne," Ursula called out.

Ethan ignored her and kept walking toward the Dragon.

After a moment, Weaver followed.

"Agent Weaver," Ursula said, upping the bitch in her voice.

"We had a demon attack at the coaster the other night," Weaver said over her shoulder. "We want to make sure there isn't a repeat."

"That wasn't in your report," Ursula said, but she caught up with them, stumbling a little, not used to the depth perception problems of the goggles.

Ethan stopped near the Pirate Cove Games, close enough that he and Weaver could cover Gus with Weaver's D-gun. He looked at the orange Strong Man and felt Selvans' seething. No wonder Gus was always worried.

"Master Sergeant Wayne," Ursula started again.

"I'm not in the Army anymore."

"I need to take you in for testing," Ursula said.

"No."

With a rattle, the Dragon began its run.

"That's my friend Gus," Ethan said. "If I go with you, he and everybody else in this park are vulnerable to demon attack. So, no."

"About that," Ursula said. "We also would like one or two of your so-called demons to examine. Agent Weaver says they're more powerful than those she supposedly has encountered so far. Of course, we have only her anecdotal evidence."

Ethan looked at Weaver. He had a feeling she was rolling her eyes behind the goggles.

"Which is why," Ursula continued, "I'm taking you in. Your blood is the only substantial thing Agent Weaver ever brought us."

"Ma'am," Weaver said, "there's a lot more going on here than you can imagine. Ethan needs to be here for this next week. He can't leave the park."

"*Ethan?* Are you losing your objectivity, Agent Weaver?"

The Dragon came swooping down the tail, and Ethan could hear the rattles. Four.

"What the hell are you doing?" Ray called out from behind them.

Ursula turned. "Who are you?"

Ethan kept his focus on Gus. The Dragon came to a halt and the lights went off. No minions.

"I own this park," Ray said, walking up, bundled up in his Burberry, towering over Ursula, his cigar chomped in his mouth.

Weaver opened her mouth, probably to dispute the *I own this park* line, and Ethan shook his head. If Ray wanted to take point with Ursula, he was all for it.

Ray scowled down at Ursula. "Who are you?"

"Senior Agent Ursula Borden. Homeland Security." Ursula lifted her chin, probably trying to look important, but her nose was red from the cold, so she just looked fussy.

"You got a warrant to be on my property?" Ray demanded.

"I have cause to be here," Ursula said.

Ethan saw that Gus was headed to his trailer, safe and sound. Time to get Mab and take her home and then, god help him, talk with Weaver. "We have somebody to meet, Agent Borden, but I'm sure Ray will be very helpful. Excuse us." He started down the midway to the paddleboat dock.

"Wait a minute," Ursula snapped.

Ethan kept walking, Weaver behind him. He could hear Ray being rude to Ursula.

"Do we really want to leave the two of them alone?" Weaver said, catching up to him.

"We have to get Mab," he told her. "And as far as I'm concerned, Ray and Ursula deserve each other."

Weaver looked back. "Yeah, but do we deserve what they'll get up to together?"

Ethan slowed.

The paddleboat dock was empty.

"Fuck," he said, and started to run.

*****

Mab had reached the paddleboat dock and climbed out, shivering in the cold, Frankie swooping ahead of her. She looked around and didn't see Ethan and Weaver. Probably off somewhere discussing the best way to kill with the thumb. Although, really, she should stop mocking them. They had a good relationship, definitely better than she and Joe, no, Fun, than she and Fun had ever had. Of course, he was a demon. It was hard to have a serious relationship with a demon. Them being demons and all.

Don't cry, she told herself as she walked down the dock, wrapping her coat around her against the freezing air. She was happy for Ethan and Weaver, they were meant for each other, people were supposed to be happy—

She stopped and squinted into the darkness.

There was a child on the path over by the Mermaid Cruise.

"Hello?" she called out. "Are you lost? Where's your mama and daddy?" She stepped off the dock and went toward the kid, mentally cursing the idiocy of parents who lost children in amusement parks. *Give the kid nightmares for years,* she thought as Frankie shrieked his own disapproval above her. "Hey," she said, when she was close enough to speak without yelling, and the child turned around, and she saw painted eyes and a wide painted smile under a black beret—

Something hit her from behind, and she went down hard, the breath knocked out of her, as wooden dolls swarmed around her in berets and lederhosen and flowered shirts, stuffing paper leis in her mouth as she tried to get her breath back to scream, their little wooden hands digging into her arms and legs, dragging her across the flagstones as she kicked out at them. Her foot struck wood, hard, and something went thump, and there was another one, there were too many, she tried to wrench her arm free and almost dislocated her shoulder, tried to get the damn lei out of her mouth so she could scream for Ethan, and then they shoved her hard and she went over an edge and fell facedown into freezing water between two cars. She spit out the lei and tried to get to her feet, but they were on her, surprisingly heavy little bastards, demon-heavy, a half dozen grabbing on to her canvas coat and sinking her to the bottom of the three-foot-deep tank with their weight, sending her into panic, she was drowning, her baby was drowning, she was going to die, her lungs bursting—

And then something red rose up inside her and said, *Fucking minions are not going to kill my demon spawn,* and she shrugged herself free of her coat and shot forward under the next cruise boat and surfaced beyond it, inside the dark cruise tunnel, gasping for breath, mad as hell, and freezing to death. She grabbed on to the side of the tank and tried to boost herself up, her teeth chattering in the cold, but they were on her again, dragging her down, and she lashed out, screaming at them, and then a strong hand grabbed her arm and yanked her out of the water and lifted her up into darkened France.

"Let go," she said, swinging, and whoever it was said, *"I'm saving you, dummy."* He kicked at one of the demons who'd tried to follow her, and she saw thick-rimmed Coke-bottle glasses gleam in the dim light and stopped struggling.

"Up there," he said, pointing, and she climbed over the wrought-iron railing into the upper part of the diorama—the Eiffel Tower—as he threw two more dolls back into the water and followed. "Get behind me," he said, and picked up a gun that looked a lot like Weaver's demon gun, so she did, her teeth chattering in the cold as her wet clothes began to freeze.

"What are you doing here?" she said, shivering hard as she leaned up against his back in the dark, more for warmth than support.

"Your bird yelled, and I came to find out why," he said, his voice calm as he looked down the tunnel toward the dim light of the opening. "What are *they* doing?"

"Some of them are still drowning my painting coat and some were trying to drown me," Mab said, her teeth chattering, and then one climbed out of the water and he shot it, blowing it back into the drink.

That doll's going to be hard to fix, she thought, and collapsed behind him, shuddering with the cold. She tried to sit up while he blasted two more demons off the walkway, and finally managed to stay upright, her shivers turning to spasms.

He looked around at her and said, "Hell," and put the gun down.

"No, no," Mab said, "*keep the gun,*" but he took off his jacket and put it around her and she didn't argue. It was a down jacket, and she was freezing for two.

Then he picked up the gun again and said, "I don't like waiting to be murdered by a bunch of little foreigners. Is there a back way out of here?"

"Yeah, farther into the tunnel, behind the scrims," Mab said, her teeth chattering less now. "They're—"

They came charging from the front of the tunnel, some running along the walkway, some paddling a cruise boat, and began to stream around the sides of the fence, the French, the Germans, and the Hawaiians, all with hateful glowing demon eyes, converging on them. The guy raised his gun and fired at the first one, blowing it back against the two behind it. He fired again and blew another one out of the boat. He aimed at another, and the first one he'd shot got up and began to run toward them.

"What the hell?" he said as the rest rushed toward them, getting temporarily blown back by the D-gun and then running again. "I thought this gun was supposed to *kill* them." He pulled the trigger and there was a click. *"Hell."* He ripped off the drum underneath the barrel and slammed another one home and fired again. "How many are there?"

"Eighteen, I think," Mab said, her teeth chattering. "Six dolls in each country, France, Germany, and Hawaii, after us."

"Hawaii is a country?" the guy said, and kept shooting, but not fast enough.

Mab rose up behind him and yelled, "Specto!" throwing her hand at the closest one, and he froze in midair, which was reassuring, since she hadn't been sure she could do that without the Guardia behind her.

The guy kicked him into the water and blew several others after him back with the gun. Then he pulled off the drum magazine and reloaded again from a bag hanging on his waist. "That's a nice trick you've got there."

"Thank you," Mab said. "I think we should leave."

"That way?" he said, nodding farther down the tunnel as he snapped the gun back together.

"No," Mab said, shivering. "There are twelve countries in this thing, and for all we know they're all possessed. What if there's another one waiting for us?"

"If it's China, they'll take a trade deal."

"It's not funny!" Mab said, in pain everywhere from the cold.

"Sorry." He sat back on his heels. "I was assured this gun killed demons, but it doesn't seem to be working. And I've only got six more rounds."

"I think you're hitting the wood," Mab said. "I don't think you're touching the demon inside. We need to break their bodies."

"Good, you work on that," he said, and picked one off as it tried to crawl around the fence. "Because this is not . . ."

His voice trailed off as he straightened.

"Crack the wood, huh?" he said, and put the gun down.

"Keep the gun!" Mab said as another one rushed them, but he picked up the doll and threw it with great force onto the iron railing below, where it cracked open and spewed something that looked like rotten purple jam all over the walkway.

They were still coming, but he was a fast thrower, and Mab specto-ed every one she could, so that after four were splintered on the railing, the others drew back to confer, babbling in little chittering sounds, like dead leaves blowing on pavement, that sent shivers down Mab's back. Or that could have been the cold.

"Here's the plan," he said. "We go out the front and then run like hell."

"You're not brave," she said. "I like that in a man."

"Stay behind me," he said, and handed her the gun.

"What am I supposed to do with this?"

"Try not to drop it." He edged his way down to the fence and shook it a little, and then he bent down. "I'll be damned," he said, and then a little Hawaiian jumped on his back and Mab raised the gun and shot the doll, sending them both into the fence.

"Ouch," the guy said. He grabbed the doll that had fallen off him and smacked it into the rail, and then he reached down and wrenched one of the wrought-iron supports free. "Come on," he said to her, *"and don't fire that damn gun again."*

"Sorry." Mab stuck behind him, shivering as they edged along the fence, his body blocking her from the worst of the wind blowing into the tunnel. He stopped at the opening and stayed there silent for several moments, and she looked down at the fence to see what had made him swear.

The bottom of the spear-shaped iron picket didn't look right.

She bent down, her hand shaking in the cold, and yanked on it, and it came out of a bracket at the bottom, it wasn't welded on at all, and then she stood up, yanking it free from the bracket at the top, and realized it wasn't a picket, it was an iron spear. All the pickets were spears, stored in brackets on the wrought-iron rail.

"This fence is all over the park," she whispered. "That means these pickets—"

Suddenly they were swarmed again, and Mab stabbed and slashed until he pulled her through the tunnel entrance and out onto the ramp, shielding her as he made short efficient stabs into the dolls' necks.

Articulated necks, Mab thought; he'd found their weakness.

"Will you *run*?" he snapped at her, and she said, *"No,"* and began to stab for the neck, too.

"Damn it." He turned back to the dolls and yelled, "Get that one, he's the leader!"

"What?" Mab said, but the demons stopped in their tracks, turning to look at one of the French demons, chittering now as it backed away, its beret askew.

Mab started to move, but the guy grabbed her arm, so she stood quietly, shuddering with the cold.

Then they all screamed and fell on the French doll, and the guy said, *"Now,"* and they tore out of the cruise tunnel and down the ramp and along the midway toward the Ferris Wheel to meet Ethan and Weaver, who were running toward them as Frankie swooped overhead, cawing at her, probably screaming, *How could you be so dumb?*

"What the *hell*?" Weaver said to the guy as he stopped in front of her, Mab running into his back.

"That leader thing worked," he said to Weaver, barely out of breath at all. "They're back in the Mermaid Cruise, killing one of their own." Then he tugged on Mab's arm. "She's freezing, so if you don't need me on this—"

"Get her warm," Ethan said. "We got this."

The guy took the D-gun from Mab and handed it to Ethan. "This does not work if they're inside wood. The pickets on the wrought-iron fence are spears. Jab them in the space between the joints, and you've got them."

"Right," Weaver said, and took off running for the Mermaid Cruise, Ethan hot on her heels.

The guy walked over to the paddleboat dock and picked up Mab's work bag from where she'd dropped it during the attack. He shoved it into her arms and said, "If we hurry, you'll be warmer."

"Who *are* you?" she said, shivering in the dark as she took the bag.

He turned to her, his black-rimmed Coke-bottle glasses gleaming in the lousy light from the cellophane-covered streetlamps. "I'm Oliver."

"Hello, Oliver," Mab said, and let him pull her down the midway, running to keep up with him, Frankie keeping watch overhead.

CHAPTER 18

Ethan and Weaver found several dolls lying near the entrance to the cruise with goo eating through the wood, and one German doll just inside the tunnel, torn to pieces and leaking purple into the water in the tank.

"This is a mess," Ethan said as he led Weaver into the dark tunnel, shining his Maglite ahead of them. "Remind me to tell Glenda to shut this ride down so we don't have to explain what wiped out France, Germany, and Hawaii. Or why the water looks like acid Kool-Aid."

"Hawaii's a country?" Weaver said as she stared at the carnage next to the fence.

"When this thing was built, it was a territory," Ethan told her. "So, that guy's your partner?"

"Yep. Oliver."

"What was he doing with Mab?"

"Following her."

"Why?"

"The same reason I followed you. She has a demon trace."

"Yeah, but he didn't shoot her."

"She wasn't trying to push Gus under the Dragon. I don't think there are any demons in here."

Ethan stopped. "I wasn't trying to push Gus under the Dragon."

"Well, it looked like you were." Weaver kept on walking past China. "He wouldn't have shot her anyway. He's against shooting. He made me promise never to kill a demon unless it was attacking something. He said it was the only way there'd be any left for him to study."

"Sounds like you have a good partnership," Ethan said.

"Very good," Weaver said, and then they were silent until they reached the end of the ride, Weaver for her own reasons, Ethan because he suddenly discovered himself feeling something he'd never felt before.

Jealousy.

When they were out in the open again, Ethan said, "So. Did you and he ever—?"

"Yep," Weaver said. "When we were done, he said, 'That was very efficient.' I think we'd been partners too long."

"Oh. So you're not now—"

"No, Ethan, now I'm with you. In Hank's trailer."

"Oh. Uh, good." Ethan looked around the park, trying to find another topic of conversation now that his future was back to bright again. Any topic of conversation. It was dark, except for the flashing light on top of the Devil's Drop and a few muted security lights here and there. "They're not going to stop coming."

"Nope."

"We need a plan."

"Good idea."

"I'm going to have to get the Guardia together tomorrow. Come up with a strategy."

"Good," Weaver said. "Thanks for being jealous."

Ethan almost said, *I wasn't jealous,* but then he shrugged. "Sure," he said, and they walked back to the trailers, arguing about the plan.

His future had never looked better.

*****

By the time they got to Delpha's trailer, Mab's hair had started to freeze and she was shuddering inside Oliver's coat. He opened the door and pushed her in as Frankie swooped in to land on his nest over the kitchen. Oliver went past her, down the short hall, where he opened the bathroom door and reached in. She heard the water in the shower come on as she shuddered with the cold, and then he came back to her and stripped the coat off her.

"In," he said. "You can take off your clothes in the shower, just get under the water," and she stepped in, and he shut the door.

She walked under the water, only warm now but getting hotter, and thought, *I can't take many more days like this,* and put her head against the shower wall and cried from exhaustion and near death and pregnancy and confusion.

Then the water got hotter and her clothes got heavier and she shoved everything off and stood naked as all the glorious warmth washed over her and brought her back.

Cold. It really shut down your ability to deal with life.

Somebody had put her soap and shampoo out—not Oliver, he hadn't had the time—and she washed off the last of the tank water, and thought, *Okay, now, what about him?* There was plenty of mystery there, Coke-bottle-glasses guy rescuing her from demons and knowing Weaver, but she was so damn *tired. . . .*

She turned off the water and reached for a towel, and then registered that there was a towel there. Somebody had unpacked her things and set up the trailer for her. Somebody had taken care of her. She felt tears start again and scrubbed them away with the towel, and then she put on her old blue terry cloth robe with the ducks and went out into the hall.

"Here," Oliver said from the bedroom, and she stepped inside and he pointed to the bed, already made up and now piled high with blankets. "Get in," he said, and she did, and he pulled the covers over her, and then stood there uncertainly while she shivered under the covers.

"Cold bed," she said, trying to explain away her wimpiness.

"Okay," he said, "scoot over," and climbed in with her, pulling the comforter over her head, shielding her wet hair from the air.

She curled against him, tentatively at first and then closer—he was putting out heat like a furnace, which made sense since he'd been a dragon—and he put his arms around her as she snuggled against his nice hard chest and buried her face in his shirt. It smelled of soap and heat and him, something indefinably pleasant and right, something that sent a primordial tingle down her spine. *This is good,* she thought, knowing her brain was addled from exhaustion and cold. *This is really good.*

He rubbed her back. "Go to sleep, you're all right now."

He was taking care of her. Mab felt the tears start again. She was turning into a needy watering pot. *Pull yourself together. Act normal.* She sniffed and said, "So you're Weaver's partner?"

He reached behind him to the bedside table and got her a Kleenex. "Here. Yes, I'm Weaver's partner. Go to sleep."

That sounded like a good idea. She blew her nose and then stuffed the Kleenex under her pillow and snuggled deeper into the bed, closer to him, sucking up his heat, relaxing in his arms until she was practically boneless. She was dry and warm and sleeping with a dragon. "You were a *great* dragon."

"What?"

There was something she was forgetting, something that nagged at her as sleep fogged her brain. Something important. Then she remembered and woke up a little, pulling her head back to look up at him. "You should call your wife."

He frowned down at her. "I'm not married." He put his hand on her forehead. "Are you delirious?"

"No. Who's Ursula?"

"My boss."

"Oh."

His cool gray eyes were warm on her now, his face so close. He had a great mouth. A great, unmarried mouth.

"Good," she said, and snuggled up against him again and sighed with exhaustion, safe in his arms.

His unmarried mouth quirked a little. "Why is that good?"

"Because I don't sleep with married men," Mab said, and fell asleep.

*****

When Ethan and Weaver got to Hank's trailer, Ethan hesitated. "I'll just go sleep in the woods."

"Right," Weaver said, and opened the door and he followed her in and down the short hall to the bedroom, where she took off her coat, and he stopped, staring at the bed, now neatly covered with a plain black comforter and thirty inches of green-and-purple stuffed dragon with gold on its wings and chest.

"What?" Weaver said, stripping off her turtleneck.

"You brought the dragon."

"Beemer? Of course, I brought Beemer." Weaver took off her jeans. "He lies 'under the shadows, in the covert of the reeds and the swamp,' don't you, baby? This is his kind of place."

"Oh," Ethan said, still staring at the dragon. "Is he going to watch?"

Weaver took off her underwear and got into bed, patting Beemer, her breasts bouncing a little as she scooted over to give him room. "Sure. I usually talk to him at night, but since you're here, he can just—"

"No," Ethan said, and put the dragon outside the bedroom door.

"Probably just as well." Weaver pulled the covers up to her chin. "We wouldn't want to traumatize him."

"We're going to do something that would traumatize him?" Ethan said, growing more cheerful as he stripped off his clothes and body armor.

"Oh, yeah," Weaver said, and Ethan sighed and got into a warm bed for the first time in a long time.

Civilization had its perks.

*****

Kharos waited for Ray to show up by recalling the various torments he could inflict on a soul once it was in his possession. There were a lot, and they were all extremely satisfying.

"Sorry, I'm late," Ray said as he slumped down on the bench.

"There's a government agent in the park. The boss of the woman with the gun that kills demons. I gotta tell you, this is turning into a real clusterfuck. I'm thinking it's better to wait until next Halloween. Maybe the one after that."

WHAT DOES SHE WANT?

"Ethan. Says there's something weird about him. I got the impression she thought he was a demon or something."

GLENDA'S SON? THE NEW HUNTER?

"Yeah."

Kharos considered that. *GLENDA'S SON.*

Ray fidgeted. "I'm going to need more minions for the attack on Friday. The good news is Tura's chalice is in the Keep. Ethan took it over there."

WHY DO YOU NEED MORE MINIONS?

"Some of them attacked Mab. It didn't work out for them."

WHY DID YOU SEND THEM TO ATTACK YOUR NIECE?

"I want the park," Ray said, sounding impatient.

I SAID THE PARK WOULD BE YOURS.

"Well, it's not, and I'm running out of time." Ray stood up. "I've got people talking back to me, threatening me, taking my gun . . . it's not right. It's taking too long. I need the park *now*—"

More of his hair fell out.

"Oh, *come on*."

GIVE ETHAN TO THE GOVERNMENT AGENT.

"But—"

TELL HER TO KILL HIM. THEN SEND ME YOUNG FRED.

"You know, he's not a big supporter of hurting the Guardia," Ray said, his face flushing red. "He just wants the whole thing to end so he can retire. He has no idea of what you're up to. So if you're thinking he's going to replace me—"

THAT IS NOT YOUR CONCERN.

"Great," Ray muttered. "You know, I've done everything you've told me to. I deserve better than—"

SOON YOU WILL HAVE EVERYTHING YOU DESERVE.

"Oh," Ray said, looking nervous this time. "I'll, uh, get on that government agent thing."

He walked away faster than usual, looking back over his shoulder once.

Not as dumb as Kharos had thought.

But still dumb enough.

Kharos returned to the new problem.

Glenda's son was part demon.

THAT CANNOT BE, Kharos thought, but if it was true . . .

Women. A problem for 2,500 years.

He thought of Vanth pressing against him, Glenda hot under his hands. . . .

Women. Worth the problems they caused.

But not worth losing everything for.

Glenda and her son were going to die.

*****

Mab woke up alone on Sunday morning, which was par for her course and which usually she preferred. But today . . .

Of course he didn't stay, she told herself. He doesn't even know you.

She crawled out of bed, found her clothes had been unpacked and put away, and got dressed in her jeans and a blue long-sleeved Dreamland thermal T-shirt. Then she put a zip-front sweatshirt on over that.

She'd been cold enough last night to last her the rest of her life.

She opened the door and looked down the short hallway to see Oliver sitting at her malachite table, his fair hair gleaming in the sunlight through the trailer window and his shirtsleeves rolled up, going through her research while Frankie sat on the malachite table and supervised.

He's still here, she thought, her heart lifting, and then kicked herself. He was going through *her work.* The fact that he looked really good going through her work was no reason for her not to be furious. Or something.

"Hello?" she said, and meant to add, *What the hell are you doing?* but he looked up and said, "There's coffee, but not for you. Tea on the counter, hot water on the stove." Then he went back to his reading.

Mab padded down the short hall and found a note pinned to a box of peppermint tea bags on the counter, something she'd missed in her hurry to get into the shower the night before. The note said, "Welcome home, Mab. Love, Glenda," and she almost started to cry again, except Oliver was sitting right there, because Glenda had unpacked everything for her to welcome her home.

So she got one of Delpha's good, thick, white china mugs down from the cupboard and put one of Glenda's tea bags in it, and poured in the water Oliver had heated for her, and thought, *People.* There were people everywhere in her life now.

She picked up her mug and turned to look at Oliver, his gray eyes serious on her work.

People. It wasn't so bad.

She sat down in the wide ebony chair across from him, and Frankie picked his way over the papers to butt his head against her hand. "Hey, baby," she said, rubbing his head with her finger, and then she looked back at Oliver. "What are you doing?"

"Finding out what you've been up to," he said, not looking up from the papers. "Apparently, you're as pure as the driven snow."

"Pure?" Mab said.

"I'm not seeing anything in here except research for restoring the park."

"That's because I was restoring the park," Mab said, confused. "What did you think I was doing?"

"We didn't know." Oliver put the papers neatly back into her binder—more neatly than she'd put them in there—and closed it, and then looked at her, his gaze steady and a little disconcerting without the big black-rimmed glasses. She could see his cheekbones clearly now. He had great cheekbones. "You're Ray Brannigan's niece, and you have a strong francium trace. So I watched you."

"That's creepy." Mab sipped her tea. It was wonderful. Then it hit bottom and her stomach said, *Hello?* but she sat very still until the urge to return the tea passed.

"Morning sickness?" he said.

"Can't anybody around here keep a secret?" Mab said, putting down her mug, annoyed. "Who told you?"

He picked up his coat and reached into the pocket and handed her his glasses. She took them and put them on, not sure what he wanted. The world looked odd through them, a little watery, but nothing really surprising until she put up her hand to take them off.

Her hand had a faint blue glow around it.

"Oh," she said.

"They pick up francium," Oliver said.

Mab looked down at her stomach. There was a tiny dot of green light there, barely visible, but there.

She took off the glasses and handed them back. "I'm scared," she told him.

"What of?"

"What this baby is. What I am." It was such a relief to say it that she sighed and picked up her tea.

"You're a human being," Oliver said. "You just have some mutant genes."

"Mutant," Mab said. "We talking X-Men mutant here?"

"It's well known that a fetus can be altered by radiation or environmental hazards," Oliver said, sounding like a PBS documentary. "At the moment of your conception, according to your mother's frequent statements, she was possessed by a demon. Therefore, you were exposed to francium. As was your baby since the man who fathered it was possessed by a demon."

Drunk Dave. "Oh, god," Mab said, gripping her mug tighter.

"Still a human baby, created by two human beings," Oliver said. "You have nothing to worry about. She'll just be like you. Different."

"I don't want to be different," Mab said, feeling her gorge rise. "I don't want *her* to be different—"

"Why?" Oliver said. "Why choose to be like everybody else when you can be—"

"A demon?"

"Gifted," Oliver said. "I have great admiration for you, Mary Alice.

You've made beautiful things in your life, recovered things that would have been lost forever. Imagine what your son will do."

"Daughter," Mab said. "Delphie."

He nodded. "Let's go get breakfast at the Dream Cream. Delphie needs waffles."

Mab laughed, surprising herself, and got her coat while he made sure the stove was off and the coffeemaker was unplugged, and then she followed him out the door, Frankie flying in advance, catching updrafts with enthusiasm. "So you've been watching me? Why?" she said as they headed for the midway, and he said, "Mostly so Weaver wouldn't shoot you," and she laughed again and felt glad to be alive.

*****

Ethan woke in comfort with Weaver in his arms, which was startling enough all by itself. Then he remembered that his bullet was gone, and after that, that Mab was going to have a baby, and that Glenda had almost died and was free of the Guardia now—

Weaver stirred and cuddled closer.

—and Weaver had slept in his arms all night. His life had changed. He was going to have to change to keep up with it.

He left Weaver sleeping, putting Beemer in his place in bed beside her, and crossed the path to Glenda's trailer just as Mab and Oliver walked by, Mab calling out to Glenda, "Thank you for unpacking for me, that was lovely, and so was the tea."

Glenda waved at her from her lawn chair, swathed in blankets, her eyes covered with big sunglasses, an umbrella drink in her hand and a novel in her lap.

All she needed was a cabana boy, and Ethan really didn't want to take that thought any further, so he said, "Good morning. I have news."

"You're engaged to Army Barbie." Glenda nodded. "I'm for it. She'll give me very sturdy grandchildren who will be able to lay down cover fire as I get older."

"The bullet's out."

Glenda pulled her sunglasses down so that her sharp eyes peered over them. "What?"

"You were right, about the Guardia, about me not dying. The bullet worked its way out." He fished it out of his pocket and handed it to her. "I'm not going to die."

"Well, of course not, I told you that," Glenda said, but her voice quavered as she looked at the bullet and she swallowed hard before she went on. "But thank you for telling me." Her face crumpled. "Oh, Ethan, I'm so glad."

"Me too, Mom," Ethan said before she dissolved completely. "Do you still have that concoction?"

Glenda blinked back tears. "What concoction?"

"The one you tried to kill me with the other night."

She shoved the glasses back in place. "Stop being so paranoid. I wasn't trying to kill you; I was trying to save you. You're on your own now, feel free to deny reality as much as you—"

"Cut the crap, Mom. It's forty degrees out here and you're acting like you're retired in Miami."

"I am retired," Glenda said airily. "I am enjoying my golden years. With my son. Who's not dying." She smiled and picked up her drink and then spoiled the picture by sniffing back tears.

"And I want to keep things safe so you can," Ethan said.

Glenda put the umbrella drink down and removed the sunglasses. "Are you serious?"

"Yes." He took a deep breath. "I'm taking this seriously. I've got a lot of life ahead of me. It's time I did it right."

Glenda put her sunglasses back on, picked up the umbrella drink, and held it out. "Get me a refill, would you?"

"Glenda, I need—"

"The big plastic jug I used to make lemonade for you is full of daiquiris. Next to the fridge is your flask. It's got the—" She waved her hand. "—concoction in it."

Ethan was surprised. "You already did that?"

"I'm your mother."

"Right." Ethan went and refilled Glenda's margarita glass and took the flask. He came back out and handed the drink to her. "You stay here."

"Absolutely," Glenda said.

Ethan paused. "Can I ask you something?"

"Certainly."

"Your eyes ever flash?"

Glenda went still. "What do you mean?"

"I thought eyes flashing was a demon thing," Ethan said. "Is it also a Guardia thing?"

"No. Try to get out of earshot when you drink that, will you?"

Ethan left Glenda to her retirement and went into the woods, out of earshot. He pulled out the flask, unscrewed the lid, hesitated for a moment, then took a swallow.

He was on his knees vomiting in a few seconds. He stayed on his knees and took a second swallow, forcing the liquid down. It felt like fire racing through his veins and like acid coming back to his stomach and up his throat. He drank until he finished every drop in the flask and purged every iota of alcohol from his system, steam rising from the sweat on his skin.

Then, hands shaking, Ethan screwed the top back on and stood up. There. A new life.

Now all he had to do was make it demon-free.

*****

"All right," Ethan said at noon, standing behind his chair at the pentagonal table on the top floor of the Keep as Mab, Cindy, Gus, and Young Fred took seats before him. "Let's get going."

He glanced at Oliver and Weaver against the wall, Weaver reading the Guardia weapons book, leaning over to show Oliver a word he needed to translate for her, and Oliver sitting silent and watchful. Glenda sat beside them on the floor, smiling at Ethan with pride. Her son, the Guardia captain.

The quiet was deafening.

"Our mission," he said to them, "is to keep the Untouchables locked up and the world safe. It's most endangered on Halloween at midnight when the boundaries between the natural and the supernatural weaken. Is that right, Mom?"

"Pretty much," Glenda said. "But most of our Halloweens have been uneventful. The last really bad one was forty years ago."

"Well, something's happening this time," Ethan said. "We've got minion demons trying to kill us. That's new, right?"

"Well," Glenda said. "Not really. One or two show up here a couple times a year. Tourists carry them in across the causeway, not realizing something they're carrying is possessed. But minions are not too smart, so . . ."

"These are organized," Ethan said. "There's a bigger plan."

Mab was looking impatient, so he added, "What?"

"If we know the Untouchables are in the chalices," she said, "why can't we just bury them in a load of cement?"

"Because if the chalice breaks in the cement, they get out," Glenda said. "And then we don't have the chalice to hold them because it's broken and buried in cement. We keep the chalices locked in the iron statues so minions can't get to them, with the keys hidden elsewhere. It's the best we can do."

"What do they want?" Cindy said. "I know I'm new here, but if we knew what they wanted, couldn't we do a deal or something?"

"You want to deal with the Devil?" Weaver said from behind them. "Very bad idea. 'He is a liar and the father of lies.' You can't trust him. Ever."

"I think Cindy's right, we need to know why they're doing this," Mab said.

Ethan rolled his eyes. "They're demons. They're acting like demons because they're demons."

"No," Mab said. "They have to want something. If we knew—"

"Despair," Glenda said. "They feed on it. They terrorize people, destroy hope, and draw energy from the pain. They—"

"No." Mab shook her head. "That's not right. Fun did nothing to make me despair."

"Hey, I was with you in the men's room," Ethan said. "You were despairing."

"I was grieving," Mab said. "And he wasn't there. If he wanted to feed on my grief, he'd have stuck around. I got upset, and he ran for the Pavilion. I thought at the time that that was because he was a guy, but now I'm thinking maybe he can't stand grief."

"We'll get him a therapist once we have his ass back in the chalice," Ethan said. "Now what we have to do—"

"Wait a minute," Oliver said from the side of the room, and Ethan turned to him, annoyed. "I think she's right. Fufluns wasn't always a demon, he started out as a god of revelry and got deposed. I bet he feeds on happiness."

"That's it," Mab said, straightening. "That's why he's always making people laugh. It isn't that he needs everybody to like him, it's that he needs to feed on happiness to survive, be strong. That's why he . . ." She stopped, evidently remembering something she didn't want to share.

"If Fufluns feeds on happiness," Oliver said when she didn't continue, "then he's naturally an enemy of Kharos, who evidently does feed on despair. You can use that."

"What about the rest of them, then?" Weaver said. "Can we turn anybody else?"

"I don't know." Glenda looked doubtful. "Tura's crazy, so she's unpredictable, and I don't think she could stand up to Kharos anyway. Selvans is his yes man, no hope there. And Vanth loves him—"

"She doesn't feed on despair," Mab said. "I've spent a lot of time with her, talking with her, and she's never made me feel despairing. Guilty, but not despairing."

"Guilty?" Oliver said.

"You should be wearing a coat, it's cold out, you know how I worry," Mab said. "Where have you been, you're late, you always start painting by ten, you know how I worry. Are you sure you want to be with him, he's not good enough for you, and you know how I worry. Although to be fair, the last one was about Fun, and she was right, so—"

"Mother figure," Oliver said. "She feeds on guilt?"

"I don't think so," Mab said. "I think it's something more that she needs me to . . ." She bit her lip. "Want to be with her? Need her?"

"Love her," Glenda said. "She feeds on love, I bet. Probably doesn't give it, but needs to evoke it."

"That's not despair, either," Oliver said. "I think you've got your secret weapon. Pit Fufluns and Vanth against Kharos because the despair he needs is the antithesis of the happiness and love they need."

"That almost makes them seem like good guys," Cindy said.

"No," Weaver and Mab said together, and Weaver looked at Mab, surprised.

"They don't . . . connect," Mab said. "They're not emotionally involved. When Fun couldn't make me happy, he left, there wasn't anything in it for him. He wants to come back because he's sure he can make me laugh, but if I don't laugh, he goes to find somebody who will. He's in it for himself, not for me. Vanth's the same way. If I reject her, she won't go on loving me, she'll turn on me, find somebody else to feed on. I don't think they're evil, but they're not good. They're demons. And I think they're all dangerous because they all really need to feed to survive. They're parasites. We need to put them back."

"Now that I can agree with," Ethan said. "So we get them to turn on each other and then we capture them by—"

Young Fred groaned. "Why can't we just let them out so we can get *lives*. They're not going to hurt anybody. They feed on emotion, not people's brains. We're not talking zombies here. Let's let them go free."

"No," Glenda and Gus said together, but Mab said, "Wait a minute."

"Not again," Ethan said.

Mab waved him away. "What would happen if we did let them out? I'm not saying we should do it, especially Kharos and Tura, I just want to know what happens when they all get out."

"The more that are out, the stronger they are," Glenda said. "All five out makes them corporeal. After that, what happens is whatever they want. I'm not even sure you can turn them against each other.

They all follow Kharos. They must, he's their king, the ruler of their underworld, and he's the Devil. We can't let them out."

"So," Ethan said, taking back the meeting. "Our mission is to keep them in the chalices. I propose a two-part plan. The first part is to move all the chalices in here. The Keep is walled with iron and surrounded by water—"

"Not running," Weaver said from the wall.

"We can start the pumps again," Gus said. "The water will run. Then the demons can't get in here unless the drawbridge is down or the door in the basement is opened."

"So we lock and barricade that door," Ethan said, "and control the drawbridge, which will make this a safe place to keep the chalices, at least until Halloween is over. Even if they get out of the chalices, they can't get out of the closed-up Keep. Right, Mom?"

Glenda nodded. "Even a full Untouchable can't go through iron."

"So this week we move the chalices in here," Ethan said. "It's our Alamo."

"Alamo?" Mab said, alarmed.

"Not the Alamo," Ethan said fast while Weaver looked at the ceiling. "Fortress. Our fortress, our fall back position. The real prison inside the prison, the most defensible and safe place. So the chalices . . ." He looked at Mab. "What's the status on Fufluns' chalice?"

"I still need the two pieces—," she began, but Gus pulled two small pieces of wood out of his pocket and handed them to her.

"One in the bottom of the statue, other one on the floor of the Tunnel," Gus said. "Fished your paint coat out of the cruise tank, too, but the demon goo in the tank had eaten through—"

"I don't need the coat back," Mab said. "Thanks for the chalice pieces. I'll get Fun's chalice repaired today. As for the rest of them, I bet Ray has the keys. He gave me the panpipes, and I found the dove in his RV two weeks ago. What other keys do we need? Fun's pipes are still glued to the top of the carousel, but since his statue is broken, it's worthless anyway. We've got Tura's chalice up here already. So we need the keys to Vanth, the orange Strong Man, and the Devil." She stopped, frowning. "Do we even know what the other keys look like?"

"We have Selvans' key. It's the green jewel Dragon's eye," Glenda began.

"You found the Dragon's eye?" Mab said, straightening. "That's great, now we can finish the Dragon . . . oh. No, we can't. It's a key." She sat back, disappointed.

"So we can get Selvans' chalice any time we want it," Glenda went on. "Vanth's key is a crystal ball that goes on top of the Oracle booth."

"There's one in the Fortune-Telling Machine," Mab said, and Glenda shook her head.

"That's just a piece of glass. The real key is bigger and it's real crystal. Then Kharos's is a silver trident that goes on the top of the Devil's Drop. We don't have that one, either." She looked ill as she said the last part, and Gus looked over at her, his eyes full of worry and sympathy.

"So we hit Ray's RV and look there first for the ball and the trident." Ethan nodded to Weaver. "You up for that?"

"Definitely."

"Good," Ethan said. "Any discussion on the first part of the plan, or can we move on?"

"Me," Mab said, holding up her hand. "Why haven't the chalices always been in here?"

Ethan looked at her, exasperated.

"Well," she said, "it sounds like a really good idea. Why are we the first ones to think of it in eighty-some years?"

"Because it's our turn," Ethan said.

"Because the Keep has always been a safe house," Glenda said. "It's true that if we keep them in here, they can't get out, but if they're out there and we're in here, they can't get in, either. The Keep is really designed to keep them out, not in."

"So it really is just that nobody ever thought of that before?" Mab said. "That seems odd."

"The second part of the plan," Ethan said loudly, "is us. Most of us are new, and aside from Gus, all of us are untried. We need to find out what makes the Guardia strong, make ourselves a fighting unit."

"We know how to fight," Gus said.

"We can fight better," Ethan said. "Last night, you and I put Tura in her chalice without Glenda there to bind her. I don't know how, she just gave up and went in, but we need to know how we did that and how we took Selvans without Mab. We need to know the extent of our powers and how to use them to best advantage. We—"

"We need a handbook," Cindy said. "With diagrams."

"Oh." Mab dug the Sorceress's book out of her work bag. "Forgot. This is for you. It's in Italian."

"Oooooh," Cindy said, taking it. "Italian. I don't read Italian."

"We'll get you a dictionary," Ethan said. "Now about *the plan*."

Mab sighed, Young Fred rolled his eyes, Gus looked grumpy, and Cindy was engrossed in her book. He looked over at Weaver, who gave him a thumbs-up, and at Oliver, who was watching everything, his face blank.

Oliver, Ethan thought. Probably over there thinking he could do this better. "You have anything else to say, Oliver?"

Oliver thought for a moment. "I think your demons are getting smarter. Every time they're out, they learn something more about human beings. If they've been escaping for twenty-five hundred years, they have a pretty good knowledge of human behavior. Has the Guardia changed its capture process in all that time?"

"No," Glenda said.

"Then I'd suggest you do what Ethan says and think outside the chalice this time."

Oliver, Ethan thought. *Good man.* "So here's what I'm thinking. We need to get faster, and we need to be able to improvise, to take over each other's jobs if we have to."

Cindy looked up at that. "I don't even know my job."

"You will," Ethan said. "Because we're going to practice. There are minion demons in the park, at least half a dozen got away last night after trying to kill Mab. So we're going to hunt them at night and put them in boxes using every variation we can think of, including doing without one of us in the capture and swapping jobs. And we're going to get faster, no more hesitating."

"Yeah, sorry about that," Mab said.

"And we're going to get angry," Ethan said, and saw Cindy frown at him. "What?"

"I get angry, there's going to be dragons."

"Good," Ethan said. "Nice diversion. Strong emotion makes the magic stronger. If you see a minion, don't think about being afraid, think about how they slaughtered Delpha."

The room seemed to grow colder suddenly, even Cindy looking grim.

"Yeah," Ethan said. "Think about how they tried to push Gus under his own coaster, about how they tried to drown Mab and her baby. They're not abstract evil, they're coming after us, they're coming after—"

"Family," Glenda said. "And nobody fucks with our family." She nodded at Weaver and Oliver. "You can be second cousins. You count."

They looked at each other, and Ethan thought, *Second cousins? That's the best you can do, Mom?* He shook his head and went on. "So this week, we meet every night at midnight, and we go demon-hunting. We practice. We *train.* And during the day, we move all the chalices in here. On Halloween night, we hunker down here and wait the sons of bitches out."

"Well, it's a plan," Mab said doubtfully.

"Maybe they just want to be free," Young Fred said. "Maybe they're not all evil." He looked back at Oliver. "Right?"

"No," Weaver said. "All demons are evil."

"It's very possible they're not all evil," Oliver said, earning a snort from his partner. "And shooting everything in sight is draconian. But if we're talking the Devil here, we're talking draconian. I think on this one, I'm with Ethan."

Oliver, Ethan thought. *Great guy.* "So Mab will do the research, and we'll meet by the Dragon at midnight. Any questions?"

"The pirates are all destroyed, so the Pirate Ship is closed," Mab said. "The cruise tank is stained with purple demon jam, so that's off the midway. Can we try to not do anything else to the rides? Because I can't fix them now. It's just too late. And Halloween is going to be our big money-making day."

"Sure," Ethan said, not amused. "From now on if a demon attacks, we'll protect the ride first."

"She's right, Ethan," Glenda said. "We have to keep Dreamland running or we can't maintain the prison. Falling on hard times is what got Ray into the park in the first place. If you can avoid damaging a ride, it's really important that you do." She nodded to Mab. "I'll talk to the Pirate Ship and Mermaid Cruise families, let them know they're not working, but that you'll have them up again by next spring."

Mab looked surprised, but she nodded.

Wonderful. "Protect the rides, folks," Ethan said. "See you tonight at midnight."

They got up, none of them enthusiastic, and some of them—Young Fred, in particular—clearly skeptical.

Tough.

They were going to be a team if it killed them. Because that was the only way he could keep them from dying.

Mab patted his arm on the way out. "Nice job, chief."

Weaver didn't pat his arm. "You need a better plan than 'We're going to do things differently.' You need—"

"I know," Ethan said. "Keep reading that damn book while I figure this out."

CHAPTER 19

Mab waited for Glenda outside the Keep, Frankie fidgeting on her shoulder. "Can I talk to you for a minute?" she said as Glenda came out.

"Absolutely." Glenda put her sunglasses on. "I have all the time in the world. Where are you headed now?"

"Oliver said something this morning," Mab said. "I need to talk to Vanth."

"Want me to go with you? It's not a problem. My daiquiris will keep."

"Boy, getting out of the Guardia really agrees with you," Mab said.

"You're never out of the Guardia," Glenda said. "But sometimes you get lucky and you're not *responsible* for the Guardia anymore." She looked at Mab ruefully. "Of course, now you're the one holding the demon bag."

"I think it's more Ethan," Mab said.

"No," Glenda said. "He needs you to balance him. It's the two of you. Did you want me to go with you to Vanth?"

"No, I can handle Vanth." Mab hesitated. "But I could use a favor. Could you maybe clean out Old Fred's trailer?"

Glenda blinked at her. "You want to move into Old Fred's trailer?

Honey, that's no good. We'll move Young Fred in there, and you can have the apartment over the paddleboat dock. Much better for the baby."

"No, no," Mab said. "I like Delpha's trailer."

Frankie rasped his approval.

"Besides, we've got nine months before Delphie gets here, so—"

"Delphie?" Glenda's eyes got bright suddenly. "You're going to call her Delphie? Oh, Mab, that's wonderful."

Mab nodded, moving on before Glenda cried all over her. "I just thought Old Fred's trailer might be nice for . . . guests."

"Guests."

"Well, Oliver. He's on our side, and I could use help with the research, and the more people we have here in Dreamland, the safer we'll be, and he's stuck in that B and B in town with the teddy bears on the bed. . . ."

"Of course," Glenda said, her face straight. "We have to get him out of there. I'll clean out the trailer today, and he can move in tonight."

"Well, maybe he won't want to," Mab said.

"He'll want to," Glenda said, and put her sunglasses back on.

She set offdown the midway, her shoulders swinging, and Mab said to Frankie, "We have to keep her safe. She's finally happy, we have to keep her safe."

Frankie pushed himself off her shoulder, flapping into the air, and Mab watched him for a moment and then looked back at Glenda, the sun gleaming on the top of her platinum head as she moved across the flagstones, nothing threatening near her—

Mab blinked, suddenly disoriented. She shouldn't be seeing flagstones, she shouldn't be seeing the top of Glenda's head, *she had an aerial view—*

Frankie circled around as the world circled around Mab and then swooped down and sat on her shoulder, and the world righted itself.

He moved from foot to foot on her shoulder, very proud of himself.

Mab looked at her bird cautiously. "Okay, I said we had to make sure she was safe, so you went to look for . . . enemies?"

Frankie bobbed his head several times, clearly exhilarated by his excellent work.

"Good job, bird," Mab said, and thought, There goes any hope of faking normal.

Frankie rubbed his head on her cheek.

"Normal's overrated," she told him, and went to talk to Vanth.

*****

Ethan knocked on the door to Ray's RV behind the Dream Cream. He waited several seconds, then knocked again.

"He's probably off buying Satan a slushie." Weaver drew Ray's Desert Eagle and pointed the massive pistol at the lock. "I'll shoot it off."

"Hold on a second." Ethan pulled out the key ring he'd taken off Ray. He found a small modern key among the old iron ones, slid it in, and turned it. "See. The softer, easier way."

"Oh yeah, that's you."

The interior was neat and clean, clearly set up as an office. There was a picture on the wall of Ray in camouflage fatigues with a bunch of guys brandishing their weapons in front of a Blackhawk helicopter in a desert somewhere. The usual *I've been there and done it* thing.

"Let's trash the place," Weaver said.

"What are you? In college?"

"He's a demon groupie," Weaver said.

"Let's find the keys. Crystal ball. Trident. Stay on task."

Weaver began searching, none too gently, and Ethan figured he'd let her vent a bit on Ray's stuff. The trailer wasn't very big, and there weren't many places to hide things, so it only took Ethan five minutes to find a locked gun box inside the cover of the window air conditioner.

"Let me," Weaver said.

Ethan put it on the desk, and using the butt of the Desert Eagle, Weaver smashed it open, narrowly missing the six-inch glass ball that was inside.

"That's Vanth's crystal key," Ethan said. "Where's the trident?"

The door to the trailer swung open, and Ray stepped inside. *"What the fuck are you doing?"*

"Where's the trident?" Ethan asked.

"This is my trailer," Ray snapped. "This is my *office*. You have *no right* to be in my office. *I'm calling the police—*"

"Like you'd bring the cops in here," Weaver said. "Besides—" She flashed her badge. "—I am the cops."

"Not anymore. I'm calling your boss and having you fired," Ray said.

"Where's the trident?" Ethan repeated.

Ray looked at him with loathing. "Fuck off, you're way out of your league."

Ethan held up the ball. "We got this, Ray. Whatever you're planning, it isn't working."

"Get out," Ray said. "And *stay out.*"

Ethan led the way out the door, Weaver reluctantly behind him, as Ray slammed the door practically on her heel.

"What the hell?" she demanded as they walked away from the trailer. "He's got the damn trident."

"It's his ace in the hole, and he's keeping it close," Ethan agreed. "But it's not in the trailer, his eyes didn't go anywhere when I asked where it was, and he's not going to tell us where, so keeping at him would be a waste of time."

"We could torture him and find out."

"Torture doesn't work."

"You're just going to let him do his thing?"

"No," Ethan said. "I'm going to destroy him. But remember what Glenda said, if we get rid of him now, Kharos finds somebody else to work with that we don't know about."

"Something stinks about all this," Weaver said.

"Yeah. Ray. I'll take care of him after Halloween." He hefted the crystal ball in his hand. "I'm going to go find a ladder and pick up Vanth. You coming?"

"Can't," Weaver said. "I have to report to Ursula." She frowned.

"I've been thinking. Is it possible she and Ray knew each other before last night? Because somebody here in Dreamland has been giving her information, good information, that Oliver and I aren't passing to her."

"Anything's possible," Ethan said. "This is Dreamland."

Then he headed off to stick a crystal ball on top of an Oracle tent so he could retrieve a demon and put it in the Keep.

*****

Mab stopped in front of the Fortune-Telling Machine. The glass was like crystal now, and she could see Vanth sitting inside, very lifelike.

She stepped closer to the glass. "Are you my mother?"

WHAT?

"My mother. My human mother thought I was a demon. Where were you thirty-nine, no, forty years ago on Halloween night? Did you possess my mother?"

The machine was silent for a long time, and Mab thought, *Don't you dare stonewall me,* and kicked the carefully painted front. "*Talk to me*. I need to know this. I'm in trouble, and I need to know—"

DON'T KICK THE BOOTH.

"The booth? The *hell* with the booth, I want to know what you did forty years ago!" Mab pounded on the glass, suddenly upset, another mother ignoring her, another mother rejecting her. "Are you my mother? Are you? Answer me!" She raised her fist to pound again and then caught sight of her reflection.

Glowing blue eyes.

YOUR EYES.

"I know," Mab said. "I don't know what it means."

IT MEANS YOU'RE MINE. HOW?

"I don't know," Mab said, her anguish suddenly chilled. "I don't even know for sure that you—"

FORTY YEARS AGO. THAT LONG? IT WAS ME. IT WAS US. WE'D BEEN TRAPPED FOR SO LONG, AND WE WERE OUT, AND WE SAW THEM GO INTO THE TUNNEL OF LOVE ARGU-

ING, AND I SAID, "THEM" AND HE LAUGHED AND WE TOOK THEM AND IT WAS GLORIOUS—

"Too much information," Mab said, stepping back.

—AND THEN WE MADE YOU! WE NEVER IMAGINED. IT'S A MIRACLE!

"Okay," Mab said, not sure how to take a Fortune-Telling Machine that was suddenly claiming her as its own. This was what she wanted, but . . .

Maybe she should have thought this through. *She feeds on love,* Glenda had said.

OH, DARLING, I'M SO HAPPY.

"Good," Mab said, really uneasy now.

YOU ARE NOT THAT MISERABLE LITTLE WOMAN'S DAUGHTER. YOU'RE *MINE*.

"Actually, I'm all grown up now," Mab said, taking a step back. "Really probably don't even need a mother—"

WE HAVE SO MUCH TO *TALK* ABOUT.

"Well, that's certainly true," Mab said.

I'M JUST SO HAPPY YOU'RE *OURS*. . . .

"Okay, about the 'ours,' " Mab said. "That would be you and Kharos."

OF COURSE, DARLING. HE'LL BE SO THRILLED WHEN HE FINDS OUT.

"So I'm the daughter of the Devil," Mab said, confronting what had been haunting her since she'd talked with Oliver.

ISN'T IT WONDERFUL?

"Fabulous," Mab said.

SO NOW YOU'LL LET US OUT.

"I can't." Mab took another step back. "I'm sorry, but Kharos kills people."

HE GETS TENSE. WE'VE BEEN LOCKED UP A LONG TIME.

"I know, and that's rough," Mab said, trying to see it from the demon point of view. "But he kills people. So does Tura."

TURA HAS NO SELF-CONTROL.

"Well, demon," Mab pointed out.

LET US OUT, DARLING, AND WE'LL BE A FAMILY!

"I can't," Mab said. "I'm Guardia. I'm sworn to keep you locked up."

YOU'RE PUTTING CAREER OVER FAMILY?

"I sort of live for my work," Mab said. "Look what a nice job I did on your machine."

MY PRISON.

"Don't play the guilt card. I have enough emotional baggage already just from Fufluns."

WHAT DID HE DO TO YOU?

"Seduced me—"

I'VE HEARD HE'S A VERY GOOD TIME.

"—and knocked me up," Mab said.

YOU'RE HAVING A BABY?

"Evidently."

THAT'S WONDERFUL! AND WE'LL ALL BE TOGETHER! LET US OUT!

"Okay, look, that's not happening. I will bring the baby by in nine months so you can see—"

NO! LET US OUT!

Mab took a step back. The glass appeared to be steaming up. "Vanth—"

MOTHER!

"Mother, try to stay calm."

I AM CALM! MY DAUGHTER IS KEEPING ME A PRISONER IN A FORTUNE-TELLING MACHINE!

"Okay, that's something we should put on cards," Mab said. "Come on, you've been in there for almost a century. I'm not respons—"

LET US OUT.

"No," Mab said, and walked farther away before the machine melted or shattered or did whatever demon cells did when their contents went rogue. The box rocked a little, but basically, as long as Vanth was locked inside the Fortune-Teller, she was stuck.

Of course, if anybody ever let her out . . .

Frankie spiraled down to sit on her shoulder.

"I think I just made a tactical error," she told him.

He cawed, and she saw Ethan coming toward her, carrying a ladder.

"We got the key," Ethan said. "I'm taking Vanth."

"Be careful," Mab said. "She's not happy."

He climbed up and put the ball on the peak of the Delpha's Oracle roof with an audible click, and then turned it.

Inside the Fortune-Telling Machine, the rear part of Vanth's statue rotated open, banging into the back of the booth.

YOU'RE LETTING US OUT? OH, THANK YOU!

"No, no," Mab said as Ethan climbed down and came back and opened the rear of the machine, reached into the statue, and removed the chalice. "We're just moving you to a safer place."

"Who are you talking to?" Ethan asked.

"Vanth," Mab said. "My mother, the demon."

"What?"

"The demon eyes we have? It's from a conception possession. Vanth is my mother. Well, one of them. And guess who I inherited the angry red eyes from."

"You can talk to her?" he asked, holding the chalice securely.

"Yeah. I can hear her voice in my head."

Ethan looked over his shoulder at the Devil's Drop, and she knew what he was thinking.

"You going to go have a word with Dad? Such a bad idea," Mab said as he stepped back onto the midway in the direction of the Keep. "Hey!"

"What?" Ethan said.

"We have the same damned father. Delpha said you were my brother, but I didn't think she meant literally—"

"Delpha was never wrong," Ethan said.

They stared at each for a moment, perplexed by their newfound siblinghood.

"So we're the Luke and Leia of hell," Mab said. "This is going to take some getting used to."

Ethan held up the chalice. "I should take this to the Keep. I've still got to pick up Selvans."

WHAT'S GOING ON? WHAT IS HE TALKING ABOUT?

"Absolutely nothing, Mom," Mab said, and watched her brother carry off her mother in a wooden cup.

Then she opened her work bag, took out the broken chalice lid, and began to repair the prison for her daughter's father.

*****

Later that evening, Ethan followed Gus on his walk along the maintenance track of the Dragon, hooked to the outer railing by a safety line. He tapped on the rails every twenty feet or so with a wooden hammer to make sure the structure was sound, putting his good ear just over the track. Despite his age and arthritis, Gus could pull himself up even the steepest incline of the coaster.

They reached the top and looked out over the park. There was a low fog on the river, and the trees had lost all their leaves, giving the land a barren appearance. Gray clouds hung low over the land, and a stiff breeze added to the cold. The light on top of the Devil's Drop was slightly above their level, flashing in the early evening. Ethan felt a chill.

"The trident goes on top of the Drop, doesn't it?" he asked Gus.

The old man was breathing hard, but he nodded. "Yeah. Keys always go on top. Carousel, Mermaid, Fortune-Teller, Dragon, and Drop."

"My father died there."

Gus simply nodded.

"Tell me," Ethan said.

Gus sighed, reluctant, and looked away.

"I need to know," Ethan said. "My eyes flash. Glenda wouldn't tell me. I deserve the truth from a fellow Guardia."

"Forty years ago, on Halloween," Gus finally said. "It was the last time any of the Untouchables was out. Petra, our Sorceress, the one before Glenda, was sick. Real sick. None of us knew it, she cast a glamour that kept us from seeing it. Kharos promised her health and life if she set the five free and left the drawbridge to the Keep down.

She was desperate but she wasn't stupid. She set four of the five free, kept Vanth locked up because she knew Vanth was the most important to Kharos. She told Kharos she'd let Vanth out when he cured her.

"Kharos—" Gus shook his head. "She should have known better, but none of us had ever faced an Untouchable. He told her to set Vanth free or he'd kill her. Gave her an hour to do it. She went to find the Guardia. She knew it was over for her, but she thought she could save us. Kharos went looking for the others and found your mom and dad instead. Nobody had escaped on Halloween for a long time. They were in the woods, celebrating another year of Dreamland . . ."

"And he possessed my dad while I was conceived," Ethan said.

"Yeah," Gus said. "Your dad knew it, told your mom to go back to the trailer, and he went to look for the rest of us. Your mom, she didn't know about any of it, so she was pretty upset. So was he."

Ethan nodded. "All right."

"Then Kharos took another body. Came here to find Selvans. I ran the Dragon and heard only one rattle and then there were the four of them. I knew it was them, coming toward me."

"What did you do?" Ethan asked.

"I ran," Gus said, jaw tight.

"I'd run, too, facing four Untouchables," Ethan said. He got the feeling Gus didn't believe him.

"Kharos let Vanth out, and they went into the park to . . . celebrate. Your dad found us all, brought us together—he was a hell of a leader, Ethan—and we went hunting. Fufluns gave up pretty easily. To tell you the truth, I don't think he wanted all five out. We tracked Selvans down pretty easily, too. He doesn't move fast. Then we went hunting for Tura at the Tunnel of Love and that's when Kharos caught us. He didn't even use magic to kill Petra, just backhanded her in the body he was in and broke her neck. He and Vanth went into the crowd near the Tunnel because without a Sorceress we couldn't—"

"Mab's parents," Ethan said.

Gus looked surprised. "What?"

"Mab's parents were taken in the Tunnel of Love."

"Maybe," Gus said. "That's where Delpha found Glenda, scared out of her mind because she'd just been called and she didn't know what was going on. It was bad, trying to explain what was going on, what your father had never told her, right before she had to go into battle for the first time. She was scared out of her wits but she was a fighter. We caught Vanth first as they came out of the tunnel, and Kharos went crazy. Everybody thought he was just a drunk, but then he took off down the midway and we had to follow, back to the Devil's Drop. He climbed. We followed."

Gus fell silent and Ethan felt a cold wind blow across the park.

"We caught him at the top, trying to smash the key so he couldn't be put back in his statue," Gus finally said. "Glenda was wonderful. I still don't know how she climbed the Drop the way she did, but we did the ritual, and your father took Kharos, but pulling him out of the host body made it stagger. He grabbed for the host just as Glenda said, 'Redimio,' and the rush as Kharos was pulled out of him knocked him off balance. He shoved the host to safety but he couldn't save himself. He fell."

Ethan felt sick. "So Kharos killed my father."

"Yeah," Gus said. "Kharos and the rest of them, trying to escape. And now it's all happening again."

There was no sound but the wind howling through the struts of the Dragon Coaster for a while. Finally, Ethan stirred. "Okay. Let's get Selvans and call it a night."

"Yeah," Gus said.

The wooden tunnel that was the Dragon was bolted to the top of the coaster. Making sure his safety line was in place, Ethan climbed up the iron framework until, one arm looped around the dragon's neck, he could reach out toward the empty eye socket. The crystal eye was pulled out of his hand as it got close. It snapped into the socket with a solid click. Ethan felt a shiver go through his body.

He climbed back onto the service track and followed Gus as he finished the walk. Then they went over to the orange Strong Man statue together. A panel in the rear had rotated open, and Ethan reached it and picked up Selvans' chalice.

It was heavier than the others had been, pulsing with a kind of dull, confused anger.

"Vicious son of a bitch," Gus said.

Ethan put the chalice under his arm. "I'll take him to the Keep with the others. You okay?"

"Yeah," Gus said, but he didn't sound good.

"It's okay," Ethan said. "This time the good guys will survive." He patted the old man on the shoulder and turned to go.

"I just want it over," Gus said, and went back in the booth.

*****

Mab stood in front of the empty Fortune-Telling Machine, trying to figure out why she felt so bereft. She fished a penny out of her bag and put it in the machine and turned the lever, and a card slid into the tray. A real card.

She picked it up.

YOU WILL HAVE MANY INTERESTING ADVENTURES.

"Somehow, that's not reassuring," she said to the booth, but Vanth was gone, so she was just talking to an empty statue. Alone. "I used to love being alone," she told the statue. "What the hell happened to me?"

"Happiness," Fun said from behind her, and she turned to see him smiling at her in the cold sunshine, warm and real and looking like Joe.

"Does Dave know you're taking him for a ride again?" Mab said.

"His request." Fun came closer, and Mab steeled herself not to step back. "If I possess him for an hour every day, his hair stays curly. Women love it."

"He can't use a curling iron?"

"Dave? He'd put his eye out." Fun smiled down at her, warm and real and treacherous. "Look, I know you're mad at me, but give me some credit. You're a lot happier since you met me, you're—"

"Pregnant," Mab said, and Fun lost his smile. "Yep, and you're the daddy, so you want to tell me again how good you've been for me?"

"There's a baby?" Fun said, dumbfounded. "But it's Dave's, not mine."

"Wrong again." Mab smiled up at him, feeling some vindication in turning the tables. "Conception possession. Since you were in Drunk Dave when he was in me, you're the dad, too. And she's definitely got your demon genes along with mine."

"She?" Fun said, still looking stunned.

"Delphie. Little girl. Redhead. Green eyes. Crooked smile. Green glow. Demon spawn."

Fun sat down on the cold hard ground as if his knees had given out.

"Of course, by the time she's born, you'll be back in your chalice," Mab went on. "Off the hook completely. But that's okay because I have family here." She stopped, a little startled by how easily she'd said *family,* but then she went on. "Glenda's going to be a kick-ass grandma, and Ethan's going to be the uncle every kid should have, and Cindy's going to be the best aunt ever, what with the ice cream and the dragons, and I'm sure Weaver will teach her to maim and kill."

"I'm going to be a father," Fun said, dazed.

"Okay, just for the record, *this is not about you.* This is about keeping this baby safe and happy and . . . undemonized for as long as possible. So you are not actually going to be a father in the pick-her-up-from-high-school, first-dance-at-her-wedding sense of the word. You're going to be in a *chalice.*"

"Does she look like me?" Fun said. "I mean, you've seen her, right? In the future?"

"She has your smile," Mab said, relenting. "Although I don't know if I actually saw—"

He stood up, his face dead serious. "I'll take care of this. I'll take care of you."

"No," Mab said, alarmed. "No, no, I have backup, really, don't—"

But Fun was already striding down the midway to the back of the park, his shoulders set in determination.

Frankie flew down to Mab's shoulder.

Mab bit her lip. "Follow him," she said after a moment. "Find out where he goes."

Frankie bobbed his head once and then launched himself into the air.

"This is all just too complicated," Mab said to nobody, and went to find Oliver.

Research would save her. And if it didn't, she was pretty sure Oliver would.

*****

Kharos was annoyed by the soul who sat down beside him, young, dressed in a blue pin-striped shirt, lounging on the bench as if sitting beside the Devil meant nothing—

YOU WANTED TO SEE ME? Fufluns said.

Kharos was startled. This was not a soul; it was an Untouchable. How had he missed that?

I HAVE THINGS TO DO, Fufluns said. PEOPLE TO MEET. LET'S GET THIS OVER WITH.

Kharos looked at him more closely and realized that Fufluns had been playing in Dreamland too long, so saturated in human emotions, human thoughts, that the demon in him was obscured.

That could be a problem, especially if he'd developed the human flaw of not following orders.

I NEED YOU IN THE KEEP ON HALLOWEEN. GO THERE BY ANY MEANS NECESSARY.

SURE, Fufluns said. ON ONE CONDITION.

Kharos went still. Nobody asked him for conditions, especially not this upstart ex-god debased by humanity.

NOTHING HAPPENS TO MAB, Fufluns said.

Mab. Ray's niece.

YOU TOUCH HER IN ANY WAY, THE DEAL'S OFF.

Kharos cursed whatever demonic fate had made this clown part of the Untouchables.

DO WE HAVE A DEAL? Fufluns said.

OF COURSE, Kharos lied.

WHY DO I NOT BELIEVE YOU?

WHAT CAN YOU DO ABOUT IT?

Fufluns smiled up at him. I CAN WORK AGAINST YOU WHEN YOU NEED ALL FIVE TO BECOME UNTOUCHABLE AGAIN. YOU NEED ME, KHAROS, AND I NEED MAB UNHURT AND HEALTHY. SO WHEN YOUR NATURAL INSTINCT TO DESTROY ZEROES IN ON HER, REMEMBER YOU'LL BE COMMITTING DEMONIC SUICIDE IF YOU GIVE IN TO IT.

Kharos seethed, knowing what he said was true. But he also knew that if Fufluns had been affected by the human cattle, then he probably had some of their traits. He was making this deal out of fear.

Fufluns stood up. SHE'S MY LINE IN THE SAND. CROSS ME THERE, AND YOU'RE DEAD. LEAVE HER ALONE, AND I'LL JOIN YOU IN THE KEEP.

He turned and walked away without waiting for an answer.

WHAT LINE IN WHAT SAND? Kharos thought, confused, and began to brood on a way to make the Mab woman weep with despair without paying Fufluns' price.

*****

For the rest of the week, Ethan focused on sharpening his team, spending his off hours looking for the Kharos key, the last piece of his puzzle. The team-sharpening went better than the puzzle search. Minion demons were infinitely easier to catch than Untouchables, and after several captures each night, the Guardia had built up a library of demons trapped in Tupperware, coin purses, Jack Daniels bottles, milk cartons, ziplock bags, and Altoids tins. If it had a lid, the Guardia could put a minion in it. Some of the minions were more optimistic about this than others—the demon in the not-quite-empty Jack Daniels bottle seemed happier than most—but they were all stuck, no matter how the five-beat chant was performed. Their only real disagreement was that Weaver wanted to kill all the demons, and Oliver preferred to keep them alive for study purposes. Ethan let them fight it out and concentrated on the big picture: living through Halloween.

The rest of the time, Ethan focused his energy on the tangibles: repairing the outer fence, preparing the Keep for any assault, planting iron weapons throughout the park along with the ever-present spears in the wrought-iron railing, and patrolling nightly with Weaver at his side, snatching a few hours of sleep with her in Hank's trailer, which somehow had become their trailer by Friday. Ethan wasn't exactly sure how he'd ended up living with a woman in a committed relationship, but now that he was, it wasn't bad. At least he felt no compelling instinct to return to the woods and the rock under his sleeping bag. And it wasn't just Weaver; he was feeling the same sense of responsibility and loyalty to the Guardia that he had to his team in Afghanistan. He was responsible for them, even if they weren't sure they wanted to be part of his team. Especially Cindy, who seemed more perplexed than involved, although she redimio-ed like a champ whenever called upon.

Being responsible felt normal, like the way things should be, but sometimes, late at night, he woke in a cold sweat, memories of what had happened in Afghanistan terrorizing his subconscious. Responsibility for other people brought risks. He didn't need any more ghosts in his dreams.

So on Friday, he got up, put Beemer in the warm spot he left in the bed, walked down to the Dream Cream, and sat down at the counter,

Cindy came to put a coffee cup in front of him.

"Hey, boss."

"Not boss," Ethan said. "We're equals."

"Right. You want breakfast?"

"No, I want to make sure you're okay with all of this." Ethan tried to find his warm, sympathetic, understanding side and then realized he didn't have one. "You're the newest, and you weren't paying much attention at the meeting in the Keep. I—"

"Yes, I was," Cindy said, unfazed. "And I've been paying a lot of attention to the book Mab gave me. It's slow going, but I'm learning many things. Including how to control the dragons. Most of them. Really, my skill set is vastly enhanced, as Mab would say."

"Well, that's good," Ethan began, and the door opened and a teenager came in, gangly and goofy and happy looking, and sat down one seat away from him.

"Be right back," Cindy said, and dished up a waffle.

Then she took the bowl into the storeroom and came out with a pile of orange ice cream on top of the pastry and put it in front of the boy.

"You look like somebody who'd be up for experimental ice cream," she said, beaming at him. "Cinnamon Surprise. On the house."

"Great!" the kid said, and dug in as Cindy moved back down to Ethan.

"So it's good you're learning, uh, many things," Ethan said. "But what we need—"

"Like it's not all spells, although Glenda gave me some of that, too. She says I'm a natural," Cindy said, watching the kid shovel ice cream.

"That's good," Ethan said again, "but what we need are practical skills—"

The boy dropped his spoon on the counter with a clatter and began to choke.

"Like now I can spot a demon as soon as he walks through the door." She leaned over the counter to the boy and said, "That's for knocking up Mab and lying to her."

Ethan saw the yellow flash in the kid's eyes, grabbed him by the scruff of the neck, and hauled him to the door as Cindy dumped the bowl of ice cream into the trash and the entire Dream Cream froze, watching them. Then Cindy said, "Everything is just *fine*!" in Glenda's overbright version of these-are-not-the-droids-you're-looking-for, and they all went back to chatting and eating.

Ethan dragged Fun around to the deserted side of the building and slammed him against the striped paneling.

"Easy," Fun said, still gasping. "I'm dying here."

"As long as it's you and not the host, I don't care," Ethan said, and then Cindy came out and joined them, looking very Midwestern and cheery in her pink stripes, the sequins on her turquoise cardigan glittering in the October sun as she hugged herself to keep warm.

"What was in that?" Fun said, starting to recover.

"Iron rust," Cindy said. "Looks just like cinnamon. And I have *gallons* of it."

"Look," Fun said, smiling at them as he choked. "I know about the baby, and I think it's great. I've never had a kid—"

"You're not going to have one now." Ethan hit him, knocking him cold, and then let him drop to the ground. "You knocked up my sister, you bastard."

"Might want to go easy on the body," Cindy said. "That's Jerry Ferris Wheel."

"The Ferris Wheels are having a bad week." Ethan picked up the unconscious teenager. "I'll take him to the Keep, you call Mab to bring the chalice and get everybody else you can."

"I'll go with you," Cindy said, and made her calls while she walked beside Ethan, who had Fun over his shoulder. They got some looks, but Cindy would smile that amazing smile and say, *"We're fine, thanks,"* and people would nod and move on.

"Okay," Ethan said after he loaded Fun into one of the paddleboats. "I apologize for doubting the new skills."

"You haven't seen anything yet," Cindy said, and got in the boat with him.

*****

Mab had just settled in on the velvet banquette in her trailer with a bowl of vegetable soup when she heard a knock at the door. She slid out from behind the malachite table and opened the door.

Weaver stood there with a pained look of friendliness on her face.

"You don't have to fake it," Mab said. "I'm good with open hostility."

Weaver's smile disappeared into her sigh. "I'm not hostile. You're hostile. I'm . . . exasperated."

"Come on in, Exasperated," Mab said, and stood back to let her in.

"Wow." Weaver took in the gold-starred walls and the branch crown molding with Delpha's urn ensconced next to Frankie's nest. "This is . . ."

"Delpha's," Mab said, sitting down again. "Oh, I forgot. Can I get you anything? Coffee, Diet Coke, vegetable soup . . ." She looked up at Frankie. ". . . sunflower seeds?"

"No," Weaver said. "Thank you. I've come for a, uh, psychic reading."

"Whoa." Mab sat back. "Either you really want to make friends or you really have a problem."

Weaver pulled out the chair on the other side of the table and sat down. "Look, you and I don't get along, and that's okay. But if we're going to work together to defeat the demons, we need to at least respect each other. And Oliver seems to think you're the real deal."

"Really?" Mab bit back a smile. "Well, we've only been working together for a week. He doesn't really know me at all."

"Right," Weaver said, dismissing that. "So, I want a reading. You know what I do; I want to see what you do."

"Ten bucks," Mab said, and ate some more of her soup.

Weaver looked taken aback.

"That's the going rate," Mab said.

Weaver reached in her pocket and pulled out a wallet and found a ten. "Okay," she said, sliding it across the table. "Here."

Mab nodded. "If you don't think the reading is real, you get to take it back." She put her soup bowl to one side. "What's your question?"

"Question?"

"What did you come to find out? Matters of the head or heart?"

"Head," Weaver said firmly.

"Right hand, please."

Weaver stuck out her right hand, and Mab took it. "Nice long life line. Clearly the military isn't going to kill you any time soon."

"I'm not in the military."

"Really? 'Cause that black helicopter looked very Ethan to me. Never mind." Mab took a deep breath. "You have a specific question in mind?"

"No, I just wanted . . ."

"Wanted to see if Oliver was right and I was the real deal," Mab finished for her. "God knows." She put her palm flat on Weaver's and closed her eyes.

Images raced by, thoughts even faster: demons, Ethan, guns, Oliver, training, Ursula, guns, Ethan . . . Weaver was evidently on overdrive 24/7.

"You're going to have to slow things down," Mab told her. "I'm getting bombarded here."

"With what?" Weaver said.

"Ursula's being a pain in the ass, but she scares you; Oliver wants you to stop shooting demons; you're wondering if you can adapt the demon gun to the Untouchables; you think Ethan can probably help you, *whoa*—" Mab dropped her hand.

"What?" Weaver said again, this time wide-eyed.

"I did not need that memory of you and Ethan naked," Mab said, scowling at her. "Concentrate on business, please."

"Oh." Weaver cleared her throat. "You can read my mind?"

"No," Mab said. "That would be too easy. I get pieces of things unless the person is concentrating on one question. Then I can see what he or she is thinking and extrapolate from that. You won't ask a question."

"Okay," Weaver said, holding out her hand again. "Can I be of help to the Guardia?"

"Good question." Mab put her hand on Weaver's and concentrated, and the flood of images slowed down, Weaver seeing herself as a guard to the Guardia, Weaver seeing herself defeating something that looked like the Devil statue, Weaver standing with the team . . . "Well, you certainly think you can." She shifted in her seat, which moved her hand on Weaver's palm. "And—"

A new image, this one of Weaver smacking a chalice lid down and yelling, *"Servo!"* and the chalice sealing—

"Oh, god."

"What?" Weaver said. "What's wrong?"

"You're going to *be* Guardia." Mab pressed down on her palm, but there was nothing there. She took her hand back. "You're going to be the Keeper." She met Weaver's eyes. "You'll be here forever. It doesn't matter that Ursula is a pain in the ass and Oliver is cramping your style, because you'll be quitting to join us. Let's just hope that Gus will be retiring, not dying, to let you in."

"No," Weaver said firmly. "I won't be joining the Guardia. I'll be the Keeper, if that's what happens, but I won't quit my—"

"What happens when you tell Ursula that the demons are real and the five worst ones are imprisoned here?" Mab said. "What's she going to do to the park? Blow it up? Or come in and shut down the place, make it a new Area 52?"

"Well," Weaver said. "That would make sense. And it's Department 51."

"No," Mab said. "That would be very, very bad. You're going to have to choose. You're either with us or them. You can't be both." She frowned. "Have you told anyone at work about the Untouchables?"

"Oliver," Weaver said.

"Oh," Mab said. "So does he want Dreamland to be Department 51?"

"He thinks it needs to be researched. You mean has he told Ursula? No. He's thinking about it. Oliver spends most of his time thinking."

"And you spend most of your time acting." Mab nodded. "Good team. You're going to have to choose between him and us."

Weaver got that mule-stubborn look on her face. "No."

"Well, then, we're going to have to keep Gus alive. I'd vote for that plan anyway."

Weaver took her hand back and stood up. "You know you could have made all of this up."

"You're right." Mab slid the ten back across the table. "Here you go."

Weaver looked down on it. "Keep it. You worked for it." She turned for the door.

"That was what you really came here for," Mab said, knowing suddenly that it was true. "You wanted to find out that the whole powers thing was a crock."

"Easy guess," Weaver said.

"And now you owe Ethan twenty bucks because he bet you it was real," Mab said. "You were so sure I was faking it."

"I'm not sure you aren't."

"Is Weaver your first name or your last?"

"Last," Weaver said. "Why?"

"What's your first name?"

"None of your business," Weaver said sharply.

"Oh, my god," Mab said. "Bathsheba? Jesus wept, that's child abuse."

"How did you . . ." Weaver pressed her lips together.

"You ask somebody a question, they think the answer," Mab said. "I read your mind. And I was not expecting that."

Weaver stayed silent for a moment. Then she said, "Don't tell anybody."

"Absolutely," Mab said. "Your secret is safe with me." She pulled her soup bowl back in front of her. "You have a nice—" Her cell phone rang, and she picked it up. "Yeah?"

"We have Fun," Cindy said. "Come to the Keep so we can put him back in the chalice."

"Oh," Mab said.

"We can try to do it without you—"

"I'm coming," Mab said, and clicked off the phone.

"Trouble?" Weaver said.

"No," Mab said, feeling a little bereft again. "Trouble's over."

Then she got up and went to the Keep to imprison her ex-lover.

*****

"You sure you're ready to do this?" Ethan said to Mab when she reached the top floor of the Keep.

"Yeah," Mab said, but she looked torn.

"Let's do it," Ethan said, and patted Fun's cheek none too gently until he started to come around.

Then Young Fred said, "Sorry, dude, but *frustro*," and Fun shot up out of Jerry Ferris Wheel and stood before them, curly-haired and goat-horned in a blaze of sunshine yellow. He said, "Wait!" and Mab stepped forward and said, *"Specto,"* and Ethan said, *"Capio!"* and took him.

He braced himself for the pain in his heart, but instead he was filled with sunshine, all that light warming him, no squeezing or death, just a lift in his chest like happi—

"Redimio!" Cindy said, and the sunshine left him and leapt into the chalice, and Gus clapped the lid on and said, *"Servo,"* and Fun was back in his box.

Gus put the chalice beside the other three and closed the doors on the armoire.

"Okay, then," Mab said, looking not okay. "So that was good. And once we practice . . ."

Jerry Ferris Wheel stirred on the floor, and Ethan helped him up.

"Uh, you passed out," Ethan said, hoping somebody there could explain to Jerry what he was doing at the top of the Keep.

"Damn demon," the kid said, sounding surly as he rubbed his jaw. "Did you get him?"

"Uh, yeah," Ethan said.

"Good," the kid said, and headed for the stairs.

"We've got them all but Kharos," Mab said, eyeing the armoire uneasily. "You know, I'm just not sure—"

"I am," Ethan said. "Thirty-six hours from now this will all be over. We're right on track."

Mab hesitated and then said, "Okay," and Ethan felt himself relax as his cell phone vibrated. He flipped it open. "Yeah?"

"Ethan, it's Ray. I want to make a deal."

"Why?"

"To save my ass," Ray said, which Ethan found somewhat believable. "I'll give you the trident. You give me half your ownership of the park."

"That's not saving your ass, Ray."

"Come on," Ray said. "I'm trying to be reasonable."

"You don't know what *reasonable* means."

"Look, you—" There was a pause; then Ray spoke again, his voice friendly again. "How about I give you the trident, you get those feds off my ass. You tell that—You tell Weaver to have her boss back off."

"Might be doable," Ethan said, not really giving a shit what Ray wanted.

"All right. Meet me, alone, at the OK Corral in ten minutes."

"You gotta be shitting me."

"What?"

"Nothing. I'll see you there. Make it fifteen minutes. Something I have to do first."

"Who was that?" Mab said as he hung up.

"Ray."

"You're making a deal with Ray? So not a good idea."

"You stay on the research," Ethan told her as he headed for the door. "I'll handle Ray."

"Okay," Mab called after him. "But if I never see you again, remember I told you so."

*****

Back at his trailer, Ethan checked his Mark 23, making sure it had a round in the chamber and was off safe. He wished Weaver were around as backup—Ursula had called her in to work—since he couldn't call any of the other Guardia on this: Gus was too old, and Mab and Cindy—well, the OK Corral wasn't their thing. Young Fred wasn't even on the reliable radar. He needed Doc Holliday.

Ethan walked past the Devil's Drop, glaring at the Devil statue in front, sensing Kharos's evil, then up to the three booths that made up the OK Corral games. He went to the gunslingers booth and stood to one side as he flipped down the plywood covering the front.

No shots rang out, so he peered around the corner, muzzle of the Mark 23 leading. Ray was standing there beyond the counter, among the statues of two Clanton brothers, the two McLaury brothers, and Billy Claiborne. At least Dreamland had some aspect of history correct, Ethan thought as he watched Ray raise his empty hands.

"You alone?" Ray called out.

"Yeah. You?"

"Nah, I'm not that stupid."

Ethan spun about. A man standing twenty feet away fired a Taser, the metal barb striking Ethan in the leg.

Electricity coursed through his body, causing his muscles to contract, and Ethan fell to the ground as Ray laughed. Then a second man came up and whipped a black hood over his head, and through the pain Ethan felt the pinprick of a needle jabbed into his arm and then there was nothing.

*****

Ethan woke to darkness.

He was bound horizontally by straps across his body. The air was damp, and Ethan picked up an odor of evil permeating whatever enclosure he was in. He'd sensed this before, in Kandahar, when he'd dropped off a high-profile prisoner his team had captured to the CIA at their special facility near the airfield. He'd gotten the hell away from the place as quickly as possible.

He knew he wasn't getting away from here anytime soon.

He lifted his head and saw a small red light, indicating he was being watched by an infrared camera. A shaft of light cut into the room as a door opened. Ethan blinked, trying to get his eyes to adjust. It got harder to do that as a floodlight hanging five feet above him came on, bathing him in its glow.

"Master Sergeant Ethan John Wayne," a woman's voice came out of the darkness surrounding the cone of light.

Ethan closed his eyes and remained silent.

"Actually, you're not a master sergeant anymore. You never served in the Army. Never were awarded the Silver Star. You were never born. You don't exist. If you never make it out of this room alive, no one will know."

"Hey, Ursula," Ethan said. He could see the silhouettes of two figures behind her in the doorway.

"In fact, we believe there is a distinct possibility you're not even human, based on your blood work. Did you know that there's estimated to be less than one ounce of francium on the entire crust of the planet? And that it's radioactive and should decay rapidly? Yet you have it in your blood."

Ursula stepped forward into the light. Two guys came up on either side of her, sandwiching her small frame, one tall and skinny, the other short and fat, a stick and a blob.

"I don't believe in demons," she said, "despite Agent Weaver's outlandish after-action reports from the Dreamland Amusement Park. But something very odd is going on in this park. So why don't you tell me what that is? I asked nicely the other night, and you ignored me."

"You didn't ask nicely."

"It was nicely for me," she said with all sincerity. "This is a matter of national security. Don't you feel a sense of duty to your country?"

Ethan blinked. "You just told me I don't exist. What sense of duty to what?"

Ursula tapped a finger against her upper lip, as if trying to decipher what he'd just said. Ethan could see the nail was chewed down. "I need to know if I can use this park. You'll talk."

"You can make anyone talk," Ethan said to Ursula. "The question is, can you believe them?"

"Are there demons in this park?" Ursula said. "Can they be used in combat? As forces on their own or weaponized?"

Ursula weaponizing demons. Ethan closed his eyes. The fallout from that would be catastrophic, especially since the supply of minion demons seemed endless. *Their name is Legion,* Weaver had said, and Ethan could see legions of minions, swarming the battlefield, feeding on pain and despair, growing stronger, out of control—

"No," he said.

Ursula turned to the skinny guy. "He's yours."

"Now we got some options here, ma'am," he said. "Like your pliers to the teeth. Or fingernails. Ice pick in the eye is gruesome but effective, especially when the remaining eye sees it coming. Then you got your teeth drilling, aka *Marathon Man,* but the equipment is a pain to haul around. Electricity works well."

The porky one indicated the damp walls.

"Right, not here," Skinny said. "Now me, I'll take a good old phone book beating any day, nothing fancy, nothing that's more about the guy doing the torture than it is about the guy getting the torture, if you know what I mean. Plus it don't leave no marks." He looked over Ursula at his partner. "You know what I think, Quentin? I think you gotta focus on results, not drama. That's what I think. I say phone book."

"Waterboarding," Quentin said.

"Okay," Skinny said.

"Just do it," Ursula snapped.

They went out the open door and came back in. One carried a bucket, the other a wad of cloth.

Ethan tensed, losing his sense of humor.

"No one lasts more than twenty seconds," Ursula said. She looked at her watch. "I've got the time."

"The record at SERE is fifty-two seconds," Ethan said.

"SERE?" Ursula asked.

"Survival, Evasion, Resistance, and Escape school at Fort Bragg," Ethan said, trying to buy time.

"Really? Who holds it?"

"I do." And he finally knew why he held it. And why he'd survived Afghanistan. He was Guardia.

"Impressive." She smiled coldly. "I think I can spare a minute."

She nodded to the men and left, and Skinny cranked something under the wooden slab Ethan was tied to and it tilted, his head going about a foot lower than his feet. Quentin placed the cloth over Ethan's face, covering it completely.

"You know this is illegal now," Ethan said, his voice muffled by the cloth. "New administration and all."

He realized he was hyperventilating and tried to relax. He found a calm spot deep inside, a place he'd never experienced before. His breathing slowed, even as he sensed Quentin lifting the bucket. Ethan closed his eyes and shut his mouth under the cloth. Closed all off.

Water poured into the cloth, into his nose, flowing upward.

And stopped. He wasn't breathing but he felt no lack of air. Everything was still except for the sound of the water being slowly poured onto the cloth and his face. It sounded gentle to Ethan, like a summer drizzle. His mind floated away to memories of his childhood in Dreamland.

Ethan blinked away water as light blasted into his eyes as the cloth was pulled away from his face.

"What the hell are you?" Ursula demanded.

"Fifty-three seconds?" Ethan asked.

"Half an hour. You stopped breathing. You're still alive." Ursula looked ready to either have a heart attack or drive a stake through his heart. Skinny and Quentin were arguing near the doorway in low voices. Well, Skinny was saying something; Quentin was just standing there.

Ethan felt triumphant. Unstoppable. He strained against the straps holding him down, expecting to see them rip and pop and then he would . . .

Nothing.

So much for superhuman strength, he thought. Not part of being the Hunter. Not breathing for half an hour wasn't bad, though.

Skinny came up to Ursula as Quentin disappeared through the door.

"Quentin's gonna get me a phone book. Let your fingers do the walking to make them do the talking—"

"What the hell are you yammering about?" Ursula shouted at him.

Skinny blinked. "Well, ma'am, just filling you in on what I think—"

"You *don't* think," Ursula snapped. "I do the thinking. I wanted you to do a simple thing, and you couldn't manage that."

"Well, now, we did it right. It's not that sophisticated. You just pour the water into the face through the cloth. Not our fault this fellow here can hold his breath a long time like some magician, but the phone book—pain is pain—and as—"

"Shut up."

"Who put you up to this?" Ethan asked. "Ray Brannigan?"

"Ray is a patriot," Ursula said with no conviction.

"Ray works for a demon—a devil. You've been played, and if you don't get your head out of your ass, you're going to be part of hell on earth, victim number two for Kharos, right after Ray." He saw the flicker of recognition in her eyes.

Quentin came back, his hands empty.

"No phone book?" Skinny said, disappointed.

Ursula turned to her flunkies. "Kill him."

Skinny nodded. "Now normally, I'd just smother him, looks like a natural death, but seeing as this guy can breath underwater, I'm thinking—"

A sound outside the door made him stop. He exchanged glances with Quentin and then said, "We'll just check on that."

Quentin opened the door cautiously and then nodded, and he and Skinny slipped out.

Ursula leaned over Ethan. "Tell me what's going on, and I won't have them kill you—"

There was the sharp crack of C-4 explosive going off, and the door to the cell blew open. A figure in black, wearing goggles, came in and jammed the muzzle of a D-gun under Ursula's jaw. "Give me a reason." There was no mistaking the voice or the intent.

"Weaver!" Ursula exclaimed, her voice higher because her chin was jacked up by the gun muzzle. "Are you insane? Think of your pension."

Weaver pushed the gun a little higher under Ursula's jaw and said, "Think of your face," as she pulled a knife out of her belt and slashed the straps that held Ethan down.

Ethan turned, putting a foot down to ground himself. Then he got up, staggering and almost falling as they backed out of the room, Weaver covering them.

Ethan stepped over the unconscious bodies of Skinny and Quentin and went down a tunnel, where Gus waited, holding open a heavy door banded with iron. Then they were in familiar territory as Ethan recognized the brick tunnel.

"Where was I?"

"The engine room underneath the Devil's Drop," Weaver said, pulling her goggles up. "They couldn't get you out of the park, because of all the people, but Frankie still spotted them dragging you down here. We'd have been here sooner, but Mab's the only person who speaks raven, and we had to find her." She hustled ahead down the tunnel. She halted at some rungs and climbed. Ethan followed, with Gus bringing up the rear.

It was dark, and Ethan could hear the sound of crowds. "How long was I gone?"

"About five hours," Weaver said. "Friday Screamland is almost over."

"I think it's getting ready to start," Ethan said.

CHAPTER 20

The crowds excited Kharos. Knowing that he was just over twenty-four hours away from having all those souls to reap.

It was unfortunate that he was surrounded by incompetence. YOU WERE TO KILL THE HUNTER.

"Is that him speaking?" the woman named Ursula asked Ray. "It sounds weird."

"It's inside your head," Ray said.

"He's really a demon?" The woman stepped up to the statue. "Listen, if you're playing some sort of game on me, you're messing with the United States government, and no one messes with the United States government."

If he were free, Kharos would have shown her what a demon was. He corrected himself—he would show her what a demon was. Soon. Very soon. But for now . . .

WE MUST KEEP THE GUARDIA ON THE DEFENSIVE.

"The minions," Ray said. "They're gonna tear up the park, and we have one more night of Screamland to go. We need that money."

YOU WILL SCREAM TOMORROW NIGHT, Kharos thought.

"Forget the park," Ursula asked. "I'm talking about *national security.*

I'm talking about *my future.*" She shook her head. "If I don't get out of this weirdo unit, my pension will be nothing when I retire. I need—"

ASSIST RAY. HAVE YOUR PEOPLE LEAD THE MINION ASSASSINATION SQUADS. TELL YOUR PEOPLE TO TELL THE MINIONS THAT THEY ARE THEIR LEADERS.

Behind her, Ray opened his mouth and then shut it again, looking shocked.

THEY WILL ATTACK ONE MINUTE AFTER MIDNIGHT ON HALLOWEEN.

"Hey," Ursula said. "I don't take orders from a statue. I give the orders. I need you to kill somebody for me. One of my people betrayed me, held a gun on me. *On me.* She's staying here in the park. Sleeping in one of those ratty trailers with Ethan Wayne."

THE HUNTER YOU FAILED TO KILL.

"Whatever," Ursula said. "She's caused you problems, too. I want her eliminated."

OF COURSE.

Ursula nodded at Ray and spoke in a low voice, as if Kharos could not hear. "He's pretty agreeable. This might work out."

Ray rolled his eyes. "Yeah, he's a real sport."

BEGIN THE ATTACKS ON THE GUARDIA AT ONE MINUTE AFTER MIDNIGHT.

"I *got* that," Ray said.

"What about Weaver?" Ursula said.

ADD HER TO THE ATTACKS.

"Can we watch?" Ursula said. "For research purposes, of course?"

Kharos looked at the gleam in her eye. OF COURSE.

Ursula nodded, satisfied, and said, "Good. I'll see you're rewarded for this."

AND I WILL DO THE SAME FOR YOU.

Ray shot him a sharp look and then turned away, as if he didn't want to be involved. "Midnight," he said, and walked away.

"He doesn't really have the liver for this," Ursula said, scorn soaking her voice.

TOMORROW, YOU WON'T HAVE A LIVER, Kharos thought, and stayed silent until the woman was gone.

*****

Ethan covered Gus as he locked the front gate, shooing the last drunk out of the park. It was just before midnight, and the moon was high overhead, casting short shadows in the park.

"Just one more night," Gus said as he walked back over the causeway.

A stiff breeze blew off the water, the cold cutting into Ethan's skin under his armor and clothes. Discarded paper and other trash blew across the ground as they reentered the park.

"Let's do the midnight run," Ethan said, "and get to the Keep. Weaver's there already, on watch. And get Glenda, too, while I do the last patrol around the park."

"She probably ain't gonna want to go."

"Convince her otherwise," Ethan said. He could see lights on in the Dream Cream to the right and decided to check in on Cindy after the run.

Gus pulled his long worn coat tight around his thin frame. "Good idea."

They passed the Double Ferris Wheel, and then the Dragon Coaster loomed ahead, and Ethan halted short of it. "All yours, Gus."

Gus walked up to the control booth.

Ethan flipped down the demon goggles and scanned the area. All was quiet.

His cell phone vibrated.

"Yeah?"

"I've got multiple bogeys," Weaver said.

"Where?" Ethan asked.

"Everywhere. Got a pack heading toward the Dream Cream. A pack heading toward the trailers. One toward the boathouse and Young Fred. An army heading toward you and Gus at the Dragon Coaster."

"They're trying to take us all out at once."

"I'm coming to you," Weaver said. "You're going to be overwhelmed—"

"Negative," Ethan ordered. "Get Glenda to safety, then cover Young Fred in the boathouse. I'll deal with things here, then go to the Dream Cream."

"There's a *lot* of them," Weaver said.

"I've got a lot of bullets." Ethan ran up to the control booth of the Dragon, where Gus was looking at his watch. "We got company," he told the old man as he turned to face the park.

*****

Mab had told fortunes right up to eleven, then pulled out the Seer's diary she'd been studying all week and went over her notes one more time. If Ethan wanted them all in the Keep, she could use the opportunity to ask him about some of the stuff she'd found. The problem was that the diary Seer was a little erratic—*whack job,* Mab thought—so it was hard to tell what was truth and what was her fevered imagination. Some of it seemed really out there, like her belief that demons took on the attributes of the thing they possessed if they possessed it long enough, which meant that demons who possessed humans would become more . . . human.

That was food for thought.

And the idea that inanimate objects could take on emotions from the humans that were around them, like well-loved stuffed animals or prized artworks, and that demons who possessed those things often absorbed those emotions—

Frankie screamed up in the rafters and swooped down to her shoulder, and Mab slammed the book shut and stood up.

She'd learned not to ignore Frankie when he yelled.

She closed down the Oracle booth and came out onto the midway, moving slowly, looking in all directions before she stepped out onto the flagstones. Frankie was still hollering, so she said, "Show me," and he flapped up above the park—

"You and that bird are really something," Fun said from behind her, and she jerked around. "Probably the only real friend you got."

He was in Drunk Dave again, but evidently Dave had been drinking even more heavily than usual, because he stumbled and slurred his words. *How the hell did you get out of that chalice?* she thought, and then he took a step closer and she stepped back.

Frankie was going crazy up in the sky, but she couldn't concentrate on him now, there was something really wrong with Fun—

"You stupid bitch," Fun said. "You had to get pregnant. You know what that kid is going to look like? Horns and a tail, cloven hoofs, she's gonna get *stoned* on the playground and you won't be able to save her."

"Stop it," Mab said, taking a step back. "What's wrong with you?"

"She's gonna hate you the way you hate your mom," Fun said. "She's going to spit on you every day she's alive."

"I don't hate my mother," Mab said, surprised to find it was true. "She did the best she could."

"She was bat-shit crazy, and you're a demon who's bat-shit crazy, and your kid is the Antichrist, born to bring this world to hell." Fun was lurching toward her now, and she backed toward the Dream Cream, ready to make a break for it as soon as he stumbled and fell. "Mutant bastard devil baby—"

He was saying all the things that were her worst nightmares, all the things she woke shaking about in the middle of the night, but they made no sense when he said them, they weren't what he'd say, something was very wrong—

"You're not Fun," she said as she backed onto the flagstones of the midway. "I don't know what you are, but I know the father of my kid, and you are not him."

The thing followed her, stupidity plain on Drunk Dave's slack face, and she tried to think of how to stop it. If it was a demon, iron would kill it, but it would kill Drunk Dave, too, if she stuck it in the wrong place. She kept backing across the flagstones until she hit the wrought-iron fence, and then she turned around and yanked one of the picket spears out and turned to face the thing.

"I'm Fun!" the thing roared at her, and lurched onto the flagstones and fell flat on Drunk Dave's face.

"Not even a little," Mab said, and stabbed Drunk Dave in the arm with the picket.

The thing screamed, and the demon rushed out, a dark purple splotch with legs like a spider and she stabbed the picket down into the middle of it and watched it explode onto the flagstones, jumping back to avoid the splatter.

Beyond it, Drunk Dave groaned.

"Get out of here," she told him.

Dave passed out on the flagstones.

"Oh, hell," Mab said, and took a step to help him, but then Frankie screamed again and she listened to him, concentrated on him, and saw what he saw: skeletons filing into the Dream Cream with Skinny and Quentin behind them. "You're on your own," she told Drunk Dave, and took off at a run for the Dream Cream.

*****

Ethan knew the demons were out there, he could feel them, but even with the goggles, the park looked empty to him.

"They're after both of us," Gus said, grabbing an iron-tipped spear from inside the control booth. "We split up, we got better odds. I'll draw whichever is after me off."

"No," Ethan said. "We stay—" But then one of Mab's ghosts flew at him, untriggered, and he thought, *Fuck,* and blasted it as half a dozen more swooped down, crashing into him so fast that he couldn't shoot and batted at them with the rifle instead. They backed off for the moment, encircling him.

Ethan blinked as the skull on the closest ghost morphed into a head, the face familiar. He paused, finger on the trigger as it floated less than ten feet away.

"Captain Martin?" Ethan's mouth was dry. He knew it wasn't real, but there was no denying the face was that of his team leader. Behind the apparition were four other ghosts—bearing the faces of the other members of his team.

Ethan took a step back as they moved forward.

You failed us.

The words echoed in his head.

"I did the best I could." He was talking to Mab's ghosts. It was insane.

You failed us.

The muzzle of the demon gun went down, the words slamming inside his head like sledgehammers.

Then the one that looked like his team leader raced forward and blanketed him with cheesecloth, and then the others swarmed him, and he couldn't breathe.

You failed us.

Ethan went to his knees, letting them take him. He needed to join his team. This was the only way to make amends.

You failed us.

But he didn't need to breathe.

The cheesecloth tightened around his mouth, around his neck, but he was fine. He was Guardia.

He hadn't failed his team, that team or his new one; he was Guardia, and that was why he had survived when the others perished. He'd survived because his team here needed him. He'd survived because he had a mission. . . .

He whipped out his Hunter knife and slashed upward, parting the cheesecloth and splattering demon goo on the midway. He cut again and again, demon goo flying outward, until there were no more ghosts.

Then he stood up, free and furious. Somebody was playing mind games using minions, somebody was—

He heard a yell and turned and saw Gus facing down the Worm as it jerkily advanced down the midway toward him, each of its jointed cars moving as if possessed, now free of its old tracks over by the Tunnel of Love.

"No!" Ethan yelled as Gus hit the controls on the Dragon and then jumped into the coaster as the Worm chanted, "Coward, coward, you let him die," and lurched up onto the Dragon tracks to follow him. The cars began to move, and the Worm turned and went on an intercept course, inching up the track in the opposite direction, going to meet the old man standing in the front seat with his iron spear.

"Damn it, Gus, get out of there!" Ethan yelled, and ran toward the ride.

He reached the control booth and yelled, "Get off, Gus!" trying to stop the cars, but instead, Gus lowered the iron spear over the front of the first car. The cars began to accelerate, and the Worm raised up, mouth opening, its "Coward" chant deepening as it crawled the rails into the sky to meet Gus.

Ethan fired at the Worm, but the steel cars deflected the iron, so he grabbed an iron picket spear out of the fence and began to run up the service path behind the Worm, praying it would slow on the way up so he could catch up to it. But the demons pushed it faster, and they all rode the rails until inevitably they met at the top, Ethan not far behind on the service walkway, staring in disbelief as Gus came out of the Dragon tunnel straight at the Worm, bracing the haft of the spear against his chest, his arms holding it up and forward. Then they collided, the tip of the spear hit the jaw of the Worm with a scream and a splash of purple goo, and then the cars slammed into the body, Gus plunging into the wreckage, his spear still thrusting forward, until the Dragon emerged on the other side, splintered Worm parts and demon goo flying everywhere, and made the final splashdown descent into the water below.

Ethan raced down as the Dragon came to a halt at the platform.

Gus was lying in the front seat, his hands still gripping the wooden haft of the spear. It was broken about two feet beyond his hands.

"Gus?" Ethan jumped into the car and checked for a pulse. It was there. But very faint.

Gus's eyelids fluttered. "Did I get it?"

"You got it," Ethan said, fumbling for his cell phone to call 911. "Never seen anything like it. You got them all—"

Gus nodded and gasped out, his voice faint, "I'm no coward."

"Of course not," Ethan said. "You—"

Gus's hand fumbled with his coat and pulled out his broken pocket watch, smashed in the battle. "For the Keeper."

"Gus!" Ethan said.

And then Gus died.

*****

Mab ran around to the rear of the Dream Cream and came in through the back door, stopping in the hall at the closed door to the shop. She could hear demons chanting inside, something like "Hungry, hungry, you can't feed us," and she thought, *Oh, hell, Cindy's worst nightmare,* and opened the door.

There were twelve skeletons with purple demon eyes in front of Skinny and Quentin, who waited by the door, guns drawn, watching the whole thing as if it were a floor show.

The guns were going to be a problem, Mab realized.

"Why are they chanting that?" Cindy said in a high voice, and Mab edged over to join her against the storeroom door.

"It's your worst fear, honey," she said, trying to figure out if making a break for the back door was better than barricading themselves in the storeroom.

"Not anymore, it isn't," Cindy said, staring appalled at the skeletons as they began to advance.

"Go get 'em!" Skinny yelled, pumping his fist in the air. "Take 'em out!"

Thank you, Mab thought, and called out, "That guy, he's their leader, they take orders from him!"

"No kidding," Cindy said, but the skeletons stopped for a moment, confused.

Go on, attack him, Mab thought and then realized that these minions were smarter, if they were channeling the worst fears of their victims, they were *a lot* smarter, they'd figure out—

"What the fuck are you waiting for?" Skinny said. *"Get them!* I'm your boss, and I'm telling you—"

The skeletons turned and fell on Skinny, and Quentin fired into the melee, trying to blast them off him, but he had real bullets, so the demons didn't flinch.

Skinny screamed.

"This way," Mab said, and yanked Cindy toward the back door, and Quentin fired at them, splintering the wood in the door frame.

"This way," Cindy said, and threw open the storage room door and then dived inside as Quentin fired again, real bullets whistling overhead as they hit the floor and slammed the door shut behind them.

Skinny's screams reached a crescendo and then stopped.

"Yuck," Cindy said. "In my nice clean ice cream shop."

"Better him than us," Mab said, looking around to see if there was another way out. "Why aren't there windows in this place?"

"Because it's a storeroom," Cindy said. "But I'll have some put in—"

They heard the gun fire again, and then the door began to splinter.

"Oh, *hell,"* Mab said, and tried to think of a way to stop human beings with guns. She'd been concentrating on demons, forgetting that humans were worse.

The lock splintered, and Quentin wrenched the door open, his face twisted with rage.

"Specto!" Mab said, hoping for a miracle, and Quentin raised his gun and pointed it at her.

"Sorry about the baby," he snarled, and Mab heard a gunshot and braced herself for the impact, only to see Quentin fall forward onto his face, Oliver standing behind him with a non-demon gun and a grim-as-hell expression.

"Sorry about the baby, my ass," he said, and Mab heaved a sigh of relief. "Your bird is upset again," he said to Mab, and she concentrated on seeing what Frankie saw.

Giant spiders attacking Young Fred, cowboys hitting Glenda's trailer, lovers from the Tunnel rushing Weaver's trailer, and out at the Dragon—

"Oh, no," she said, and ran for the midway.

*****

Ethan ran down the midway to the Dream Cream, stopping to blow away half a dozen large spiders that had surrounded Young Fred and were chanting, "Betrayer!" at him while he screamed, *"No!"*

"Come on," Ethan said, and Young Fred collapsed to the ground in the middle of papier-mâché spider parts and demon goo and screamed again. "Okay, then," Ethan said, and started for the Dream Cream, only to have Mab, Cindy, and Oliver run by him.

"Trailers," Mab yelled back. "Frankie sees demons there," and Ethan reversed direction and ran after them, catching up as they arrived at Glenda's trailer, where demon-splashed wood cowboys from the OK Corral were strewn around with iron-tipped crossbow bolts in them as Glenda sat smoking on the trailer steps, a daiquiri in her hand, the crossbow on her lap.

"Weaver had some trouble," she called to them, and then drank another slug of daiquiri as Cindy stopped to see if she needed help while the rest ran past.

Hank's trailer looked like Glenda's, except this time the bodies were the lovers from the Tunnel of Love blown open with a demon gun, leaking purple goo, and the trailer door was open and empty.

Mab stopped to catch her breath and survey the carnage. "She really does have relationship issues."

"Where is she?" Ethan said, his heart pounding as he went toward the trailer door.

Weaver was sitting inside, breathing heavily, staring at Beemer, who sat on the table in front of her, staring back at her with glowing, purple demon eyes.

Ethan raised his gun to blow the little son of a bitch away, and Weaver said, *"No!"* and put her hand between them.

"That thing is possessed," Ethan said, trying to shove her hand out of the way, and she rose up and pushed him hard enough that he stumbled backwards and fell down the trailer steps onto his ass.

"Maybe if I tried," Mab said, looking down at him. She went up the trailer steps and said, "Well, what have we here?"

"It's Beemer," Ethan heard Weaver say.

"Yes, it is," Mab said. "But there's somebody in there with him."

"That's Beemer, too," Weaver said, and Ethan thought, *Oh, hell, she's lost it.*

He climbed back into the trailer and said to Mab, "Get her out of here, and I'll take care of it."

"No." Weaver's eyes were wide but not crazy, and she stared at Beemer as if trying to understand something. "That's Beemer. I know it's a demon, too, but it's not . . . evil."

Ethan and Mab looked at Beemer's crazy purple demon eyes and then at each other as Oliver climbed in to join them.

"He's not evil," Weaver said to Oliver. "You said that maybe demons could be good."

"Yes, I did," Oliver said, staring at Beemer. "What evidence do you have that Beemer is . . . good?"

"I just know."

"Did he save you from the other demons?" Mab said.

"No." Weaver frowned. "I think he jumped into Beemer when I blew Romeo away."

"So he was attacking you," Ethan said.

"Until he jumped into Beemer," Weaver said. "Then he stopped. He . . . he *absorbed* Beemer."

Ethan turned to Mab. "Get her out of here. I'll take care of Beemer."

"Wait." Mab slid onto the banquette next to Weaver, keeping a cautious eye on Beemer, who appeared to be seething. "He absorbed Beemer. Like Beemer's personality?"

"Yes," Weaver said tensely.

"It's a *stuffed animal*," Ethan said.

"Shut up, Ethan," Mab said, not taking her eyes off Weaver. "So since the night Ethan gave him to you, you've talked to Beemer a lot, right?"

"I'm not crazy," Weaver said, sounding like her old self.

"I know. But you talked to the dragon a lot, right? You've had him for a week, two weeks? You talk to him every day?"

"Yes," Weaver said. "But I knew he was a stuffed dragon. *I'm not crazy.*"

"Just let me get the demon out of it," Ethan said. "I'll stab it . . . close to a seam or something and then Mab can fix it—"

"No," Weaver said.

Ethan looked at Mab.

"I've just been reading about this," Mab said. "In the Seer's journal. She thought strong emotion could exist in inanimate objects if it was constantly stoked. That's why some prisons radiate hate after they're deserted, and why stuffed animals are—"

"You are kidding me," Ethan said.

"No. The Seer wrote about a demon that grabbed on to an artwork, a statue that a woman talked to every day, and the statue changed the demon. . . ." Her voice trailed off.

"Statue?"

"Sorry," Mab said. "I just realized something. Anyway, this demon has grabbed on to the emotion Weaver invested in Beemer, which means . . . the demon is Beemer now."

"And it's still *a demon*," Ethan said, trying to keep everybody on point.

"But it's emotionally linked to Weaver," Oliver said, gazing at the dragon with a lot more interest now. "And she's protecting it, which ties it to her closer."

"It looks like it's going to eat her liver," Ethan said.

"Well, there's always that," Oliver agreed.

"I'm keeping him," Weaver said.

"He's not a *puppy*," Ethan said. "He didn't follow you home from *hell*, he's a *demon.*"

"Don't be a bigot, Ethan," Mab said. "Weaver's a big girl. If she wants a demon as a pet, she gets it."

"Thank you," Weaver said.

"Of course, if it rips your heart out in your sleep, you're going to be in a world of I-told-you-so," Mab added.

"No, this is right." Weaver took a deep breath. "I looked into its eyes, and I felt myself change. We're supposed to be together."

"That wasn't Beemer, that was Gus," Ethan said, and Weaver jerked her head up.

"Gus?"

"He's dead. You're the new Keeper."

"No," Weaver said. "Not Gus."

Beemer moved across the table and butted her arm with his head, and she put her arm around him automatically as his eyes glowed demon sympathy. Or demon something.

Ethan reached into his pocket and pulled out the watch. "Gus wanted you to have this."

"Oh," Weaver said, swallowing hard as she took it.

Ethan stepped back, really not ready for an emotional Weaver. Or a demon stuffed dragon. "We're going to the Keep. Now. All of us. I've had enough death."

"I have bodies to get rid of," Oliver said. "I'll join you later."

"Bodies?" Ethan said.

"Skinny is now giving Quentin his opinion of hell," Oliver said. "In hell."

"That works for me," Ethan said.

"What about Kharos?" Mab said.

"I'll go get him when the rest of you are inside the Keep." Ethan looked at Weaver, her arm around a demon dragon. "We'll leave the dragon here for the night."

Beemer snarled at him, and Weaver patted his olive-green velvet side. "It's okay, baby, you're coming with me."

"The Keep it is, then," Mab said cheerfully, getting up. "Lots of room there." She went past Ethan and muttered, "Lots of weapons there if the thing turns on her. We're good."

"Right," Ethan said, and stood back to let Weaver and her dragon out, wondering how Beemer felt about him. He'd put him out in the hall every night for a week. That could make a dragon surly. "You're not going to sleep with him, right?" he said to Weaver as they went out the door.

Beemer looked over Weaver's shoulder at him, purple eyes glowing.

"Wonderful," Ethan said, and followed them back to the midway.

*****

Ethan walked the battlement at dawn, looking out over Dreamland, now littered with pieces of the Worm and giant exploded spiders and dead cowboys and lovers, the park almost destroyed, Gus gone—

"You okay?"

Ethan looked over his shoulder at Mab as she came out onto the roof. "No."

She came to stand beside him. "I'm sorry about Gus. He was a great guy."

Ethan looked back at the park.

"At least he went out fighting," Mab said. "He probably enjoyed that. It must have been spectacular."

"It was," Ethan said. "Living would have been better." Anger rose up and cut through his grief. "What the fuck just happened here? What were those things that attacked us? They *knew* things about us, they—"

"Minion demons," Mab said. "Plain old minion demons. But it's Halloween now, and the supernatural has more power. Oliver thinks they got smarter and reflected our fears back at us to drive us to despair. That's what Kharos wants: pain, despair, guilt. He feeds on it."

"I'll get Kharos," Ethan said. "And then we'll hunker down here and wait until after midnight." He looked over at her. "Unless there's something I'm missing?"

"Kharos's plan," Mab said, looking out over the battlements. "Those attacks on us were to demoralize us, not set him free. He has to want to be free, but he's not doing anything about that. What is he waiting for?"

"I don't care," Ethan said. "I'm socking his ass in here with the rest of his gang, and then I'm going to find a way to keep him locked up forever. We're not going through this every Halloween."

"Yes," Mab said, still staring out over the park, and Ethan knew she was mourning the destruction of her work along with mourning Gus. "I'll fix it," she said. "I'll make it better than it was before."

"I know," Ethan said, and they stood together looking out over the wreck of Dreamland under the orange-colored lights.

CHAPTER 21

Mab spent the morning supervising cleanup crews until the park opened at noon. Then the people swarmed in, most of them in costumes, and the park came alive. The Dream Cream was packed when she got there, the college help slinging waffles and scooping ice cream like pros, but the storeroom door was open, and Mab went inside, brushing her fingers over the bullet holes in the wood door.

"We almost died," she said to Cindy, who was bent over her worktable, reading the Sorceress's book. "It's making me rethink things."

"Well, that's good," Cindy said, straightening. "Especially if you're rethinking that asshole Fun. I can't tell you how much I enjoyed poisoning him with rust." She looked at Mab closely. "You're not still hung up on him, are you?"

"Not exactly," Mab said.

"Not what I want to hear," Cindy said briskly. "We find out they're cheating demons, we move on."

"Well, I owe him." Mab pulled over a bowl full of chocolate chips and took a handful. "He kind of jump-started my life. He really did make me happy."

"Yeah, so he could feed." Cindy crossed her arms. "He was using you."

"Yeah, but he loved me, too. He just couldn't love me very much. Which explains why the sex never quite worked even though everything . . . worked. He wasn't there for me, he was there for the happiness I felt, but I still felt really happy so . . ."

Cindy was shaking her head as if warning her.

"What?"

"Nothing," Cindy said, and went back to her book. "So what's the plan for today?"

Mab was still thinking about Fun. "It's just that I've thought about it, and I don't think making me come my brains out so he could get high on the happiness is a killing offense."

"So we almost died last night," Cindy said. "We should talk about that."

"What is wrong with you?" Mab said. "You love to talk relationship stuff."

"I'm just saying we almost *died*," Cindy said, raising her eyebrows.

"*Almost* being the key word," Oliver said, and Mab jerked around to see him behind the door with some kind of wood filler, spackling in the holes from that side.

"Hi," Mab said, and turned back to Cindy, glaring at her.

Cindy leaned forward and whispered, "I wanted him to hear you say you were over Fun, not get into the sex stuff."

"Well, you didn't *tell me that*," Mab whispered back, and then turned back to Oliver. Possibly if they all pretended he was deaf . . . "So, did Glenda tell you about Old Fred's trailer—?"

"Moved in last night," he said, his eyes on the door. "That was thoughtful of you to ask her."

Cindy snorted over her book.

"Something interesting?" Mab said, going to look over her shoulder and kick her on the shin.

"Ouch," Cindy said. "Well, the Sorceresses are evidently the whack jobs of the Guardia. You would not believe what this woman thinks is real."

"Actually, I'm a lot more open-minded about reality these days." Mab squinted at the book. "You can read Italian?"

"No," Cindy said. "But I can read most of this. And Oliver *can* read Italian, and he can't read it."

"Magic," Mab said.

"Whack job. But good recipes." Cindy straightened. "So what's the plan for tonight? Because tonight is the last of it, right? Tomorrow we go back to normal?"

"Sure," Mab said. "It'll be like none of this happened. Except I'll still be pregnant, and you'll still be making dragons, and Glenda will still be pretending that Dreamland is Cancún, and Weaver will still own the only green velvet demon in captivity. Other than that, perfectly normal."

"I just meant no demons trying to kill us," Cindy said. "My baseline for normal is a lot lower than yours."

"A low bar benefits everybody," Oliver said, his voice cheerful as he moved to the other side of the door to finish spackling.

"So we have a plan, right?" Cindy said.

"We're taking turns watching the chalices. Weaver's got first watch today, then Glenda, then Young Fred, then Ethan. You and I are supposed to keep the Dream Cream and the Oracle running until closing, when we take the last watch."

"Okay," Cindy said. "I'd feel a lot better if we had some kind of super-mojo."

"Keep reading, then," Mab said, and headed out to the Oracle, stopping by Oliver on her way out. "Nice job on the door."

He looked up, his face as serious as ever, just different without the glasses. "When you're partners with Weaver, you get handy about fixing bullet holes."

"I can imagine." Mab hesitated, trying to find something to say that wasn't lame. "We really appreciate your help, especially the part where you saved our butts. I know you don't believe in shooting people—"

"In general," Oliver said. "It's not a hard and fast rule."

"—and I know you have no investment here, so it's doubly appreciated."

"I have an investment," he said, still spackling.

"Oh," Mab said.

Cindy snorted again.

"I'll go open the Oracle," Mab said, and headed for the midway, cursing the luck that had saddled her with Fun as her one true love instead of . . . well . . .

Frankie flew down to her shoulder.

"Delpha was always right, right?" she said to him. "If she says Joe is it for me, he's it?"

He dipped his head.

"Maybe she was wrong this time," she said, and headed for the Oracle booth.

*****

Darkness was falling and Kharos was growing impatient. He was so close—

Ray came scurrying out of the tree line, the government woman with him.

"They've been looking for me all day," he complained as soon as he arrived.

OF COURSE.

Ray looked over his shoulder. "You sure this is going to work?"

YES.

Ursula had a clipboard in one hand, a video camera in the other, and a bag slung over her shoulder. She looked officious and confident.

Ray was the smarter one. He looked uncertain and worried.

Down the midway, Ethan walked toward them.

BEGIN.

Ray went over to one of the legs of the Devil's Drop and began to climb.

"Can I ask you some questions?" Ursula said. "For my report."

NO, Kharos said, and concentrated on Ethan.

*****

Ethan and Weaver saw Ursula standing next to the Devil's statue and Ray's bulk halfway up the Drop.

Weaver raised her voice. "Hi, Ursula."

Ursula turned in surprise, and Weaver pointed the large muzzle of Ray's gun at her. "Make a move," Weaver said. "Please."

Ursula stood as still as the statue until Beemer dropped out of the sky with a complete lack of aerodynamic grace and landed on the statue's head, making Ursula scream and then frown as she saw what he was.

"That's a stuffed dragon," she said.

"No, no," Weaver said. "That's the bluebird of happiness. Touch it and you'll lose an arm."

Ethan looked up and saw Ray's large butt disappear as he reached the top of the tower.

"Step away from the statue," Ethan ordered Ursula. "Don't shoot her," he reminded Weaver.

Ursula shuffled a few steps away, keeping an eye on Beemer, who chittered at her, giving away the little minion soul inside the velvet and lamé.

"Got it!" Ray's voice echoed down from the top of the Drop.

A panel on the back of the statue rotated open, and Ethan felt a blast of evil wash over him as he walked behind Ursula and grabbed the chalice.

Beemer chittered faster.

"There are minions in the tree line," Weaver said, looking that way through her goggles.

"Then we run," Ethan said, and took off toward the midway, Weaver behind him, Ray shouting curses from the top of the Devil's Drop and firing ineffectually at them with a new pistol. Beemer launched himself from the empty devil statue, labored to attain altitude, and dive-bombed Ray, giving them enough time to get out of range, not that Ray's marksmanship was anything to worry about.

Which was odd, Ethan thought as he pounded toward the Keep. The guy was a Ranger. He should have been able to hit them, no trouble at all.

Glenda and Young Fred were waiting on the other side of the Keep drawbridge, and as soon as Weaver and Ethan ran across, they raised it, Beemer swooping in just before it clanged shut, to drop like a sack of potatoes onto the stone floor.

"We've got the last one," Ethan said as he raised Kharos's chalice.

"I'd rather get Ray," Weaver said flatly as Beemer climbed up her body to sit on her shoulder, giving the chalice the same unenthusiastic look, dragon-style.

"Lock it up," Glenda said, taking a step back.

Ethan took the stairs two at a time and opened the armoire. He placed Kharos in the center of the other four chalices, then swung the door shut and locked it. There. All of them. The park was safe.

Why hadn't Ray shot them?

He came back downstairs. "Ray is still out there with Ursula. And some minions. He's up to something."

"*Now* can I shoot Ray?" Weaver asked.

Ethan nodded. "Let's go get him, Ursula, and the minions." He turned to the others. "Lock up after us and let no one other than Guardia in."

"We've got it," Glenda said.

"Okay," Ethan said, but he felt uneasy.

Ray really should have shot them.

*****

Mab had shut the Oracle at six and begun to walk through the darkening park, running into Oliver almost as soon as she stepped down onto the midway. He had his glasses on again, which made him easier to talk to but was disappointing at the same time.

You are hopeless, she told herself. First you fall for a demon and now for a government agent with weird glasses who turns into a dragon.

"Hi," she said, and fell into step beside him. "See anything?"

"Minions. They're lying low."

"How many?"

"Maybe half a dozen so far. Of course it could be a couple just shifting from host to host, too. I think they're doing the same thing we are."

"Which is . . . ?"

"Watching," Oliver said. "Nothing has happened all day. Weaver called me and said they got the Kharos chalice locked up in the Keep. If I didn't have goggles, I'd say the demons were gone."

"They're waiting for something," Mab said. "Ethan's midnight."

"I'll feel better when we're locked in the Keep with those damn chalices."

"I'm not sure I will," Mab said. "But if I see the sun come up tomorrow and nobody else I care about dies, that'll be a good day."

Oliver looked at his watch. "We've got about twelve hours till sunup. Let's get a funnel cake."

They walked through the park, eating food that tasted like summer, talking about demons and Delphie and prenatal care—"You're a doctor?" Mab said. "Why does that sound like a line?" and then she blushed because what would he need a line with her for?—and the moon came up as they talked and walked, watching for demons, moving closer to each other as the temperature dropped, the fires in the barrels along the midway working with the orange lights to make Dreamland a fantasy hell, screams and laughter, fire and funnel cakes, dates and demons.

"I love this place," Mab said, and Frankie cawed his approval from her shoulder.

"I know," Oliver said. "It gets to you." He smiled down at her, briefly, a flash of a smile that made her breathless in a way Fun's crooked grins never had.

Fun made me happy, she thought. Oliver makes me hot. And with the worst timing in the world.

Get away from him.

"I need to get back to the trailer. Frankie needs . . . pistachios."

Frankie cawed his approval of the plan.

"So I'll meet you at the Keep," she went on, and he said, "No, you shouldn't be alone. I'll walk you."

"Okay," Mab said, and tried to think cool thoughts as they headed for the trees.

And prayed Oliver would keep his dumb glasses on.

*****

Kharos felt the lid of his chalice loosen and then—

Expansion.

He stretched out his arms as he broke free, no longer bound within wood and iron, and raised his head and laughed at the sheer power of it all.

Before him, in the round room at the top of the Keep, Young Fred, the Guardia traitor, cowered.

"RELEASE THEM ALL," he said, and Young Fred hurried to do his bidding, first Vanth, rising up in blue smoke, her face blissful over her beautiful, free body; then Selvans, stolid, orange, and enraged; then Tura, writhing in blue-green glory, her great, long, muscular tail flipping as she swam free through the air; and finally Fufluns.

Fufluns. Eight feet tall—they all grew taller and stronger as the next was released, which was the only reason to ever set Fufluns free—golden-horned, golden-eyed, and a pain in the ass.

"WELL, WELL," Fufluns said. "THE GANG'S ALL HERE." He folded his arms and stared down disdainfully at Young Fred. "BEAT IT, YOU LITTLE TICK."

"I just want everyone to be free," Young Fred said, but he backed out of the room anyway.

"NOW WE ARE ONE!" Kharos said.

"OH, YEAH," Fufluns said. "I'M FEELING THE BOND."

"TODAY IS HALLOWEEN," Kharos said, ignoring him, "THE DAY WHEN THE BOUNDARIES BETWEEN OUR WORLD AND THE WORLD OF THE CATTLE SOULS IS WEAKENED. TODAY, WE ARE MOST POWERFUL. TONIGHT, WE WILL *RULE THIS WORLD.*"

"THAT'S LOVELY, DARLING," Vanth said, gliding up to him and sliding her arm around his waist. "WE'LL BE SO HAPPY."

She stretched up and kissed him, and the warmth from her embrace, her body, her mouth, flooded through him, and he lost his place in his speech for a moment. *VANTH—*

"AND JUST HOW ARE WE GOING TO DO THIS?" Fufluns said.

Kharos drew himself up, taller than the trickster demon, still holding Vanth. "WE WILL *OPEN THE HELL-GATE.*"

Selvans nodded, grim but approving; Tura smiled as if she were confused; and Fufluns closed his eyes and shook his head.

Kharos glared him down. "WE *WILL* OPEN THE HELL-GATE."

"FINE," Fufluns said. "WHATEVER MAKES YOU HAPPY."

"IT ISN'T ABOUT HAPPINESS," Kharos snarled at him. "IT'S ABOUT *POWER*. IT'S ABOUT *FEEDING*. FEEDING ON ALL THAT DESPAIR, FEASTING ON HOPELESSNESS." Vanth was frowning now, pulling away, so he added, "WHAT?"

"WE ARE GOING BACK TO HELL, AREN'T WE?" she said.

"NO," Kharos said. "WE'RE SENDING THE CATTLE SOULS TO HELL. WE WILL REMAIN HERE, RULING DREAMLAND, GATHERING MORE SOULS, SOULS UPON SOULS, FEASTING ON THEIR DESPAIR, UNTIL THE EARTH SUCCUMBS TO US!"

"THINK OF HELL AS A BIG FREEZER," Fufluns told Vanth, "FULL OF UNHAPPY MEALS."

Vanth turned to Kharos, distressed. "BUT WHO WILL TAKE CARE OF THE SOULS IN HELL?"

Kharos glared at her. "WHO CARES?" She shrank away from him, and he forced a smile. "WE'LL BE TOGETHER HERE. WE WILL RULE TOGETHER HERE!"

"BUT WE HAVE RESPONSIBILITIES," Vanth said.

"WE DO AS WE PLEASE!"

"OKAY, THIS IS HOW EVERYTHING WENT SOUTH THE LAST TIME," Fufluns said. "PEOPLE STOP WORSHIPPING YOU IF YOU DON'T DELIVER AND THEN YOU LOSE YOUR POWER. TRUST ME, I KNOW."

"SO?" Kharos snarled. "I DON'T NEED WORSHIPPERS; I NEED TO FEED. THE DESPAIR THE HELL-GATE WILL DELIVER ME WILL MAKE ME POWERFUL BEYOND—"

"SO MUCH FOR ALL OF US TOGETHER," Fufluns said. "IT'S ALL ABOUT YOU, RIGHT?"

Kharos scowled at him. Ray was looking better every minute.

"WE GET TO STAY IN DREAMLAND?" Tura said. "I LIKE THAT." She flipped her tail and swam through the air to put her arm around Fufluns. "YOU LIKE THAT, DON'T YOU, DARLING?"

"LOVE IT," Fufluns said, folding his arms and staring back at Kharos.

"WE'RE BETTER IN HELL," Selvans said from behind them. "THE OLD WAYS ARE BEST."

"YOU'RE BETTER IN HELL," Fufluns said. "SOME OF US LIKE THE LIGHT."

"YOU ARE NOT LOYAL," Selvans said to him.

"I USED TO BE A GOD," Fufluns said to him. "LOYALTY IS NOT IN MY JOB DESCRIPTION."

"ENOUGH!" Kharos waited until all eyes were turned to him. "WE'RE OPENING THE HELL-GATE. NOW. AND THEN WE WILL FILL IT WITH SOULS. RAY AND THE GOVERNMENT WOMAN ARE GATHERING ALL OF THOSE WHO HAVE BEEN POSSESSED, SINCE THEY HAVE ABSORBED SOME DEMON NATURE AND WILL BE DRAWN TO THE HELL-GATE. LATER WE—"

"WAIT A MINUTE," Fufluns said, his face dark. "NOT ALL WHO HAVE BEEN POSSESSED. NOT MAB. WE HAD A DEAL."

"NOT ALL THE POSSESSED SOULS," Kharos agreed smoothly, thinking, AND THAT WOMAN OF YOURS WILL BE THE FIRST ONE IN.

Fufluns did not look reassured.

"WE GO NOW TO THE LOWEST LEVEL OF THE KEEP," Kharos said, "AND OPEN THE HELL-GATE. RAY WILL BRING THE SOULS IN THROUGH THE TUNNELS, WE WILL CAST THEM INTO HELL, AND DRINK THEIR TERROR, FEED ON THEIR DESPAIR—"

"I DON'T DO THAT," Fufluns pointed out. "FORMER GOD OF HAPPINESS HERE, REMEMBER? FEEDING ON DESPAIR GIVES ME GAS."

Kharos gritted his teeth. "—AND OUR POWER WILL BE INVINCIBLE—"

"I DON'T KNOW," Vanth said. "I DON'T LIKE LEAVING THEM ALONE DOWN THERE. I'M THEIR GUIDE, YOU KNOW. THEY LOVE ME. I—"

"THEY'LL BE FINE," Kharos snapped.

"OH, YEAH," Fufluns said. "COLD DESPAIR AND NEVER-ENDING HOPELESS TERROR. THEY'RE GOING TO *LOVE IT* DOWN THERE."

Selvans lumbered forward, scowling at Fufluns as he raised his fist. "INSOLENT!"

"BRING IT ON, MEATHEAD," Fufluns said. "THE LAST TIME YOU WON A FIGHT, THERE WAS A STAR IN THE EAST."

Selvans stopped, confused. "WHY DOES HE TALK LIKE THAT?"

"HE HAS LISTENED TOO LONG TO HUMAN SOULS," Kharos said.

"I GET OUT A LOT MORE THAN YOU DO," Fufluns translated for him. "YOU'RE THE ETRUSCAN HULK, EXCEPT NOT SO LIGHT ON YOUR FEET."

Selvans swung at him, and Fufluns leaned back to let the massive fist pass in front of him.

"YOU SEE MY POINT," he said.

"ENOUGH!" Kharos said, angrily aware that he'd said that once before.

"I DON'T KNOW," Vanth said.

Kharos looked at her, exasperated.

"DON'T BE CRANKY, DARLING," she said. " IT SOUNDS LIKE A REALLY GOOD IDEA, BUT I HAVE TO WONDER, WHY HAVEN'T WE DONE THIS BEFORE?"

"BECAUSE IT'S TIME TO DO IT NOW," Kharos said, not in the mood to discuss the finer points of the ebb and flow of cosmic power. He turned to the others. "WE OPEN THE HELL-GATE BY CIRCLING THE GATEWAY IN THE DEPTHS OF THE KEEP. AS WE CALL ON THE GATE TO OPEN, WE WILL—"

"IS THIS GOING TO TAKE LONG?" Tura said from the window. "THERE ARE PEOPLE IN THE PARK. I WANT TO PLAY."

"I SAY WE TAKE A BREAK." Fufluns went to join her, putting an arm around her and pointing out the window. "SEE THAT GUY DOWN THERE IN THE AEROSMITH T-SHIRT AND THE MULLET? MARRIED. AND THAT IS NOT HIS WIFE."

"OOOOOH," Tura said, leaning forward. "MINE."

THIS ISN'T GOING TO WORK, Kharos thought, looking at them all. Trying to bind them together had been foolish. He didn't need them agreeing, he was the Devil, they would follow him or they could go to hell with the cattle souls. Because he was going to feed whether they cooperated or not.

"WE GO NOW," he said, and opened the door to the stairway.

"OH, ALL RIGHT," Tura said, and swam past him and down the stairs, followed by Selvans, obedient as always, lurching after her.

Vanth patted his arm on the way out. "I LOVE IT WHEN YOU'RE COMMANDING, DARLING."

Fufluns didn't pat his arm. "YOU KNOW THE GUARDIA ARE GOING TO BE ALL OVER THIS."

"FUCK THE GUARDIA," Kharos said. "THEY CAN SCREAM IN HELL WITH THE SOULS. THIS IS MY PARK NOW."

" 'FUCK THE GUARDIA'?" Fufluns said, laughing at him. "WHO'S BEEN CORRUPTED BY POSSESSION NOW? YOU'RE MORE HUMAN THAN YOU THINK, BIG GUY. EVER THOUGHT ABOUT WHAT THAT'S GOING TO DO FOR YOU?"

"YES," Kharos said. "HUMANS ARE SELFISH, CRUEL, AND RUTHLESS, PREYING ON THEIR OWN KIND. THAT MAKES ME A BIGGER BASTARD THAN ANY OTHER DEMON IN THE HISTORY OF MANKIND."

Fufluns lost his smile.

"NOW GET YOUR ASS DOWN TO THAT BASEMENT AND HELP ME OPEN THE HELL-GATE," Kharos said, "OR YOU'RE GOING TO BE THE FORMER GOD OF HAPPINESS IN *HELL.*"

Fufluns hesitated and then went down the stairs.

"DAMN RIGHT," Kharos said, and followed him.

*****

Mab and Oliver left Frankie gorging on pistachios in Delpha's trailer and went down to Old Fred's, where Oliver loaded his demon gun while Mab put extra rounds in his bag. He'd taken his glasses off, and Mab tried to distract herself from her libido by reminding herself that she was going to be facing the apocalypse shortly.

It did the job nicely.

"This feels very OK Corral," she said to him. "Not that we have an OK Corral anymore." She zipped the bag closed and then gripped it as she heard the sounds of "Alcohol" drift up from the Pavilion. Ten thirty. They were running out of time. Whatever Kharos was going to do—

Oliver shot the bolt home on the gun and took the bag from her. "Don't worry."

"Don't worry?" Mab heard her voice rise and took a deep breath. "We could all die tonight."

"No." Oliver put the bag and gun by the door and turned back to her, folding his arms and leaning against the table. "We'll win."

"Why? Because we're the good guys? This is reality and we're up against *the Devil*."

"Because the universe bends toward justice."

His gray eyes were steady on her, and his voice was relaxed, and his biceps pushed against his shirtsleeves because his arms were folded and Mab thought, *I'm scared out of my mind, and I want him.* "That makes no sense," she said, but there he was, tall and broad-shouldered and calm and powerful and smart, so smart, and competent, and—

"Are you okay?" Oliver said.

—he'd been a great dragon. Okay, that had been an illusion, but she was a Seer, so what she'd seen had been true—

"Mab?"

"The universe bends toward what?" she said, trying to keep her libido in check. It was just because she was going to die tonight. Adrenaline. Or something.

"The arc of the universe is a long one but it bends toward justice," Oliver said. "A nineteenth-century minister named Parker said it. I like it."

He smiled at her, not a charming, crooked grin, not trying to trick her or jolly her along, just his usual flash of a smile while he looked into her eyes, and she lost her breath.

"It means the universe is on our side," Oliver said, his voice kind but sure. "If we fight for what we believe in, the universe will put its thumb on our side of the scale."

She loved his voice, she realized. No lilt in it, no laughter, just a steady low voice that told the truth. And then went into her bones and hummed there.

"We'll be okay," he said, when she didn't say anything.

"We could all die tonight," she said to herself, and thought, *And I'll never know what it's like to make love with a dragon.*

"Mab?"

He bent down to look into her eyes, and she took one step forward and kissed him, her eyes closed and her hand on his chest as her mouth moved against his, and he pulled her to him and kissed her back, competent and powerful and—

He bit her lip and she gasped and his tongue invaded her mouth as he pressed her against the wall, his body lifting hers up as she clung to him, shocked and breathless. He broke the kiss, his eyes hot on her, his breath coming heavy, and then he said, "You're right, we could die tonight, we should live for the moment," and kissed her again, and she wrapped her arms around his neck, arching into him, trying to get closer, too many clothes—

He bounced her up to his waist and she wrapped her legs around him, and he carried her down the short hall into the tiny bedroom and put her down on the bed, easing on top of her, all without breaking the kiss. *This,* she thought, *this is right,* and then she remembered that Delpha had said Joe was her one true love and stopped and looked up into Oliver's gray eyes, not so steady now, pupils dilated and hot on her. "I don't care," she said, "it's you, I want you," and he nodded and kissed her, slipping his tongue into her mouth as he shoved up her

Dreamland T-shirt, catching the edge of her bra so that he stripped her naked from the waist up in one smooth move while she gasped again. Then his mouth was on her breast and she arched against him as she felt the pull deep inside her, and yanked at his shirt, wanting to feel his skin against hers, and he stripped that off, too, as she raked her nails down through the fur on his chest and felt him shudder under her hands. "Naked," she said, but he was already shoving off his jeans, and she kicked off hers and then he reached for her.

He caught her roughly, bore her down, his hands hard on her as his mouth moved over her, nipping at her skin with his teeth, little flickers of pain that made her shiver and drove her higher as he bit his way down her body, parting her legs, his hands hot on her. Then he licked into her and she writhed as he held her down and the heat spread, prickles under her skin, building and twisting inside her, and then she cried out as she came. He moved back up her body and she kissed him hard, wrapping herself around him, biting him on the shoulder, her hands everywhere as he shuddered against her, exploring him as he'd explored her, loving the way she made him moan, the way he came back for her and made her moan, too. And when she said, "I can't wait any longer," he reached for his jeans and got a condom because of course Oliver would have a condom, and she kissed him because he was Oliver and because she knew he'd always be there for her.

Then he rolled her on her back and she felt him hard against her and then thick inside her and the shudder began again. He looked in her eyes, and he must have seen the blue glow there, but he never flinched, and she gave herself up to him, rocking with him, letting the shudder build as she wound tighter and tighter under him. She bit him on the shoulder, and he laced his fingers in her hair to pull her back so he could kiss her again and again, moving hard inside her until the heat was too much, and she cried out and let the spasms take her, over and over and over again while she clung to him. Then she was quiet, gasping, and he came, holding on to her, his fingers digging into her until he collapsed, and she wrapped her arms around him as he rolled onto his back, taking her with him, his face buried in her neck. They breathed together for a few minutes and then Oliver let his head fall back and she saw the exhaustion on his face, completely spent from loving her.

He smiled at her, and this time the smile stayed, and he said, "We're not going to die tonight."

"Really?" Mab said, still trying to breathe. "How do you know?"

"Because the universe wants us to do this again," Oliver said, and kissed her, pulling her back against him, demanding and strong and hot and sure.

Dragon lover, she thought, and kissed him back.

*****

Ethan and Weaver met Mab and Oliver on the boat dock at eleven thirty after the park closed.

"Well, hello," Weaver said to Oliver, laughing, and he said, "You have no room to talk," and she laughed again.

"Am I missing something?" Ethan said.

"No," Mab said, her chin out, and Oliver looked down at her and grinned, and Ethan thought, *Oh, for Christ's sake.*

The end of the world was coming, and Mab was fooling around. *Way to concentrate on battle,* he thought.

Not that there was a battle. There'd been no sign of Ray, Ursula, or the minions, and now that they were on the dock, no sign of movement inside, and the drawbridge remained in place.

"We just got here," Mab said. "Young Fred's not answering his cell phone."

"That's not good." Ethan checked his watch and then breathed a sigh of relief as the drawbridge cracked open and slowly lowered into place on the dock.

Young Fred came racing out as if the Devil himself were behind him, and Ethan and Weaver grabbed him as he tried to run by.

"What happened?" Ethan demanded.

"They got out," Young Fred said, gasping with terror.

"How?" Ethan asked.

"I don't know, they just . . . *got out."*

"Where's Glenda?"

"I don't know!"

Ethan slapped Young Fred on the back of the head and made him stumble. *"Not a problem.* We'll just all go to the Keep and *put them back."*

"No." Young Fred shook his head, trying to back away, and bumped into Weaver. "They're real. *Big. Evil."*

"Walk." Weaver prodded him in the back with her demon gun, and they trekked back across the bridge, Young Fred looking over his shoulder, desperate to escape.

They entered the defunct restaurant, and Ethan said, "Keep him here," to the others, shoving Young Fred at Weaver.

He took the stairs fast, weapon at the ready. The armoire was wide open, and inside he saw five open, empty chalices on the shelf. There was banging on the door at the top of the stairs going to the roof, and Ethan ran up there, slid the bolt back, and threw it open. Glenda and Cindy were framed against the stars.

"What happened?" Ethan asked.

"Young Fred called us up here and then left and locked the door," Glenda said as she came down the stairs behind Ethan. "And now I'm going to kill him because you don't play pranks on Halloween in Dreamland."

"He wasn't playing a prank."

Glenda froze as she saw the open armoire and empty chalices. "They're *out?"* She looked at Ethan, her eyes desolate. "A *Guardia* let them out?"

"We'll take care of it," Ethan said.

Glenda sank down onto one of the chairs. "You have no idea what he's just done."

"Well, I'm about to find out," Ethan said. "You stay here." He picked up two of the chalices and handed them to Cindy. "Ready for the Mother of All Demon Battles?"

"No," Cindy said, but she took the chalices.

"Too bad," Ethan said, taking the last three. "Let's go kick demon ass."

*****

Five minutes later, Mab quietly followed Ethan down the stairs into the darkened Keep basement, hugging the wall behind him and carrying the empty chalice he'd given her. Cindy and Weaver followed, carrying the rest of the chalices with Young Fred sandwiched between them, and Oliver brought up the rear, carrying a demon gun. Halfway down the stairs, Mab slowed, seeing by the purple light that glowed in the center of the basement that the Keep junk had been blown away from the center of the floor, as if something had exploded there, propelling everything into the walls. The weird light in the middle of the room left the edges in shadows darker than anything Mab had ever seen, but in the center, the Untouchables stood, united after 2,500 years: a hulking orange warrior carrying a sword in his hamlike hands; a beautiful blue madonna dressed as a Roman huntress; a smoky-eyed mermaid, full-breasted, full-lipped, and full-hipped, floating in shimmering blue-green; and a goat-footed golden boy with little round horns buried in his curly golden hair; all of them dominated by a furnace-red devil with eyes like coals and obscenely ripped muscles, his head topped by curved horns ending in points. They were all at least eight feet tall, and Kharos was even taller, his arms upraised in triumph, hovering over a shimmering, seething, oily pool of something the vile dead purple color of demon goo, the source of the unhealthy light in the room.

"AND NOW IT BEGINS!" Kharos said in a deep voice, and the others looked down with varying degrees of enthusiasm at the pool below.

"YAY," Fun said, his voice flat.

Kharos ignored him. "BRING THEM."

Ursula stepped into the light at the edge of the pool, pasty in the purple glow, her officious little face smirking over a clipboard. "We need records of this if we want to track them."

"You have to be kidding me," Ray said from the shadows, his presence marked by the glowing end of his cigar.

"I need to know if this has military applications," Ursula told him.

"We could use a place to drop people where they'll never be found. And besides they may have assets they won't be needing."

"Oh." Ray sucked on his cigar. "Good point."

"Damn it," Ethan said under his breath, and Mab looked into the darkness beyond Ursula and saw what they were talking about.

People. Dreamland people. Ashley, Drunk Dave, Carl Whack-A-Mole, Sam, Laura Ferris Wheel and her brother Jerry, and more, empty-eyed and slack-jawed and shuddering with despair, herded into a line that went out the tunnel door. And beyond them, Mab could see, were still more, a tunnel full of them, all of them ashen and shaking and immobilized with terror, some of them sweating and some of them weeping, straining against something that was pulling them toward that vile dead pool of purple beneath the feet of the Untouchables.

"What is that stuff?" Ethan whispered as they reached the bottom of the stairs under cover of that awful darkness.

Mab shook her head as Oliver came up behind her, Weaver next to Ethan, Cindy with a firm grip on Young Fred behind Weaver.

Ethan put Kharos's chalice on the floor and then put his mouth next to Mab's ear. "First we get the people out. No collateral damage."

Mab nodded and went up on her toes to put her mouth next to Oliver's ear. "There are more people in the tunnel. Go in there and get them out of here, out of the park." He nodded and started to move away, and she grabbed his arm. "Be careful, there might be minions," she whispered, and he held up his gun and then crept toward the tunnel door, hugging the debris-plastered wall in the dark, Weaver close behind him.

"I'M AGAINST THIS," Fun was saying to Kharos, rubbing his hands over his short horns. "THESE PEOPLE, WE'VE USED THEM ENOUGH. DAVE'S LIKE A BROTHER TO ME." He looked back at Dave, now catatonic with terror. "A DUMBER, DRUNKER BROTHER, BUT I'M AGAINST SENDING HIM TO HELL."

Hell? Mab thought as Oliver put his hand over Jerry Ferris Wheel's mouth and dragged him into the darkness toward the tunnel door. Weaver followed close behind with Laura, and Cindy followed her, reaching for Sam, none of them struggling, and then Mab kept her eyes on the Untouchables, waiting for them to notice that something was going on in the impenetrable darkness behind them while they argued with each other.

Ethan put his mouth close to her ear. "We're going to have to go into the light to get Ashley and Dave," he whispered, and she nodded, pretty sure that was going to be very bad but also sure they had no choice.

Oliver came back and pulled Carl Whack-A-Mole out of the edge of the light, and Mab held her breath, sure they had to notice as Ethan stepped forward and took his place behind Dave.

"DAVE CHEATED ON HIS GIRLFRIEND," Tura was saying, her voice like syrup with a reverb. "PUT HIM DOWN. BUT NOT ASHLEY. SHE'S NOT BAD."

"BRING THEM ALL," Kharos commanded. "WE'LL FEAST ON THEM ALL."

"That wasn't the deal," Young Fred said, coming in out of the darkness, his voice shaking but rebellious. "You said we'd all be free. You didn't say anything about sending people to hell. I did my part, you're free, let them go—"

"I WILL SPARE YOU, BOY, IF YOU LEAVE NOW," Kharos said. "STAY AND YOU DIE WITH THE OTHERS." He raised his arms again. "AND NOW WE WILL *FEAST*!"

"NO," Fun said, and Kharos jerked back. "*YOU'LL* FEAST, WE WON'T. YOU'RE THE ONE WHO GORGES ON DESPAIR. ME, I LIKE HAPPINESS. I VOTE NO."

Good for you, Mab thought.

Kharos rose up over Fun and Young Fred, larger, redder, angrier. "THERE IS NO *VOTE*."

Young Fred slunk back into the darkness, but Fun stared up, defiant, as Mab crept up behind Ethan, and somebody moved in behind her, and she realized it was Cindy, the Guardia forming a new line to take the place of the old.

That's gonna be a nasty surprise, she thought, and began to feel better, although she was definitely going to hurt Young Fred when they were done.

Assuming they survived.

"YOU WILL OBEY ME!" Kharos raged.

"OH, ALL RIGHT, THEN, TAKE ASHLEY," Tura said, petulant, her massive tail lashing in the air as she folded her arms. "BUT IT'S A WASTE. SHE WAS A GOOD RIDE."

"MAYBE IF I WAS DOWN THERE WITH THE SOULS," Vanth said, gliding closer to Kharos. "TO TAKE CARE OF THEM, SHOW THEM THE WAY. THEY LOVE ME WHEN I'M WITH THEM."

"NO," Kharos said, and Vanth pulled back from him, frowning.

"SHOW THEM THE WAY TO WHAT?" Fun said to her. "HAVE YOU FORGOTTEN HELL? ALL THAT'S DOWN THERE IS COLD DESPAIR."

"It's cold?" Ursula said, clicking her pen nervously. "I thought hell was hot, burning fires."

"YOU'D PRAY FOR FIRES DOWN THERE," Fun said, and he sounded sick as he said it.

"IT SEEMS CRUEL TO SEND THEM DOWN WITHOUT US," Vanth said. "WE'RE THEIR GODS. I'M THEIR *GUIDE*."

"WE'RE THEIR DEMONS," Fun said. "WE'RE THEIR WORST NIGHTMARES. YOU THINK IT'S BETTER IF YOU GUIDE THEM THROUGH HOPELESSNESS?"

"IT'S WHAT I DO," Vanth said, her voice virtuous.

"IT'S NOT ABOUT YOU!" Fun snapped, and Vanth jerked back again, scowling at him, while Mab thought, *I'm not forgiving you yet, but you're getting closer.*

"*ENOUGH*." Kharos spread his arms. "BRING THEM TO THE FEAST."

Ursula clicked her pen again, put it on the clipboard, and laid it down. She took a tracking collar out of her bag and strapped it around Ashley's neck, ignoring Ashley's sobs. "Come on," she said, and Ashley tried to pull back, her face twisted with fear. "I'll just take your purse," Ursula said, reaching for the bag on Ashley's shoulder, "and any identification you have. Don't worry, the United States government will know exactly where you are."

Ashley crossed her arms in front of her, too terrified to let go.

Ursula tugged on the bag. "Give me that purse. As a government official, I command you to *let go*!"

Ethan moved forward, and Mab followed him into the light. He grabbed Dave by the neck and thrust him behind him, taking his place in line, and Mab shoved him behind her where Cindy caught him and passed him to Weaver and then he was gone into the darkness, as Ethan pulled his knife and moved up behind Ashley, who was crying in big gulps now.

"Please," she sobbed. "Just let me go. Whatever I did, I'm sorry, just let me go, *please—*"

"*Give. Me. That. Bag!*" Ursula snapped, greed in her eyes, her lips pulled back over her teeth, and then she gave one final, huge yank on Ashley's bag just as Ethan cut the strap with one smooth move.

Ursula staggered back a step—the suddenly freed bag clutched to her chest, her mouth a perfect round O—and then another flailing step and then one last step into the pool, where she dropped straight down as if in a vacuum tube, sucked into the dead purple nonmatter of that hell, nothing left but her echoing scream as Ethan yanked Ashley behind him into Mab's arms, and Mab passed her on to Cindy and then stepped up behind him.

Ursula's scream continued as if she were falling a great way, but the rest of the room was silent as Kharos faced Ethan across the gate.

"YOU," Kharos said.

"Yep, me," Ethan said. "Now we can do this the hard way or the easy way."

"WHAT?" Mab whispered behind him.

"I've just always wanted to say that," Ethan said over his shoulder.

"WHAT?" Kharos roared.

Ethan spread his arms, the knife still in his hand. "It's like this: You can agree to go back in your box, or we'll kick your ass and put you back. Your choice."

"Are you nuts?" Mab whispered behind him. "That's the Devil."

Kharos snarled and flung his hand toward Ethan, and even standing behind him, Mab felt the force of the blow.

Ethan rocked back on his heels and bumped into her, and then he straightened. "That's all you got?"

But Mab had felt him shudder with the impact, and his voice sounded gaspy, as if he'd had the wind knocked out of him.

Kharos raised his hand again, and Mab said, "Wait a minute," and circled around Ethan to stand in front of him. "I think if we just *talk this out—*"

"Damn it, Mab," Ethan said, trying to pull her behind him.

Mab pushed him off. "—we can find a good compromise here . . ."

Deep in the pool, Ursula screamed on, her voice growing hollower and fainter as she fell, but the Untouchables all ignored it to close in around the pool, staring at Mab.

"DARLING," Vanth said to Mab. "YOU REALLY SHOULDN'T GET INVOLVED. THIS IS MEN'S WORK."

"WHO ARE YOU?" Kharos said, and then he looked at Vanth . *"WHAT DO YOU MEAN, 'DARLING'?"*

"I'm Mab," Mab said. "And here's the thing. We're not going to let you put anybody else down there. No souls in hell in Dreamland." She cast a cautious look at the still-screaming pool. "Aside from Ursula. You can have her."

Kharos lifted his hand to strike her, and Fun said, *"HOLD IT.* WE HAVE A DEAL."

"I DON'T DEAL," Kharos snarled, and threw his hand at Mab just as Fun stepped in front of her.

A bolt of red slammed into Fun, ripping through the golden curls on his chest, and he took it, staggering sideways into the edge of the darkness, bumping into Young Fred, who ducked behind him, using him as a shield. *Coward,* Mab thought, and then Kharos threw another bolt, and Fun evaporated, turning into a golden mist so that the bolt slammed into Young Fred.

He went down without a sound.

"No!" Mab said, then Oliver was there next to him, and she went to her knees beside him.

"He's breathing," Oliver said to her, ignoring the murderous demon and the gate to hell to concentrate on his patient. "But he's not responsive. Is he in there?"

Mab reached inside Young Fred and felt only emptiness and a dead brain. *No,* she thought, and searched harder for a spark, and then she heard Weaver say, *"No,"* and looked up to see Ethan moving toward Kharos. Mab thought, *I hope he knows what he's doing,* and then she bent closer to Oliver, concentrating on finding some kind of spark that would bring Young Fred back.

*****

I *have no idea what I'm doing,* Ethan thought, as Kharos roared, "PUT THEM ALL INTO HELL!" and Vanth said, "WELL, NOT MAB, SHE'S OURS. BUT I SUPPOSE THE REST—"

"ALL!"

Vanth put her hands on her hips. "NO." She walked up to him, her glowing blue edges crackling in the cold air, and smiled, leaning into him a little. "MAB'S OURS, DARLING. WE MADE HER. SHE LOVES US!"

Kharos stopped in midroar, and Ethan thought, *This isn't good,* just as Young Fred heaved in a breath behind him and tried to sit up. He heard Oliver say, "You stay down, you treacherous bastard," and then he felt Mab stand behind him again, and thought, *That's better.*

If he had to face the family from hell, it was good to have a sister by his side.

Weaver with a demon gun would be even better.

"WHAT ARE YOU TALKING ABOUT?" Kharos said to Vanth, confusion mixing with rage, and Ethan realized that Vanth was Kharos's weak spot.

"MAB'S OUR DAUGHTER," Vanth said, delight in her voice. "ISN'T THAT WONDERFUL?"

"NO," Kharos said, really taken aback now. "SHE ISN'T—"

"Hold it," Ray said, coming into the purple light looking mad as hell. "We had a deal. I get the park. If Mab's still alive, I don't get the park. So Mab goes to hell. Even better, just kill her, so the coroner can rule it a natural death. I'm going to need a body." He looked down into the pool where Ursula was still falling, her screams much fainter now and growing hollow with despair. "If you put her down there, I have to wait seven years to declare her dead."

"You *bastard*," Mab said, trying to see around Ethan.

"NO," Vanth said. "NOT MAB—"

"Look, lady, I don't have much time, seeing as your husband is gonna take my soul whenever he feels like a snack, so Mab's gonna have to die now. It's her own fault, she should have given me the park when I told her to—"

"*NO*," Vanth said.

Ray waved that off. "Oh, the hell with it, throw all the Guardia in. Starting with Mab. I have things to do."

Vanth drew herself up, a tower of blue rage.

"What now?" Ray said, taking the cigar out of his mouth, and she raised her arms and a wind blew up in the room, and Ray said, "Now, *wait a minute*," and she threw the full force of the storm at him, and he screamed as his hair blew back and then off, as his skin stretched as if he were in a wind tunnel and his screams sharpened, and there was a tearing sound and blood flew and only his skeleton stood there until it, too, was blown into pieces to clatter against the wall.

Vanth drew the storm back to herself. "THAT'S FOR MY DAUGHTER, YOU *MINION*," she said in the direction where Ray used to be, and turned back to Kharos.

Mab stood openmouthed with horror.

"You okay?" Ethan said, not so good himself.

"That's my *mother*," Mab said.

There was a click and the lights came on, illuminating the entire basement with the exception of the pool, which repelled all light.

Four of the Untouchables stood there, bigger than life but a little tawdry looking, as if they needed the shadows to impress.

"The darkness was giving me the creeps," Cindy said from over by the light switch. "Did I miss anything? What was the screaming about?"

"Ray's dead," Weaver said. "Mab's mother grounded him."

Mab moved closer to Ethan. "Now what?"

"We put the easy ones back in the chalices first," he said, not feeling as confident as he sounded.

Kharos stepped forward, seething at them. "YOU TOOK THE CATTLE SOULS AND YOU THINK THAT WILL STOP US? WE WILL FEED ON YOU FIRST, BOY—"

"Kharos!" Glenda said from the door at the top of the stairs. "Ethan is your son!"

"Oh, crap," Ethan said. "Mom, *go home*."

"NO," Vanth said, stepping closer to Kharos, glaring up at Glenda. "MAB IS OURS, BUT THAT MAN ISN'T."

"Mab is yours and Kharos's," Glenda said, coming down the stairs, and as Mab watched, she grew younger with every step until she reached the bottom and was twenty again, with a face like an angel and a killer body and a smile like a razor as she looked at Vanth. "Ethan is Kharos's . . . and mine."

She doesn't haven't any power, how did she do that? Mab thought, and then saw Cindy concentrating very hard.

"GLENDA?" Kharos said, sounding almost human as he stared at her.

"*WHAT*?" Vanth said, her head whipping back and forth between them.

"*YOU CHEATED*?" Tura said, swimming closer, her tail lashing.

Kharos blinked as the two demons drew closer. "I AM KHAROS! I TAKE WHAT I WANT!"

"HOW COULD YOU?" Vanth said, her voice breaking as she shrank away from him.

"ARE YOU KIDDING? SHE'S REALLY HOT," Kharos said, and then stopped, stunned. "I DIDN'T SAY THAT!"

"*OH*!" Vanth said, and turned away from him, her face twisted with rage and hurt.

"YOU *CHEATER*," Tura said, her voice snarling as she swam up in his face.

"You're going back in your box, you bastard," Glenda said, her voice sure as she took a chalice from Cindy and held it up.

Selvans stepped forward, grabbing for it, and Cindy said, *"NO!"* and the chalice turned into a wooden dragon that snapped at him and then flew up into the rafters.

"Okay, we're gonna need that," Glenda said to Cindy as Weaver came up behind Selvans with his chalice and tapped him on the back with it.

"Frustro, Big Orange," she said, and he turned and grabbed her by the neck and lifted her off the stone floor.

"No!" Ethan said, but even as he lunged for them, seventy-five bucks' worth of velvet demon dragon launched itself from the landing above, chittering as it dive-bombed toward Selvans, followed by four ounces of angry raven, cawing his support. The demon looked up in confusion as he choked the life from Weaver.

"BEGONE, MINION, I HAVE HER," Selvans said to the dragon, and turned back to finish off Weaver only to catch the full weight of Beemer in the back of his head, which made him stagger, and then Oliver shot him, which made him loosen his grip, and then Frankie went for his eyes so that he had to drop Weaver to bat him away.

Weaver fell to the stone floor, heaving in gulps of air as Beemer flew off then reversed direction in midair and came at Selvans again, chittering with rage.

"MINION, I COMMAND YOU TO HALT, FOR I AM YOUR MASTER!" Selvans said.

Beemer's eyes glowed purple as he dived into Selvans' face, blinding him as he staggered back, and Oliver shot him again, which made him scream, and then Young Fred stood up and said, *"Frustro,* meathead," and Mab said, *"Specto!"* her voice like a lash, and Ethan said, *"Capio!"* and took all that orange rage inside him.

Angry orange mud again, everything about him slowing and thickening as he felt himself dragged down into a paralyzing stupidity until Cindy said, "Redimio!" and pulled the sludge out of him and into the chalice Weaver was holding, and Weaver clapped the lid on and said,

"Servo," her voice raw and rasping from being choked, and the chalice sealed.

Weaver put it on the floor.

The little wood dragon flew down from the rafters into Cindy's arms and turned back into a chalice, and Weaver said, "Good boy," as Beemer flew down with it and tried to wedge himself under her arm.

It all had taken less than ten seconds.

Kharos looked over the heads of Vanth and Tura and said, "No!" trying to throw his hand and stun them again, only to find himself blocked by demonesses as they screamed at him, their wrath rising in a blue-green fog around him, blinding him for the moment.

Women, Ethan thought.

They all looked shorter now, and Ethan realized they'd shrunk a good six inches with the loss of Selvans' power.

"*ENOUGH*!" Kharos said. "GET ME THAT CHALICE!"

"*YOU SLEPT WITH HER WITHOUT ME,*" Vanth snapped, and stormed off to the other side of the pool, her arms folded.

Kharos looked confused, and Ethan almost sympathized.

Then Kharos said, "TURA'S A BETTER LAY THAN YOU ARE ANYWAY," and Ethan thought, *Are you insane?* as the real Kharos roared in anger.

Vanth spun around to the mermaid, her face twisted in fury. *"TURA!"*

"I DIDN'T," Tura said, backing away. *"I DIDN'T! I WOULDN'T*!"

"Frustro!" Young Fred said at the same time Kharos said, *"THAT WASN'T ME, YOU IDIOT, THAT WAS THE TRICKSTER*!" but Mab had already specto-ed Tura, nailing her to the stone wall of the Keep, and Ethan said, "Capio," and took her in again, all that blue-green screaming inside him like old times as Cindy said, "Redimio," and bound Tura into the chalice, and Weaver sealed the deal.

Tura's chalice went to join Selvans', and Kharos shrank down another six inches.

"*GIVE ME THOSE CHALICES,*" he said, striding toward them, and Ethan thought, *Oh, crap,* and prepared to have the father of all Oedipal conflicts.

*****

Mab grabbed the two filled chalices and shoved them at Glenda. "Upstairs!" she said, and Glenda ran with them.

Okay. If they took Kharos out now, while he was angry and confused, Vanth would go quietly, nothing to fight for. Ethan was standing braced for the Devil's attack, but he wasn't going to be able to do it alone—

"Here's how it's going down, Dad," Ethan said as Kharos tried to loom over him with the six-inch advantage he had left. "Your time is done. You get back in the chalice, or we vanquish your ass forever. You keep fighting, we'll put you d—"

Kharos grabbed him by the throat and lifted him up off his feet, and Mab saw that Ethan still had his knife in his hand.

If that's iron, she thought, but Ethan couldn't strike him, Kharos held him too far away, and she couldn't wait any longer. She slid around the hell-gate pool, came up behind him, and tapped him on the shoulder.

When he turned around, bringing Ethan, who was turning blue, closer to him, she smiled and said, "Hi, Dad," and Ethan thrust the knife between his ribs.

Kharos grunted and threw Ethan against the wall. Then he grasped the iron hilt of the knife, his hand smoking around the metal and yanked it out and dropped it, the imprint of the Hunter's arrow symbol from the hilt burned into his palm.

Ethan got to his feet slowly, staggering, and Mab thought, *It has to be me*. She stared into Kharos's eyes, trying to see what was in there, where his weakness was, what he feared, *anything,* as he reached for her, radiating rage, and then she sucked that in, furious with him, rage calling to rage, feeling her eyes glow red.

He stopped, staring at her eyes.

"Frustro!" she said as the red mist took her, *"Specto, capio—"*

He fought her, but she pulled him in and then fell to her knees as all that red murderous, vicious inhuman hate wrapped around her heart and squeezed. She felt Oliver's hands support her, heard Cindy scream, *"Redimio!"* but Kharos hung on, squeezing harder, his laughter in her head, everything falling away, her last thought, *At least Oliver knows CPR—*

And then Ethan was there, whispering, "Capio," in her ear, and she felt Kharos leave her, sucked out of her as Oliver caught her, and her heart loosened and beat again as Cindy snarled, "Redimio, goddamn it, you get *out* of them," and held out the chalice, and Ethan arched up as Kharos rushed out of him and into the box, and Weaver slapped the lid on, and said, "Servo, you *fucking* son of a bitch."

Mab slumped in Oliver's arms, exhausted but triumphant. "You were right, we won," she said, looking up at him, but he was staring across the pool.

"Not yet," he said.

"THAT WAS VERY WRONG OF YOU," Vanth said, and Mab looked at her and saw the warrior madonna inside the pretty blue huntress, the madonna that had disintegrated Ray. "*GIVE ME THAT CHALICE,*" Vanth snarled, and raised her arms again.

"Ah, hell," Ethan said, as the wind began to blow inside the Keep.

*****

Ethan knew he couldn't take Vanth. Her fury made Kharos's look like a tantrum.

"YOU TOOK MY MAN," she said, gliding toward Ethan, her eyes glowing with blue rage as the wind began to pull hard on him. "YOU GIVE HIM BACK."

Weaver stepped in front of him, her demon gun at the ready, her hair blowing in Vanth's wind.

"THAT CANNOT STOP ME," Vanth said.

"This guy is *my* man," Weaver said. "I understand your anger, but you can't have him."

"Get out of my way," Ethan said, trying to move Weaver to one side.

"And he's my brother," Mab said, moving up beside Weaver. "You know how important family is, Mom. I can't let you hurt him."

Vanth stopped, still furious but listening, the wind swirling around them but not decapitating anybody yet.

"The problem with Dad," Mab said, smiling at her as she stepped closer, "is that he wants to kill us. I know that's mythologically not that big a deal, but we're human. You're not supposed to kill your children."

"I KNOW," Vanth said, sounding almost apologetic. "BUT YOU HAVE TO LET HIM OUT. HE'S *KHAROS!*"

"Yeah, that's why we had to put him back," Mab said.

Vanth's face grew dark again, and she raised her arms, and the wind picked up.

"Because if he kills me," Mab said, "you get no grandchildren."

Vanth stopped, her arms upraised.

Mab took another step so she could look up into Vanth's face. "The baby's a little girl, Mom. Her name is going to be Delpha Vanth. Isn't that beautiful? We can call her DV—"

"Delpha Vanth?" Vanth said, sounding displeased.

"Or Vanth Delpha," Mab said hurriedly. "And then we could call her . . ."

Don't say it, Ethan thought just as Mab realized what the kid's initials would be.

"Vanth," she finished brightly.

Vanth's face was stony but thoughtful now.

"Little Vanth?" Mab said, trying again.

Vanth shook her head. "I'M SORRY, DARLING, BUT I NEED YOUR FATHER BACK. I'M SURE ONCE WE EXPLAIN—"

"Mother," Mab said. "He's going to *kill* me. And Delphie—*Vanth*."

"NO," Vanth said, and raised her arms and the wind began to cut at them.

Weaver fired her D-gun and caught Vanth midtorso, and she screamed and the wind rose higher, painful now as they huddled together. Beemer and Frankie launched themselves from the landing above, only to be caught in the wind and flung against the walls. Young Fred yelled, *"Frustro!"* but his voice was lost in the storm. And

Ethan took a step forward, ready to tackle an Untouchable to the ground, pretty sure the consequences of that weren't going to be good, but Mab was there before him, her choppy red hair electric in the storm as she shielded the others from Vanth's wrath.

Oliver said quietly, "Show her the baby," and Mab hesitated and then raised her arms in a perfect copy of her mother, closed her eyes, and frowned as if concentrating, and in the middle of the maelstrom, in the space between them, a little green light began to glow, expanding out to make an eye in the storm, floating up and forming the shape of a child with glowing red hair who stood looking up at Vanth, curious and unafraid.

Vanth looked down and froze, staring into the green eyes of her granddaughter.

"He'll kill us," Mab whispered to her.

Vanth put her hands down, the storm disappeared, the baby vanished, and they were back in the Keep, windblown and exhausted.

"SHE WAS BEAUTIFUL," Vanth whispered.

"She's your granddaughter," Mab said "And if you wait nine months, you can see her again."

"CAN I HOLD HER?" Vanth said.

"Only if you promise not to let Dad out," Mab said.

"I DIDN'T WANT YOU TO GO TO HELL," Vanth said to her. "NOBODY SHOULD BE DOWN THERE WITHOUT ME."

"I know, Mom," Mab said.

"AND HE DID CHEAT ON ME," Vanth said, frowning as she remembered.

"Serves him right to be in that chalice," Mab said with enthusiasm. "Can't cheat in there."

Young Fred stepped up behind Vanth, but he didn't say anything, a world of sympathy in his eyes.

"You have to go back in your chalice," Mab said. "But I promise that if you swear not to let Kharos out, I will release you when the baby's born so you can hold her. I swear on my life, I will do that."

"Wait a minute," Ethan said.

"Stay out of this," Mab said out of the corner of her mouth, and Weaver nudged him and said, "Shut. Up."

"IT JUST GETS SO LONELY IN THAT FORTUNE-TELLING MACHINE," Vanth said. "HALF OF THE YEAR, NOBODY EVEN COMES BY."

"We can move the booth into the Dream Cream," Mab said.

"Uh," Cindy said.

"People are in there all year round. *Happy* people," Mab said. "They'll *love* you."

"REALLY?" Vanth said.

Mab nodded. "Really. And they'll put in pennies and want a fortune. You can tell them anything you want."

Vanth considered it while Mab held her breath. "ALL RIGHT," she said finally. "I BELIEVE IN YOU."

Mab blinked back tears. "I believe in you, too, Mom." She stepped closer to Vanth and put her arms around all that glowing blue, and Vanth's arms went around her, enveloping her.

"This isn't good," Ethan said, seeing disaster ahead.

"Oh, *shut up*," Weaver said, and Ethan heard Cindy sniffing behind him.

"You know, we're demon *fighters*," he said, and Weaver and Cindy both said, *"Shut up, Ethan,"* so he shut up.

Then Mab stepped back and said, "In nine months, I swear," and Vanth nodded, and then said, "WAIT!"

"I knew it," Ethan said, but Vanth walked over to the hell-gate, raised her arms over it, and said, "TERMINO," as she brought her hands together.

The hell-gate closed, shutting off Ursula's faint cries, and the floor was stone again.

Vanth turned back to Mab. "THAT WOULD HAVE BEEN VERY DANGEROUS FOR THE BABY."

"Yes, it would," Mab said, her voice heartfelt.

"ALL RIGHT, THEN," Vanth said, sounding resigned.

Young Fred stepped up and looked into Vanth's eyes and said,

"Frustro," very gently, and she looked at him, startled, and then Mab said, "Specto, Mom," and she sighed, and Ethan said, "Capio," not exactly sure what was going on, and felt all that blue flow into him, filling him, and then a motherly voice in his head saying, "You drink too much. You should stop before my granddaughter is born, it's a bad example. And take off that stupid vest. You're in Ohio."

Tura's screaming would be better, he thought, and then Cindy said, "Redimio, Vanth," in a very gentle voice, and Vanth flowed into the chalice, and Weaver put the lid on and said, "Servo, Vanth. See you in July."

"We're not really going to let her out, are we?" Ethan said, and three women turned to him and said, *"Yes, we are."*

"Give it up," Oliver told him.

"It's that mother-daughter thing," Young Fred agreed. "Don't mess with it."

"And now you," Ethan said, glad to have somebody to fight.

"I'm sorry, I don't know what I was thinking of," Young Fred said, backing up a step. "I'm young, I make mistakes, I thought I was helping, but I can learn. And you need me. I'm your Trickster!" He grinned at Ethan crookedly.

"You're Fufluns," Ethan said. "And your ass is mine."

"All right," Fun said. "You're not my type, but I'm open-minded—"

"Wait a minute," Cindy said, looking at Young Fred for the first time in the light. "My god, you *are* Fufluns."

"Don't piss Ethan off," Mab said to Fun. "He's just looking for a reason to put you back in your box—"

"I *have* a reason," Ethan said. "He's a *demon.*"

Fun stood there smiling at him. "Here's the thing. You need me. I'm your Trickster. Plus, I saved you from Kharos. You owe me."

Ethan shook his head. "Can't trust you, can't do it. Sorry." He picked up the empty chalice. "Got to go back in."

"That could be harder than you think," Fufluns said, not worried.

Ethan looked at Mab. "Can you take him without a Trickster?"

"Yes," Mab said. "I'll always know where his spirit is. I love the dumb son of a bitch."

Ethan looked impatient. "Will you take him?"

Mab nodded and said, "Spec—" and then the sound caught in her throat. She coughed and said, "Spec—" and choked again.

"What's wrong?" Ethan said.

"I *can't* ," Mab said. "The words won't come out."

"Well, I can," Ethan said, and went for Fufluns' throat. "Cap—" before he choked, too, his hand stopping millimeters before he touched Fufluns' neck.

"Before you hurt yourselves," Fufluns said, "may I remind you that Young Fred is Guardia."

"Young Fred is dead," Ethan said.

"Well, the part that was really Young Fred is gone," Fufluns agreed. "But this body? It's still breathing, and it's still Guardia, and none of you can harm it. So I'm, basically, safe. I'm also your Trickster, which is going to be different, but I can work with that. We did pretty good tonight, I thought."

"We can't trust you," Cindy said, coming closer, clearly intrigued.

"Of course not," Fufluns said. "But you couldn't trust Young Fred, either. We're Tricksters. That's what we do."

"You're going to have to leave that body sometime," Ethan said.

"Young Fred is twenty years younger than you are," Fufluns said. "Want to make bets on which one of us gives up the earthly shell first?" He looked Ethan up and down. "Especially since you look like crap."

Ethan reached for him again, felt himself blocked, and gave up. "I've had enough," he said, picking up Vanth's chalice. "We're locking all of these in the armoire and shutting the Keep up tight and getting some sleep. Because it's not Halloween anymore. We won."

The last things he heard as he headed for the stairs were Fun saying to Mab, "So about us," and Mab saying, "Not in this lifetime."

Ethan felt cheered. He might not be able to strangle Fun-the-Guardia, but Mab could still do a nice job of choking him off. And if she didn't, he was pretty sure good old non-Guardia Oliver would kick his ass.

Things were definitely looking up.

*****

A week later, Mab sat on the carousel roof between two clowns and considered her work in the morning sunshine. Much of it was gone.

The Pirate Ship was empty of pirates, currently painted half pirate-black and half ark-red. It looked awful, but by spring it would be a wonderful Noah's Ark, full of color and pattern and life, not just elephants and horses but aardvarks and llamas and dragons, too, wonderful weird animals that Delphie would love. The Tunnel of Love had been denuded of its doves and flowers and sat like a glowering pink lump next to the Worm tracks that were currently Wormless, but she could fix those, too. She envisioned butterflies on the Tunnel along with a lot of green vines. Delphie Vanth would like butterflies. And green. The Mermaid Cruise was dry-docked, its tanks drained so the remains of the demon goo could be neutralized, and the shooting gallery was empty, its guns pointing at a newly whitewashed blank space that would be filled with demon targets later, reconstructed from the OK Corral shooters who had tried to take out Glenda.

"I'm okay with shooting demons," Mab had told her.

"Me, too," Glenda had said, back to her old self again, as Sam and some newly hired college help were getting ready to put up the Demon Shoot sign—SHOOT A DEMON, SAVE A SOUL—over the top of the old OK Corral sign.

And at the back of the park, painters in rigging worked their way up the Devil's Drop, painting the five-sided tower blue and attaching big white wood clouds to it, preparing to put up the new sign, this one saying PARACHUTE PEAK, no devil anywhere in sight. The skeletons and the ghosts and the giant spiders were gone, and the orange cellophane was finally off the streetlamps, and above all, the Ferris Wheel, the Dragon, the Roundabout, and the carousel she was sitting on top of now were as wonderful as ever, unharmed in the Demon War.

Dreamland was beautiful again.

"I like it," she said to the clown to her right, the one who was alive, looked like Young Fred, and kept trying to put his arm around her.

"That's a lot of your work gone," Fun said.

"The good stuff is still there," Mab said, patting the upflung wooden arm of the clown to her left. "And what isn't needed changed anyway. Some change is good. I don't ever want to see those little monsters from the cruise again. They were always creepy, even before they tried to kill me."

"Where's the money for all of this coming from?" Fun said.

"You're worried about money?" Mab said. "That's not like you."

"This is where my kid is going to grow up," Fun said. "I want the place safe."

"From Ray," Mab said. "He left me everything, and his lawyer is putting the will through since Oliver certified his, uh, heart attack as his attending doctor. So far, nobody's come looking for a body. And the good news is, Ray was one rich bastard. We're going to be fine."

She turned to look at him in the bright sunlight, still a little disconcerted that he was Young Fred, although the real Fun was starting to seep through already, the nose sharper and beginning to hook a little, the hair curlier, the grin crooked. By the time she got back, Young Fred would be . . . well, a Fun Young Fred. He might have liked that.

Down below, Glenda put the last bag in Ray's RV, got in, and honked the horn.

"I have to go," Mab said, standing up. "I have many adventures ahead."

"You sure you're okay?" Fun said. "I mean, you know, the baby?"

"Delphie Vanth will be fine. Although God knows what she'll turn out like."

"She will be unpredictable, hardworking, fun-loving, and intelligent," Fun said. "The world may not be ready for her yet." He sounded proud.

"Well, the world has eight and a half months to brace itself."

"But I'm the kid's father, right?" Fun said. "I mean, you'll tell her it's me."

"Yeah," Mab said. "I'll tell her." Then I'll tell her to count on Ethan and Oliver, not on you. You'll love her all you can, but . . .

"I'll be here for her," he said as if he'd read her mind. "I like Dreamland." He leaned back a little to smile up at her. "You sure you don't want to give us another shot? I can't leave this body without it dying, so—"

"I'm positive," Mab said. "You're a liar, and you're always going to be a liar. It's your nature. And lies kill love, eat it away like acid. If I stay with you, you'll take away everything you gave me, all this happiness, all this confidence, all this joy. So we're done."

His smile had faded. "I can change."

"No, you can't," Mab said. "And you don't want to. I don't want you resenting me any more than I want me resenting you. Let it go, Fun. The world is full of beautiful women who would love to be with you for a weekend."

"They're not you," Fun said.

"I'm not the me you knew anymore," Mab said. "Now I'm somebody who demands love and honesty and respect and connection. I deserve it all. And with a little luck, I'm going to get it."

"Oliver, right?"

"Maybe," Mab said, smiling as she remembered Cindy saying, "So is Oliver a demon in the sack?" and the look on her face when Mab had said, "No, he's a dragon." She looked down at Fun and shook her head. "It's not about Oliver. I love you, I do, but you can't give me what I need." She took a deep breath. "And now I'm free."

Fun smiled up at her, sitting in her shadow, not quite as sure as he had been. "Anything I can do for you before you go?"

"Tell Ethan we left," Mab said. "We decided to go on the spur of the moment last night. Glenda's idea. I haven't told him, because you know Ethan. Overprotective."

"Oh, thanks," Fun said. " 'Hey, Ethan, I have good news and bad news. The bad news is your sister just took your mother on a road trip. The good news is, she took the crow, too.' "

"Raven." Mab patted his arm. "Just tell him to put up the bat signal if he needs help. And you have a good time seducing Ashley."

Fun grinned. "Caught on to that, did you? Of course, you did." He stood up, too. "It won't be the same."

"I should hope to hell not," Mab said, and tried to move by him.

He bent and kissed her swiftly, and she stayed in the kiss for a minute because it was good, and because she did love him, even if he was a lying, cheating, evil, Trickster demon clown, but she kept her eyes shut because he still looked too much like Young Fred for the whole thing to be anything but weird.

Then she patted him on the arm again and climbed down the ladder to the RV, really glad to be leaving him behind.

*****

"What's happening in Department 51?" Ethan asked, looking out over Dreamland from the top of the Keep, where he'd been keeping an eye on his sister and her demon ex-lover. "Why isn't Oliver here?"

"He's swamped," Weaver said. "He got Ursula's job since she disappeared, and nobody else knows what the hell goes on in the department. He'll cover for us. He still wants to research demons, but he thinks it's done best without sending anything up the chain of command—or someone like Ursula will get stupid ideas."

"That's good." He looked at the destruction in his park and thought, *Hell*, but overall, the park was in decent shape, and Mab had big plans for its future and probably hers, if Oliver would get his head out of Department 51 and come back. "How about you?"

"How about me what?" Weaver said.

"You work for the government."

"Not anymore," Weaver said, turning to him. "I don't exist anymore. Oliver saw to that for me."

"But your career—"

"I'm Guardia." Weaver put her arms around him. "That's more than enough." She frowned and rapped on his chest. "Where's the vest?"

Ethan pulled her close. "I'm in Ohio and the demons are all gone. What do I need a bulletproof vest for?"

He leaned in to kiss her, and Beemer flapped down to land on

Weaver's shoulder, shoving him aside, much lighter on his wings after a week of practice but still one big-ass velvet demon.

"Well, not all the demons are gone," Weaver said, reaching up to pat Beemer on his gold lamé chest.

Ethan stared at Beemer, and Beemer stared back. Then the dragon curled his tail around Weaver's neck and ducked his head to the side, giving Ethan room to lean in and kiss her.

Dreamland, Ethan thought. Where anything is possible.

And then he kissed Weaver.

The purple velvet dragon claw in his ear didn't bother him at all.

*****

"I do not approve of you kissing demons," Glenda called back to Mab as she loaded her suitcase into the RV. "Did you tell Ethan we were going?"

"No, I told the demon to do it." Mab slammed the back door shut and then moved up to look through Glenda's window into the back-seat. "Everybody strapped in?"

Delpha's ashes sat on the seat behind the driver's seat, secure in their brass dragon urn, taped down with duct tape. Frankie rode shotgun on the same seat, looking vaguely interested in the new routine. On the other side, behind Glenda, Vanth's booth was crammed in.

"Ready, Mom?" Mab said.

There was a whirr, and a card plopped out.

Glenda picked it up. "She thinks we should bring your father."

"I'm still not over him trying to kill me," Mab said to Vanth. "I hold grudges. But you're going to love the Statue of Liberty."

"We're all going to love the Statue of Liberty," Glenda said, and then she nodded past Mab. "Somebody wants to talk to you."

Mab turned around and saw Oliver standing in front of the Dream Cream, his hands in his pockets, regarding the RV with puzzlement, so she walked over.

"Well, hello, stranger," she said. "You never call, you never write—"

"I have called you every night," he said, and bent down and kissed her lightly, and she smiled against his mouth.

"It's not enough," she said softly.

"I'm here now and I have the whole weekend," he said, and then nodded to the RV. "Why do I have a bad feeling about that?"

"Because I'm leaving on a road trip," she told him. "My newly acquired mothers haven't been out of Dreamland for forty years, so I'm taking them all to see the Statue of Liberty."

He nodded solemnly. "Good idea. How long are you going to be gone?"

"A couple of weeks," she said, and he closed his eyes. "We'll definitely be back by Thanksgiving. Glenda and Cindy want to do a big Thanksgiving dinner deal. You'll be here for that, right?"

He nodded. "I'll be here for that. By then I should have gotten everything straightened out at work, and I can really be here. No more phone calls."

"Work. I bet they all love you there," Mab said, and looked up into his handsome, sane, serious face and thought, *Delpha made a mistake.* This guy was her destiny, he had to be—

"I think love may be pushing it," Oliver was saying. "They seem grateful for the sanity."

"I'm grateful for the sanity," Mab said.

"Hurry back, Mab," he said, looking down at her.

Fun would have been smiling. Oliver looked like he was going to miss her.

"I will," Mab said. "I want to get to know you a lot better." She laughed. "I don't even know your last name."

"It's Oliver."

She blinked at him. "Your name is Oliver Oliver?"

"No, my name is Joe Oliver."

"Your name is Joe," Mab said, and heard Delpha say, *His name is Joe,* and the park swung around her and settled into place.

"I don't like the name Joe much," Oliver said, "but you can call me anything you want," and she laughed in the sunlight in front of the Dream Cream, and said, *"Joe."*

"I'm missing something, aren't I?" he said.

She took a step closer to him. "It's *very* good to meet you, Joe," she said, suffused with happiness, and then he leaned in and kissed her, and she put her hands on his strong arms to steady herself because the kiss was a mind-bender: strong and sure and dark and hot, the dragon of her dreams, her one true and future love.

Delpha was never wrong.

"Hurry back," he said again against her mouth, and she laughed, and then went around the RV and climbed into the driver's seat.

"I approve of you kissing that nice boy," Glenda said.

"I do, too," Mab said, and punched up "What Love Can Do" on Ray's cassette player, waved good-bye to Oliver, put the RV in gear, and drove across the causeway, heading east out of Dreamland with no worries at all.

She'd seen where they were going, and it was good.

THE END

Thank you!
Please leave a review as they are extremely valuable.

An excerpt from Rocky Start follows About the Authors.

Also by Jennifer Crusie and Bob Mayer

Lavender's Blue: https://books2read.com/u/boqdN9
Rest In Pink: https://books2read.com/u/m0WdwM
One In Vermillion: https://books2read.com/u/mlqG2W
Rocky Start: https://books2read.com/u/bPzkRx
To be followed in the Rocky Start series by
Very Nice Funerals
The Honey Pot Plot
Agnes and the Hitman: https://books2read.com/u/meqyWEa

Wild Ride: https://books2read.com/u/bW69X7
Don't Look Down: https://books2read.com/u/bQex80

Questions or comments for Bob and Jenny: email to bob@bobmayer.com
For updates, sign up this email list:
http://goo.gl/XnSgtB

ABOUT THE AUTHORS

crusie
MAYER

Jennifer Crusie is the New York Times, USA Today, and Publisher's Weekly bestselling author of twenty-three novels, one book of literary criticism, miscellaneous articles, essays, novellas, and short stories, and the editor of three essay anthologies. She was born in Wapakoneta, a small town in Ohio, and then went on to live in a succession of other small towns in Ohio and New Jersey until her last move to a small town in Pennsylvania. This may have had an impact on her work. She has a BS in Art Education, an MA in literature, an MFA in fiction, and was ABD on her PhD when she started reading romances as part of her research into the differences between the ways men and women tell stories. Writing a romance sounded like more fun than writing a dissertation, so she switched to fiction and never looked back. Her collaborations with Bob Mayer have pretty much proved everything she was going to say in her dissertation anyway, so really, no need to finish that. For more information, see: https://jennycrusie.com/

Bob Mayer is a graduate of West Point and former Green Beret. He's had over 80 books published including the #1 series The Green

Berets, The Cellar, Area 51, Shadow Warriors, Atlantis, and the Time Patrol. He's also written two sequels to *Agnes and the Hitman*: *Shane and the Hitwoman* and *Phoebe and the Traitor*. His latest series is the Will Kane Green Beret books.

Born in the Bronx, having traveled the world (usually not tourist spots), he now lives peacefully with his wife and dogs.

For information on all his books, please get a free copy of the *Reader's Guide*. You can download it from his home page at www.bobmayer.com or sign up for his newsletter for the latest on his books and the collaborations.

ROCKY START

ROCKY
START
FROM THE NY TIMES BESTSELLING AUTHORS
Jennifer Crusie
& Bob Mayer

TUESDAY, OCTOBER 27

CHAPTER 1

Rose

On Day Three of what was shaping up to be the second worst week of my life, I was trying to glue a naked doll's head (I'd stripped off all its paint with acetone so it was a blank, flesh-colored stare) to a very old paregoric bottle (paragoric was a medicine made of alcohol, honey, and opium, which was sounding pretty good to me right then) when somebody rattled the front door to the secondhand shop where I worked, which was locked because we weren't open yet. I thought the CLOSED sign on the front door pretty clearly communicated that, but this was Rocky Start. Not a lot of people obedient to signs here. I didn't look up as I was focused on putting that head on that bottle. Something I could control.

I was standing behind the marble-topped counter, trying to be Upbeat and Positive About Life, but it wasn't working. I'd put Bob Marley's "Three Little Birds" on the iPod because that always starts the day right, but today . . . just no. I'd switched over to Lenka's "Trouble is a Friend" because that had an aura of plausibility. We were in big trouble, but maybe that would turn out to be a good thing . . .

No. No, it wouldn't. My boss and landlord had died two days ago, my future was unknown which meant my daughter's future was also unknown, and I just wasn't in the mood to cheerfully sell junk.

The door rattled again.

Ozzie had been a real character, aka an unreplaceable pain in the ass and a great guy. The weather-beaten sign out front said "Oddities. Mostly Old Junk Nothing You Want" and I'd tried to get Ozzie to get rid of the second line for nineteen years, but no luck. Ozzie wasn't a fan of customers. I did take down the sign that said, "You break it, we shoot you," but that was as far as I'd gotten. In nineteen years. Change was not Ozzie's byword. Until two days ago when he'd died on our kitchen floor. Change is bad.

So now I was trying to glue a doll's head on an old paregoric bottle Ozzie had given me—"This looked like something you'd want," he'd said as he handed it over—without getting glue on my apron which was hard because I was using the wrong glue and it was going everywhere. The head kept falling off and rolling away. I was losing my head. Joke. Kind of.

Where was I ?

Right. My aprons are frumpy with huge pockets so I can keep things I'll need like scissors and a craft knife and Kleenex and a measuring tape and a calculator and several pens and—well, you never know what you're going to need—but frumpy is actually good because nobody pays attention to a middle-aged woman in a frumpy apron unless it has glue on it because people do like to judge. The last thing I needed was for people to notice me.

Lenka finished up explaining that trouble was a pal with her last oooh oooh, and that's when I realized I was using the wrong glue. My mind was all over the place. I was putting the tube in my apron pocket, trying to remember where I'd put the right glue (not in my pocket), and the door rattled again.

Honest to God, read the sign people. That sounded like Dottie, our postmistress. "It's a sign, Rose," she'd say, when something happened. "It's a sign that Ozzie died now." Yeah, Dottie, it's a sign that he's dead and I'm screwed.

The thing was, I had to call Barry, Ozzie's lawyer, to find out if he'd made a will, and I really didn't want to know. Barry Mason is one of two lawyers in Rocky Start, the other being my good friend Lian.

(Yes, his name is a joke. Ozzie always said somebody in Witness Protection had a sense of humor. I don't know if that was a joke, but it wouldn't surprise me if Barry was in Witness Protection.) Lian is clever, honest, fit, well-dressed and professional. Barry is sly, underhanded, pot-bellied, badly dressed (ill-fitting white suits that are speckled with cigarette ash), and a criminal lawyer, emphasis on the criminal. So of course, he's my boss's lawyer.

Was my boss's lawyer. My former boss. Ozzie Oswald. The best savior a woman could have. He died two days ago. I keep saying that to myself because it's so unbelievable. I heard him fall in the kitchen which is right off the shop, and I ran in, and he was on the floor, gasping, and I tried to help him up, and he said, "That fuck--" and died on me, died right there in my arms with an obscenity on his lips. Damn it. I'd tried CPR and screamed for help, but in the end, nothing could bring him back.

So now, I was technically jobless, and my daughter Poppy and I were homeless if anybody noticed since we lived in one of the two apartments over the shop Ozzie owned (we shared the kitchen on the first floor off the shop, the one Ozzie had died in), so that wasn't good. I mean, everybody knew Ozzie was dead, it had been two days (it was unbelievable that there had been two days with no Ozzie) and I was just waiting for the other shoe to drop for everybody about my living and employment status.

Somebody rattled the door again, and I finally looked up to yell at them to go away only to see Coral Schmidt, my good friend and the proprietor of *Ecstasy*, her amazing German coffee shop and bakery next door. (I was pretty sure Coral named the shop that so she could say, "This is Coral in Ecstasy," every time she answered the phone.) The CLOSED sign didn't mean a thing to her; Coral tended to go where she wanted to go.

I started around the counter to let her in, but then I heard her key scrape in the lock, and she came in, saying, "Rose? Why didn't you open the door?"

"I was coming . . . " I started and then stopped because Coral was dressed head to toe in tight, shiny, black mourning, topped with a huge black picture hat. She looked like the Angel of Death. If the Angel of Death was a voluptuous blonde in her seventies.

Ozzie would have loved it.

I wasn't sure.

I mean, I knew Coral would be in mourning because Ozzie had been one of her friends-with-benefits, and she loved him and drama, but I was not expecting Elvira, Queen of the Dead.

"That's a lie, you haven't come in years, Rose," she said as she closed the door behind her. "I don't know how you stand it." She handed me a necklace. "Can you fix this?"

I took a deep breath, and then I took the necklace. Coral was a good person who was never rude, so I was sure she was just upset about Ozzie's dying. It would be bad if I snapped at her from grief, rage, anxiety and sexual frustration. That I did not have because who needs sex? All that naked thrashing about with somebody who lies to you? I mean, really. I never think about sex. Or men. I try to keep a positive outlook on life.

I spread the necklace out on the counter. It was a beautiful, ornate locket that she'd once told me had locks of hair from her lovers—big locket—but its chain had tangled and knotted as chains kept in jewelry boxes often do, so I began to isolate the knot carefully; the necklace was old and finely made, much like Coral.

"I worry about you, honey," Coral was saying, standing on the other side of the old counter, frowning at the blank doll head beside Ozzie's paregoric bottle as I teased out the knot in her necklace. The blank eyeballs stared up at me from the counter. "It's not good to go without sex for years. And years. And years." She looked closer. "Is that one of Betty Baumgarten's dresses under that horrible apron? You've been thrifting again, haven't you? Are you braless? You're fifty years old, Rose--"

"I'm not fifty until Sunday," I told Coral. "And the shop's closed, there's a sign and everything, so underwear is unnecessary. And uncomfortable." I looked down at the top of my loose apron. "How could you tell I'm braless in this?"

"You're a C cup and things were shifting under there." Coral shook her head. "Beauty is pain. Put on a bra. Somebody wonderful could walk through that door at any time, and there you'd be. Not ready."

Coral was always ready.

I kept working on the knot in her necklace.

She was flashing enough seventy-four-year-old cleavage—D cup—over a wasp-ish waist to cast doubt on her mourning, although I had to give her credit for maintaining her figure or at least corralling it with powerful undergarments. She would have pulled it off, too, except for that thing on her head, resting on her long dyed blonde hair: a wide-brimmed black picture hat full of black tulle bows with a black spotted veil that she could lower to swath her face.

"That hat needs a crow," I told her, squinting at it as I handed back her now unknotted necklace.

The thing was huge. I would have put a crow on it, first thing out of the box.

"No," Coral said, rejecting my crow. "Thank you for fixing my necklace." She clasped the locket in her hand, pressing it against her heart, and moved on from my non-existent sex life and my equally non-existent underwear. "Have you heard from Barry yet?"

"Barry? Why would I hear from Barry?"

"About Oz's *will.*"

Coral really loves drama. I think it's the heat from the ovens at her place and all the caffeine.

"Do you think he left anything to me? Or Pike?" Coral leaned forward, and her breasts came with her, threatening the black satin that bound them. Ozzie used to call her The Couch because he said she was well-upholstered. "I'm spending the night on The Couch," he'd say, "If anybody calls, tell them I'm in Ecstasy," and then he'd head over to her apartment above her bakery.

He didn't call her the Couch behind her back; that was his nickname for her, in front of her face. Ozzie didn't go in for tact. He didn't go in for people, either, although he went into Coral with surprising frequency for a seventy-eight-year-old misanthrope.

Damn it, I *missed* the old bastard.

"He surely left Pike something," Coral was saying. "They were so close."

Well, she would know. Pike, her other friend-with-benefits, was her younger man. Seventy-two. I was pretty sure that Ozzie and Pike were two of the locks of hair in her heart-shaped locket, although there could have been more in there. It was a pretty big locket.

I don't mean to be disapproving at all. I admire Coral for having threesomes in her seventies. I'd been mostly dating myself for nineteen years.

The bell rang again on the shop door, and a man came in: middle height, maybe in his forties, tanned and dark-haired, expensive suit, probably carried his wallet in his inside breast pocket—his right hand was more calloused than his left, so right-handed, so the wallet would be on the left--good-looking except for his beady eyes and air of superiority. Your basic upper-class weasel who shared Coral's inability to read a CLOSED sign.

Trouble, I thought, but not Lenka's kind of trouble. I always figured Lenka's kind of trouble would be kind of hot. This guy was just sleazy. Here to sell you a Bible sleazy.

Still, I flashed the weasel the Cheery Boost smile I gave everybody who came into the shop. It's about as authentic as Coral's hair color. "We're closed."

"You must be Rose Malone." He smiled at me with cold, dead, weasel eyes.

"Must I?" I don't like strangers who know my name, but I kept smiling anyway, hiding my instant dislike behind my teeth, because that's what I do. I smile at people and I fix things so everybody will like me and not rat me out to the cops if they come looking for me.

Yeah, I smile a lot.

"Rose Malone, my father's right-hand woman and who knows what else," he was saying. "Unfortunately, since my father is dead now, he doesn't need a right hand."

"Wait a minute," I said, losing my Cheery as Coral swiveled to look at him.

He smiled at me, weasel to the teeth. "I'm Oz Oswald's son, Joseph

Stafford-Oswald, Junior, and I've inherited this building and the business. I'm sorry for your loss, but you have to go."

I just stared at the jerk for a moment, my nightmare come true. He was evicting us.

But he looked nothing at all like Ozzie. And he didn't seem to have any proof of ownership. Just a huge sense of entitlement.

So, no on that.

When I didn't move, he said, "What part of this don't you understand?"

He smirked and I hate smirkers, and he was ordering me around, and if you want to see me go ballistic, try telling me what to do (unless you're Ozzie), plus under all that bravado, he was nervous, so he really was a weasel and this was definitely a scam. I walked out from behind the counter and around him, opened the front door, and pointed to the street. "Out, Limb of Satan."

His smirk got smirkier. "Don't be ridiculous."

"This is a con, a truly stupid one," I said to him. Twelve years traveling the magic circuit with Poppy's father and then nineteen years working with Ozzie, and I had mad skills for spotting the crooked. Just not for avoiding them. I picked up the heavy reproduction of the Maltese Falcon from the shelf by the door, the statue that Ozzie had called our security system, feeling all my grief and tension and fear and frustration spiraling into rage. "Get out, Junior, and I won't beat you to death with a movie prop."

"Oz never mentioned a son," Coral murmured from behind Junior.

"Look." He reached into his left inner jacket pocket, retrieved his wallet—told you so—and took out a paper. A photo fell out as he did, and he held the paper out to me as Coral scooped up the photo. "Here's the DNA report. Oz Oswald was my father."

I took the paper, which was basically a bunch of numbers I didn't understand under abbreviations I didn't understand, but at the top it stated that Joseph Oswald-Stafford was a 97% match as a son of Joseph Oswald. "This is just a paper," I said, handing it back to him. "Anybody could have typed this up. And his first name was Ozzie, not Joseph."

He shook his head. "My mother gave me that. It's real. She would know who my father is. I'm Oswald Junior."

Coral was looking at the picture, rapt. Then she came to the door and showed it to me.

A young man with a sharp face, dressed in dull green fatigues, was looking at a tall slender woman with the blackest, straightest hair I'd ever seen, framing skin so pale she looked dead. Beautiful but dead. Morticia Addams in the flesh.

"That's my mother, Serena Stafford," Junior said, still smirking. "And my father, the man you knew as Oz Oswald. We thought he was dead all these years."

"That could be anybody," I said, and gripped the heavy Falcon tighter, but Coral shook her head.

"It's Oz," she whispered as if seeing a ghost. "I remember. God, he was so handsome then. Six-pack abs. He could crack a walnut with his glutes."

I glared at her, not pleased to know about Ozzie's glutes and even less pleased that she was supporting Fake Ozzie Junior and his fraudulent DNA test. "I don't care if it is Ozzie. He's just standing next to a vampire, that doesn't mean they made this guy together."

"This is ridiculous," Junior said, frowning now. "You need to get out of here *now*."

I opened the door wider and gestured with the Falcon. "Ozzie's estate hasn't been settled yet, so nobody has any idea who gets what. And I have a bottle that needs a head. Get. *Out*."

Coral was still staring at the photo lost in her walnut-cracking memories, but Junior took it from her and put it back into his wallet with the DNA test, and tucked both away in his inside jacket pocket, his eyes darting all over the shop as if looking for something.

Then Poppy appeared in the kitchen doorway, home late from high school, dark curly hair flying every which way, tall and beautiful and eighteen and not like me at all. Well, I'm tall.

"I saw the lasagna. Is that for our wake tonight?" she said to me. "Ozzie would have loved that."

Junior moved toward her. "Hel*lo*. *You* can stay."

"*No*." I moved around him fast to block him from my daughter, Falcon in hand.

He grabbed my arm to move me out of the way as Poppy said, "Mom?"

I tried to jerk my arm away and said, "Get out!" as Coral reached up and pulled something out of the crown of her hat. He didn't let go, still smiling a creepy invitation to Poppy. That's when all that fear and anxiety and rage at fate overwhelmed me, and I whacked him hard on the shoulder with the Falcon.

Trouble is a friend, my ass, Lenka.

He yelled and staggered back, and I drove him toward the open doorway, swinging the Falcon at him, fully expressing my inner Rose as I snarled, *"Stay away from my kid, you perv*!" until he was out the door, dragging me with him as he stumbled onto the sidewalk.

Poppy said, *"Mom!"* and Junior let go and backhanded me.

I went dizzy from the blow for a moment, but Coral snarled and lunged at him, and I saw a line of red blossom on his sleeve as I slapped my left hand on his chest to push him away. I started to swing the Falcon again with my right hand as I slid two fingers into his jacket and onto his wallet while his eyes went to his reddening sleeve and then the incoming Falcon. When he pulled away from me, half a second later, the movement of his body pulled the wallet out of his pocket, the lift hidden in his motion, and I dropped the wallet into my right apron pocket, the one where I keep the scissors and the craft knife. He reached into his jacket and I thought he'd felt the lift after all —I am a very good pickpocket so that was unusual—and I swung the Falcon in an arc, low and hard, aiming up for his hot spot, just like Ozzie had taught me—

And then he disappeared.

Momentum from the missed swing to the nuts kept me moving and I staggered a little, but I could see Junior sprawled out in the street now, courtesy of a new guy standing in front of me who turned to look at me with no expression at all: Middle-aged, dark hair with grey at the temples, weather-beaten, unshaven, gaunt in dusty black, a man who looked like he'd traveled far and hadn't enjoyed it and hadn't eaten much on the way. He was carrying a massive backpack, and beside him was a dog that looked like a big black wolf.

Trouble in the flesh. Also possibly the Angel of Death if Coral changed clothes.

I frowned at the new guy. My cheek throbbed, and I was still dizzy, so I snapped at him.

"I *had* that," I said, annoyed because I do not need rescued, and I'd really been looking forward to neutering Junior.

"You did not have that," he said calmly, which irritated me further, another one of those Master of the Universe guys, but then I saw Junior get up off the street and charge him, and I yelled "Behind you!" and the dog barked, and the new guy took a step sideways and took Junior down with a sweep of his foot.

His expression never changed. Stoic R' Us.

Okay, I was beginning to warm to him.

Junior rolled to his feet, his arm bleeding from whatever Coral had done to him. The new guy shrugged off his ruck, dropping it to the ground. The two of them looked at each other, sizing each other up, the dog baring its teeth by the good guy's side, and I thought, *This is dangerous.* Junior was looking actually threatening now, but the new guy was scarier, grim and expressionless, just waiting.

Then Lian ran out of her law office across the street with her pink taser, and Coral was at my side with a long, skinny knife I was pretty sure she'd pulled out of her hat and then out of Junior's arm, and Poppy came out of the shop with Ozzie's shotgun, which was a nice gesture but useless since I'd taken the shells out a long time ago.

"I called Pike!" Lian yelled, and I glared at Junior.

"Pike's the local law, and you hit me in front of witnesses," I snarled, the side of my face aching from his blow. "And my friends are armed and dangerous. I'd *leave* if I were you."

Junior ignored me, staring at the new guy who stared back, expressionless, almost bored, like he didn't give a damn. Then a dark window in the rear of a large SUV across the street powered down, and a woman's low voice called out. "Joseph Junior. Enough."

Junior said, "I'll be back for what's mine," and walked to the car. He opened the passenger door, and the woman said, "Go, Jane," and the car was moving before he shut the door.

Lian reached us, breathless, taser at the ready. "I saw what happened. Are you okay, Rose?"

"Yes." I said, ignoring my throbbing cheek as I watched the massive car roll down State Street. "Did you really call Pike?"

"Yes. As soon as I saw that guy hit you, I yelled 'Oddities!' into the phone and grabbed my taser." Lian looked at the new guy. "And you are?"

He nodded at her once as he picked up his pack and shouldered it. "Just passing through. You ladies have a nice day."

"*Wait*!" Poppy called and came down the steps with her shotgun. "Your dog—"

"*Wait*!" I said at the same time, feeling guilty now. The guy had helped and I'd snapped at him, the least I could do was . . . something. Offer him a drink? Lasagna? My body?

Okay, that last one was Coral's fault. And maybe Lenka's.

But he really was sort of attractive, if you liked serious, dusty, underfed, expressionless, middle-aged men with cheekbones and an overwhelming aura of gravity and menace who looked like trouble but rescued you.

Which evidently, I did. Weird after years of going with "men are the devil" on a knee jerk basis, I was suddenly having warm feelings for somebody who actually looked devil-adjacent.

So of course, he shook his head at Poppy, nodded to me, and walked away with his dog down State Street, the same route the Mercedes had taken, his back straight, and his stride strong, except for a slight limp on his right side, evidently not having warm feelings about me.

"Stripes," Poppy said.

That's the family code for danger. I used to panic and Ozzie would say, "Rose, if you hear hoofbeats, think horses, not zebras. Unless you see stripes. Then come get me." So our code for danger has always been "stripes." Except now we couldn't get Ozzie. Damn it.

"That dog hasn't been brushed in months," Poppy said severely.

"That's *neglect*." She handed me the shotgun and started down the street after the guy and his dog.

This was all wrong. Ozzie dies, Coral comes in looking like First Mourner, a jackass in a Mercedes tries to take my home, and then hot Trouble with a wolf shows up just in time to protect me?

No. Poppy was right, we were looking at stripes.

"What the hell is going on?" Lian asked.

"I don't know," I said, looking down the street after the stranger. "But I don't like any of it." *Except maybe him.*

Except I have terrible taste in men, so not him.

I looked around for Coral, but she'd disappeared, which was not like her, not in the midst of drama.

"You know," Lian said, watching the stranger, "that guy was attractive in an experienced Johnny Cash man-in-black kind of way."

"He didn't look anything at all like Johnny Cash." *Springsteen, maybe.*

"No, the vibe," Lian was saying. "Like he had been interesting places and done dangerous things. I find that very hot."

"Then stop dating younger men."

Lian waved that away. "So what are you going to do about this?"

I gave it two seconds' thought. "Go after Poppy so she doesn't annoy that last guy about his dog. Lift his wallet to find out who he is and why he was in town just in time to interfere with Junior because two strangers here in the same ten minutes is suspicious. Put the lasagna in the oven so we have dinner tonight." I looked at Lian. "Thank you for coming to tase the enemy. You are a good, true friend."

"Here." She handed me the taser. "In case a stranger gets ugly again. That last guy was not ugly, but if he catches you in mid-lift of his wallet, that might change." She looked off down the street. "No, he still wouldn't be ugly."

"He's too old for you," I said and handed her the empty shotgun so I could go hunt zebras.

CHAPTER 2

MAX

I headed to the post office with my dog, Maggs, to pick up the package that my old boss had sent to this oddly named town of Rocky Start and to get away from the four women and the SUV.

Maggs and I had been shadow-walking the Appalachian Trail for months, and today we'd headed for the town Herc had sent my boots to. It was a pretty little place, off to itself in the woods, spread out for a half mile covering a flat bend in the river away from the highway. When we got into town, I heard some shouting from a store, and then a guy stumbled backwards out of the door, dragging a crazy lady swinging a black statue. Parked across the street was a big black Mercedes with the subtle but important modifications indicating it was armored, windows tinted, engine running.

All of that seemed odd, but none of it was my problem.

But then he backhanded her. I don't care who started it or who was in the right or wrong, you don't hit women. You might have to kill one if she's trying to kill you, but that's a different scenario. I went closer, noting that the woman was a furious, middle-aged version of the girl-next-door, all curly dark hair and flashing dark eyes. Cute in a she-demon kind of way, but then I'd been on the trail for months, some trees were looking good to me. I didn't know who the guy was, but he had a telltale bulge under his jacket on his right hip.

He was reaching for that bulge as she swung the statue toward his balls, so I grabbed the guy's collar and pulled him backward and behind me into the street to save both of them, just as a middle-aged Asian woman carrying a taser came bursting out of an office behind the SUV, yelling something about a pike.

The guy rolled to his feet while the crazy-lady-next-door bitched at me for saving her, and then Maggs barked and she said, "*Look out,*" and I had to deal with the jerk as he charged me. I got him with a leg sweep but he handled it like a pro, going with the fall, rolling and immediately back on his feet.

I dumped the ruck and we were squaring off when a woman in the Mercedes called out and brought him to heel and he left, so he probably had some mother issues. Those are the worst. The SUV drove off, smooth on a jacked-up suspension to handle the weight, the powerful engine rumbling, so that problem was gone.

Two more women had come out of the shop, a dark-haired teenager who was obviously not afraid to use a shotgun and an older, stacked woman in a big black hat who was holding a small version of the classic Fairbairn-Sykes fighting knife in a way that showed she knew how to use it. And then there was the middle-aged Asian-American woman in the sharp suit with a pink taser in her hand and a look on her face that said somebody was going to die. And weirdest of all, the feisty, grown-up girl-next-door, blazing eyes and dark curls bouncing, swinging what appeared to be the Maltese Falcon. That last was a new one for me, and I'd seen a lot of weapons in my life. Being wise to the ways of the world, particularly those that involved danger, I moved on down the street, away from the quartet of females ready to inflict pain.

Definitely not going back there.

I continued down the main drag. There was no sign of the Mercedes; it had turned, probably heading out of town if the people in it had any sense. All I could see was a handful of folks going about their business, most of them middle-aged or older. Rocky Start did not look like the kind of place that kept its young. The trees were turning at the higher elevations, and it was going to be a beautiful fall here in a week or two, but it would also be beautiful miles down the A.T. where I planned on being shortly, where there would be fewer armed women.

The guy bothered me. He was definitely hinky. The woman must have caught him by surprise—who expects a Maltese Falcon?—but he'd recovered nicely and the stance he'd assumed to face me spoke of someone who'd had training but not enough since his foot placement was slightly off and he'd run into the leg sweep at full speed.

The armored Mercedes also bothered me. It did not belong here. Very Important People rode in those, particularly VIPs who were worried about threats to their well-being. I knew because I'd taken down one or two in my time and also ridden in them on protective gigs.

Still, not my business.

I checked my map app and found out there were two post offices because the town was bisected by the state line between Tennessee on the north and North Carolina on the south where the jagged line that separated the two states ran east-west for a mile or so. That explained the blue line running down the center of the appropriately named State Street and evidently up through the building called *Oddities* behind me. Two post offices seemed extreme, but I'd done contract work for the government and knew redundancy and stupidity were built into all elements of the bureaucracy. It had kept the country running this long through a lot of shit, so who am I to complain? Plus, it had paid me pretty well for many years.

I noticed several on-lookers who'd come out of the storefronts during the kerfuffle, the most notable of which were an older black woman dressed in a pure white suit in front of *Merriweather's Funeral Home,* and across the street a big, doofus-looking guy wearing glasses, headphones and a black suit. He had come out of the shop called *Nice Funerals*. I was wondering if they were waiting to see if there would be any business. Both of them eyeballed me as I walked the line down the middle of the street, as if measuring me for a wood box.

So. Two post offices and competing funeral homes. What the hell kind of town was this? Because there wasn't much of a town outside of this main drag, perhaps a block or two on either side. None of the buildings were higher than two stories, most of them old and worn brick, the ground floors being small mom and pop shops. The place dated back at least a century when these mountains had been harvested for timber before that same bureaucratic government stepped in and made things like National Parks and National Forests. Score one for the bean counters and bureaucracy.

The two POs were directly across the street from each other, and North Carolina had a CLOSED sign on the door. Tennessee won by default, although I had little doubt that my boots had been shipped to the North Carolina side because that was my life.

Maggs and I stopped at the Tennessee PO, and I signaled for her to wait outside the door and went in. There was no one behind the counter, but there was a bell. Before I tapped it, given the weirdness I'd already seen here, I surveyed the place, noting a pair of expensive cameras in the far corners of the room. Pretty high tech for a small town. Then I leaned over the counter to take a look. Nothing suspicious to see except a M1014 Benelli semi-automatic shotgun with a collapsible stock in a specially made sheath, ready for quick deployment. Not standard post office issue. Last I'd seen one, it was issued to Special Operations close quarter battle teams for sweeping rooms with a half dozen blasts as fast as one could pull the trigger. I hoped my package wasn't postage due.

I lightly tapped the bell. It took several seconds, then an older fellow in USPS uniform—blue shorts, white shirt, plus gray hair and bushy white eyebrows—came out. He looked me up and down, then nodded and swallowed, dabbing his lips with the napkin tucked in his collar which was already crowded with a bow tie.

"Max Reddy?"

I tensed, half-expecting dark figures to lunge out of the shadows. "Yes."

"We received your package yesterday."

I had to ask, although I didn't want to. "How do you know it's mine?"

"The wife and I know everyone in town and the package was sent care of the post office to someone we never heard of. Max Reddy. So we figured it was a stranger passing through. We don't get many strangers. Passing through. None staying. You are him, right?"

"I am he," I said, for lack of anything else and noting the emphasis on 'none staying'. So far, this wasn't turning out to be a friendly town. I waited for Postmaster Lionel Ferrell (according to his name tag) to produce the package, but he just stared at me.

"The package?" I finally prodded.

"Oh," he said, as if surprised. "It was sent to Rocky Start, North Carolina. Across the street. My wife has it there."

"That post office is closed."

"Yep," he said. "Post mistress is out doing the route. We flip every morning for that. She lost today. Made her none too happy, not that she's ever happy. A grim woman, she is."

"Could you perhaps get it for me?" I asked.

He shook his head. "Nope. Not my jurisdiction. The United States Post Office is a branch of the federal government, son, and as such we are governed by very strict laws regarding the storage and delivery of mail." He said this by rote, bored and apparently willing to ignore the coin flip thing, which most certainly wasn't in the official manual.

The door opened behind me and the young shotgun girl came in, sans weapon, looking like she owned the place. Maggs padded in after her from the porch. Which Maggs isn't supposed to do. I waited for Ferrell to throw a fit about the dog being inside. I was, of course, wrong.

"Hiya, Poppy," Ferrell said, changing demeanor in a flash.

The girl smiled at him. "Hiya, Mr. Ferrell." Then she transferred her big brown eyes to me and lost her smile. "You're not taking care of your dog. She hasn't been groomed in a long time and she looks underweight. What's her name?"

"Maggs. But—"

She shook her head. "Let me help clean up Maggs and feed her, I'm good at that."

"Yep," Mr. Ferrell agreed. "Poppy's pretty much the town vet these days since that moron Alfie ran off to Peru with his assistant. *Louise*." He said the name with loathing. "I give it a couple of weeks and he'll be back, tail between his legs, poorer and no wiser. No Louise, neither." He looked at me. "She's a dangerous woman, that Louise, with her womanly wiles." He shook his head. "Women. They'll turn on you in a second. No offense," he added to Poppy.

"None taken," she said, cheerfully.

"I'll see to Maggs," I said, irritated by the accusation that I wasn't taking care of my dog, even though the girl was right about the lack of grooming, although the same could be said of me. I turned back to the postmaster. "Could you unlock the door across the street so I can get my package?"

He shook his head. "The wife doesn't like me messing with her stuff. She doesn't like me much in general right now. That woman can carry a grudge. She should be back before dinner."

I sighed. "You want me out of town? Get my package and I'm gone."

He looked at me keenly. "You here because of Oz?"

"What's Oz?"

"Not what. Who. Friend of ours." Ferrell nodded at Poppy, whose smile faded. "Died two days ago. Terrible thing, but he was getting on in years. Just keeled over. Message there for all of us." He pursed his lips. "I hear tell there's some stranger in town claiming to be Oz's son, giving Rose at *Oddities* some trouble. That you?"

"Nope," I said, and beside me Poppy shook her head vigorously in support, which helped alleviate some of my irritation.

"Good," Ferrell said. "Don't like vultures winging into town. Not much for strangers either."

No shit. "Could I just get my package?" I pointed at my toe sticking out of the boot. "It's boots. I need them."

Poppy made a small distressed sound as she looked down.

Ferrell's chin went up. "I also hear there's a fellow who ran off the man claiming to be Oz's son. That you?"

"Apparently."

"Yes, it's him, he's the good guy," Poppy said firmly. "But now I need to clean up his dog and feed her as a thank you."

I said, "No," but the door opened again, and this time it was Feisty, out of breath and bosom heaving, her cheek red from where that jerk had hit her. "Hi, Lionel," she said cheerfully, and Lionel said, "Hiya, Rose. Looking good."

"Thank you, Lionel," she said, practically twinkling at him. Just a cute woman in an apron who'd tried to beat up a guy with a Maltese Falcon and was now holding a taser.

And smiling at me.

I really needed to get out of this town.

CHAPTER 3

Rose

I'd tried to make a plan as I'd followed Poppy and the new guy up State Street. First, I had to get a grip on my anger and outrage at getting hit by a guy trying to scam me. Anger and outrage are not attractive or charming, which is what I needed to be to get through life. My daughter called me Cheery Boost because I smile at everybody and make them feel better as a survival trait while I fix their problems, so they'll love me and not rat me out if the cops show up looking for me.

Poppy said she did not intend to become Cheery Boost Two, which I agreed with. She didn't understand that I was Cheery Boost One to keep her safe and fed so that she could grow up and leave Rocky Start and be whatever she wanted to be and never come back. She was heading to college in ten months, and once she was gone, living her best life someplace exciting and full of possibilities, I intended to become Resting Bitch Face and probably starve to death, but at least I wouldn't have to be fucking *cheerful* about it.

The new guy and Lionel Ferrell were having a stare down when I walked in, which wasn't good. I didn't need this guy annoyed. Poppy was kneeling next to the dog which also probably wasn't helping.

Lionel said to the good guy, "So you planning on staying long?"

The new guy shook his head. "I'll be gone once I get my boots. Sooner I get the boots, the sooner I can be on my way. Not staying. Don't want to stay."

"And after I take care of your dog," Poppy said. "Please?"

"No, thank you," he said, so I put my hand on his sleeve and smiled up at him. Cheery Boost at work. Always.

"Poppy will take good care of her," I told him, upping the wattage on the Cheery.

It didn't do a thing for him. "Maggs stays with me."

Poppy started to protest, and I said, "Go home, Poppy, the man wants his dog with him."

"But—"

"Stripes."

Poppy huffed and went out the door, and I held out my hand to the new guy, smiling, of course. "Hello. I'm Rose Malone. And you are?"

He looked at my hand as if having an internal debate, then sighed and took it. "Max Reddy." He dropped my hand and turned back to Lionel. "About my boots?"

Lionel looked at Max. "I told you; I can't get your package because it's in North Carolina."

"You mean across the road." Max closed his eyes for a moment, and that's when I saw my chance to get close enough to lift his wallet to see if he and Junior were in this thing together.

Yes, I have trust issues.

And yes, I was attracted to him, but this was about the weasel trying to make my kid and me homeless. My kid trumps everything else.

"Lionel." I leaned on the counter beside Max Reddy, brushing his sleeve. If men didn't like it when you moved in close, they moved away.

Max did not move away.

Lionel frowned at me.

I smiled up at him, not easy when you're 5'9" and the guy you're smiling up at is 5'8", but I have skills. Here's a tip: Leaning across a counter makes you shorter. "This man just saved me from somebody who *hit me*. I mean, *look at my cheek*! Max Reddy is a *hero*." I leaned closer which made me even shorter. "The government should reward heroes. *You're* the government here, Lionel. You have the *power* to get him his boots. C'mon, be a hero, too. All he wants is the package that is legally his." I smiled again, looking up up at him from under my eyelashes, just between us, a secret we could share. It's a trick so old it has whiskers, but it always works.

"You know how Dottie gets," Lionel said to me, but I could see a smile breaking through. He was a cheating husband; they always respond to flirting with women who aren't their wives. Dottie was going to kill him for invading her space, of course, but that was his problem. My problem was getting Max's boots for him so he'd trust me so I could steal his wallet.

"Lionel." I leaned a little closer to Max, a little farther across the counter, too, tilted my head, and hit Lionel with my smile and my dimples. Those dimples are worth their weight in moisturizer. "You're not afraid of Dottie. I don't believe that for a second. A tough veteran like you? You've faced down much worse. And this hero needs his package. I bet anything he's ex-military, all you guys have that *devastating* confidence. He's your *fellow soldier*, Lionel. *Esprit de corps*. And he really needs his package. C'mon, man. *Be a hero*. Get this guy his boots."

Lionel looked at me and sighed, probably knowing I wasn't going to quit, and turned to Max. "You wanted some boots?"

"Yes," Max said. "I wanted some boots."

Lionel took the napkin out of his collar, and I said, "Wait,", and leaned closer to straighten his bow tie. It was a clip on and I almost knocked it off as I fixed it, but Lionel seemed happy to have my hands that close to him and relaxed some.

When I had it straight, I patted him on the chest and said, "Looking good, Lionel," and he beamed at me and grabbed his big key ring, lifted the countertop, and headed across the street at a run, probably trying to get there and back before Dottie caught him.

When he was out the door, Max looked at me, grim as ever. "Don't bother trying that on me, it's not going to work."

I gave him my best smile. "Of course not, I can tell you don't charm that easily." I watched him relax a little. Compliments often did that for men. "That was a big ask, for Lionel to invade Dottie's territory." I looked across the street where Lionel was at the door, unlocking it. "I lied, he couldn't take Dottie in a fight. Actually, I think he thought that was a plus in the beginning. Lionel likes strong women."

Max frowned at me.

"They're divorcing," I told him. "It's played merry hell with the mail. Some days, nothing gets delivered if they're really feuding and don't do the coin flip." I moved a little closer. "So anyway, thank you very much for defenestrating Junior. Or whatever throwing somebody into a street is. I was rude back there, and you were helpful. I apologize. It was my pleasure to charm Lionel for your boots in return, don't mention it." Then I stopped. "But I really did have that."

His expression didn't change. "He had a gun and he was going for it. And you weren't armed." He looked at Lian's taser in my hand. "Then."

Junior had a gun? Maybe I hadn't had that. *Stop doubting yourself, Rose, you had a Maltese Falcon.* "I just needed to thank you." I smiled and flashed the dimples again.

He was still frowning, negating all my dimple power, which was just wrong. I mean, I'm not young anymore, and I never was a beauty, but when I put my back into it, I can be cute as all hell.

"That guy who hit you said he was coming back," Max said, after a few moments of silence. "Why was he going to shoot you?"

"I hit him with the Maltese Falcon. It's a movie prop—"

He shook his head "I know what it is, why were you hitting him with it?"

"It was the first thing to hand—"

"No, I meant—"

Lionel came back into the office, out of breath from running, and handed a large Amazon box to Max. "You owe me, stranger. Good thing you're just passing through." He held out an electronic handheld device. "Sign here. You can use your finger."

"Right." Max slashed his forefinger across the screen while awkwardly holding the box.

"Have a nice day," Lionel said in his usual, flat voice, a signal that his being nice was over and we could leave.

"You're a sweetheart, Lionel," I told him. "Dottie is a lucky woman."

Lionel cheered up a little at the first part, but the mention of his wife's name put the grumpy back.

Max opened the door for me and stepped back so I could go out first. What Coral would call A Real Gentleman. So I tripped and fell into him, and he caught me with his free hand, jamming his foot against the door to keep it from closing, and I looked up and met his eyes and he really was grimly attractive, and for half a second I forgot why I'd fallen. I mean, I came to my senses fast, we needed to know more about this guy, but there for a moment, it was just nice to have somebody's hands on me. Especially his.

I said, "Sorry," and patted his chest while I pinched his wallet between two fingers, and he moved away from me to call Maggs as I straightened, which pulled the wallet from his jacket as I turned my back to him to drop it into my left-hand apron pocket. I went outside, and he and Maggs came out, too, and he closed the door behind us. "I didn't know about the gun," I told him. "So. Thank you."

"You're welcome."

"You know, Poppy would take good care of Maggs," I told him. "Comb her out and clean her up and feed her. She'd feel so much better. You know where we are, right?" I pointed down the street to the shop, back the way I'd come. "That blue line runs down State Street and ends right at the shop. Goes through the shop, actually. You can't miss it. I can walk her down there while you put on your boots. It's the least we can do for your help."

If I took Maggs to Poppy, I could give him back his wallet when he came to get her after I checked it out. I'm not a *thief.*

He shook his head and sat down on the curb just as Pike's truck rolled to a stop next to him, missing his feet by inches. He didn't flinch.

We don't know if Pike is officially the law. He has a badge he keeps in a pocket, but I understand you can buy those online. He's one of those guys who's not so much elderly as seasoned, as if the years have worn away all the weakness and just left this teak-tough ancient force of nature that nobody messes with. He and Ozzie definitely ran Rocky Start together, so whether or not Pike is official law enforcement is kind of moot. It's his law and he enforces it.

Pike looked down at Max now. "This the guy who helped you, Rose?"

"Hey, Pike," I said, moving to the window. "This is the guy. Do not maim him."

Pike shook his head. "Go home, Rose. I need to talk to him."

"*Do not hurt him,*" I said. "I mean it, Pike. He *helped* me. That guy who hit me had a gun."

Pike frowned. "He did?"

I nodded. "He drove off in a big SUV with some woman after telling me he was Ozzie's son. Did Ozzie have a son?"

Pike ignored that. "What kind of gun?"

Like I'd know. I am personally anti-gun. I looked down at Max, who was reaching inside his own coat to pull out a very sharp knife. So that was two people carrying concealed knives in less than an hour. Plus, Junior with a gun. Of course, I was carrying a taser.

Welcome to Rocky Start.

"It was a Browning Hi-Power in a hip holster on the right side," he told Pike.

Pike stared at him. Max started to cut the tapes on his box, ignoring him, which isn't easy. Pike has a very sharp stare.

Max added, "They were in a black Mercedes G63. Ballistic protection, heavy suspension for the armor, souped up engine, probably run-flat tires."

"You know this how?" Pike asked.

"I have eyes."

"That so?" Pike said.

"That's so," Max said.

"Rose?" Pike said to me, his voice flat.

"Yes?"

"I left a shirt at Coral's that needs some mending. Now would be good."

"Of course," I said. "But--"

"Rose," he said.

I sighed, knowing what was coming. "Yes, Pike."

"Go home."

Right. Okay. I leaned over Max as he slit open the box. "Really sorry about this," I whispered.

I started back down the street at a good clip as Pike said to Max, "You got a name? Any ID?"

Great, now the guy would look for his ID. I wanted to make it back to the shop before he noticed his wallet was missing, him being the observant sort—there was a gun?—but then he called, "Wait a minute, Rose," and he walked over to join me, looking stern. Grimly stern. Didn't this guy ever smile?

"My wallet," he said.

I immediately moved into this-is-my-innocent-face. "Hmmm?"

"Cute. Give me my wallet, or I will take it."

"I don't know—" I started and then I stopped because he was patting me down. Everywhere. He hit the left apron pocket just as he was getting to my good parts, so that was a letdown—

"If you wanted to see the wallet, all you had to do was ask," Max said as he took his back.

"Really?" I said.

"No."

"That's what I thought." I put my hands on my hips, trying for the spunky little woman this time since innocence wasn't working. Well, the spunky little woman who was 5'9," but still such a cute archetype; you'd have to forgive a spunky little woman—

"Don't do that again," he said and I gave up on the spunky little woman, too.

"I wasn't after your money," I said, trying for outraged virtue.

"I know," Max said.

"I just wanted to know more about you."

He leaned forward then, almost nose to nose with me and said, "You don't need to know more about me."

His dark eyes were hot on mine, and that's when I began to think seriously about sleeping with him. Because men will tell you anything if you're naked, not because I *wanted* him, I'd given that up a long time ago when I'd realized that I had a genius for finding the only cheating alcoholic in a room full of good men, and when that happens to you two or three or four times, you just say, "The hell with this" and concentrate on being a single mother and selling odd secondhand—

He narrowed his eyes at me, and I realized that being naked might not work with Max, either, him being the suspicious type, so I put my hands on his chest to hold him off and when he moved away, I lifted his wallet again.

Maybe I could get him to pat me down again, too. That was fun.

"Whatever you're planning, the answer is no," Max said.

"That's really mean," I said, and walked away with his wallet.

CHAPTER 4

MAX

I watched Rose go down the street for a moment, ignoring the old guy glaring at me from his truck. She was kind of hot, braless as she was under that loose dress—you can find out a lot when you're searching for a wallet—and she had a nice swing to her step as she walked away. Insane and definitely bent, but cute. Then I looked at the old man in the truck who seemed impatient and apparently knew what a Mercedes G63 was, so I retrieved the shoe box from inside the Amazon box and sat on the curb again. I tugged off my old boots and replaced them, wiggling my toes, reveling in the feel. Sometimes it's the little things in life. I laced up and shoved the old boots into the box. I should change out the socks, too, you learn that early in the Infantry, but the old guy was getting testy and I didn't want to dig through my ruck in front of him.

He was still frowning at me as I stood. "Where you headed?"

"Back to the A.T.."

"Get in. I'll give you a lift to the highway." This had echoes of the opening to *Rambo*, except I was too old and too tired to burn the town down and my knife was a lot smaller. More useful, but definitely smaller. I could spend a lot of time talking about knives, which I used to do with various operatives while sitting around, waiting for the action, and everyone had their own preferences.

I tossed the box with my old boots in a nearby trash can, put my ruck in the bed of the pickup, opened the door, signaled for Maggs to get in, and climbed aboard the old rust-colored truck. Maggs sat between us on the bench seat and I noticed she did smell a little raw. The girl was right. Maggs could use a good cleaning up. Of course, so could I.

Pike was rolling before I had the door shut, but he wasn't moving fast as he did a leisurely U-turn to go back up the main drag. I noticed a pistol in an open top holster bolted to the driver's side door, within easy reach of his hand and ready to be pulled. He noticed that I noticed.

"Name's Pike. I'm the law." He shot me a glance. "And you are?"

I'd had to give my name to Ferrell to get my boots, and I was pretty sure it was all over town by now, given the speed of the local grapevine, so I said, "Max Reddy."

"Where you coming from?"

"Up north."

"Where you going?"

"Down south."

"Uh-huh," he said, stopping at the lone stop sign on State Street and turning to look me over. "We don't get many strangers here. No A.T. through hikers. Town's too far off the trail." He made it sound like I'd broken the law.

And we weren't moving. Probably so Pike could stare at me. I noticed in the side mirror that Rose was on the sidewalk, slightly behind us now and thought it interesting he hadn't invited her in for the ride, although it would have been a tight fit with Pike, Maggs, me, and her. That would have been even more interesting.

"I meander," I told Pike, taking my eyes off the mirror.

"You meander," he said as if evaluating the statement. "So, you're walking the trail, is what you're claiming."

"Yes," I said, watching as Rose swung by, passing us. A lot of energy in that woman. Hips that moved, too.

"There aren't many trails from here to the A.T. so you have to move cross-country, which is tough bushwhacking in these hills." He nodded his head toward the west. "A.T. is five miles yonder where it cuts this road. Hikers resupply in Bearton farther down the line. Post office there is just a half mile off trail. They welcome through hikers."

The implication there was obvious.

Pike went on. "Either you're really lost or up to something."

I pointed down. "My boots were mailed here."

"Really?"

"Really."

He was studying me now and those eyes were keen, but after several moments, he put the truck in gear and drove through the intersection, arriving at the end of the street just as Rose was going into her store. He turned right and drove out to the highway, turned left on it and drove past the edge of town. He pulled off the road to let us out.

"Thank you," I said, opening the door.

His next words got my attention. "I expect you'll be moving on right quick now, won't you, stranger?"

Subtle he wasn't. "Did you find the guy claiming to be this Oz's son?" I asked, trying to level the playing field.

"Funny thing about that," Pike said. "I did not. He seems to have vanished."

"Isn't that kind of odd, given its your town and it's not that big and they were in a pretty conspicuous vehicle?"

"Do not push me, son."

"I have no intention of doing so." I got out of the truck and called Maggs to join me.

He nodded down the road. "Keep going straight and you'll hit where the A.T. crosses in about five miles," he said. Then he grinned at me. It wasn't heartwarming. "Got your wallet?"

I patted my pocket, and yes, it was gone. Great.

"Don't be going back for it," Pike warned.

"I have no plan to," I said. I nodded to him, grabbed the ruck out of the truck bed, and he pulled away laughing as I barely got it out. He pulled a hard u-turn and headed back the way we'd come.

There was a story there, and I was going to move on before I heard it. Rose could have the damn wallet. It didn't have anything irreplaceable in it, just a cover ID and money, and I had more cash in the backpack. My old boss Herc could get me another valid, backstopped ID and mail it to my next pick-up spot. Hopefully one closer to the trail and with fewer crazies.

I ignored Pike's order to take the road to the A.T. since following the highway would take me even farther out of the way. I could cut cross-country and save a mile and a half. Checking my app, it indicated that up ahead there was a forest road crossing the Little Melvin River which delineated the south boundary of Rocky Start and was now to my left. I shouldered my ruck and ambled down the road until I was sure Pike was out of sight as he turned into town.

It was perfect timing as a clearing in the trees, car-width, appeared to the left. I crossed over the two-lane highway and into the woods. Within twenty feet, I reached a one lane steel trestle, wooden planked bridge over the Little Melvin River which was a fast-moving, dangerous looking mountain stream. On the far side was a gravel and dirt road. Perpendicular to that, following that side of the river, was the remains of an old narrow-gauge rail line where lumber had been hauled out. The rails were gone, but there was a level four-foot-wide byway with a very narrow, footpath etched in it. Looking that way, I could see the old railroad embankment running along this side of the water, overgrown and muted by erosion.

I paused. Part of the reason I had walked so many extra miles was because I did meander. I looked in that direction and noticed something, an anomaly in the vegetation about fifty meters away. Intrigued, I dumped my ruck on the side of the road.

"Come on," I said to Maggs.

We walked along the trail, the river to our left. The ground to the right rose up sharply about ten feet. And then, pretty much hidden by tangled growth, was a run of stone stairs set into a narrow cut in the embankment. I forced my way up there, Maggs following. When I got to the top I saw what was hidden from view: An abandoned stone cottage almost disappeared in the forest. It had probably been cute once upon a time, but that only works in fairy tales. Nature had reclaimed the outside, although the slate roof looked solid. Some of the old glass in the windows was broken, and they all looked like empty sockets peering out into nature. A few of the trees around the house were fruit trees which had been planted a long time ago and were still looking good, but a lot of it was just weeds and brambles. There was a padlock on the thick wooden door.

I wondered about whoever had built this place and the first people to move into when it was new and pretty and a place they could call their home. Possibly it had been a company house for railroad workers or loggers and they'd been crowded into it and paid pauper's wages. But it looked like a home to me. It must have been hard to leave it, for whatever reason. If I wasn't in a hurry to get away from the town and its odd inhabitants, I'd consider bunking up next to it, but there was plenty of daylight left.

Maggs circled the place, curious, sniffing, as if also wondering what the story was. Perhaps a dog had lived here once upon a time? Her tail was wagging and she went and pressed her head lightly against the door.

I turned back to the stairs and noticed farther upstream a three-rope bridge crossing the river, which brought back memories of river crossings in faraway lands it was best to forget about. I went back down to the rail line and paused at the bottom. Completely covered by plants was a stone bench, overlooking the river. Which made me think whoever had lived in that stone cottage had come down those stairs and sat here, watching the water splash by. I was tempted to clear it off to sit, but the trail was calling.

I went back to my ruck and shrugged it on. I turned away from the bridge and followed the road for a quarter mile. On the right, I passed a cute white one-story cottage, shutters painted blue, with a white picket fence, except there was also a four feet deep overgrown trench on the inside of the fence with a gated wood bridge over it, which was weird. The mailbox had *Baumgarten* written on it. I saw movement off to the side of the house, and then a llama came out of the bushes and stared at me across the trench, clearly warning me off.

Yeah, a llama.

If anything tells you it's time to move on, it's when you start seeing llamas. I looked down at Maggs who was staring at the beast, her head cocked, as if puzzled.

"I don't blame you," I said. "Let's keep moving."

I crossed another one-lane bridge over a stream, then found a narrow trail branching more to the west and I took that so we could shadow the main trail again. Maggs moved parallel to me, but off trail to the left, which was her way.

About ten minutes later, I hit the tripwire.

Rocky Start: https://books2read.com/u/bPzkRx
To be followed in the Rocky Start series by
Very Nice Funerals
The Honey Pot Plot

Cool Gus Publishing
www.bobmayer.com

WILD RIDE by
Jennifer Crusie and Bob Mayer

Book cover design by

eBook ISBN: 9781621254188
Trade paperback ISBN: 9781621254287
Hardcover ISBN: 9781621254294

Created with Vellum

Printed in Great Britain
by Amazon

45467421R00245